C0-CCO-103

DISCARDED

DISCARDED

Books *by* **BERNARD WOLFE**

IN DEEP (1957)

THE LATE RISERS (1954)

LIMBO (1952)

REALLY THE BLUES (*with Milton "Mezz" Mezzrow 1946*)

In Deep

No diver has so far reached . . . one hundred fathoms. . . . The main obstacle is a compulsion, the "drunkenness of the deep seas," which affects different people at different depths. It has been observed at fifteen fathoms but is more usual at thirty. Some exceptional divers have only felt it at fifty. A man becomes aware of great sleepiness, a euphoria leads man to the abyss, so that he welcomes death and seeks suffocation. No myth has ever equalled the tragic grandeur of this scientific truth. When he made his fatal dive in 1947, Fargues, of the Submarine Research Group, fell victim to this "drunkenness" of the deep seas. As he went down, he made scratches on pieces of slate attached to an anchored rope. The last mark he left was at sixty fathoms. . . . But as we are still on the brink of this submarine language . . . this is the time to invent common nouns. —Philippe Diolé THE UNDERSEA ADVENTURE

BERNARD WOLFE *In Deep*

New York **ALFRED A KNOPF** 1957

UPSALA COLLEGE LIBRARY

813.5
W855i

L.C. catalog card number: 56–5777   © Bernard Wolfe, 1957
This is a Borzoi Book, published by Alfred A. Knopf. Inc.
Copyright 1957 by Bernard Wolfe. All rights reserved. No part of this
book may be reproduced in any form without permission in writing from
the publisher, except by a reviewer who may quote brief passages in a
review to be printed in a magazine or newspaper. Manufactured in the
United States of America. Published simultaneously in Canada by McClel-
land and Stewart Limited.   FIRST EDITION

The epigraph is reprinted by permission of Julian Messner, Inc., from
The Undersea Adventure, by Philippe Diolé; copyright 1953 by Julian
Messner, Inc. The quotation on pp. 307–8 is reprinted by permission of
Scientific American, Inc., from "The Deep-Sea Layer of Life," by Lionel A.
Walford; copyright 1951 by Scientific American, Inc.

119380

TO DR. EDMUND BERGLER

Contents

Contents

In Deep

... *going* ...

  Going down, I forgot about Barto. The last I saw of him he was leaning over the deck rail, scolding at me with his "Rob, no tricks, twenty fathoms is the limit," then I beat him to the dive. Under, and feeling muscles slack, I forgot him.

  The water was congested with sun. Amniotic against the skin. Heat, up this high, was a stuff on its own, slow turps. . . . Down three fathoms, close over the reef spires, I turned on my back and looked up.

  No sign of Barto. Where did he get off with those safety Chautauquas?

  I couldn't locate any one brightness that was the sun. Light down here wasn't something that came at you from one source far off, it was a stampede you bent against.

Explosion: the surface tore, to one side of the boat's blue-black hull. Another milk cloud popped, close by the shredding one I'd left.

Barto, coming after me.

I turned and started down again, past the reef's carbuncle side. I was in no mood for visiting lecturers, I was busy keeping my mind off my breathing. Trying to. If I started to think about my nose gone and the air tube in my mouth, let my thoughts go, in two seconds I would be out of control and tearing at the mask to pull some saving stuff through my nostrils—ocean, anything, to stop suck-feeding on a breast of air.

"You think too much, you're a damn philosopher in the water," Barto had been telling me.

Dropping, I thought of the air tank strapped to my back, knapsack to hold off big sleeps. . . . The mask, too, the mask annoyed me. Without it I wouldn't be keeping any distances against the water's blue invites, in touch everywhere.

The bottom, I knew from soundings, was fifty-some fathoms down, a place where jumps stopped. I kept sinking past the reef and its kinked backbone formations, past the caves with stalactite tusks, and I wasn't so much thinking the bottom as feeling it.

Going down was like dreaming, it didn't take fighting the water, just knowing there was a pulling bottom somewhere and an agreement not to buck the pull. . . . Some saupes scatted by in convict stripes. I wondered if Barto was catching up.

Dropping, no effort, in a dream fall, thoughts running with the sarguses that flicked in and out of the reef's gape mouths . . . and this time, for a big joke, I thought dreamily, Barto or no Barto, the bottom was helloing hard and it was time I got there for once, in reunion spirit. At ten fathoms, the chill currents came across. My flippers, in on the joke, seemed to be moving by their own will, pushing me in answer to the floor's pulling.

A deep cave went by, in it I saw a rock cod studying me through sentry eyes. I sang to him without opening my mouth, "Bartolome Caro is right behind, Bartolome Caro is loyal and kind." But the clotting in my chest was worse, it was working up the throat muscles.

Another cave, carpets of cobalt moss. Another, hung with tapestries of orange slime. A third—something looking at me again.

At first all I saw was the eyes coming at me from the dark, two yellow ones like gold pieces, separated by a black line. Yellow thyroid eyes mounted in black water.

"Big beautiful doll," I said to this octopus, behind my lips. "Who needs eight arms, ticket takers? Card sharps and switchboard operators? Deaf mutes, the gabby ones?"

Thinking it was here and I had to open my nose and breathe . . . then my muscles had a spasm. Something touching me on the neck. I pulled yards away before I circled to see.

Barto. He was looking at me too. Jerking thumbs up, wanted me to come up. He was turned sideways and I could see the two dents in his flesh, back of the left armpit.

I dove again and swam straight down, four or five fathoms, in no time. The reef at this level was a tree trunk with roots exposed, gnarling, unplanned, coated with weed fans. Waterlogged jungle, pinks, madders, lemons, plums, smalts—the spectrum's junkyard. Bubbles from my breathing apparatus rose for the surface in strings, my soft brain fizzing.

In another cave below, another octopus, playing possum.

"Where," I said into his eyes, Barto's unapproving eyes, "where's there a possum wants to play octopus?"

But it was too small for an octopus. Small, and the head was flat and disc-topped. Besides, there were only five legs, thin as garden hoses, not boa-muscled and prehensile.

A brittle star! As I live and.

"Ophiurian," I said without making a sound. "Ophiurian of the group Ophiurida, generally encountered in South Cali-

fornia waters. Oughtn't to hang around the Keys, pretending
to be an octopus for all bad mathematicians."

He kept on watching me, like an A-1 octopus. His five
hoses jumped with worry as I came down.

"Nor is it polite to stare," I said in my throat.

For answer, his disc head topping fell off, then his five legs,
one after the other. I hung there and watched his parts float
down to some idiot roll call. Marching home to Pop and the
folks. I had a sense of loss, as though they were my head, my
legs.

The Ophiurian's way of handling danger: surrendering
frills to save vitals. But do you just nod like three wise men
when Mother Nature comes up a maniac?

The eyes were still on me.

"What's the opposite of blowtop?" I said. "Blowbottom?"

The eyes went on taking inventory of me.

"Lady should not drop her Red Sox cap and snakes," I
said. "You stay right there, I'll go and get them back."

All this politeness made me bite on my mouthpiece to
keep from laughing.

I started down again, full of W. C. Fields mission, and the
panic broke and was over me. Heat had weight, light had
weight, in this broth where a man was the only weightless
unlit thing and destroyed, and my panic was the heat and the
light, weight itself, and sticky. An albumen of sun and hotness,
secreted by nobody but me, and I was in it, dropping. Who
can breathe butter? I cursed my father and all of them.

My flippers heard the bottom's pitchman voice, father's
voice, they were moving first and making my legs snap second.
Dying to get there to rancid bonanzas. That I knew was the
central part of the joke, the best joke of all, the way my
flippers took the bait. I had to get my mouth free for the
laughing that was in my chest, and for the yawning. Year's
need of sleep in me, had to yawn.

Then I couldn't stand it with mouth leeched to tube and
I was tearing at Pop and at the mask, spitting out the plastic

nozzle between my teeth and Barto was alongside with the wrinkled holes in his side . . . I was fighting off his octopus arms and shouting, making a fry of bubbles, shouting something about walking papers, then something about Nagasaki and run, soldier, run.

Barto's octopus eyes through the lucite, yellow and with no approval . . . cold water pumped in through my nose and mouth, made red oceans in my throat.

BOOK ONE: *Key West*

ONE For epochs, I thought about opening my eyes. I addressed my father and he became a floating white silk bag, so soft. On the edge of laughter, I considered this proposition: Look into the hole long enough and the hole will look into you.

I opened my eyes. A pulsing Barto, bent, looking into my face with no approval.

My throat and sinus areas felt raw. I was coughing like a lunger. But my God, I felt better. I was stretched out on deck and my God, weight in arms and legs again, flesh cramming on something without give.

Past Barto's long-templed head, past the cabin with its antenna stalks, tenting over everything, a blue vacancy with no pressure in it. I was sucking in that pastel nothing as though it was homebrew.

"I pumped two quarts of water out of you," Barto said.

"No papaya juice?"

"What got into you?"

"Two-thirds of the Atlantic, roughly."

"Philosopher. What, what do you think is always one yard past your fingers?"

His head was giving off its outlines in concentric waves. I watched the contours of his elongated features peel off and re-form and the words came to me: You and your pipes. "Something that would keep my fingers busy, I guess." Was I supposed to like his making it worse?

My shoulders were shaking. He took hold of my arms and said, "Are you feeling all right?" His lips, that were emanating larger and vaguer lips, humped into a line again. I thought: There were no pipes. "That time last May, when Dino the Greek went down far for sponges and didn't come up, who made the guess that if Dino got drowned and there was nothing wrong, he must have, past a certain point, wanted to get drowned? Who said maybe everybody has his limit in the water? Who?" He got up off his knees, took a towel from the railing and blotted the sweat on his neck and shoulders. "One thing I don't get. If you want to breathe, you come up."

"Twice two."

"You're down. So to breathe free you go farther down. Smart, smart." He kneeled next to me and wiped my mouth with the towel. "Are you sure you're all right? You're still leaking. Here, wipe your nose."

I managed to sit up. The deck boards flowed. I remembered the brittle fish, so profligate with his members, and the word Nagasaki came to my lips. Then I was angry, burning angry. "How does a big safety expert get two—bullet holes in him?"

The stretched skin of his face stretched some more and his eyes went empty. He moved closer, a trick of his when his thoughts backed off and he was making himself unavailable. "Hombre, I have been to the wars." When he used Spanish like that, to mock, it was for purposes of changing the subject. "Many wars, compadre. I am a busy soldado."

"My co-ro-nel, I salute you. You have the true valor."

"All the same," he said seriously, "you're through and finished with the water, Rob."

I got to coughing again. Barto said something about hearing a motor and stood up, hand shading eyes, to look in the direction of Key West. "You're having company." I made it to my feet, Barto supporting me.

Connie cut the motor as her speedboat came alongside. "Two men without clothes on," she called. "I'm really living." Barto caught the line she threw and made it fast, reached for her elbows and pulled her on deck. "Sweetie," she said to me, "you don't look your shining best. Are you going to fall down?"

"I just washed my legs. Can't do a thing with them."

"Everybody's full of suicide today," Barto said. "Who told you to come this far out in a speedboat?"

"Honey," she said, "I'm a strong-willed girl. I might get it into my head to cross the Atlantic in a thimble."

"Thimbles," Barto said, "would hold your wardrobe."

She was wearing a Bikini, strips of white silk on which were printed old French menus in different colors. Tossing her streaked blond hair, she struck a stripper's pose, one hand across her breasts and the other over her crotch for a fig-leaf effect. "Mr. Caro," she babytalked, eyes so wide it looked like the sound was coming from them, "would you be happier if I covered up my considerable charms?"

"You can't do anything to make me happy," Barto said.

"I can do a whole lot of things. Ask Rob."

"Connie," I said, "stop throwing it around. Where's Boyar?"

"Mr. Boyar," she said, "with tears in his eyes, told me I'm very juicy but for the next three days he's got to go potch-kying around Cuban waters and catch him a marlin. I said fine, fish well, and I'd try not to die. Sweetie," she said, coming up and rubbing her cheek against mine, "we've got three— whole—days."

"I've got to work," I said.

"You mean pouring that stinky fish glue from one test tube into another? Counting up those nowhere algaes and formanifera whatchums?" She remembered everything.

"Mustn't sell oceanography short."

"You can always count up your watchums. You can't always have my lovely white body to do with what you will."

After working her way into Barnum teases she almost believed it, her mouth went come-and-get-it loose and she took
on the look of a lotus-eater. Boyars from the Riviera to Malibu
couldn't get enough of those preview flutters, though the pay-
off was less gorgeous than the build. Maybe the Boyars didn't
notice the discrepancy.

"I'm going to stay home and work," I said.

Her eyes got veneered. "If I didn't know you better, Robbie boy, I'd think you were trying to give me the fast shuffle.
I really would." Then something happened to her face: the
muscle went out of it. Her face was capable of this sudden
melting and regrouping, as though inside was a hand holding
the flesh and periodically going loose. She stared out at the
water and looked forlorn and unsalvageable. "I know why
you come out here, to get away from me and everybody like
me. I wish I had some place to go to get away from myself.
Some quiet place. I'd bring my eyes and my skin and leave
the rest behind." The clamp came over her face again as she
turned back to me. "Oceanography. Listen, you meet me at the
Late Watch. You be there."

"I wouldn't advise you to wait."

"I wouldn't advise you not to be there."

"Well," I said, "everybody's full of advice."

"Anybody thinks he can give me the duster is full of more
than advice." I began to think, from the way her eyes wouldn't
stay put, that maybe she was a little drunk. "Say, why don't
you both come down to the Late Watch? The three of us could
have a party."

"I can't make it," Barto said. "I'm getting up early to go
on a trip."

It was the first I'd heard about any trip. "Havana?" I said.
It was usually Havana.

"I figured the boats won't be in before Sunday so I'll have
five days."

"Listen," Connie said to Barto, "I never see you with
girls."

"It is my big tragedy," Barto said, "that when a desirable woman like you comes along, she is already spoken for. By battalions."

"It's people like you," she said, "who keep the art of conversation alive. Say, what do you do on these trips, anyways? I'll bet you've got a harem of two hundred over there on the Isle of Pines someplace, you little sneak."

"Only one hundred and fifty. Naturally, their hours are staggered. Only fifty work the swing shift."

Connie climbed over the railing and backed down the rope ladder into the boat. "You ought to come tonight," she said to Barto. "We could ball."

"I'll be there in spirit," Barto said.

She shifted her eyes to me. "Robbie, you better be there."

"You don't want to go around scaring people."

"Eight sharp." She caught the line Barto threw down and started the motor. "I'll be waiting."

"You wait." She gunned the motor and the boat slammed off like a panicked duck. We stood at the rail watching. "The worst of it is," I said, "I *like* that girl."

"You have to head for the bottom," Barto said. "In all departments."

"It's just a hunch on my part, just a sneaking suspicion, but you know something? I think you're losing your zest for diving."

"The way you do it, it's to die. I'm too busy to be dead."

"And I'm too dead to be busy?"

He turned his eyes to me, and I thought he looked scared. "I saw your face when you pulled the mask off. You know what I saw there? Celebration. Big joys. Does any Connie see that look on you?"

"What do you dive for, Barto?"

"Not the sensation. The end of the dive, the rest and easy breathing afterwards. You, you look for all that *in* the dive."

I watched the speedboat a while longer, it was shrinking down to baby mallard size. "Tell me—" I was going to ask whether Nagasaki and walking papers meant anything to him but I felt a chill, remembering how the brittlefish came apart, then I didn't need his answer.

Once before I'd seen an intact animal break into its constituent pieces. A human animal. On a Pacific strip of beach east of the Manggar and Klandasan beaches of the Balikpapan invasion area, Northeast Borneo, July 7, 1945, at 5:17 in the morning, just after Barto and I had finished our predawn survey of the hardwood post clusters and concrete pilings. We were hiding in the water behind a reef hump, with eight fat minutes before the LCP(R) was due back, cursing the boats for not coming and not coming, and the Japanese sentry came over the dunes running toward us jabbering and aiming his rifle. We could see him running, sharp as a paper cut-out with the moon framing him, when he tripped the land mine that in his devotion to his work he forgot was there. Nose to the grindstone, men! My head was full of sloganeer words. It was not too cold but my teeth were going and everything looked yellow. The sentry came apart too, in many distinct pieces, I saw one leg go up in the air twenty feet and running all the way. My throat was bursting with messages for the world and I said, "Much obliged, Nagasaki. Where the fellers chew tobacky." Then I felt I hadn't made it clear, so I said, "Nose to the grindstone, soldier. Deport yourself as an alert soldier at all times. Eternal vigilance is the price of. Run, soldier, run. In all directions." All Barto said was, "Shut up, goddamn it! You listen to me! Rob!" Minutes later, in the boat, we were going out fast and more sentries were on the beach and their bullets were blanging off the boat's side, Barto had to hit me with all he had because it was growing in me again and I was yelling, "To the grindstone, leg, deport yourself as an alert leg at all times," feeling my nose passages were packed with breadcrumbs and I was suffocating. Barto kept saying: "Why are you so yellow? You're yellow through and through." I heard it as I went down and I resented it. Just before I went out I saw the two holes in Barto's back and after my eyes snapped shut

I went on studying the two precise round holes, they were filling with reluctant yellow blood and had replaced my eyes.

"Tell you what?" Barto said.

What way was there to talk about it with him? Words being built to hide crisis, not communicate it? "I like her. What I can't stand is the act she puts on. Always at the grindstone—"

"Connie? She's got her work to do, like everybody."

"There's something else there. But how do you get under the brass?"

"She's not all brass. Some of her's molybdenum." He yawned. "Wipe your mouth off, you're leaking again."

TWO   Two hours later we tied up at the dock. I didn't have many plankton microorganism samplings to pack because I only dove three times that afternoon and the third time I dropped without traps. I stoppered whatever test tubes were full and stowed them in the wooden rack, and Barto helped me carry them over to the parking lot behind the yacht basin, to my car.

"Have a good trip," I said as I climbed in.

"I'll be back Sunday at the latest."

"You're your own boss. If you feel like taking off, that's it."

"This isn't a pleasure trip, you know that." He tapped me on the shoulder and I pulled away because my muscles were still jumping. "Rob, don't do any diving while I'm away."

"I won't even breathe, dads. If I want to take a breath, I'll cable you first." I got the motor running, then I held my hand out. "Sorry, Barto. My head's full of salt water. If this trip's important, I hope it turns out well."

As I swung into the road I had trouble seeing past the fuzz in my eyes. There were multiple edges around objects that made everything look like it was shedding, my insides felt sore each time I swung the wheel and it was hard keeping the car on a straight line.

The sun was still up, fizzing over the mangroves and scrubby pines, when I got home and carried the test-tube rack into the shed I used for a laboratory. I tried to eat a salami sandwich but with this much soreness in the throat, food went down with grapples on it. I got a bottle of Canadian ale from the icebox, took four Empirins, and stretched out on the settee.

Keeping a log of dreams is like charting the course of a banana peel through the Sargasso: where are the lessons in flotsam? Still, I had some offbeat dreams. There was a square-rigger ship, some brigantine with a skull-and-bones flag waving from the mizzenmast. Grandfather Heixas was there, of course. I was standing on a plank reaching out over the rail, my hands were in irons behind me and I was hotheadedly refusing to walk until they slipped an oxygen tank on me or at least one lousy snorkel. "You got your walking papers, now walk," Grandfather Heixas insisted, prodding at me with his cutlass, no, fish-chopping knife, and twirling his glossy half-moon moustachios that were arched like cutlasses. He kept growling his name was Manuel but for a joke I kept calling him Man-O'-War, Portugee Man-O'-War. "Run, diver, dier, run," he said. "Your dear down daddy's waiting." Finally he got sore and told me bums who walk the plankton don't get no fancy breathing apparatus, and his cutlass was making cube steak out of my flesh, so I jumped, Grandfather Heixas yelling, "Since you always got to get to the bottom of things." The water was boiling. Down, far down, I saw the two holes in Barto's back, spouting blood, then they were two gold pieces twinkling and I thought, ah, my countrymen, the lost doubloons, sunken treasure. But when I got down they weren't gold pieces but eyes, yellow eyes, and there at the bottom Connie was under me with bright red skin and bright green lips and shining gold-piece eyes. "Better than celebrations, better than oxygen," she said. She locked her legs around my thighs, saying, "Honey, not too deep, Dino hon, stop at twenty fathoms, you're hurting me bad," and blood came in thick rubies from her green mouth. Her mouth subdivided paramecium style and was two mouths, the two holes in Barto's back, agates of blood still blobbing from them, and they spoke in unison, saying, "This is not a pleasure trip." I said, "How do you expect celebrations on my face if you won't give me oxygen?"

It went like that, Grandfather Heixas, Connie, and other things. Coming out of it, I saw it was not me in the water but my father, Connie, no, my mother was trying to clamp a breathing-tube nipple in his mouth and he fought like a madman, tearing it off. When I woke my headache was better, I was in a good mood. Crisis? Me in a crisis? Barto was the one in crisis. I saw by the luminous hands of the electric clock on the bookcase that it was almost 8:30 and the thought came: Some kind of trouble was on Barto.

I got up and looked out the window: past the lights on the point the moon was hanging, jogging a little, and under it the water ripples, streaked with phosphors, looked like radium eels. I thought I saw porpoises jumping there, through the silver smears. My thoughts jumped with them, and I remembered the tightness in Barto's tone when he told me he was too busy to be dead. What did he know about easy rests after dives? All he was busy at was not resting.

I took a shower to get the fog out of my head, put on poplin pants and a T-shirt, and started along the beach. The usual light was on in Barto's living room and through the bottom slits of the rusted Venetian blinds I saw somebody walking around. I called out as I went around to the front door. At the door I banged on the frame and said, "Barto? Barto?" Still no answer. I went in.

A man was standing in the living room. He was average size, in his low thirties, dressed in rayon summer suit and wearing a spattercolor bowtie, and his collar was marble-smooth with starch, which made me dislike him more. There was some-

thing too damned hardworking and cleancut about him, he
reminded me of a YMCA counselor who gives a good account
of himself on the parallel bars. His hair was despicably neat,
and he didn't blink enough.

"I know this looks funny," he said, "but it's really O.K.
Caro knows me."

"You generally drop in on people you know, or say you
know, when they're out?"

"I didn't know he was out. There was a light."

"That's an invitation to stay out."

"Depends." He smiled a youth-counselor smile and held
his hand out with manliness, straight from the shoulder. "My
name's Caprio. Unless I'm wrong, you're Mr. Garmes."

I didn't take his hand. "How do you know about me?"

"I know a lot about Caro. I know, for example, that he's
got a partner who's five nine, stocky, lightish brown hair, not
talkative, owns four boats, does a pretty good business in shark
livers, suspicious of strangers. Robert Heixas Garmes—right?"

"What business have you got with Caro?"

"It's a private matter. Look, I'm not kidding about the
name." He took out his billfold, which had many compartments and was undoubtedly cross-indexed. He picked a card
out and handed it to me. The name Vincent Caprio was en-
graved on it, and under that an address in Chevy Chase, Mary-
land.

"This doesn't say who, or what, you represent."

Caprio, or whatever his name was, grinned. "Well, Mr.
Garmes, let's just say that what I represent right now is a strong
desire on the part of certain people to keep your partner
alive. That, I might say, is an enterprise in which Caro doesn't
always give us his best cooperation."

"Is your being here connected with this trip Barto's taking?"

"Oh? I was given to understand he didn't tell you much
about his personal affairs. You wouldn't know *why* he's going
to Havana, would you, Mr. Garmes?"

"I wouldn't."

"That's what I thought. Mm. Well, to answer your question, yes, my being here has a lot to do with Caro's impending expedition to Havana." Impending expedition. It went with the sincere manner and the starched collar.

"If Barto wants to contact you, where are you staying?"

"The Concha." His face turned solemn. "You're a good friend of Caro's."

"He's my partner."

"He's the only man you met in the Navy whose bones you didn't want to break. You liked him enough to make him your partner when you set up in business here. That's a lot of liking, for you." He took a turn around the room, examining the furnishings like an auctioneer. "Garmes, if Caro's your friend, if you value him at all, keep him here. You understand me? Keep—him—here. Once he's in Havana, he's dead." He had an annoying habit of sticking a silent Q.E.D. on the end of every sentence.

"He was born and brought up in Havana. He goes there all the time."

"Things are changing in Havana."

"You keep on not saying anything."

"I just said a lot. Make sure Caro stays on the Key, Garmes."

"I'll see what I can do."

"I and my associates would appreciate it." Caprio picked up a light gray porkpie hat that was too light gray, the kind with perforations running around the crown in diamond patterns, and put it on the side of his head, too far to the side. "Get him to call me tonight, will you? No matter how late it is." He nodded and moved toward the door. "I'm not being secretive for the fun of it, Garmes. Nobody's playing games." The starched grin came back over his face and he said, "You won't find anything missing, except your manners," and went out.

I looked around the room. It looked the same as it had for four years, tired wicker furniture, Maxfield Parrishes on the walls, doilies that were coming apart, dining table with the cheap blond veneer chipping off. One wrong note. The flaking maple desk in the hall was open and there was a mess of papers lying on the top. I'd never seen that fly-top desk open. The papers seemed to be mostly faded, cracking clips from Spanish newspapers. The top one was from some Barcelona newspaper, *Workers' Future*, dated May 2, 1937. Pieces had broken off from the right side but I could make out phrases:

Beloved Cuban Militant Disapp
No Trace Found of Arturo Ca

A hero of the Cuban toiling masse
carried on his lifelong struggle for
proletariat with glorious militancy du
Madrid's darkest hour, has today been rep
missing since Friday. Prof. Arturo Car
last seen in the headquarters of the C.N.
kidnapped, and it is suspected that he
taken aboard a foreign ship presently
the high seas, rumored bound for Ri
fessor's son, a young miliciano in
International Brigade, was recently
ualty during the Huesca retreat. Thi

I left the house and headed for town. I looked in all the bars and greasy spoons, without finding Barto. While I was standing on the corner of Oyster and Duval, not knowing where to try next, Kimon came along sucking on a Good Humor. Kimon was a Greek kid whose old man, Aristides, sold us bait and sometimes shipped on our sharking boats when we were short a hand. Yes, he'd seen Barto about an hour before, standing in front of the Late Watch talking to a man. Some billionaire. Came into the basin this afternoon on a cruiser a thousand feet long. The *Easy Rider*. Crazy name. Cruiser a thousand feet long, how else is it going to ride but easy?

It was almost 9:00. I went along Oyster to the end, where it fades out in a stretch of sand and pulverized shells, and went on through the parking lot into the Late Watch.

Barto wasn't anywhere, but Connie was slouched in a corner booth, looking like she was going to throw something. "You," she said when I went over. "Oh, you."

"You seen Barto? This is important, Connie."

She jumped up. "Important! Me, I can wait! Any barnacle-crusted son of a bitch who thinks—"

Two people came through the door, Barto in front, behind him a man. I waved.

THREE   "Professor Owen Brooke," Barto said.

"Professor of fish?" Connie said. "Like Professor Garmes?"

"Sociology," Brooke said. "You might call it professor of fish, you might indeed. Sociologists study some pret-ty queer fish." He laughed, but it was something he did with his body more than his face.

"If you ask me," Connie said, "sociologists look like fish."

Laughing heartily, the professor took a seat. He was tall without shoulders and awkward, he didn't know for sure where to put his arms and legs and kept trying out positions. The smile looked like a strip of court plaster stuck on over the lips. Aging boyish type, nursing an uncomplicated Ivy League face into his forties because he didn't know what complications to put on it. In lieu of them he wore a pencil-line moustache.

"If sociologists study fish," Connie said, in tones of the interested hostess, "is that why they look like fish?"

I motioned to Barto to sit next to me. When he got placed I pulled my chair close and said, "Something funny—"

"Don't let on about Havana. This Brooke, he used to visit my father in Cuba. He wants me to go to Havana with him but I don't want him on my neck there. He's nothing."

"Listen. Half an hour ago I stopped by your place and found a man there. He was interested in your belongings."

Barto sat up, his eyes widened. "What kind of man?"

"Youngish, my height, efficient. Said his name was Vincent Caprio and he knew you."

Barto smiled as though it was funny. "Oh, him. You know what I call him? Vinnie Sisyphus Caprio, after the poor Greek who kept rolling the stone up the hill."

"He not only rolls stones, he jimmies desks."

"He's seen those clippings before. I leave them so he'll have some reading matter when I'm not there." Barto's face got thoughtful. "He was just looking?"

"He sends you some travel information. Go to Havana and you won't come back."

Barto hit the table with his fist. "At last! Well! So! It's about time!" You would have thought he'd just been elected to high office. "This means what I'm looking for in Havana is there, Vinnie would know. Now I have to go."

"And get killed? You, the eminent safety man?"

"Oh, killed. Vinnie likes to dramatize."

"He sounded to me like he had facts. What's it all about, Barto? I've never butted in, I've never even asked about those scars on your back, but when—"

Connie shoved her elbow in my ribs. "Know something?" she said. "This one's traveling on a nice shiny yacht. You know what yachts do? They contribute, definitely contribute to moral looseness. I know, I've been on lots of yachts, and by now my morals are so loose they rattle. He talks through his nose, too. He ought to blow his nose, the sociologist."

"Nasal inflection," Brooke said. "Characteristic of certain Hudson valley regions." His smile was beginning to look

UPSALA COLLEGE LIBRARY

embalmed. "You've got a well-developed sense of humor, Miss Overton."

"This fish-lover on my right," Connie said, jabbing me, "has contributed, definitely contributed, to my moral looseness. All day long I've been asking him, begging him, to contribute some more, and he won't. The test-tube-loving—"

"You're ravishing tonight," I said. I got a good hold on Connie's elbow and pulled her to her feet. "Let's dance." The Cuban quintet was just getting up on the stand. Connie wobbled, but I managed to get her to the dance floor as the band started on a bop-bongo arrangement of "The Way You Look Tonight."

Two teen-agers drifted past, looking like they'd just garroted the faculty of their progressive school. "Sitting in an orgone box wouldn't give you a vaginal orgasm," the boy said. "You're too retracted, pelvically, I mean. I don't mean that critically, it's just an observation." "Well, I'm trying," the girl said. "My mother should only know how I'm trying. She thinks I'm in Winston-Salem, visiting Civil War monuments with Cousin Libby." "Your mother's got a very bad case of muscular armoring," the boy said. "She looks to me like a definite clitoral type, with a real pelvic retraction." "I've noticed that," the girl said. "I think that's what gives her her terrible backaches." "With her lack of vaginal release," the boy said, "she might get cancer of the uterus at some future time." "Well," the girl said, "I don't want to get cancer of the uterus. I'm really trying." "Understand," the boy said, "there's nothing personal about this. It's an objective observation. I'd like to see you loosen up that pelvis." An older couple danced along. "I don't care what anybody says," the redfaced woman said, "a Porsche is too flashy. Now, the Mercedes-Benz is a lot of car."

I tripped over Connie. She was beginning, as usual, to take steps my feet weren't even hinting at. "Want to toss a coin to see who leads in the next set?"

Her nails dug into the small of my back. "You don't want a woman, you want a doormat. In and out of bed."

"Doormat? You're a magic carpet—flying solo. In and out of bed."

Two crewcut young men danced by, blending cheeks. "That was one reason I was so fascinated by Gide," one said. "There was no dissembling with that one." "Oh, Gide, she was a very sincere person," the other said. "I respect that in a person," the first one said. The band finished its Afro-Cuban camouflage of "Tenderly," and a rattling of bongos announced the set was over.

"You can come back to the table on one condition," I said. "Shut up and behave yourself."

She giggled. "Talk tough to me. Black-and-blue me and satisfy my soul."

"Remember, get out of line and you're leaving on your ear." I meant it, but it sounded like words in comic-strip balloons.

When we got back to the booth Brooke was saying, "We came all the way from Varadero. You can't let me down, Barto."

"I can't get away," Barto said.

"I was sure you'd be glad to see me. After all."

"Our boats are due in from the Gulf any day. That ties me up."

"I have all the equipment," Brooke said. "I need a man like you to handle things. Of course, I wanted to see you, too. It's been a long time."

"Thirteen years."

"It was wonderful news when we heard about you. Ever since '37 we'd been thinking you were dead."

"Many people thought I was dead."

"Too bad your father couldn't be here now."

"My father thought I was dead too. Then, a little later, many people thought my father was dead."

Brooke stopped playing with the swizzle sticks. "What're you saying! Arturo died in '37, during an air raid on Barcelona! There's no question about *that!*"

"Well," Barto said, "some were said to be dead in 1937, and later they sit in a bar in Key West and drink bourbon and talk of old times and 1937."

"But there's no doubt about Arturo, surely? I've never heard—"

"Nobody saw a body. He could be dead."

"Barto," Brooke said with real pain, "a lot of people died in those tragic days and their bodies were never found."

"Yes, a lot died and a lot were not found."

"Look, man, Michael was there. He's always been sure."

"Michael," Barto said. "Yes. You've seen him?"

"Well, no." The professor looked with care at his glass. "Not for years, I mean, not since before the war. He told me about Arturo then, it was just after he got back from Barcelona, the last time I saw him was then. Before the war, the *world* war, I mean."

Barto came close to smiling. "You know the last time I saw him? We were running fast, on a mountain below Huesca. They were shooting at us. More were shooting at me than at him. One more. Tell me, Owen, how did you find out I was living here?"

"Why, no, it wasn't from Michael."

"I didn't say it was from Michael," Barto said very mildly.

"Why, what happened was, in Varadero we ran into some Americans over at the Internacional Hotel. They'd been fishing around the Keys, and they went down to your sheds a couple times to buy bait and saw you. The man who waited on them, somebody named Aristides, told them your name and they remembered it. It was one of those things." Brooke began to laugh with his chest and thin shoulders again.

"Yes," Barto said without any expression, "we have a man in our sheds named Aristides. Sometimes we have extra bait that we sell."

"Barto, you don't get the picture. It's taken me years, but I've got my research center going, the thing I used to talk about with your father, the Sociedad por la Música Afro-

Cubana, to preserve the old music. We've got headquarters in Havana."

"S, O, M, A, C. Yes, I've heard of it. Yes."

"This year I'm on sabbatical leave, I'm going down there to make tapes of the old ceremonial music for the annals of this Society. It's all set up. But the thing is, the ceremonies I'm after, the authentic ñañigo and such, well, they're banned, you know. That's where you could do a job for us. You know your way around Havana, you could contact the right people and get them to stage some of this voodoo stuff—"

"There's no way for me to leave now," Barto said.

"Come on down to the boat, anyway. We'll have a drink and go into it some more."

"I'm having a drink here."

Old Aristides came through the door, red suspenders looped over his baggy sweater. Barto saw him at the same time I did. "There's our man Aristides," he said to Brooke. "Now you'll know him, in case you run short of bait." He turned to me: "He wants to know how much ice to order for the sheds. I told him to meet me here." He rose and moved off toward the old man.

"What was all that about Barto's father being dead and not being dead?" I said to Brooke.

"He was killed in Spain during the civil war. Barto can't seem to accept the fact."

"Who's Michael?"

His hands jerked. "Michael Brod, he was a friend of Barto's father. I used to see him in Havana, at the Caros'."

"Is it true you haven't seen him lately?"

The hands did their ballet again. "Mr. Garmes, you ought to be careful about calling anybody a liar. Barto said he couldn't go to Havana when he was planning to go. *You* let him say it and you knew it wasn't so."

"Who said Barto's going anywhere?"

"Miss Overton."

I looked at Connie. She stuck her tongue out at me and

squinted her eyes. "Miss Overton seems to be a mine of information. Why don't you ask her why your hands dance when
you're asked about seeing Michael Brod?" His head went back
as though he'd been slapped, his cheeks turned red. "Thanks
for the full answer," I said. "It shows good breeding." I didn't
know what it was about him that irritated me. Maybe his way
of talking, as though there was an apple in his mouth. My
father had had that elocution lessons manner.

Barto came back and took his seat. There was another
rumble of bongos and the band leader, a little Cuban with
oversized teeth and a fancy ruffled shirt, stepped into the
spotlight.

"Ladies gennelmeh," he bubbled into the mike, "you are
good audienh and show appreciatieh of Cubano good music
and this make us verh, verh hoppy. So tonigh we are honor
to presenh a man famoos all the leng and bread of my native
counhry, the one an donly Rey del Bongo! Weener of all
bongo contess in his own lanh and known everaywhere by
the mambo lover! Julio Rodríguez! Coolio Rodríguez anh his
real cool bongos, ha, ha! Juss arrive from Habana, anh for
this nigh only! Coolio! The King!"

A tall fleshless Negro in a starched white suit and with a
mouth full of gold stepped up on the stand, moving without
goal. He was carrying a set of bongo drums. Professor Brooke
sat up with a bounce. He seemed both puzzled and elated.
"I'll be!" he said. "Coolio! He's the greatest, cuts everybody
in the business!"

"Did he cut you?" Connie said. "You look like you've
been cut."

"We've recorded him at the Society a dozen times! Wait'll
you hear those polyrhythms, you'll think you're deep in
Dahomey country, listening to tribal bashes!"

"Can I ask you something?" Connie said. "Why'd you
grow a damnfool moustache like that?"

Barto was studying the bongo player. "He works with

your Society?" he said to Brooke. "I suppose many people do." Then he stopped staring at the drummer and watched Vincent Caprio come through the door with scoutmaster briskness and approach the bar. Caprio ordered a drink and turned around to survey the room. "I know why you grew the damnfool thing," Connie said. Caprio's eyes met Barto's, he considered Barto for a while and went back to his drink. He seemed sure of himself, sure Barto would make some move. "Show you can grow something besides older," Connie said. Caprio was right. In a few seconds Barto excused himself, got up and walked to the bar.

FOUR   The band went into a racheting version of "Perfidio" and King Coolio, face in a washboard composure, began to play, making oinking sounds that the mike picked up. The kids stood up and began to oink back. "Go! Go! Go!" they yelled. "Vaya means go!" "The end!" "Do the thing, pops!" Brooke, his head making whooping-crane dips and his heel hammering the upbeat, leaned over toward Connie to tell her that African drums, the fundament of true jazz, America's one indigenous art form, were a means to trance, whereas the European bluenose restraints in our culture were against trance and all primitive letting go. Connie wanted to know if he was a professor of letting go, too. At the bar Caprio was talking and nodding with briskness, Barto listening and once in a while slowly nodding. I asked the waiter to bring the bottle and I had some straight drinks in a hurry, my raw throat protesting.

"Musicological analysis shows," Brooke was saying, "that the African tribal songs of derision and work chants lead in a straight line to the classic Storyville two-beat blues form," and Connie was giving him back a big eyes-wide "Well throw

gravel down my throat and call me Ma Rainey." Then Barto
was alongside the table, saying, "Afraid I have to go now.
Owen."

"Oh, come on," Brooke said, climbing to his feet. "You're
not just taking off like that, are you? Without one drink at the
boat, for old times' sake?"

"I'll have to pass up that drink. Maybe another time."

"All right. I rather thought I'd get a warmer reception,
after all these years, but. In case you change your mind, you
can reach me at the Ambos Mundos in Havana."

"Take it easy, Connie," Barto said.

Connie jerked her shoulders. "Buy yourself a rubber duck.
You don't even like girls."

I walked toward the door with Barto, and we went out
into the parking space. "Where to?" I said.

"Caprio wants to talk some more. I'm going over to the
Concha, to his room." There was some private ferment working
in him, it had put extra red in his darkish cheeks around the
compressed cheekbones. His head was pushing in a friendly
way toward me to highlight the fact that there were no gaps
between us, sure sign that his thoughts were in the next county
and traveling. "If he wants me to say I'm not going, I'll say it."

"Barto, you can't go now. Connie told Brooke about
your plans."

"Oh?" Barto was quiet for a second, then shrugged. "It
doesn't make any big difference."

"I don't get you, I swear I don't. One minute you're
giving *me* big-brother talks about not going past twenty
fathoms, the next minute *you're* going to Havana. How many
fathoms down is that, Barto?"

"They haven't taken any soundings yet." The fun evapo-
rated from his face and he was meaning it. "Don't get me
confused with you, man. More and more, lately, you dive to
push the limits, that's all. For the sensation of everything at
once instead of in sequence. You want all the aftermaths without surfacing, the dive and the dive's end together in one

prize package. That's a philosopher's aim. Next time you won't come up and that'll be your everything."

I had him dead to rights and he kept at me.

"There's only one way to dive. Find some water, and jump."

"Wrong. It can be to telescope now and later, because you're fed up with waiting for one measly thing to follow on another—just to be touching something and out of vacuums. That's one way. Or it can be not for the sensation but to make deep alterations outside and inside, to know a thing's done. That way takes patience, and planning." He massaged the knuckles of one hand with the open palm of the other, methodically. "On the boat this afternoon, when I was pumping water out of you, you know what you said? 'Let him stay down if that's his way. All he treasures is sunken treasure. Let him inhale the doubloons and the plankton if he must walk the plankton.' You were speaking textbooks, Rob. If I had the time and the vocabulary, I would try to translate them into English. *You* try."

"All right!" It made me wild to listen to words I never knew were in my mouth coming back at me via another mouth. "You're the big authority on diving who never gets his feet wet! Ten years now you've been standing in one place, with your knees bent and your feet together and your hands out and pointing, waiting for some special signal to dive! And all you keep on doing is not diving! I've known people jealous of you because you looked like you had your direction all picked. Sometimes I envied you too—your seeming to know the way you had to go, so you could clear your head of all the irrelevancies. The Connies. But you never once jumped! Now you're taking off, is that it? This is the big one! To stretch the muscles!"

"You said it yourself." With his mind that made up, nothing in view but the good chance of extinction, he could take pleasure in the fencing—was that it? "First you've got to find the water."

"Listen, compadre. Do you mind if I call you compadre? If you've got to go, how about my coming along?"

"We go to some wars together." He was grinning again. "In some wars a big soldado like me doesn't want company."

"You talk about wars like some people talk about private property."

"This war is my own exclusive baby, yes, compadre."

"Like the Spanish war?"

"It belonged to other people, but a part of it, one small segment of it on a mountain below Huesca, became mine and nobody else's. That one part detached itself from the public war and became my private war at the point where two private bullets made a home in my private left shoulder blade." His smile had in some way stopped being a smile. Its shape had not changed but it was now of another substance than flesh, a study in steel mesh. "Let's work over your metaphor one more time. Twelve years ago I *started* a dive. All the years since then I haven't been inactive, I've been looking for the right time and place to finish. Incomplete dives are very bad on the nervous system." And there I was out of his areas again.

"So you're going tomorrow." I felt helpless. "Watch it, then. Don't pull any fool tricks."

"Fool tricks!" There was no masking smile on his face now, but some boil there was no name for. He was close to shouting his words. "You call it tricks if a man is dying of thirst and hunger, and for twelve years is dying this way, then one day there's meat and drink of the best for him, just one inch away from his fingers if he will reach—you call it fool tricks if a man reaches! You think hunger and thirst is the whole program!" His voice actually broke, he glared at me. I'd seen the kind of look on his face before. On the faces of troops riding for a beach in assault boats and knowing there was no backing away from it now and in the final moment of being trapped losing the fear that comes from having choice or the illusion of choice, with the outs used up losing fear and so leaning forward with rifles ready into the next crisis minute,

anticipating the shore and what waited on shore with something not too far from lust.

"I don't know what to call it. Something it would be
better to have over."

"Now you've said something! That's why I'm going!"
With that his face was masked again with on-top-of-everything
nonchalance. "I guarantee I'll be back by Sunday. I wouldn't
make you handle the boats. Oceanographers can't count shark
livers right."

"So long, Barto. Remember your safety lectures."

"Seguro, hombre. Take it easy." We shook hands almost
formally, then he waved his long index finger at me and said,
"You envied me? Truly? That's wild—I envied you. I never
for a minute thought the Connies were irrelevancies. What I
couldn't understand was your treating them as though they
were, and picking them for that—without your mind being
occupied in side streets like mine, without even that excuse.
Well, don't inhale too many wooden doubloons." He waved,
making half a circle with his finger, and walked out across the
parking lot, a refugee behind his skin again and cracking sea-
shells underfoot as he went.

When I got back to the table Brooke was standing and
trying to say goodbye to Connie. "I hope you trap some truly
gorgeous ñañigos," she was saying. "I really do. Clap those
hands and roll them eyeballs." I really liked her at such moments.

"If you can't trap them yourself," I said, "maybe you
can get Mr. Brod to help you."

His chicken-bone shoulders hunched by inches. "Mr.
Garmes, I don't have to take your insults."

"I take yours. Your face is an insult." I couldn't stop the
words and I wanted to. He talked entirely too much like my
father, and I'd had too much to drink.

"I don't get in barroom brawls."

"Try. Make an effort."

"I wouldn't give you the satisfaction."

I stepped in front of him as he turned. "Yes, you'd better go. You lose face if you go, but you'll lose more if you stay. All the insipid Groton face you've got." He tried to move and I stepped closer. He even looked like my father, with that lippy embarrassment. "I'll try to make the point. Barto's in some kind of danger and you're part of it. If anything happens to him I'll be coming after you." Then I turned away, feeling dizzy. It felt like a stopper was pulled somewhere back of my eyes, a salty discharge came down my upper lip and over my chin. When I looked up again Brooke was moving fast toward the entrance.

"My hero," Connie said. "Making faces at the nasty professor mans." But in a matter of seconds the quills were out of her voice and she was playing with my earlobes and saying, with tin cups in her words, "Let's get out of here, Robbie. Let's go to your place, please, Robbie."

"You really want to?"

"Yes, Robbie. Yes, Robbie. Yes, yes, yes, yes."

"Not if you keep talking like a paperback novel."

It was a way of saying yes in the grudging form of a no, but she wasn't overly concerned with form. She brightened up immediately and clapped her hands. "Going to your place! Going to do the thing! Vaya means go!"

On our way out the band began to blare again and there was a spatter of fingers on the bongos, but when I turned involuntarily I saw without understanding that it wasn't Coolio fronting the band, it was another man, the leader with the ruffled shirt, and Coolio was nowhere in sight. I said, "Somebody was telling me tonight you weren't an irrelevancy." The truth was, I needed her with me, somebody. My voice was saying in my ear, "All he treasures is sunken treasure," saying, "If he must walk the plankton," and I didn't want to be sitting alone in a room listening to the words.

FIVE   The last half mile we left the road and went on up the deserted beach. The coral dust, left damp-packed by the going tide, made whining noises under our rubber soles. "I'm Polly Rhythmic!" Connie shouted. "My name is Polly and I'm from Dahomey and Polly wants a rhythmic!" I told her to pipe down before the seismographs cracked. She said she would take my words under advisement and immediately began to pull her clothes off, first the turtleneck sweater, then, in spite of my telling her to act her age, with her explaining in high-dignity severeness that she was at the age where men were forever begging her to act her age by taking her clothes off tooty-sweety, the tight velvet toreador pants. I let it go. Tell gazelles to put on kimonos. Nobody was around.

"The moon is my step-ins," she said, rubbing against me. "I shall not want."

I tried to pull her along. "You always want. Every time you're tried, you're found wanting."

"I adore the direction this is taking."

As we went along, the moon got blotted and night thickness came down over our heads with gunnysacks. Connie danced near and ran her fingers down my sides. "Penny for your thoughts. Two bucks for the rest of you."

"After twelve o'clock I never talk money. It's vulgar."

"After twelve o'clock is the best time to be vulgar. If you can't arrange it earlier."

Why were my teeth put on edge by that boarding-school talk of Brooke's, the mouth gorging on each word as though it was an apple? My father went on talking like that up to the time he went under. . . . The moon swung out again. I looked at Connie. She was a deep tan from following the sun from Capri to Acapulco. Mermaiding along brown and silver, cupping hands under her breasts with self joy or a try at it, toes springy and chin stretched whippet long and knowing she looked good and with boldness that came from the knowledge —she was a D.P. porpoise, and without lacks anywhere. Not where they showed. It was rightness enough for the eyes, at least.

"You're nice to look at."

She stopped ponying around. She came up facing me and put her hands to my shoulders. "I love to hear you say that," she said in a high, thin, failing voice. "It empties me of my spine."

I kissed her. Lips soft and not asking for everything but only stating nice facts. "You're fine, in so many ways." I meant it, almost meant it, though I was irritated, as always, by the little-girl forlornness in her voice. "Why are you throwing your time away on the Boyars, or guys like me, either? You could do better."

"You're what I want, Robbie."

"You want me because you don't want anything."

"Well, honey, you're not anything to write home about, maybe. But you're for me. When you say things like that to me, you make me feel, oh. Besides, I haven't got a home to write about anybody to."

There it was: her whole story. She knew she was the world's orphan, and she knew the world was down on orphans. "You're right about this much, Boyar's nice shiny yacht isn't much of a home."

"It keeps the rain out. Also, it gives me mink coats, which keep the rain out."

"You don't keep the important rains out."

"Who does? The big ones are manufactured inside." Who could hate a girl with that kind of style?

The sand was still sending out its petitions of protest. It moaned in its throat and said, They-step-all-over-me. "Connie, you're two things. You're great to look at, and you're a self-appointed orphan."

But all she could say to that, in a voice again full of lollipop hungers, was, "I'm really really in love with you, Rob. Be good to me, honey." Meaning: I can be had, oh boy, that is my gift, but where are those with wish or skill to take? Ouch, went the bullied sands.

"Let's go through the lab. I left the door open."

She went straight for the bedroom, but I stopped in the kitchen to pour myself a double shot of Scotch. When I slipped in next to her she took hold of me and pulled at my shoulders as though she was going under and I was the only log in the vicinity. It gave me a moment of panic, it echoed too much, not only dreams, and I jerked back and said, "You're not drowning, this is a bed."

"Rob. Honey."

"There's sand in the bed."

"Honey, it's been so long."

"We ought to shake out the sheets."

"Never mind the sheets. Robbie."

"Easy, baby. There's nothing but time."

When her body stopped being a board from head to foot, one warped board without hinges, when she stopped taking initiatives and was falling in with mine and encouraging them by that, it was only a concession, not anything felt, muscle rhetoric, but it was better than nothing. But how long can you play the orphan, perennial shutout? So, very slowly, very subtly, with just perceptible shifts, the least quickenings, rolling head from side to side and whispering as though out of her mind with the magic of it and so not responsible, she began the searching again, the searching and the exploration, with drive that had to be dictator. She, her deposing body, was announcing that my time had to be over, now it was her time, and she began to fight the clock, crowd ease to the far corner.

Changing of the guard. I did what I always did, froze. She did what she always did, looked up at me in shock and interrupted joy. Up wide-eyed at me, the lollipop thief. "What's wrong?" Me, the scourge of orphans.

"You know. It's no good this way."

"But it's wonderful, darling. Please don't stop." She was going to hold on to the lie with both hands and her teeth.

"Like the dancing tonight was wonderful?"

"Dancing? The—" Tin cups in the eyes. We'd been through this twenty times, and each time her eyes had backed off to the cradle and whimpered, What, what, love me, love me.

"How can two lead, Connie? Especially when you lead with a part of you that isn't involved with me." As though, between her great body being a liar and my wanting it to stick to the facts, or at least lie better, talk could work out any truce terms.

Her eyes widened again. As fast as she could she sucked her anger inside and fell back on the everready dodge, the passion that makes madmen of us all: "I'm so sorry, Robbie. I didn't mean to, I—I got carried away, darling, it was so wonderful."

So we let ourselves get carried away again, with this wonderful thing she didn't feel, this tidal wave of no-feeling she didn't ever want to end. Each with his wary third eye on the other, until the phone rang.

SIX "Mr. Garmes? Owen Brooke. I hope I didn't wake you." He sounded as though he'd been running.

"Where are you?"

"I don't know exactly. It's a gasoline station near where we're anchored. Look, I don't know if this means anything, but you see, we had a passenger on our boat, a man. He was anxious to talk to Barto. The thing is, I just got back and, well, this man isn't here. He said he'd wait for me—"

"Did you go to school to learn how to use words sideways?" I said. "What the hell are you trying to say?"

"I'm sure it's nothing, this fellow probably just got bored and decided to take a walk, but if you're so worried about Barto—"

"So you're calling out the Marines. Because a man took a walk." I wanted to add: The human race didn't go to all the trouble of inventing hysteria so it could be recited like elocution lessons.

"Mr. Garmes, I'm calling *you*. I just thought—"

"You and thinking haven't been introduced yet! What do you expect *me* to do, comb the Key for a man with six thumbs? How do I recognize this walker who takes such harmless walks, you're practically tearing your hair out? Is his name by any chance—"

"I thought you'd want to know. Sorry to have bothered you, Mr. Garmes." The phone went dead.

I dialed Barto's number, there was no answer. I tried Caprio at the Concha but the night clerk, a fellow I knew, said he'd just gone out. Barto and Caprio had come down in the elevator and stood talking in the lobby, then they shook hands and Barto left. Caprio called a man from the cocktail lounge and this man left in a hurry, and right after that Caprio himself went out.

"Come back to bed, Rob," Connie said, wriggling her fingers at me.

"For more photo finishes?" I said. But this was under my breath, she didn't hear, as her hands urged at my neck I let myself sink down. Thinking that I was one thing trapped in shape, and the rest of the world another shaped thing, and between us there were no transactions. Grindstones everywhere. . . .

Salt water ran down my lips.

"Darling, it gets better every time."

"Yes."

"Why are you so quiet, darling?"

"It's because I'm not talking."

That strained hollowness, big gift to me, when her need was to jut and press.

"Is anything wrong? Darling, wasn't it just as good for you?"

Sisyphus with shoulder to stone, uphill all the way. At the time for leaving off effort and becoming final passenger, the grinding.

"Connie, leave it alone. All right, it was good."

I reached for the phone and tried Barto again. No answer. The desk clerk said Caprio was still out. Connie was raised on one elbow, face full of over-fulfilled love and asking little over-loving questions about why I wasn't lit up with over-love too.

"It was the best ever for *me*."

"Connie, it's all right. It's as good as it can be."

"You mean, under the circumstances?"

"Under the circumstances."

"The circumstances being?"

"Exactly what they've always been. You're a wonderful girl and we should never be in the same town together."

"Will you explain to me how it happens that you're the only one ever has any complaints?" Her voice was less loving now. "When all the others just about die? . . . I make all kinds of concessions. I try like the devil." Her voice was going wobbly. "I lean over backwards with you."

"That's one of the troubles."

I made myself a promise there and then: never would I again touch a woman not a full siphon for my thoughts and a full partner in needs. How long could I live up to the promise? Last time, it had been two weeks.

Grindstone glories. All the together she knew or could know.

"Connie," I said, with no fight, "I don't care how many men you've had, you're an incorrigible virgin. You've never been had. You've only been touched on the outside, where it doesn't count."

"Well. You're the world's authority on how it should and

shouldn't be. Accentuate the inside and eliminate the outside
for sonny boy. . . . Listen! How do you know so much about
where a woman's feelings are? Outside! Inside!" She sat straight
up. "No woman ever felt anything where you say. I'm telling
you. . . ."

"All right. You've told me."

"It can't be that way. . . . All the way inside? The whole
thing inside?" She raised her fists. "Damn you! If I have to
listen to any more of that!" She was all over me, pounding
on my chest and screaming. "You! You!" I had to put real
effort in it to push her over on her back. She began to sob,
making rattling noises.

"Come on, Connie. It isn't that bad." I patted her on
the shoulder, rubbed her scalp.

"Love me, Rob." Her whole body was going. "I try and
I try and nobody. . . . It's so hard. . . . You can't win. . . ."
When she stopped shaking and opened her eyes, the tears still
running, she was the little girl in pigtails again. "What's so
funny?" she said uncertainly.

"I just thought of something. It's six weeks since I walked
into that hamburger joint and you asked me to pass the ketchup
and we got to talking."

"That's not funny."

"Yes, it is. People don't generally get this edgy with each
other until their silver anniversary, at least."

"It's that Henry Ford did it all." She wiped her cheeks
on the pillow case. "He had to get his two cents in. Him and
his goddamn speedup."

I leaned over and took her in my arms and kissed her,
with plenty of warmness. "We're no good together, that's for
sure, but I'm real fond of you, Connie."

"I love you, Rob," she said in the high, small voice. She
saw me pull in a little, as I always did when the pigtails crept
into her tone. "I love you," she said, with strength and quality,
"and I want to be touched by you. Deeply. Maybe I ought to
go and study letting-go under Professor Upbeat Brooke."

"Don't study anything under anybody. You're fine as you are." I kissed her again, and turned to get the phone. Barto was still out and Caprio was still out.

"I didn't like the way that Brooke kept after Barto to go down to his boat. He's a wrong one, Rob. Who's the other man on his boat?"

I stared. "Other man? How do you know?"

"Is it important? On my way back from seeing you this afternoon, I passed this big cruiser idling, I saw the name was *Easy Rider* and I went over. There was a man at the wheel, a sort of thin fellow, in his forties but well preserved, blond. I was a little high, you know, so I waved at him and yelled something about what a nice boat he had, but he ducked."

My watch said 2:43. "Honey, I'm worried about Barto. I'm going over to his place and see if he's all right. You stay here and get some sleep." Before leaving I leaned over to rub the back of her neck. "Don't pay any attention to what I said. I like you fine."

Going along the beach I walked fast, trying to clear my head. I thought about the thin blond man who ducked in a hurry, his name could be Michael. The moon was out, and about halfway along to Barto's house I saw a tall, thin, familiar-looking figure coming toward me, hurrying. There wasn't any place to hide, so I dropped down on the sand. He came closer, looking like he had a lot on his mind. I waited until he was a few yards from me, then I jumped up and said, "Evening, Professor."

He jerked as though from an impact. "Huh? Oh—why, it's you! Garmes!" He looked up and down the beach. "You scared the dickens out of me. What are you doing out this time of night?"

"Suppose I asked you that, Professor?"

"Why, I, I was looking for Barto. The lights are on at his house, but he's not there."

"Come on along with me. We'll make sure he's not there."

"I'm sorry but I'm in a hurry. We're due to leave tonight, I'm late now."

"I'm going to insist. If you want to be balky, fine."

He studied me with no enthusiasm. "Oh, very well. If you're going to be nasty about it."

He turned and began to walk just ahead of me. Before I knew it he was stopped and turning around fast with his fists coming at my jaw. He didn't look like much with his Brooks Brothers underfed look, but coming at me that way, with me off guard, he had considerable strength. I went down and sat on the sand, wagging my head. When I came out of it and looked down the beach I saw the professor about fifty yards away, sprinting. Even in good shape I couldn't have caught him.

I got up and ran. At Barto's window I stopped and looked in through the bottom blades of the Venetian blind. Barto was there. He was on the floor, the upper half of his body naked, just wearing chino pants. Blood was coming down his back from a place on the left shoulder blade close by the two bullet holes, there was a knife in his back at that place and the blood was coming from there. He was face down and not moving, except for his fingers going absent-mindedly at the carpet.

SEVEN   He was conscious, just about. "Barto. It's Rob." I put my arm around his right shoulder. What is to be done when a man is spitted, in the place of his heart and best substance, with an inch-wide spit? "Barto." Blood was coming from his back in unrelated thin lines. Mucus, spotted with blood, ran down his chin from the corner of his mouth. "Barto, can you hear me?"

His eyelids fought their way open. His dedication had pulled in, he was dedicated to the unifying steel camping in his lungs and dearest gristle. He looked puzzled, interrupted in important work. "Who did it, Barto?"

The lips moved, the throat thickened as the muscles in it worked. "Caa. Ca-ap."

"Tell me who did it. Try."

"Cap. Ap. Ri."

"Caprio? Caprio did it?"

"Tell. Ap. Ri, ri, o. Phono."

"Phone? Telephone Caprio?"

"Teléfono. Tell."

"All right. Try not to move, I'll phone Caprio." I let his face down on the mat, easy, and ran to the telephone. I dialed the Concha, and in seconds Caprio was at the other end with his scoutmaster preciseness. "I'm at Barto's. He, I think he's—"

"Where is that bastard?" There was a new push and harshness in his voice. "We were keeping an eye on him, trying to, but he got away."

"He's here. He's got a knife in his back. Caprio, all I can do is look at it and I'm afraid to touch it. He's alive but not much—"

There were noises at the other end, it sounded like blowing. "They got him? Here? The dirty, ah, the dirty. . . ." Now it sounded like he was hitting something with his fist. "Listen, Garmes."

"He wanted me to call you. Can you get a doctor over here?"

"Garmes, try to keep him alive."

"I can't touch the knife, it sticks out of him and moves when he breathes." I hung up and went back to Barto. "All right, Caprio's on his way over." I reached down and cupped his cheek with my hand. "He's bringing a doctor."

He took several chugging breaths. The knife handle jumped each time. "Loose." I thought that was what he said.

"What, Barto? What's loose?"

"Pobre, pobre. Loose."

Something was poor, and something was loose. "Qué es pobre? Quien es pobre?"

He made a sound I thought was "hair." He repeated it and it got lengthened to "hermana." Sister. He said, "Ai, la pobrecita. Mi. Hermana. Pobre hermana mia. Loose."

It came to me that if he was talking Spanish, maybe he was saying "luz" and not "loose." It was the word for light, but it was used for a girl's name. "Donde está? Donde está tu hermana?"

"No sé." He had a sister named Luz, whom he'd never mentioned in eight years. He didn't know where she was, and he thought of her being poor as he was dying. "You. Rob. Find her. Must. Muy importante."

"I will do everything. Voy a hacer todo."

"Padre. Pobre padre. Disparado. Barcelona. Completamente disparado. Ai, mamacita, mamacita. Mi pobrecitita. Luz."

His poor father had disappeared, completely disappeared, in Barcelona, probably, and his head was full of his little mama, poor little mama. Also of Luz, the equally poor. "Barto, you've got to tell me. Who did it?"

He looked at me, eyes empty, and he said, "Pero es muy conocido que el hombre es inglés." Someone, some man, it was well known, was English.

"I'll say a name and if you want to say yes, close your eyes. That's all, just close your eyes. Was it Brooke?" The eyes kept looking at me. "Caprio? Was it Caprio, or somebody connected with him?" The eyes said nothing. "Who was that drummer in the Late Watch, Coolio? Did you know him? Was he the one, Coolio?" No sign. "The man you call Michael? Tell me, Bart."

Something like a smile came over his lips. "Ah, sí. La sociedad. Verdad."

"La sociedad? Qué es verdad? Dígame."

"Seguro. Entonces. En toda casa, el milagro, casa milagro. Casa del milagro. Vamos a ver el milagro glorioso. Mil milagros y Luz y Miguel, Michael. Ai, el cabrón. En la espaldilla, dos veces, a espaldas, detrás del olivo."

He was talking about the miracle, the house of the miracle, saying we should go and see the glorious miracle, the thousand miracles and Luz and Michael, Michael the son of a bitch, in the shoulder blade, twice, behind the back, behind the olive tree, then black clots came from his mouth. His eyes rolled back to their more important work, his face went slack. The last expression he had, as the mouth fouled itself, was surprise.

The eyes were reversed, fixed in all-white surprise. I put his head on the floor and pressed the eyelids down. There was blood on my hands, I saw. I went wildly into the kitchen to wash, it was hard to get off. Then I remembered Connie. I went to the phone and called my place, she took a long time answering and when she did her voice was dragged with sleep.

"Get your head clear and listen. Barto's been killed. You've got to dress and get out of there."

"What? Barto? What are you—"

"You want the news to get out that the night Barto was killed you were at my place? You want that news waiting for Boyar when he gets back?"

"Never mind that. My God, Barto. How can it be?"

"Somebody put a knife in his back. We were in speaking distance of each other for eight years and neither spoke. Five minutes ago he wanted to speak to me but he couldn't, the knife was there. . . . Remember the waterproof minks, Connie. Remember how you like to stay out of the rain. Get home fast, do you hear? I'll call you." I hung up so she wouldn't hear me crying.

EIGHT "Technically, suffocation," the doctor said. He was a small brush-haired man who dismissed his words before he spoke them, as though everything not done with his sure hands was only for protocol and a waste. "Blood in lungs, when blood detours, nnnn." He stood and faced us, returning his wave-edged panama to his head and snapping black bag shut. "You won't be needing me here. I'll make out a report." Caprio thanked him and saw him outside, then came back.

"Neat job," he said. "This time it had to be."

"We'd better call the police."

"You recognize there are civil aspects to a corpse? I'm surprised." He came toward me, pulling his wallet out. "I'm police enough." He flipped the wallet until a transparent plastic holder came up and held it out. Inside was an identification card with government seals on it, establishing Vincent Caprio as something official without getting too precise. What the card lacked in precision was made up for by the signature of a Cabinet member. "Some of us in Washington have been giving a lot of thought to Barto. I was assigned to think about him full time."

"Then why—"

"It was important to keep him alive." He was doing a free-lance talking to the walls, letting me listen. "Important to everybody but Barto. Seven months of careful, careful thinking down the drain."

"You could have told me."

"Yes. Sure." He decided to recognize my presence finally. "I know you, Garmes. You don't care for institutions any more than Barto did."

"Do your institutions know who did this?"

"Do you?"

"On my way here I met Owen Brooke, if you know him. He'd just been here."

Caprio looked bored. "These people use an Owen Brooke to run errands. If knives are going to be used they don't even tell Brooke, he's squeamish."

"You were supposed to be watching Barto."

"I'm afraid," Caprio said, looking irritated, "I didn't give you all the facts over the phone. I said Barto got away from our man but it wasn't quite that way. Our man made a bad error in judgment. It was understandable." All the same he looked disgusted. He kept turning to the phone as though he expected it to ring. He got out a cigarette and put it in his holder, the kind that has another cigarette inside for a filter. I noticed that the cigarette itself had a filter tip. "When Barto left the Concha this man, Seward, went after him. Then a third party appeared ahead of Seward, also trailing Barto. Barto must not have seen him too well and figured him for one of *my* men and decided to lose him. He wanted to sneak up to Miami, I think, and take a plane from there. I was counting on that, I had a man up in Miami waiting."

"To stop him?"

"To keep him company without his knowing it. I also had a man waiting in Havana."

"Then you weren't serious about warning him not to go."

"I was, very. But I knew how serious he was about going. I'd had this out with him before." He frowned at the telephone.

"Why'd you bother to warn him at all?"

"New situation. The man with reason to kill him was back in Cuba. Well, Barto started to shake the third party. After several turns and backtracks, Seward found he was still with the third party but the third party was no longer with Barto. Seward couldn't stop to check with me. He thought it out on his feet and decided to stick, instead of trying to pick Barto up. This lad led Seward on a tour of the Key. Then he cut down a side street, went up the steps into the Late Watch, changed back from dark clothes to white ones, got his drums and climbed on the band stand."

I blinked at that. "Coolio?"

"Seward knows Coolio is connected with Barto's enemies. So long as he kept Coolio in sight, he figured, Barto was safe. Just what he was intended to think."

"Somewhere around two Brooke called me. He was upset about a passenger on his boat, a man who'd come here to see Barto."

He looked unhappy, staring at the phone. "The *Easy*

Rider's manifest doesn't say anything about a passenger. There *isn't* any manifest. That boat left Havana without getting clearance from the port authorities."

"That explains why Brooke was worried. He was smuggling somebody in here, and traveling illegally himself—he knows that's serious business." I dropped into a wicker chair. "Was it the passenger who killed Barto? Brooke said he was missing."

"That," Caprio said, "is a possibility."

"Then what're we sitting here for!"

"It's better than standing."

"This is crazy!" I jumped up. "I'm going—"

"You don't go anywhere until that boat's out to sea." He sighed, fell on the settee, crossed his legs. "We want the *Easy Rider* where it's going, which is, I'd say, somewhere on the north coast of Cuba." I started for the door. "Sit down, Garmes. Stop bucking the institutions." He didn't move. "If you try to shove off, the police will stop you. If you get away I'll have the Coast Guard bring you back, after which I'll have you thrown in jail for obstructing justice. Sit down."

I came back and sat down. "What justice have you got to obstruct?"

Ignoring me, he got up and went for the phone. "Operator 21," he said into the mouthpiece, his finger tracing spirals on the wall. "Operator 21? Major Caprio. How about that call to Cuba? . . . I see. Keep trying, it's urgent. I'll be at the same number." He took his place on the settee again, studying a cigarette burn in the fabric cover and scowling. He took a deep breath and let the air out with an escaping-steam sound. "Let's talk about that passenger for a minute. I can tell you two things about him. He's almost certainly the one who killed Barto, and I don't see how his name can be anything but Michael Brod. I'll know for sure when my call comes through."

"Thin, blond, in his forties? That's how the passenger was described to me."

"That's him. Have you guessed yet that Brod's what Barto was looking for on all his trips?"

"Still, when Brod was mentioned last night Barto just looked remote."

"Garmes, Garmes. Haven't you noticed how lovers act when the objects of their affection are mentioned—how bored they try to look? For twelve years Brod was Barto's one passion. Most of the time it took the place of sex. One head isn't big enough for two passions like that. Barto was in love with the idea of Brod's death, he wrote sonnets to it."

"What did Brod do to him?"

"For one thing, he put those bullet holes in Barto. April 21, 1937, at 4:19 in the afternoon, on a hill south of Huesca, in a pretty olive grove. Brod botched the job—Barto didn't die. Brod did a better job on Barto's father. Arturo was kidnapped in Barcelona, carried on board a freighter, and never heard from again."

"What about Barto's family? He never talked about them."

"The mother died before Barto could get back to Havana. The kid sister disappeared. Barto was never able to find her though a lot of people helped him look, myself included."

"Then Barto felt Brod had destroyed his family?"

"It was a documented fact." He pointed again at Barto's body. "One of the slugs is still there, it shows up clear in the Navy X-rays. Brod was very much with Barto, part of him, you could say."

"Didn't Barto expect to get shot at in a war?"

"Ah." Caprio nodded. "But Brod and Barto were in the same army. It was a very peculiar war. Those on the Loyalist side had big differences about how to fight the war, about what, exactly, they were fighting *about*. Sometimes the differences got so bad that they would stop shooting at the enemy and shoot each other. Brod was highly skilled at shooting his comrades in the back while they were trying to shoot Falangists at the front. It was his main function in the Loyalist militia, he was what's known as a spetz, a specialist. In back-shooting."

I sat for a long time, numbed. Finally I said: "What are you a specialist in?"

"More and more things. After Spain, Brod found other wars. Less spectacular, with little shooting, the kind that go on miles underground in the sewers on seven continents. These newer wars interest us. Lately we've been learning the special techniques and sending our people in, here and there. Brod came to our attention because he's been operating on our doorstep—Canada, Mexico, Cuba, sometimes right in the States."

"It doesn't make sense! If he's that dangerous—you could get him for this!"

"The new-style wars aren't fought that openly," Caprio said lazily. "You don't go after your man as you would in a clean, open, shooting, Marquess of Queensberry war. Most of the time you don't get your man at all, don't even want to, you just try to get something from him or outwit him in some maneuver, or stymie him. You practically never grab him and clap him in irons. Sometimes you sit and drink a cup of coffee and chat with him."

"You're trying to get something from Brod?"

Caprio smiled. "Take my word for it, he has something we want very much. Eventually we may get it, if amateurs with appetites for personal justice don't get in the way. There's nothing personal—"

The phone rang. Caprio was across the room in three steps to answer it. "Yes," he said. "This is Major Caprio. . . . Good. Put him on. . . . Carlos? Barto's dead. What the hell happened down there? . . . The regatta. Yes, I heard. That was smart. . . . You've been keeping a twenty-four-hour watch? . . . Then how. . . . Who *did* leave the building? Describe everybody your men reported. . . . No. . . . No, doesn't sound right. . . . Army officer? I don't think so, too risky. . . . Negro woman? Give me that again. . . . Old. Withered foot. Surgical boot. . . . That could be it. Yes. I think—in Ottawa —yes. The day he got away there was a report about an old woman with a bad foot. We never could fit it in. It got filed away. . . . No. You couldn't be expected to know. . . . Wait there for me. I'll see you tomorrow. Keep me informed about where the boat puts in. . . . Right."

After hanging up he stood for a moment, hand to chin, thinking. He looked up: "Do you know what a paradoxical race of pragmatists we are? If we can't see a thing, hold it in our hand—we won't grant it exists. That's pragmatic, right? Pragmatists don't appropriate cold, hard cash for rumors and shadows. That means—no adequate funds for those who make themselves invisible to keep tabs on their invisible opposite numbers. Inadequate funds—limited manpower. . . . I had every available man from my department in position to cover Barto from here to Havana. Had to call back the few who were working in Cuba. Of course, the Cubans help us out, and they've got good men. But they don't have enough to go around either. So—the *Easy Rider* sets out innocently from the Havana Yacht Club to join the regatta—no port clearances, nothing to arouse suspicion—Brod sneaks out of the house in Vedado where the Cubans think they've got their eye on him —limps out as an old Negro woman with a surgical boot—nobody wants to lay a hand on a crippled old lady—manages to board the *Easy Rider*—sneaks in here and. . . ." He went over to the body and looked down at it. "We did our best, but we were short-handed. It was the pragmatists that got him."

"Didn't you see Brooke sitting with us at the Late Watch?" I said. "That meant the *Easy Rider* was here."

"We knew the *Easy Rider* was here before then. The Coast Guard reported it. We searched it—no sign of any passengers. I had only one man to spare, Seward. It seemed wiser to keep him near Barto than have him watch the boat." He sat down again. "The Europeans are a little more sophisticated about these things. They learned a long time ago that what's *visible* is the thing to be distrusted. . . . They accept the sewers. Undercover work is for them simply that part of international relations that isn't seen—the foundation work. Routine. Diplomacy's big brother. Kept in the cellar when there's company, of course. Its party manners aren't of the best. . . .

Well, all I had was Seward." He was beginning to look tired.
"Brod knew that. He did something absolutely desperate, the
one thing we didn't expect. He came *here*, himself. . . ." He
drummed on his knee, thinking. "And brought Coolio up, to
get the tail off Barto. . . . Damn, damn, damn." He hit his
knee with his fist, hard. "If I'd had two more men."

"Didn't Coolio's coming here make you suspicious?"

"He's traveling all the time. Most places he just plays his
drums." He grimaced. "Not that we were taking any chances.
As soon as I saw him I started calling Washington for two more
men. That's where *I've* been the last three hours—on the
phone." He saw that I was still puzzled. "Look, here's the
whole story. Barto told me Brooke was trying to get him down
to the boat. I thought Coolio might be here for that reason—
to get Barto on that boat somehow and bring him down to
Cuba—to Brod—whether he wanted to go or not. It didn't
make sense otherwise, Brooke taking the fool chance he did
coming up here illegally—Coolio could have been here to help
him—Brooke isn't a muscle man. Seward saw it that way too.
That's why he stuck with Coolio. . . . The whole thing is
this: we were getting hourly reports from Cuba saying Brod
was still holed up in his apartment—still being watched. He
couldn't have been here. But he was."

"You were bound to find out what happened to Barto
fast enough. Wasn't Brod worried that you'd understand he
was on the *Easy Rider* and come after him?"

"Brod's only problem was how to sneak *in* here. He can
relax going back, he knows that. . . . All we can do now is
try to keep him in sight. Oh, he understands. Only too well."
He stopped and looked at me speculatively. "I'm sorry there
aren't more dramatics in this. I know you like wars to be spectacular, even if they take a little insubordination to arrange."

I looked at him hard for that. "Insubordination. All right.
Which of my ribs is the birthmark between?"

Without any try at being funny he said, "Between the
fourth and fifth ribs, on the left."

At this point there were steps on the porch and four men came in, one a police lieutenant, two others who seemed to be plainclothesmen, another whose medical bag and dyspeptic eyes identified him as from the coroner's. "All yours, Lieutenant," Caprio said, as though he'd been expecting them. "Just see that it doesn't get in the papers right away. I'll go over it with you in the morning. . . . Let's get some air, Garmes." On the way out he told me he'd had the doctor make some calls to the local police. He hadn't let me know because he wanted me angry enough to continue barking at him until the *Easy Rider* was away. We sat down on the porch steps and he said, "Northeast Borneo, morning of July 3, 1945."

"8:45, roughly."

"Hitting the lieutenant (j.g.), knocking his incisor out."

"*He* was insubordinate. To his own common sense. He had a vision of pipes."

"You don't get my point," Caprio said mildly. "I didn't say you were wrong. All I said was, you knocked an incisor, upper jaw, left, out of the lieutenant's mouth."

"I had to do what I thought was called for. The same as Seward did tonight. When your man's wrong you call it understandable. When I'm right—"

Caprio nodded. "I didn't say what I intend to do about Seward. It was an understandable mistake but, you see, technically Seward didn't follow instructions, and in this highly technical war you've got to take your work—well, technically. My report will call Seward's mistake insubordination."

"What's that mean to him?"

"I expect and earnestly hope he'll be fired from our service and permanently blackballed. If he ever tries to get an official job again I'll see to it that he's thrown out of the building." He stopped to put another filter-tip cigarette in his long filter. I wondered if the cigarette that served as the filter inside the holder was also a filter-tip. "Incidentally, you may be interested to know that Seward and I went to college together. Up in Chevy Chase where we both live, his wife is my wife's friend.

We play bridge together once a week. Does that make my point?"

"You're an institution man."

"And I strongly suspect you're going to be a nuisance to the institutions I work for."

I stood up and said: "I don't know about them but I know this. You were interested in Barto as bait."

"Of course. Obviously that's how you'd see it. . . . Don't you think there's something funny about my sitting here telling you things you've no right to know?"

"I began to find out some of them myself."

"Absolutely. What I've told you is my carefully considered estimate of just how much you might find out if you went galloping off on a one-man mission. It was intended to save you a lot of work."

"Thanks."

"I didn't do it for your sake. I don't want another quixotic loner messing up my work." He stood up and stretched.

"Tell me this. Is there any chance you people will make a serious effort to get Brod for this killing?"

"For the time being, no. There've been other killings."

"Then we've got nothing to talk about."

"Except this: You're a hothead, you don't like institutions. All right—so long as you work off your angers in personal ways, being generally truculent and playing around with brass-knuck dames and taking crazy chances diving, that's your business. But I'm telling you now, stay out of *my* business. I warn you, I'll cut you down myself in two seconds when it's necessary. There's a lot at stake here, man. The parties involved are potential murderers of populations. On both sides. Keep—your —nose—out of it."

The screen door squeaked open, the police lieutenant was in the doorway asking if Major Caprio would come in. "I'll be there in a second, Lieutenant," Caprio said. He took a step toward the door, stopped and considered me again. "You think I'm quite a cornball, don't you? Judging from the way you cased my haberdashery last night." He relaxed and grinned. "I want you to know, back in my closet in Chevy Chase I've got five J. Press suits. My bureau's full of shirts with soft button-down collars, I hate starched collars. Don't sneer at anybody's working clothes, friend." He turned serious again. "By the way, I considered that Barto was a friend of mine too, one of the best." He went in then, without any more backward looks.

NINE   Down the road from Barto's house there was a broad-bodied man in an open-neck sports shirt, leaning against a willow tree. I went by him, passed two or three cross streets, turned quickly into another. When I reached Duval Street the man was still in sight, walking unhurried and observing the local architecture. The all-night hamburger place was just ahead. I waved at the half-awake college kid behind the counter as I ran past and out the back way into the alley. I went full speed down this alley, then down another that branched off from it. When I stepped out on a real street again, Oyster, there was nobody in sight. I started west, toward the inlet just below the Navy base, making sure the roads both ways were empty before I went to Aristides's back window and tapped.

It took him awhile to come to the door. He was an old man, with knuckles and cheekbones permanently cancered from the sun, and he looked older still with the gray hair tangling over his eyes and his bagged corduroy pants, that he'd just slipped over his nakedness, pinned in place by his elbows, the fireman-red Stork Club suspenders that a gentleman fisherman had once given him down around his knees. He pulled a shredding sweater on and got his sneaks tied while I told him what to do. He went without asking questions.

Kimon was fast asleep at the other end of the house, I was

safe in using the phone. I put in a call for Maury Catums,
whose pharmaceutical laboratory up in Tampa bought most of
our shark livers. He'd had a big night and was suffering from a
hangover, but the news about Barto shook him sober. I explained that I had to get over to Cuba, without being seen,
and he reacted as I'd expected, by offering to get his plane and
fly me down. I told him how to spot the bight near Aristides's,
using Fort Taylor and the Navy installations as landmarks.

Aristides was back from the office in thirty minutes with
the valise, the clothes, and the gun. Nobody had seen him,
either along the way or at the shed. While I got into the sum-
mer-weight flannel suit, I began to relax. I could hear Caprio
with the what's-what tone in his voice, saying, "We can't think
too much about this or that man," and I was more than relieved, I was celebrating, to be out of his orbits. I sat down at
the window to wait, watching the sun come up and brush carnival colors on the cloud humps, the corrugations of the water.
For the first time in hours I was aware that the roof of my
mouth and my throat were sore all through.

An hour later the Cessna set down in the cove. I was waiting when it taxied in, and in a minute I was strapped in alongside Maury, waving to Aristides as his answering arm became a
matchstick and the scrubby pines behind him shrank to moss.
"The poor, poor bastard," Maury said when we got on the subject of Barto. "He had a family? I thought he was born in the
hollow left foot of an albatross." The sun was on our left, an
ascending blast furnace. I remembered that sixteen hours before I'd been fathoms under the water, trying to locate the sun
and not finding it. "Poor bastard," Maury said again. "He was
a damned good businessman but wherever his heart was, it
wasn't in shark livers." Maury asked if I needed any money. I
told him I had banking connections in Havana, I would cash
a check, but he pulled a roll of bills from his pocket and held
it out. "Six hundred, it's all the cash I had on hand. You
sound like you may be too busy to get to banks."

I talked about Caprio, trying to get that part of it straight in my own mind, the warnings to Barto that weren't exactly warnings, the friendliness that had qualities of skilled angling. When I ran out of words, Maury let air through his teeth in a silent whistle. "Wow-wee. It's wild, sure enough. The wildest thing is that you and me are taking this ride." I looked at him blankly. His bloodshot eyes were staring, his meaty red face exploded in something worse than anger. "You got rocks in your head, man? This Caprio kept warning Barto off, and kept watching him, and Barto took his trips. Now Caprio's warning you and watching you, and here *you* are a traveling man. Think, Robbie!" Planes never bothered me, but instantaneously this two-seater was coffin close around me and I felt my lungs were stoppered, heart pounding, sweat was swimming over my skin. "You bonehead! He lost a good bait in Barto, now you step up and volunteer! He was counting on your doing just that! He didn't stop you on the Key because he wants you in Cuba!" I was suffocating, and trying not to look down at the copper-sheeted sea. "Robbie, what say we turn back?"

"No." I was under again, long fathoms down and dropping, I had to breathe immediately and unmetaphorically and the top was too far away.

... *down* ...

At La Jolla I sat and waited for Barto. There was little to do, the crews from Navy Electronics and U.S. Hydrographic were rigging the research ship with echo sounders and net-pulling equipment. I took up cigars, less for the taste than to watch their helixing smoke: my mind was still in hospital rest, unable to turn over by itself, and anything that moved, had inner propulsions, interested me. Afternoons I went out to the end of the pier and braced myself against a bulkhead, barnacle-set, studying driftwood for tendencies, reconstructing the night off Balikpapan when Barto kept hitting me and saying I was yellow all through. He hadn't been making a moral valuation but stating physical facts. My face, nails, earlobes, eyes and eyelids were turned a sick and sallow saffron. By the time they got me back on our converted destroyer escort I was running a 104 temperature and raving about the curdle colors of the world. In the Borneo seas I had succumbed to the least of the yellow perils, yellow jaundice. Nobody had noticed the first signs. Biliousness was expected from me anyhow, Barto later wrote me in the hospital: if my bedpan hues had been seen they would have been taken as the seepage of an attitude. But why, I wrote back, not sold on the joke, did such inside souring come out as a loudmouth sunniness? Then shouldn't all glow-face Americans be examined for catarrhal stoppages in the common bile duct?

Through the Larrañaga smoke I considered my family. On my convalescent leave I had gone down to New Bedford. My folks were dazed with war prosperity. My mother had contracted all her catches to the quartermaster at Fort Devens and with the steady Army money bought a second trawler and fixed up the old one, as well as hired some crews. She was for the first time tasting the rhapsody of whole days off, days when nothing was required of her but breathing, and my father, though he had only to go on loafing as before, could for once call it no crime but his right.

They were dislocated by the money. It robbed them of their definitions. Not having to fight for his freedom to do nothing, my father had, so to speak, lost his one steadying occupation. With his idleness endowed and underwritten now, instead of stolen, he seemed less a defender of unpopular causes than somebody hanging around. His gray eyes were felty, and the sidelines jokes gone. This was the last time I was to see him. Months later, at the golden upturning in his life when my mother let him throw out his patched and skinned clothes and buy a wardrobe, he was one day sitting on the porch in new gabardines and loafers, his boyish baby-toned face freshly shaven, graying straight hair newly barbered and combed, disheartenedly doing a drawing on his sketchpad of the busy harbor at the foot of the hill, and in some manner

the commotions of the working world down there must have
got through as some final dig at him and his sketches and sidelines looking because his pinkish cheeks turned purple and he
mumbled, according to my mother, "Goes on forever, they
load and unload," and he slid to the floor and died that way,
blue-faced, neat-combed, in the first new clothes he'd had in
better than twenty years. But that was later. At the time of
my visit he was just moody and absent-aired and often could
be found in the glass-enclosed studio porch my mother had
built for him, tearing up old sketches and water colors and
saying to himself some such thing as, "No vision. Just a lot of
fingers." He said to me once at supper, "Rob, here's a riddle.
When is a hobby a hobble?" and limped away from the table
before I could even pretend to answer.

My mother too was punctured. Do something: push: keep
a hold had been the motto and program of her days, but now
when she said the words it was without conviction, as an after-
thought, her tone increasingly puzzled—as though rebuttals
were being prepared behind her back. She, who for years had
done a man's double chores on the boat and thrived, now in
her first vacation from the hauling and carting developed all
sorts of aches and pains, arthritic twinges, fiery bursitis, a
permanent stiffening inflammation in the lower spine, bad
migraines. Maybe she had worked too hard to feel anything in
these stalled hours but the postponed and now reaped hurts
in her bones. She lost her appetite. Her once stocky body
looked spent, the skin hanging loose and with the rippled
bleach texture that comes from being in water too long. In one
year her hair had turned from its streaked silken auburn to
almost pure white. What went on in her mind I never knew,
but I felt she blamed this downhill chemistry in her on my
father. Since it was so clearly a visitation. She never turned
her eyes to him any more. She had built the studio to banish
him from the rest of the house and now she would not even
sit in the same room with him. It seemed that if she could not
hold him an offender she could grant him no space at all. But

having dismissed him from her thoughts she had no other thoughts to fill in—she was deprived of targets, and unpurposed. Prosperity, maybe, had robbed her of the indignation that held her together so long. She was to follow my father to the grave before the year was out. With her last breath, addressing herself to some album snapshot of me in the molding, she said earnestly, "Robbie, wherever you are, do something. Watching is too little." But this time it was a plea to be agreed with. I was sitting by her side, but she didn't recognize me.

On the front porch, the fishing boats unloading in the harbor down the hill, old Manuel played with his cane and talked to me without stop and with much gaiety of the West Indies buccaneering he had never done but remembered in sprouting detail. Money had stirred his fantasy life to a last outburst. He now had a different sweatshirt for each day of the week, some with Mickey Mouse and Captain Marvel figures on the front. He reminded me that there were jokes, too. But I had to get away from the house: my mother and father were more alien bodies to cut off the vision. Foreign matter. Part of the clutter to be stepped around, to reach the free air on the far side. When I sat at the table with them and saw how their eyes avoided each other's, drawing in, I shrank from the yellow scene and wished I had some of Barto's indifference to scenes in general.

I had never had any extended talk with Barto, though we had been in the same demolition team and in daily contact from Maui across to Seppinggan. He was not much of a talker. But when I spoke of my family, the conglomerations, I sensed from his quietness and merely polite nods that he considered all objects not himself part of a debris easily brushed away. He was so inattentive to the hampering masses in the world that he went through his entire Navy service from boot camp to the Japanese occupation, doing every detail of his job flawlessly, with a steady air of not being conscious the Navy was there. His vision, you gathered, could not be cut off by outside

structures because he was never looking at anything but what
was inside himself. When I asked if he had any family he said
no, and let it drop. About the only matters we discussed in
any detail were the best ways of crimping hot primacord and
the concussion effects on the body of underwater explosions,
but I liked him.

I was satisfied with my orders to proceed from the hospital to California to join the oceanographic research group
being assembled there. When they told me at the La Jolla base
that they were still shorthanded, I took a chance and did some
fast talking about Barto, his U.D.T. record, his underwater interests, etc. They made inquiries and found out that after
V-J Barto and most of the team members would be hanging
around Japan on routine occupation duty, he could be spared.
He flew in during my third week in California, looking as contained and without grievances, and as busy with himself, as
ever. With the same quiet style of marking time. He didn't
mind my having suggested his transfer. A man had to be
someplace, he said; La Jolla and Tokyo Bay, and for that matter
Galaxy M 31 in the Constellation of Andromeda, were all the
same and all beside the point, he meant. Hanging around the
La Jolla pier, drinking beer out of cans, we talked about the
D.S.L. that the Navy wanted us to investigate. D.S.L., I explained, was short for Deep Scattering Layer, the migratory
mass of passive plankton life recently proved to exist in all
oceans and which displeased the Navy because it confounded a
ship's measuring instruments. When 18-kilocycle sound waves
were sent down to chart the ocean bottom, what came back
was not one set of echoes but two: the styluses on the drum
traced two bottoms, one true and one false. The phantom
bottom appeared only during the day, at depths from 150 to
450 fathoms down. Research started during the war suggested
that this layer most likely was a suspended mass of animal
and plant life—comb jellies, heteropods and other mollusks,
crustaceans like the copepod, sea and arrow worms, sauries,
squids, euphausiid shrimps—which rose to the surface at night

and with the appearance of the sun regrouped in dense strata far down. Our job when we went out on the research ship was to plot these movements in designated offshore waters, and with long sleeve nets to bring up plankton samples for further study. Barto listened and said fine, sounded like a reasonable project but what was I getting so intense about? The Panama Canal and the making of salvarsan had also been reasonable projects, did I get emotional about them? There was no way to make him see the obsession, the downright anger, you could develop over these untold tons of living matter falling and rising all over the globe, day and night, in answer to the sun's orders. All that drift: so much protoplasm in everlasting drill. Barto said my father and mother were too much on my mind, and laughed, without malice. Projects were projects, to be carried through but kept on the outside where they belonged.

Our work on the ship was routine. For the first five days, as we cruised back and forth over the canyon, Barto and I were chiefly busy with the sleeve nets, handling the winches that lowered them to various depths and seeing that they were dragged the prescribed distances before we cranked them back on board and emptied their squirming contents into tins for the planktologists. We had long stretches of time, as the nets streamed along underwater terrifying the dwarfed and luminous monsters huddled down there and scooping up the most stupid and dilettante of them, to rest our elbows on the rail and talk, or just smoke. The sea was placid, uninspired old-mop gray. The thin sauries rose to break the surface at the appearance of our night lights, the air was still and in general the cruise was not thought-provoking, which suited me. We smoked more than we talked. But on the sixth day we ran into a snag, literally. One of the nets had hooked onto some underwater obstacle and couldn't be maneuvered free. The nets were valuable and had to be salvaged if possible. The captain had immediately reversed the engines and was now moving the ship slowly in a circle to avoid snapping the tow line. Barto and I were instructed to go down and free the net if we could: our first diving job since we'd gone out, and my first time down since Borneo. This was at daybreak, sluggish fogged reds were beginning to stain the eastern horizon.

We put on our trunks, flippers and breathing equipment and climbed down the ladder. The water was chilly and colloidal near the surface, and got colder as we descended. Since we were after predawn plankton samples that day, hoping to catch the marine animals before the sun sent them on their regular morning dives, the nets had been let down to relatively shallow levels. The trouble was that the snarled net was one of the deepest, down thirty fathoms or more. Neither one of us had ever been that far down. We located the net without trouble, it was caught on a sharp hooked arm of rock projecting upward from the western sheer wall of the canyon; the ship must have run off course slightly and come closer to the wall than planned. It took only a couple of minutes to work the silk mesh clear, then Barto waggled his flashlight at me and made a sign that he was starting up. I signaled to him to go first but as he began rising slowly, long rubber fins paddling with lazy strokes, I realized with little surprise that I was watching him float away and making no effort to follow him. The sight of those slapstick shoes hitting at the water in slow motion, like the webbed feet of a pompous duck seen from underneath, struck me as a truly comic thing and worth watching from one place.

The upper waters were just now beginning to come alive with a cold blue-white neon glow, infused with the first frigid and bloodless rays of sunlight, and there was good old Barto the self-propelled, the self-trending, air cylinders humped on his back, feet under their own power, a contained and capsuled unit, going his own sweet way up into the smear of light with sublime indifference to the downward trends in all the tons of less willful protoplasm about him. That was the biggest joke, I suppose. He was in step with no migrations but his own. I watched his feet pumping steadily, with duck determination, and I thought it was the funniest and most note-

worthy sight I had ever seen. I felt an exhilarating lightness
all through me that was in some way part of the joke too. It
was not just the buoyancy of the body in water. It was somehow a lightheadedness, the sense of pressing weights lifted
from inside my skull and thoughts suddenly thinned, all the
muck filtered out and head clean and coldly lit like the
waters into which Barto was diminishing above. I hung motionless in the thick but dissipating blues some thirty fathoms
down, and the thick weighted blues in my head were being
sponged away and the lightness, the cleanness, the expansive
intensifying brisk spring sunniness that came into me, the in-
vading daybreak, was too encouraging and precious to lose.
There was a giddiness in me, and the need to laugh.

I hung still. Straining to hear something: the swish and
burble of the sun-regimented plankton animals on their forced
march downward, throbs of their coerced gills, clanking of their
small chains. I was on the alert, extraordinarily aware that
living matter was falling past me on all sides by the ton, sure
that this rain of life stuffs was a significant event and anxious
to see and hear it in its full pitiful glories. But the parade was
taking place in secret. There were no signs of these lockstep-
ping mum organisms. They were slinking away from the spreading surface lights by the billions, everywhere, but furtively. I
took my eyes from the shrinking humped bubble-sprouting
form that was Barto, and looked down. In the depths of the
canyon it was intense crowded blue, touched with black. Down
in all the murk, way down in the plankton nesting grounds,
was one white and moving thing, my father. There he was,
all white, sitting in a white rocking chair and swinging back
and forth in the blue heart of the waters. Looking up at me, I
could see his face clearly, smiling and waving his hand. Back
and forth he rocked, with the laziness of easy tides, with the
unhurried rhythms of Barto's duck-majestic flippers, all white
in a white rocker, and as he smiled and waved he called out to
me, "Come on down, Robbie. Down is best. Down is fun.
Do you think you're happy either?" I saw with delight that he

had grasped the whole joke. There was no fun in going down like a miserable copepod or arrow worm, just because the sun instilled a down chemistry in your slave neurones and it was your chemistry diving, with you a helpless passenger. The fun, the truly incomparable joke, was to go down as a free agent, electing to go, following the crowd but not chemically tied to it. I had enormous respect for my father's subtle thinking then. "Be right with you, Pop," I called.

I turned head down and began to propel myself in his direction. I was excited, lips sucking faster on my mouth plug. My father reached his arms up, incredibly long arms stretching up across the miles of blue, and got a strong grip around my neck and pulled, to help me go faster. "Thanks, Pop. I'm for reunions." Down I went, faster and faster, toward the white man on the white rocking chair, while he pulled. His white face grew large as I approached, big and bright as the sun, and he was smiling and I smiled back, glad that we shared the joke. Then I was very close and saw that the white rocker was not exactly a rocker, it was lower and longer and had sides enclosing it and my father was lying flat on his back inside it, it was a sort of crib that my mother, her vigorous old self, dressed all in black and with black face, black eyes packed with indignations, was rocking back and forth vigorously, making my father's head snap and his whole body jerk with each push, she was standing directly behind and pushing violently and the rage was black in her face as with each push she said, "Do something! For once will you! Up! For once in your life!" She was trying her best to dump him out of the crib. But he refused to get up, he lay tenaciously on his back and kept looking at me and saying "Son, son. Do you think I'm happy either?" This alarmed me and I started to struggle against his hands as they closed tighter around my neck and pulled me down, down, I couldn't breathe. "Help me," I said in despair to my mother. "Help me. I can't breathe." She said not a word, wouldn't look at me. "Do something!" I bellowed. "Since you're the dour!" I was stricken with shame. My mother had always been so proud of my spelling. Doer and dour were pronounced the same but I knew I had had dour in mind when I had tried to say doer. "Since, since you're the dower," I stuttered. That wasn't right either. I was afraid she would notice how I was getting even the simplest words mixed up, and I had so desperately to breathe. I reached out to take my father's windpipe and bend it in half, break it, break him to bits, and my hands closed on soft, smooth, giving silk, disgusting bodyless all surface silk, nobody was there and nothing but the white softly glowing silk mesh of a sleeve net. The net was half full of soft struggling things in a thick mass, a bundle of uneasy protoplasm. It was one of our nets, palely luminous with the first rays of sun reaching it and lit further maybe by the slight glowing of some of the creatures trapped in it. They heaved and squirmed, the blobbed animals. Feeling the first beams of the sun and desperate to go where they were told, and the silk bag keeping them from their never questioned mission. I held the bulging bottom of the net in my two hands and felt the desperate minor lunges and heaves of the living things inside, fighting to obey. Rapture of the deep? Here in the deep was supposed to be the drunken rapture. These crusted and spider-legged things were fighting terrible barricades of silk, that was their rapture. I was fighting the thought of sure suffocation, that was my rapture.

The hardest thing was to keep my hands from reaching for my mask. I wanted insanely to pull it off and sweep stuff into my nostrils, immediately. I started up along the tow rope, watching the bubbles stringing from my exhaust tube. No faster than the bubbles. Even with the bubbles. Slow, you don't want nitrogen residues in blood and tissues. I tried to count in time with the flipper strokes, to take my mind off the sure feeling that I was about to smother. Aimed toward the dark hull of the ship, pleading with it to come closer, trying to pull it down to me with the rope and making myself go too fast again. When I broke the surface I grabbed a rung of the ladder and tore the mask from my face. I gasped like a winded dog, my body shuddering. Barto was on deck, looking down at me with worry.

When I was sitting in the mess, covered with a blanket, still shaking in spite of the brandies, I began to tell him too fast and anxiously about the flier I'd met at the hospital in Manila, Maury Catums, whose family ran a pharmaceutical plant down in Tampa. There was a growing market for shark-liver extract, Maury said, if I could get a couple boats and go for sharks around Florida he'd guarantee to buy all the catches. My mother had some money put away for me and I could get financing under the G.I. Bill, and so could Barto if he wanted to go in with me, I said, rubbing my burning knees and try-ing to keep the urgency out of my voice. Suddenly I was leary about being out of the Navy I could never stand being in, I didn't want the possibility of one open minute, any unclaimed time in which I might drift and be without clear direction. I needed a partner. I would be working around the water, it was what I knew, and I didn't want to go near it again without company. At what fathoms would my closest relations be wait-ing next time?

Barto looked thoughtful and said it was a possibility, the Key might be a good location for him.

I watched his aimed, future-devoted face and I thought that if sound waves could be sent down him no false bottoms would be registered by the styluses, he had no scattering silts or sediments to send back secondary echoes. But where was his one true bottom? He knew, and he wasn't drawing con-tour maps of it for the public.

He said he would think it over, the Key might be a good place for him.

He was wearing just dungarees and an undershirt, as he leaned on his elbows and looked with careful thought into his coffee I saw the lean muscle around his left shoulder blade tighten to a ridge, narrowing to slits the two neat holes back of the armpit.

I rubbed my ignited knees, the shakes still in me, and

wondered how a man who steered so carefully clear of the cluttered world and its projects could arrange to get two bullets from another man's gun in his back.

He would think about it very seriously, he said, the Key might be just the place for him.

What Panama Canals was he going for? What salvarsans?

BOOK TWO: *Havana*

TEN My room on the eighth floor of the Sevilla-Biltmore was adequate, north off the rectangular column of space that the building was a shell around, with louvers on windows and door for ventilation. I stood at the window looking out north over the packed-tight Old Quarter to the waterfront drive, the Malecón, and to the uncramped ocean just past it. In the sun the water shifted like lazy dry goods. Freighters were cutting back and forth, hauling brown leaves and cooked sugars for the world's taste buds. Humping up offland to the right, flat gray and to no purpose, Morro Castle. I went to the phone and asked for the Ambos Mundos. No good, Brooke was not registered. I told my operator to keep trying.

It was close to eleven; I had been awake for twenty-seven hours. It was hodcarrier's work just to get my clothes off. When I was stretched out, arms and legs feeling like sash-weights, I reached for the telephone directory and without hope turned to the listings under Casa. This town was a breeding-ground for Casas. Casa de 1, 2 y 3 Centavos. Casa Edison and Casa Fanny. There were eighteen Casas de Socorros, and there was Casa Gameda Refrigeradores Montgomery Ward, and even a Casa de Salud La Milagrosa, which made me jump, but no Casa del Milagro, too much miracle to ask. I fell asleep with the directory on my chest and dreamt about houses named Centavos and Montgomery Ward falling on my chest.

At 4:30 I woke, feeling better. The sun was rampaging through the room, a runaway stain. The bleats of Havana traffic kept at my eardrums. Still no sign of Brooke at the Ambos Mundos. As soon as I was dressed and shaved I had a solid meal in the restaurant off the lobby and went out for a walk along Calle Obispo. Like most streets in the Old Quarter it was just wide enough for one car and lined with stores, you felt you could touch, or even rob, two facing stores simultaneously. I checked at the Ambos Mundos, Brooke was not there.

I passed the American consulate and continued on to the waterfront and out along the curving Malecón, looking as I went for the *Easy Rider* and telling myself the boat might be tied up a hundred miles away. For a while I watched the kids in makeshift trunks diving off the rock piles at the bottom of the escarpment into the strongarm breakers, on the hunt for the big morro crabs. A girl with pencil legs, wobbly on high heels, came from the arched promenade across the drive toward me, belly running interference for the rest of her. She had black flopping feathers in her hat, and her mouth was an open sore as it dripped the words, "Jig, jig, mister? Fun?" I thought that idiom had gone out about the time of the Spanish-American troubles. In my best gimp Spanish I said, "Much thanks, but no," and cut across into the Prado.

From the benches on the elevated center walk the louse-pocketed beggars and speed-eyed postcard salesmen reviewed the tourist parade. All along the windows were jammed with the world's shined junk, sandals, alligator bags, rums, banana liqueurs, perfumes, tinny costume jewelry of bright baked-enamel hues shipped down from fly-by-night factories in Rochester and Perth Amboy to be bought for that oversung song and worn back chestily to Perth Amboy and Rochester. Coming into Central Park, the masonry cupcake that was the Capitol just beyond, more beggars on the benches, barefoot and crust-ankled and matted in the hair, arms and legs and eyes missing and the stumps showing and the vacant puckered sockets, only the capitalists among them with homemade crutches and eye

patches; dressed, all of them, in dishrag clotted clothes, re-
minding you that in a country where so many are Bowery poor
and look it, for a beggar to look like a beggar and not just
another citizen named Juan Dó is a major job and takes real
go. I headed east until I came to La Floridita.

At the bar a heavy-set novelist who had written books
about the cojones of the Spanish civil war was drinking
daiquiris with some friends. Hard to tell what the excited talk
was about, maybe elephant shoots and white hunters and bull-
fights and the truly astonishing toreador named Manolete
with infinite cojones. Not very much about olive trees near
Huesca, most likely. Possibly nothing in reference to shooting
in the back and kidnapping in the night, or other matters of
minor cojones. But I had luck with the directory, among the
Sociedads listed was the Sociedad por la Música Afro-Cubana,
on a street off the Prado, Emilio Nuñez. Five hours ago I
looked up Casa del Milagro, not expecting to find it. It took
me five hours to look for the Sociedad, which was bound to be
there. I stalled, maybe, because I had the feeling Vincent
Caprio wasn't expecting me to.

It was there on Emilio Nuñez, a three-story chipped-stone
building wedged in between a warehouse and a garage, with a
sign across it. Fronting the first floor was a small store with
narrow windows, in them drums of various shapes and colora-
tions, some finished, others with wooden bases unpainted and
the hides for their tops lying separately. In addition, there were
some monographs and paper-covered books on display, one of
the books was called *Rhythmic Patterns in Afro-Cuban Ritual
Music* and was by Owen Warrister Brooke, Ph.D. I opened the
glass-paned door and went in. Behind the counter was a thin
Cuban with a thin moustache, dressed in a pleated, outside-
the-pants guayaberra shirt and neat bowtie, busy putting together a tumbadora drum. "Mister?"

"Good day. Perhaps you can help me."

"With all pleasure. You are of the inclination to consider
drums?"

"No, I look for a friend, the Professor Owen Brooke."

"You are friendship with the professor?"

It was a conversation that refused to jell because he insisted on speaking his lopsided English and I stuck to my lopsided Spanish. "Yes. It would please me much to locate him."

"Mister, too bad. The professor is not here for six, seven day now. Maybe he is make the field trips."

"I saw him yesterday on the Key of the West." The man seemed genuinely surprised at this. "He asked me to meet him in Havana."

"Fat chance he is in Havana, mister. When he is in Havana, we know."

"I thought you could have some message. He said he needed help to record ñañigo and I said I would help with all willingness."

The clerk was getting enthusiastic. "One more to help is good, the professor will be glad. Is there a place he can communicate?"

"The Sevilla-Biltmore. The name is Garmes. I cannot say how grateful I am for your efforts."

"For nothing, Mr. Gomez."

"Again, all my gratitude."

"Not worth the mention."

At the door I stopped. "If I can impose on you yet again, you know the whereabouts of Mr. Rodríguez?" He blinked, bit on his moustache. "The bongo drummer of eminence, Julio Rodríguez?"

"Ah! El Rey! Yes, yes! But are you not inform, mister, Coolio is distant from Havana? Only the day passed he depart to make the guest appearance in the States."

"I know this. I attended his performance last night in the Key of the West."

"An ultimate musician, do you not find? I concoct all his drums, I, personally."

"He is an artist of supreme talent, and you make instruments truly excellent. My congratulations on the quality of

your handiwork. Thank you still again for your many consid-
erations."

"It is my gladness to be of service."

"I am irrevocably in your debt."

Outside, I called the Ambos Mundos. Still no sign of
Brooke. I went to a movie and back to bed.

ELEVEN   At ten next morning I was in the open
cafe across from the Ambos Mundos, having my fourth coffee
and smoking my second H. Upmann Número Quatro. Tourists kept appearing and disappearing in the hotel entrance
loaded with aluminum and saddle-leather luggage and woven
baskets holding rum bottles. I turned the pages of the *Havana
Post*, looking for mention of the *Easy Rider*'s arrival but not
really expecting to find it. There was an editorial on "The
Menace of Noise," saying that the Anti-Noise League of the
Academy of Sciences had reported Havana as the noisiest of
all cities, filled with the kinds of sounds which cause nervous,
mental and heart disorders, split personality, madness and in
certain cases death. The *Post* urged that the general hubbub
be reduced by stringent regulation of juke boxes and motor
horns and a definite prohibition of loud-speaker vans, firecrackers and animal cries. I looked up and saw Brooke standing
by a cab across the street. I threw away my cigar and went over.

"What! Uh! Garmes!" His hands froze as though holding
a basketball. "This beats everything!" His face tried several expressions before it settled for wariness. "I thought *Barto* was
coming over."

"No, Connie got it wrong. She knew we had some business over here and she thought Barto was going, but it was
me." I tried to keep my voice easy as I added, "Were you expecting to see Barto?"

"I was hoping there'd be a message from him, in any case,"

Brooke said. His face said nothing to cast doubt on his words. "But, look, if you knew you were coming—"

"Socially speaking," I said, "it didn't seem to me that you and I had much future. Events seemed to bear me out on that."

"Yes, indeed," Brooke said. "*That.* You're—I guess you're pretty sore."

"Not me, just my jaw."

I managed to produce a smile. Brooke studied my expression, took courage from it, broke into a relieved laugh. It sounded like a man in the advanced stages of tuberculosis. "I'm really sorry about that, Garmes. I have a horror of using my fists on anybody but, well, you were being so damned unreasonable. It was late, we were sailing. . . . It's damned decent of you to take it this way. Shall we forget it and shake hands?"

"Suits me." His hand was damp, soft, it felt boned. "Next time you throw a punch, though, give me a little warning. It worries me when fists come out of the night."

"You're all right, Garmes. You see the lighter side. Oh, how's Barto?"

"Fine. He asked me to say hello." He looked as though he'd just received a bonus. "Did you have a good crossing?"

"A little choppy. Not too bad."

"I hope you didn't have any trouble. I was looking for you yesterday, I began to wonder."

"No, there wasn't any trouble." He was serious again. "Was there any particular reason why you wanted to see me?"

"Yes. About the research you're doing. If I can be of any help—"

"You're—don't tell me you're interested?"

"More than Barto. I used to be a jazz collector when I was in college."

"Garmes," he said, eyes lit up, "that's great! Really great! Come along by all means, and see the kind of work we're doing!" He looked around carefully, lowered his voice. "We've got a ñañigo thing arranged for this afternoon, we should get some wonderful stuff."

"Fine. Want to have some lunch first?"

"That's an idea. Let me see about my bags, I'll be with you in a minute."

He was gone for several minutes. When he came back from the lobby we started up Obispo, trying to keep from being pushed off the gangway sidewalks. Up on Avenida Martí, across from the Capitol, was a long outdoor cafe. On a bandstand raised over the tables were eight or nine girls wearing puff-sleeved blouses and ponking away on guitars, maracas, bongos, tumbadores, claves, doing a twitchy mauling of "How High the Moon." We took a table and ordered planter's punches. "The *Havana Post* says the Yacht Club at Miramar is crowded," I said. "Did you have trouble about docking space?"

"No, we didn't." He pointed his finger at me. "Are you trying to be the last Renaissance man? Oceanography, jazz— weren't you and Barto in one of those, what're they called, frogmen units?"

"U.D.T.s. Underwater Demolition Teams."

"That was a funny thing to get into."

"There's a story behind that." I needed another approach to the matter of the *Easy Rider*.

"Want to talk about it?"

"My grandfather on my mother's side—no, I'd better start with *his* father. *His* father was pure Brazilian Portugee, a sailor, married a Hindu girl in British Guiana, girl with a caste mark on her forehead. So Grandfather Heixas was by rights half Portugee and half Hindu. He was a sailor too, on the last whalers. In New Bedford he met and married an Irish scullery maid with no caste marks, just sunken cheeks from sometime eating. Out of their union came Annie Florence Heixas, my mother. She used to work summers in Cape Cod hotels, and there she met a dapper New York fellow, my father. He was one of the Fifth Avenue Garmeses but in disgrace—what he wanted to do was paint cubed landscapes and instead of going into the bank he'd hung around Paris for years with the early postimpressionist painters." There was no way to get from this to the *Easy Rider*. "Charlie Garmes and Annie Florence Heixas had their nuptials, then me. Am I boring you?"

"Hans Christian Andersen never bored me."

What he made of the literal truth about my roots was Hans Christian Andersen. All right. "My mother worked a fishing boat because my father never brought home anything more negotiable than his postimpressions. My father, though, had been captain of the water polo team at Harvard—"

"Is that right?" He was enthusiastic. "I went to Harvard myself."

"That's the only way. You're on your own." I smiled, to show the joke was friendly, and he smiled back harder to prove he took it that way. "Well, the Fifth Avenue Garmeses decided I ought to have an education, they put up the money and I went to Harvard too." Everything pointed, I decided, to the conclusion that the *Easy Rider* had docked at some point away from Havana. "I went in for oceanography there. It made more sense than thirteenth-century litanies. Then I got bored with studying the oceans in a dry library and signed for a research expedition to the Bering Sea, then a second to the Marianas."

"Everything's beautifully clear," Brooke said, smiling, "except how you became a frogman."

"When I was drafted they asked what I was trained for. I said I knew about cutting up whale blubber from my maternal grandfather, potato famines and how to make beds with a hospital fold from my maternal grandmother, trimming bonito to look like fancy tuna from my mother, how Picasso mixed his fuchsia and how many brioches he ate for breakfast from my father. Also, thanks to my father's swimming lessons, I'd developed a chest expansion of almost five inches and

could stay under water better than two minutes. They perked
up at that. I was a natural-born frogman, they said." And
suppose I could locate the *Easy Rider?* Would that tell me
where Michael Brod was? "See what happened? I was a mulli-
gatawny to them, so they solved the problem of what the hell
to call me with a tape measure and a stopwatch. They measured
my chest and clocked my underwater endurance, and that's
how I got to be a frogman. They asked me to volunteer for the
U.D.T.s and I did, I couldn't fight the evidence." Wondering
how many possible mooring places there were on the northern
coast of Cuba, I said, "What I like about military life is, it
gives solid definition to a man."

"Garmes," he said, "was that about Barto true? He's all
right, really?"

"Sure. Why?"

"It must—the other night you must have thought my behavior very peculiar. That telephone call. I didn't *really* think
anything could happen to Barto, but you were making such a
thing of it. . . ."

"I'm the alarmist, I guess. After I thought it over I was
grateful to you for being so concerned."

"I think I ought to explain. About that man, I mean."

"You don't have to explain anything, Owen. I'm glad I
ran into you. I walked along the waterfront yesterday, hoping
I'd find the *Easy Rider*. Not that there was much chance it
would be right in Havana Bay."

"No, I'd better say this. The man I *said* was a passenger,
was going to be a passenger, well, he *wasn't*, he, he was just on
board temporarily, hoping to see Barto. When I referred to
this man as a passenger I didn't mean he'd been a passenger
coming *up* from Cuba, I just meant he might be going *back*
with me." Somewhere in the past thirty hours he'd been given
the postgraduate course on the seriousness of confessing to
unmanifested passengers.

"Sure." The look he gave me was full of I.O.U.'s. I
brushed some sweat drops from my forehead and puffed a

little. "You know, this is perfect weather for a cruise. I was thinking about it this morning. That's not the reason I looked for the *Easy Rider*, but a cruise would be fine."

"It would be nice," he said. "I think we'd better be going, Robert."

In the cab going back to the Ambos Mundos I said, "It's too bad you had a rough crossing. If it was choppy, I'm surprised you didn't head right for Havana and cut it short."

"It wasn't too bad. I'm a very good sailor, you know."

A man was waiting for Brooke in the cafe across from the Ambos Mundos. I spotted this Negro the minute he opened his mouth. The free floater, sharp, ready, sum of a town's around-the-edges enterprise, not looking, exactly, but with plenty of arithmetic going on under the catnapping eyes and not avoiding, either. This man, anywhere between thirty-five and fifty, lazy but tight of flesh, dressed in candy-striped shirt with sleeves held by pink arm garters, jacketless, collar buttoned but no tie, stiff straw hat shoved back from friendly barricaded face—this Negro was introduced as Benjamino Francisco, of unstated occupation but unhesitatingly at our service.

"They call me Benjamin Francis, sir," he said in his thick, mellowed Isthmus accent. "Benjie to my friends, sir. Good friends from the States call me Benjie."

"How are you, Benjie," I said.

"Tip-a-top, sir. In good shape. Glad to make your acquaintance, sir." If he was not for hire, he wasn't altogether tied up. He did not look like a man who would pull the last knot of a commitment too tight.

"We're ready," Brooke said, pointing to a chrome-cased tape recorder and some photographic equipment on the floor. "Benjie's arranged the whole thing, he's got a car waiting at the corner." He was high in spirits. Benjie got the stuff and we climbed into the back seat of the Cadillac while Benjie slipped in with the driver. "By the way, Robert," Brooke said, studying the passing sights. "About that little misunderstanding the other night."

"It's all cleared up, Owen," I said.

"Fine! I just wanted to be sure. This fellow wasn't a passenger, he's an old friend of Barto's, we were planning a little joke on Barto, that was the whole thing. I got the mistaken impression he might be coming *down* to Cuba with me." He'd been getting *big* lectures on manifests. "Somehow—in the rush—"

"Sure, Owen."

TWELVE   Southwest out of the Vedado suburb the villas stopped and the boulevards faded. We went along a back road through sandy stretches, passed some junk yards. The driver took a sudden turn and what we were in was a trash pile with humans for trash. Here and there on the cityward side were fair-sized buildings, abandoned warehouses. These bins were filled with Negroes and the huts in between and stretching away in a gray corrugated-iron jumbo on all sides were filled with Negroes too, barefoot, wearing loose knee-sprung overalls and nothing else, Negroes with gaps where teeth should be and open-edged sores on cheeks and skull, old creased Negroes with faces cut from cocoanut shell and young Negroes with the sucked-in pondering eyes that belong to the old but show up in the chronically hungry. There were no streets in this Sargasso settlement, just dirt lanes where nobody had yet thought to build a lean-to or a sewage ditch. Stringy chickens walked here and there, not bothering to peck. Stench of slops over everything.

"Salsipuedes," I said involuntarily.

"What?" Owen Brooke said.

"It's the name of a slum in Puerto Rico. It means, Get-

Out-If-You-Can." Benjamino Francisco had his head turned and was looking thoughtfully at me. "Isn't that right, Benjie?"

"I have not the honor to know Puerto Rico," Benjie said. "The translation is very good. Yes."

"On the second day of our visit we drove to Get-Out-If-You-Can in our Cadillac," Brooke said. "Good God. So many people."

"Many, yes, sir," Benjie said. "Very friendly types, Habañeros. Live close together. Much singing here, sir." The helpful smile on his face did not falter as he directed the driver to make another turn into another ratrun.

"Terrible," Brooke said shakily. Black faces were looking in the windows in mass quiet asking. No hawking, no soapboxing, no begging, just asking. The professor looked back, shocked and fascinated, and said, "Terrible, what three hundred years of imperialist exploitation can do."

"I see what you mean, sir," Benjie said. "Yes, streets very narrow here, bad for driving." His eyes were steady and full of help. "Most friendly people, yes, sir. No danger of any form whatsomever. Just for convenience, sir, it will be good if I do the talking."

What drew Brooke to his Africas? They were so unlike Dutchess County. He had a big love of the wild, and found it only among the broke. But if his bottomdogs were not so broke, would they be half so wild? Here in this ultimate slum, the paresis of cities, his nose and steamy social conscience were insulted but he couldn't take his eyes from the black putty faces at the windows. Benjie understood all that and played with it and on it, under the strawberry jam of his yessir, nosir. The folk forever. Customer's always right, sir. Want to swing over hell's own sulphur pits, we provide the asbestos basket, sir.

"People who don't do much swallowing with their mouths, swallow with their eyes," Brooke said. All the same, the professor had his Leicas. Then, at Benjie's orders, the

driver pulled up at one of the warehouses. "Is it all right?"
Brooke said.

"They will be very friendly," Benjie said. "With permission, I will do the talking."

Brooke had packed along six bottles of rum, it being
Benjie's thought that these people were very, very friendly,
friendly like anything, yessir, but with three fingers of rum
spiking the gastric juices they would be friendlier. Brooke now
gathered up the bottles and headed for the building. Ahead
of him went Benjie and the chauffeur with the recording
equipment and the cameras. Inside in the one large bare room
were about twenty people, women with scarves around their
necks and men in denim shirts or cotton undershirts. Negroes,
and the men, most of them, were fooling with bongos or larger
tumbadora drums. In the middle of the crowd, bent over a set
of bongos, was a man holding a lighted candle and delicately
warming his drumheads with it, a man all bones, face a set of
interlocked hollows, with unfocused shellac eyes; Coolio. The
way the others detoured around him, he might have been in
a transparent lucite cell all his own. "We're in luck!" Brooke
said. "Coolio's here! I didn't expect him back so soon."

Rum bottles were passed around and everybody drank.
There was a lot of peppery talk from several sides about New
York, show business and guest shots on TV, road shows and
playing one-nighters. "Man, the time we play the split week in
Pittsburr an the cat shooted both his two guns at the bar
mirror, wowp," a chubby guitar player said, and everybody fell
out over the memory. "Chano Pozo? Ai-yunh, that cat was *the*
absolute most when it come to bongo," a curvy teen-age girl
said, and heads nodded religiously. "New York?" a heavy handsome woman said to me. "Good bookings, New York?" a ma-
hogany-faced man said right after. "You book into Palladium,
on Broadway, Palladium?" somebody else said. "Alway play to
capacity at Palladium, man. Gone."

The men started test runs on their drums, warming up,

and at this signal some of the younger plump girls edged to the corner and slipped their outer clothes and sandals off, showing tight shorts and bandanas around their breasts. They came back to the center of the room and made practice hip swings and shoulder shimmies and pelvic flips, faces bored. Coolio looked up, still warming his drum skins, his eyes congealed out of space to take me in. "Too tight sound like paper bag," he said. Immediately after, still with face dead, he said, "Dance mambo big New York, heh?" I said I hadn't been to New York in some time. "Funny that city," he said. "Streets go up and down and you canno go at any angle. Where you book, Cheecago and Sain Loos or someplace?" He said this with the air of not wanting to know, satirically. I said I was located in Florida, with no branch offices. "I caught you in the Late Watch night before last," I said. "You got to be too square to get caught," he said. "You're not square, are you?" I said. "You take long walks late at night," and as I moved off toward Benjie, Coolio smiled at me, nodding. "For jungle folk," I said to Benjie, "your friends talk a lot about television."

"Yes, sir," Benjie smiled. "They make some appearance on the television, when possible. From time to time, yes. We have here five, six television station, yes."

"Why all the questions about bookings?"

"They have much interest in booking, sir. They are in the show business, travel in Latin countries and in the States too. They appreciate to work when possible."

"Who told them they could get bookings from this?"

Benjie smiled, very affable. "Long story, sir. Cubano artist think very much about New York. They hear of the big success of mambo in New York, they think to get in Broadway show and make the film in Hollywood also. Tell them professor come to make record and nobody sing or dance, tell them man from New York come with big booking office and maybe will hire many for show and film, they sing and dance very much. Is that right logic, sir?"

"The professor knows what you told these people?"

"He know, sir. He want to record the true folk spirit before it pass."

"I see."

"I thought you see this, sir."

"I see Coolio Rodríguez is here too. He travels a lot. Is that what the professor's Society is for, to help artists like Coolio get back and forth?"

"Yes, sir, they give many concerts all over," he said, and in the same breath switched: "Maybe they do not get the booking, sir, in this world is very hard to get the booking. But they get the rum, much. Rum not easy to get either."

"You keep looking at me as though you expect me to say something. What are you waiting for from me, Benjie?"

"You, sir? Me?" His eyes opened wide to show me there was no design in them. "You have not the look of tourist, sir. This is all. I am friend to tourist, I am much incline to happy peoples, but tourist always say the same things. You, sir, could say some words I have not heard. I am interested to hear new things."

The room buzzed. The girls slapped bare bored heels on the cracked tiles, drums stuttered, guitar strings gave off rehearsal sounds. "Any time you say, boys," Brooke called up from his layout of machines. "Tell them, Benjie." Somebody said, "Hoo! Hen!" Somebody made an indifferent tonguing noise that sounded like "Puttee-puttee-puttee-puttee."

It broke then. Snap, and the unrelated soloists became a pulsed assembly. Nobody stamped it off or gave the signal in any way, but by mutual understanding all muscles spasmed at once, the drums came in together, behind them the strings suddenly blanging, and on the floor the young girls in their tights and the young men now stripped to the waist were facing each other and their darkish damp bodies were in high jerking acceleration. Heels tattooed the floor, arms made humped chicken motions and eyes rolled. Planned epilepsies all over the place. Coolio was attacking his bongos while his face stayed dead, and around him the other drummers were pounding with palms, hammering with thumbs, clicking the wooden sides of larger drums with kitchen knives and spoons, and from the floor somebody yelled "Ayee-ayee-aaaaa-yeeeee," and somebody else came back with a "Huh! Haaaaaoooooowww! Huh! Huh-hooonh!"

It started fast, but it got faster. It was ñañigo like my father painted Whistler's Mother on his toenail. They weren't drinking blood from the necks of ritually scalpeled chickens, or calling the dead out of cemeteries to do buck-and-wings under the chatty palmettos. This was a Shubert Alley rendition of Africa, the jungle as jazzbo sociology professors dreamed of it behind their box hedges. In this staged Africa there was one and only one rite, the invocation of Booking. Now the older people on the side, the music makers, began to sing, chanting clipped syllables behind Coolio as he rose from his bongos and began his almost monotoned solo. Brooke perked up still more when he heard these chugging "Hens!" and "Joog-joog-joogs" and "Widi-widi-widis." This was the Black Continent babble he'd come for, he never saw the ironizing New York-rapt eyes above the Congo lips.

It was his good luck that he didn't know Spanish. Most of the words were Spanish and a fair number of them, even in their careful slurrings, I understood. They came from the novocained face of Coolio Rodríguez while he played straight to the professor and the others chanted enthusiastically and looked with entire good will in the same direction, they were arrowed for the professor as he bent there in his delight and they went something like this:

It is a big, big city up in the north, heh
And he comes from the city on a visit, heh
With a whole lot of money and shine on his shoes
The money is making a rattle in his pocket
It would be nice to take the money from his pocket, hunh
And throw him in the shit behind the house, hunh
And go on a boat to the big city up north

And live in his big nice house up in the north
Wearing his fine shoes with the shine on them, hoo-wa
While he lies in the pile of shit without shoes on, hoo-wa.

It had the folk witchery. The dancers wiggled their authentic wiggles, the singers yelped their authentic yelps, and over to the side Benjie stood with permissive smile, happy that all the happy peoples were happy. Behind his smile, he kept looking at me.

The pace stepped up again and the music got still louder and wilder, the walls and ceiling themselves became drumheads, the room was one big kettledrum and in it flesh turned to noise. The dancers took their cue from the drums. The plump girls now began to agitate their frames more and this time, with many cries of "Awah! Awah! Awah!" they started to bend at the knees, sank with shudders to their knees, bodies snapping as their heads bent back to find the floor. In a minute all the girls were writhing on the floor, arching, only knees and skulls supporting them, middles snapping in the air, while the boys leaned hard over them, the bodies on the floor posing convex questions and their own bodies giving concave answers. It looked unplanned, but all the girls moaning for water and thumping against the floor were dropped in formation around the professor, he was adrift in a monsoon of bodies. He went on adjusting his dials, but he was not happy any more.

Then the girl nearest him, a sixteen-year-old with eyes that had gone corrupt about the time Caligula started sucking his thumb, this girl reached up and with trained hysterical fingers pulled the bandana from her full breasts, and with a cosmic heave got her tights off and kicked away, pelvis and eyes not missing a beat. In a second the young dripping boy leaning over her had dropped his dungarees, abdomen not missing a polyrhythm. There under Brooke's thin white nostrils the girl squirmed, her displayed middle did a showmanlike cootch and her thighs yelled squirmy footlight demands, while the boy described syncopated Immelmans back and forth over her, letting himself down slow, by controlled approximations. The performers kept up their pleas for "Awah," cooing to the professor for "Awah." His answer was to stay put, face emptied of blood and something in its place that was the stage past nausea. No adjusting of dials and knobs now. He looked like he could use an oxygen tent. I began to work my way around, trying not to step on bodies. Halfway around the room I came to the all-smiles, all-approving Benjie. "Some ñañigo," I said.

"Yes, sir. Much talent."

"The singing was very good."

"Best singers in all of Cuba, sir. Good voices, sing fine together."

"The words were unusual," I said in Spanish.

Those eyelashes didn't know what it meant to be batted. "Yes, sir," he said in careful English. "I look in your face and I think, he is man who understand many words."

"How much do you understand, Benjie? You understand words like *Easy Rider?*"

"Oh, yes." He nodded. "Easy rider. Like the Cadillac or some nice car that ride easy. Strong power and no bumps, is this the meaning, sir?"

"I intend to find the *Easy Rider*, and I intend to do it with your help. Do you understand that?"

"If I can be of service," he said with his open smile, "please, only ask, sir."

The professor bolted up from his station. He looked around prayerfully, lips moving but apparently not saying anything. His face was the color of beach sand. He swallowed hard, clamped both hands to his mouth and hopped grotesquely over the bodies, running for the door fast as his pogo-stick legs would carry him. "Owen's going for awah," I said.

The musicians were still at their instruments and the dancers still on the floor, stopped dead, all of them looking coolly as we picked our way to the door. Outside, there was

laughing. Owen was bent over, distributing his breakfast onto
the dirt road. Chickens pecked with determination around his
feet, kids gathered at the strange sight. It was a music-hall
novelty to them, the sight of a man with stomach so profligate.
To them it was like throwing away gold, they couldn't believe
their eyes, they hopped around screaming and hooting. Gay
billionaire pranks! What'll the billionaires think of next!
Benjie and I pushed our way through, each of us took one
of Brooke's arms. "You'll be all right," I said. "It's the heat
and the excitement." We got Brooke into the car and in a
few minutes Benjie had the equipment stowed away and we
were going. We made the trip back in silence. It was only
when we pulled up at the Ambos Mundos and Benjie was
out getting the machines that Brooke turned to me and said,
"There's something about you. You and Benjie. When Benjie
tells me something it's with a straight face but it sounds like
there's a joke behind it. Then he looks to you, he expects you
to be in on the joke."

"We're blood brothers," I said. "We drink homogenized
blood from the same chickens." I said into Brooke's white
face, "Thanks for taking me along, Owen, it was rhythmic."

When I got out Benjie was waiting. I was about to insist
on giving him a lift but he got there first. "I go in your
direction, sir," he said. "With permission, I walk along a ways
with you." That was all right, except that he didn't know
anything about my direction. "Good day, good sir," he said to
Brooke. "Any time you want the good singing, you call on
Benjie. Day, sir, day, Professor." Brooke looked straight at
Benjie, questioning, and Benjie looked straight at me, smiling.

THIRTEEN   We went to a small waterfront bar
across from the dock for the Morro Castle launches. Benjie,
lazy all the way, got right down to cases. "You look for some-

thing, sir, not the things of a professor. You do not mind this frankness, sir?"

"Stop calling me sir. My name is Robert."

"Robert?" He approved. "My best uncle in Panama, he was named Roberto. He was a good man, once he drank twenty-two beers without going to piss."

"I'm happy for him. What do you think I'm looking for?"

"Mm, hard to say. Alligator belts, wholesale? Absinthe in the crème de menthe labels, to go by the American customs?" He was running through his standard catalogue but there was no conviction in his voice. "Possible to locate artistic postcards, collector's items. No? Mm. Nearby is a private show tonight, one man, six lovely girls. This man is favorite with the American ladies, of unusual construction."

"We've had enough shows."

"Well, Robert. If it is to your taste, we find a tip-a-top pleasure house for you. There are fine houses in Havana, it is only the question of which is for your personality." He seemed to go into consultation with himself, while he continued to check my reactions. "Consuelita's? No, I do not think Consuelita's. Clientele very rowdy, American sailors and such boisterers, besides the girls are of inferior type and not clean, not inspected with full care. Dolores the Big-Ass? You could find it amusing, they have the girls from Paris there, excellent talent. But a certain corrupt atmosphere, not a place from the shoulder, besides they do not sweep under the beds. Black Domballa's? It is hard to say, if you appreciate the girls with color, some Americans find they are too narrow in the legs. For my own taste—"

"What's your connection with Brooke and his Society? How'd you happen to be there this afternoon, anyway?"

He was not put off by the questions. "From time to time, because I make this or that door open or maybe stop to be open, because I have the contacts, somebody pay me to arrange something. A few times, it is the Sociedad. You are asking, what side Benjamino Francisco is on? No secret, he is on the

side of Benjamino Francisco. In the heart and in the pocket-
book, I am the free-lance."

"All right, free-lance for me. One thing I'm looking for
is a cruiser. The *Easy Rider*."

He gave the matter some sober thought. "I know the
professor has a boat. It could be in Lake Titicaca, for what
I know."

I had to take a chance. "Benjie, have you ever heard of
a place called the Casa del Milagro? Any place with milagro
in the name?"

The smile came off his face like court plaster. With a
quick movement I wouldn't have thought him capable of, he
stood up. "It is very late," he said, seriously. "I have many
appointments."

I got a grip on his wrist and pulled him back to his chair.

"You do not see my position," he said, speaking rapidly.
He took a red polka-dot handkerchief from his pocket and
patted his face with it. "With me it is delicate. You know what
I do for ten years? I am on the banana boats, from Honduras,
from Costa Rica and other places, I do work of a dog and
get big callus on the hands like elephant skin, and all the time
belly empty and feels bad. I have the big experience in going
without everything, got nothing to pack in the cardboard
suitcase but the sweet free air, believe me. So one day I leave
the home in Panama, and begin to walk, I walk, and finally
I walk all across Cuba from Santiago to Havana, and here
with much work I make something from my small self and I
buy suits with jackets. Now I walk down the streets and the
police call me mister, I am somebody with a name and a
part in the hair. One bad move and foom, pah, everything
skiddoo, like that. You think I am amiable to go back to the
banana boats and get paid in callus and sore muscles again?
I am not a well man, I am weak inside from a bad, bad dose
not treated with properness, doctor say if I do not take fine
care of my insides he will not predict." Agitated, he stuffed his
handkerchief in his pants pocket. "I have a position to protect,

Robert. What the goddamn hell you look for in the Milagro? Who, in the Milagro?"

I took a deep breath. "A man named Michael Brod."

He jumped. There was intense pain on his face. "The Milagro, and then Miguel Brod inside the Milagro. Ordinary things are not good enough for you, you want the best. What you want with Brod?"

"Two nights ago, in Key West, he killed my partner."

Benjie looked as though somebody was pulling his arms and legs in four different directions. He stood up, I had to work hard to get him seated again. "Mon, you just tell me something," he said unhappily. "Now I see about Coolio."

"Coolio?"

"This is why Coolio come to the party this afternoon. Nobody ask him, not me, not professor. Coolio come to keep the eye on you, for Brod." He shook his head, greatly discouraged with me. "Excuse me. Urgent business in other places."

"Stay where you are. How would Brod have known I was going with Brooke? The arrangements weren't made until late this morning."

"Mon, mon, is your head up your rear end? You think professors don't know how to use the telephones?"

"But, wait a minute, Brooke wasn't suspicious about me. He doesn't even know my partner's dead. Why should he call Brod about me?"

"This professor is big telephone man, every time he wipe himself he call to Brod." He was really frightened. "Am I crazy or something, to sit with you and make chitchats? I got to get the terrible hell out of here."

"Coolio must be close to Brod. He was in Key West two days ago, helping him."

Benjie took this as very bad news. "Talk with you is bad, mon. More you talk, more gloom I get. If Brod bring Coolio to Key West, he take big, big chance. Coolio is known, and

Brod is not the man to take chance. This mean he is in bad
mood, impatient."

"I've got to find him, Benjie."

"You do not understand your position," Benjie said
hopelessly. "A man looks for Brod for a killing, Brod finds out
and look for the man. Mon, this is the way to lose your
health. All of your health, all over, from head to toes."

"What's your connection with Brod?"

"I tell you how I am set up, Robert. I do the little odd
job for this one and that one, sometimes for Brod too. I am
not on the payroll or something like that, it is a from time to
time thing. Only lately it happens more times. Now he loses
many close friends, it is natural, he has to use more Coolio,
and sometimes me. I do not wish to break off this little business,
not for the pay, I would like not to make this man mad. He
has a lot of tendency to get mad lately. You should see these
one when he get mad, Robert! Oh, mon, my, my!" He clapped
both hands to his cheeks and rolled his head.

"He was mad at my partner."

"If all he did was kill him, just kill him clean, without
the extras, he was not so mad."

"Benjie, where do I find this Casa del Milagro?"

"You are a man," Benjie said with exasperation, "who says
a thing, then grabs it out of the ear. You say to me, no
pleasure house, then you say you go to the Casa del Milagro.
Only, too bad for you, this is not pleasure house for Americans,
no, sir."

"It's a whorehouse?" I blinked. "Why is it called—"

"This house, it is run by American lady named Millie,
she was mistress of some bigshot in the government and for
the pin money she start house for government bigshots. This
idea come to her after she meet wives of government men,
then she decide there is big business in house for government
men. Because she is named Millie, for joke they call this house
Casa del Milagro. Funny miracles they make in that place,
take my word."

"Brod hangs around there?"

"His old friends go there but they are not friends with him any more, so he does not go. Even Millie, before, she would give him anything, seventeen girls for breakfast, now she would not speak his name. Brod is hiding someplace, but not the Milagro."

"You have no idea where he is?"

"You want to find him, ask Coolio, or maybe the professor. Go up to them with a sign on your stomach saying Kill Me In A Hurry, Please, and ask where is Mr. Brod."

"Benjie, you don't make sense. If the Milagro is just a house for government people, why are you so scared of it?"

"You do not listen with care, Robert. I say, when it start, it is place for government people. Now it is type of club, more than just house. Now, still, some government muchymuches go there, special types, the ones mixed in side lines and ready to buy and sell. Also, some political types, ones who have done business in many countries, who fight in the Spanish war, who travel much like Mr. Brod. Very tough boys. Also some plain and simple gangsters, they all go there. Some have dealings with Brod, when he is their friend. Now they do not like Brod. You think, you walk in with your happy Florida face and say, show me, please, Mr. Brod, they are going to kiss you and throw parties for you? Suppose Brod hear about this, you think he invite you for some brandy? You will need the adding machine to count up how many knives in the stomach."

"Spanish war," I said. "My partner, Barto, was born in Cuba, he was in the Spanish war. Brod tried to kill him there. Barto wanted to get him for that."

Benjie had followed this closely. "Spanish war, very funny war," he said finally.

"That doesn't explain why my partner was talking about the Casa del Milagro when he died."

"It explains much. Here in Havana we have veterans in quantity from Spanish war. We have name for them, combatientes. They are of two kinds, far apart, those who like very much all which happened in Spain and those who do not think of it with pleasure. Of those pleased with their memories, certain hard types go to the Milagro. Only those. Your friend, maybe he was in touch with the others, those unhappy about Spain. Maybe they tell him go to the Milagro, some in the Milagro do not like Brod any more and from them you will find clues to Miguel Brod. Your friend die still fighting in Spain, only now it is called Casa del Milagro."

It took a minute to absorb this: a war which had started as a crusade for rights and dignities had wound up, one small part of it had, in Millie's place. "You're the best kind of historian," I said. "You give the footnotes that are usually missing because historians don't want their pages sloppy. Benjie, will you take me to the Milagro?"

He was in a sweat. "Robert, good friend, do not insult my intelligence with such propositions! I will not take you, no! I will not hold out my hand to wild lions either and say to them, chew, have a good lunch!" He took off his straw hat and fanned his face with it.

"I've got to go. How do I get in?"

Benjie drank half his beer, very deliberately. He put the glass down with nicety and looked at me. "You insist? You are bored with living?"

"I insist."

He took a long, long breath. "Go with God, though I do not think He will get in the same taxi with you. There is just one way. I do not guarantee, but it could work."

"What is it?"

"In the Milagro there is one person who still has good thoughts of Mr. Brod. Old, old friend of Brod, young girl, one of the house girls. She is close to Brod on the personal basis. I see her sometimes, I buy her ribbons and eyebrow pencil." He looked discouraged. "She does all her business in birthday suit, and this is all right. But without the pink ribbon all over the hair she feel naked and all ashame. Crazy girl."

"What's your idea, that I go there and ask for her?"

There was severity in his look. His long fingers drummed displeasure on the table. "You would do that, heh? Go to the front door and knock, and say, the Señorita Natividad, the friend of Brod, please? It would be interesting for you, you would stand there and watch your head roll down the front steps all by itself. . . . Let us talk with two inches of sense, please. I will call Natividad. I tell her a certain Roberto from Mexico City wish to see her, it is about Brod but Millie is not to know this. Natividad was in a house in Mexico City. It is seven months now that she come from Mexico City with Brod. She like to hear everything about Brod. In case Brod is busy other places he will not find out about you immediately. Maybe it can work. It is big, big risk, but . . ."

"Make it work, Benjie," I said. "Go and call."

Shaking his head, he got up and went to the phone in the rear. I took my hand from my drink and studied it, it was shining with sweat. Cars streamed along the drive, tourists were climbing aboard the Morro Castle ferry just over the way, glasses clicked inside at the bar, but these normal sights and sounds were a million miles away. I was still wiping my palms on my trousers ten minutes later when Benjie came back. "She expects you," he said sourly. "She will say only that you are old friend, from Mexico City. Booked solid today. Go tomorrow, noon, sharp. If you do not make Millie suspicious, maybe you can make deal to hire the girl for a day and take her away. Impossible to talk there. This is best I can do. Should Brod find out, they bury you in two hours, and then me, and we will both bleed from all over." He mopped his face with the handkerchief again.

"You'll have a solid gold coffin, at my expense. What's the address?"

He took a postcard from his pocket, one which seemed to have two photographed nude figures on the front remarkably entwined, tore a corner off and wrote two addresses on the back. "Here, my friend full of suicide. First address the Milagro, second mine, plus my phone number. Memorize these infor-

mation, please, and tear up the paper quick. I do not wish
that they recover your sliced-up body with sample of my hand-
writing in the pocket."

"Thanks." I studied the addresses and the phone number
until I had them memorized. I was struck by Benjie's address,
a fashionable Vedado one. "You live well, Benjie. No dung
heaps for you."

"Until you come here," Benjie said, "I live fine. My land-
lady is retired madam with much real estate, I have excellent
picture window and private patio full of the pretty bougainvilleas. Very nice flowers. They put them over the knife holes
in my face when they bury me." He looked at me unhappily.
"I give you the phone just in case. Try to consider it is dis-
connected."

I took out my wallet and got a hundred-dollar bill. "Here.
For your free-lance work—"

He pushed my hand away with surprising violence.
"Please, Robert. I do not take money when I send a man
to be remodel into meat."

I paid the check and we went out. "You start out with
a big interest in me. I tell you about the *Easy Rider* and you
want to help. You stick with me. The moment I mention
Brod you want to run. You arrange things at the Milagro
and won't take money for it. Who are you working for today,
Benjie? When do you work for Brod and when—"

"Some days I work for Brod. On my own time I spit in
the face of Mr. Brod."

A cop came across the drive and caught sight of Benjie.
His face went genial and hat's-off, he smiled, touched the
visor of his cap. Benjie, with ward-boss style, raised a regal
finger and touched the brim of his straw hat. This made the
cop very, very happy. "Which days do you spit, Benjie?"

His face seemed to have gone on a long trip. "I am not
one for politics, I am modest businessman. But I have memories of Spanish war too. Long time ago I have a cousin,
Oliviero, big handsome man in Panama City, I love that man.

He get tired of the banana boats too, he go to New York and become stevedore on the docks. Then a man come to him and say, go to fight in Spain for all stevedores all over the world, and all black men, and Oliviero, he understand English only a little but he is sorry for stevedores and blacks, and he go to Spain to fight. There in some training camp there is a chief, some politician big man, who boss him around the way the dock boss yells at stevedores and poor blacks. Oliviero does not like that because the boss say, you are not here to ask the questions, you are only a gun here, not a mouth, and Oliviero starts fight and the boss shoots him, not on the battlefield, there in training camp. I do not know the details, this is all I hear about it. I cannot say the man who shoot Oliviero is Brod, no. But, fff he is some Brod." He stopped and looked squarely at me. "You will kill him?"

"What?"

"You have to kill him, you understand that?" I couldn't do anything but stare. "Listen to me. First you go to the Sociedad, now to the Milagro. Brod will know the meanings of this. You understand? Now there is no more play here, you kill him or he kill you. Nobody can kill this one, but you, mon, you must kill him."

"You know I went to the Sociedad yesterday. Who told you?"

"Not Brod. In Havana there is a big population of loose mouths." He took my hand and shook it, earnestly. "All right. Please, do me one favor, Robert. Try not to call me up in this century. If possible, go to some hemispheres where my name is not spoken." He turned and walked away, very lazy, very much at peace with the world, the candy-striped boulevardier. The cop was standing on the corner, they exchanged comradely salutes again.

Back at the Sevilla-Biltmore the desk clerk called to me and handed me a letter from my box. There was no return address on the envelope, just the words "Robert Heixas Garmes, Esq." written in a neat, precise hand. In my room I stretched

out on the bed, opened the envelope, and read the neat,
precise note:

My dear Garmes,

*My calculations were off: I had thought it would take
you several days to learn the facts that would draw you here.
I can only conclude that Barto did not die immediately and
that before he died he told you certain things which otherwise
you would have had some trouble in learning.*

*It does not please me to think of how Barto must have
suffered. You must understand that I was badly rushed in
Key West: and these matters are unpleasant enough without
that.*

*In any case, your being in Cuba is quite intolerable for
me. I did not remove Barto so that you could take his place
in trying to interfere with my plans.*

*No doubt, Caprio has given you all the reasons for not
coming here and, no doubt, you have dismissed them. I daresay
that, with your sharp bystander's eye, you began, along the way,
to sense that Vincent's arguments against your meddling were
less than convincing because he did not want to convince
you, quite. (Any more than he wanted, really, to convince
Barto.) In spite of which, or perhaps because of it, you came,
on the double, without shaving. People committed only to
lethargy, to an avoidance of commitment, are dangerous: they
will, at moments, jump in and outdo the windmills. Especially
when Mother was a windmill.*

*Under other circumstances I would welcome a meeting
with you: your objectless hunt for objects interests me. But I
have no time for talk right now, unfortunately. I am so pressed
for time that, if you persist in interfering, I shall have to
stop you.*

*Go home, Garmes. You're more your father's son than
you care to admit: don't fight the easy chairs. Why immerse
yourself in happenings when the supreme fact about you is
that you don't care what happens? Leave the pretenses of*

energy to those whose nervous systems are oriented that way.
Some of us, I assure you, are professionals at it.

> Sincerely,
> Brod

I slept for twelve hours.

FOURTEEN   The cab went as far as Los Cuatros
Caminos Crossing, then out Padre Varela Avenue and into a
scrubbed residential section. The houses were of middle-class
bonton, with small walled patios and sometimes colored glass
domes over them, curlicuing iron grillwork on all the doors
and windows to discourage the easy-come element. Millie's
place had its nose as high as its neighbors, it could have been
the embassy of the Principality of Lichtenstein. The bell was
hidden in a mess of stagey hibiscus. Long moments after I
pressed it there was movement behind the heavy glass-and-
grilling door, somebody pushed a buzzer and the door came
open. Inside was a dumpy, bulb-shouldered man in Basque
shirt and beret who asked in Spanish what I wanted, implying
that my demands would do well to be quick and modest. It
was exactly noon, the time I was due.

"My name is Roberto. I am expected."

"The place from which you come?"

"Mexico City. I am not expected?"

"You will permit that I see the small finger of the left
hand?"

I held my hand out. "Look to your utmost satisfaction.
When you are finished, not before, it is necessary that I have
it back."

He examined the finger. Never have I given another
human being such intense pleasure with one finger. "It is as
said. Small scar in the shape of a triangle, on the inside of

the finger, above the knuckle." That Benjie! The sly one, with
the arithmetic eyes! The finger inspector stood aside and I
went in. The patio was enclosed, unilluminated but splashed
with bright chips of color over the floor and furniture like a
spilled kaleidoscope, from the church-style mosaic glass forming
the roof. The man gestured to me to follow and started up a
staircase.

The walls were of pimpled buff stucco. Wrought-iron
chandeliers with red bulbs in the shape of dripping candles,
niches with pouty cherubim statuary, overstuffed velour sofas
and ballooning easy chairs, tapestries depicting Calvary vi-
gnettes and grandees at the court of Queen Esperanza de los
Flatfeet Somebody. The large oblong front room upstairs was
like a parlor car, little tables scattered about and men sitting
at them over beers and demitasse cups. No telling which were
the government people and which the combatientes and other
free-lancers, some looked like Humphrey Bogart and some
like Pedro Armendariz but with no hints as to their lines of
work. Those with ties on, I decided, were the government
people. Nobody showed any enthusiasm over my Florida face.
"With permission, we will go to the back," the guide said.

There was another large room down back, with swirled
linoleum on the floor and white walls. Large General Electric stove, large Kelvinator refrigerator, restaurant size, and in
the corner a jukebox, one that went on and on, bubbling
lights over its front.

"Feel that this is your home," the guide said with what
he imagined was warm hospitality.

"I feel I have lived in no other place," I said.

A woman came in from another entrance, behind her I
could see a long passageway with half a dozen bedrooms leading
off from it. She was Barbara Stanwyck padded considerably,
wearing a blue satin kimono with gold-thread roses and hyacinths running over it. She was big and wheat blond, her air
that of a Galveston hash-house cashier who has struck oil
under her chaise longue. A woman who had been around and

come back by short hops, taking notes all the way. She gave
me a big join-the-party smile. "Hello, buster," she said. The
accent in the gut tones was pure Panhandle crib, smoothed off
by two sessions at the Cornell School of Voice Culture. "You
Robert?"

It seemed the thing to get my Spanish established fast.
"I am called Roberto," I said in Spanish.

"You're from, let's see, Curaçao?"

"Mexico City. And other places."

She seemed impressed by my vagueness. "Live town,
Mexico City," she said. "What line you in over there?"

"Various things. A little crème de menthe, other things."

My words were to her liking. "Plenty of action in crème
de menthe. I'd like to have some of that going for me. Here
for long?"

"Just passing through, I've got some business in the States.
I thought I'd kill a couple days in Havana and look around."

"So, sure, you want to look up your old friends." She
studied me for a while. "You've got a friend here from
Mexico."

"That's right."

"Well. A man likes to have a little party. Nattie's just a
kid, though, we've got some that're not kids. You could take a
look."

I felt my shoulders getting tight. "Ordinarily I'd take
you up on that. I've only got a couple days, though, and
Natividad's an old, old friend."

"There's no harm in looking."

"Another time, maybe."

"Come on!" She gave me a big grin. "Let's have some
fun, Bobby. We'll get the kids out here and you act like
Nattie's just one of the kids and after you look them over you
see do you still pick Nattie! I told Nattie I'd be watching her
to make sure she acted just like all the others, no signals."
The grin was still on her face and her eyes were still on my
face. She went to the door and called down the passageway,

"Herminia! Pegita! Julianita! Boo-Boo! Mercedes! Come on, kids! Let's get with it! Hup! Hup! Hup!"

The girls began to troop out, breasts bare but wearing satin and lace cut-out panties of various bright colors and patent-leather pumps with very high French heels that they didn't seem to trust. Seven of these girls came out and lined up in a wobbling row, giving me big-promise looks. I was iced to my fingers but I still noticed this walking-on-eggs of theirs. Whores in the imperialist countries, pampered by the robber barons, have learned to negotiate on French heels, but the ones in the exploited colonies, being long oppressed and cut off from the main sources of imperialist frilly culture, never seem at home on those luxury-item spikes, they look like kids on their first pair of stilts. But which of the unsteady balancing girls was named Natividad? I cursed Benjamino Francisco for not preparing me for such tricks, and myself for not thinking to ask for a description of the girl. I was badly frightened. Unless Natividad gave me a sign I was sunk. But Natividad couldn't give me a sign, Millie was watching.

They stood there, balancing, trying to project winsome personality. They were of several varieties, bleach-haired and scroll-haired, some tawny of skin and others ivory dead, all of them young, under-endowed in the flesh, but made up in smears, a line of obscene moppets. But one caught my eye. She was a little shorter than the others, the second from the end on the right, and what held me was some almost delicate thing about her face. It was the unstable mixture, maybe. She was the most babyish of all and the most corrupt, and each quality stood out like a sore thumb on the other, that was one fragility. It was a jumbling of bloods, too. Her cheekbones came from Mayan high princesses, but her nose was straight from Estremadura and her eyes had survivals from the Nairobi back country that professors never dreamed of. And she was a baby, to boot, with the whole history of foulness tatooed in her baby softness, her pert face a Rosetta stone of the world's vices. She was thin, her legs undernourished, and her breasts

were small, put on the baby body as a playroom joke the way
kids put on their mother's party shoes. She wasn't my physical
type but if I'd come here for a girl, this was the girl I would
have picked, despising myself.

I looked at her hopelessly, aware of Millie's eyes on me.
I noticed something that made my pulse race. The girl was
wearing several pink ribbons in bows around her long black
hair. Benjie had said something about pink hair ribbons. She
was holding her hands up idly, as though playing with her
breasts, and I saw something else that maybe she meant me
to see without Millie getting suspicious. There was a big carved
silver ring on one finger, an unmistakably Mexican ring, the
kind they make in Taxco. Natividad had come lately from
Mexico. She thought I was from Mexico.

I took a long breath. I walked over to this befouled child,
stopped in front of her and said, "Natividad. Baby. You
look fine." I held my arms out, hoping their trembling wasn't
noticeable. With a delighted squeal she rushed into them.

"Ay, bay-bee, bay-bee," she said lovingly. "My big Roberto.
Beer for the girls, Roberto, play jukebox, bay-bee. Ay, ay, ay."
This was between showers of passionate kisses over my face.

Millie was tickled pink. The other girls, unemployed again,
drooped in the corner around the big enamel table. The man
in the beret looked at me questioningly, I nodded, he went to
the oversize icebox and got out bottles of beer for everybody.
Natividad held her hand out and I deposited some coins in
it, she went off to put them in the jukebox. Perez Prado's
barking saxophones filled the room, doing a bop-tense samba.
I felt a pleasant numbness, as though a guillotine had missed
my vital tubes by two important inches. Natividad grabbed me
and we went into a clipclop dance across the linoleum, she
singing along in a bobbysocks-thin voice and eyelids going,
Shirley Temple at her first grown-up dance. My legs were not
inclined to go where I did. When the number was done I got
over to a chair and sat down. Natividad followed and eased
into my lap, giggling, and began whispering graphic four-letter

nothings to me and biting my ear. Millie, sitting across the
room taking big swallows from a bottle of beer, was pleased
with the merriment. From time to time she gave us a big wink
and a nod. I got my earlobe free from Natividad's molars and
asked Millie how it would be if I took the kid away for, say,
twenty-four hours. "It's been a long time," I said. "We ought
to celebrate."

"Damn nice thought," Millie said. "Let's say fifty dollars.
Special price for you, Roberto."

Natividad jumped to her feet and began to hop around,
singing, "Twenty-four hours, a-yeh, a-yoo, twenty-four, dyah-
dar, dyah-doo." I supposed twenty-four hours meant a lot of
hard work to her on Millie's assembly line, and here now came
her hero on a white charger from Mexico City, bringing paid
vacations. It was a sentimental moment. When I took the fifty
from my wallet, plus something for the beers, and handed it
to Millie, the girl's eyes sparked like a kid's at a Christmas
tree. "I go now," she said excitedly, chewing on my ear again.
"I get dressed up crazy, have hell of party!" She skipped off
down the passageway, going to circuses.

At this point the oldest woman I have ever seen came out
from the bedrooms, a tiny, very black woman of over ninety,
with skin like tapa cloth. She was carrying a bundle of soiled
towels, also, surprisingly, a roll of toilet paper in her large
apron pocket, and between her bluish toothless gums was a
Churchill-size cigar. She seemed pleased to see a visitor and
came over to sit with us. I figured out the casting, she was
Maria Ouspenskaya in blackface. They had changed her name
for this role, though, what she was called by the girls, in Spanish
diminutives, was Maria the Bent-Over, and Maria the Cigar
Burner, and, more sentimentally, Maria the Beer Vat.

"A small swallow?" she said, poking thumb toward my
beer bottle. "To wash out the mouth? Mouth full of donkey
leavings from donkey flop cigar?" I passed the bottle to her.
It was half empty but when she put it down again it was all
empty. She tore off a piece of the toilet paper and daintily

patted her tapa-cloth lips dry. "Beer very good for loose bowels," she said pleasantly. "Better than the coconut milk. From where you come?"

"Mexico City, mother," I said.

"No good girls in Mexico City," she said with quiet authority. "Dirty like hogs, no inspection. I relieve myself on the heads of girls from Mexico City."

"Havana is to be preferred, infinitely. Here are to be found the best girls, also the best cigars."

"I relieve myself equally on Havana. On the entire city of Havana, from the Prado to the Almendares River equally, I leave the scrapings of skin from my scalp, and the phlegm behind my tongue, and the collection of dirt between my toes, and the wax from my ears." She spoke with no trace of rancor, reportorial.

"There is a city more to your liking, grandmother?"

"Grand Rapids, Michigan," she said. "There lives my grandson, who is in the profession of making false teeth." She took the uppers and lowers from her mouth, clacked them to show the quality of the workmanship, returned them. "My grandson writes of the many wonders of Grand Rapids. He describes constantly that they eat strawberry ice cream each night, and in the streets there is no dung. On all other cities of this and other lands I relieve myself from sunup to sundown and equally through the night. You are married?"

"To the present, no."

"I have been married seven times, counting only the official way. I relieve myself on the marriage. It is for harness horses, for those who drop the dung on the public streets. You do the wise thing, you come to the Casa for the one-hour marriage. To buy the marriage between trains, then to use the toilet paper or the towels at extra rates and to change the sheets before the next marriage."

"You speak wisdom, mother, and it pleases me to hear of your relative who eats strawberry ice cream. You will do me the kindness to accept this cigar?" I found a Larrañaga in my breast pocket and offered it to her. She gave me a courteous old-world nod.

"I will keep it to smoke in quiet," she said, "after I distribute to the rooms the paper and clean towels. There is small demand now for the towels because of the extra rates. A thousand gratitudes, gentleman, and take care with the dirty stinking whores of Mexico City. They never wash themselves, from Christmas to Christmas Eve they have the skins of lice and crabs. They are hotels for the vermin of all classes, equally the girls of Havana. Health and money."

"And the time to spend it, mother," I said, and she wandered away with her towels and toilet paper, puffing on the cigar.

Millie sighed audibly. "You get old," she said, "got nothing working for you. Pick up towels, put down toilet paper. Always between trains." She was getting a little drunk, I thought. "Guys used to pay for the towels."

In a few minutes Natividad burst from the passageway. She was wearing something that looked like a bedroom robe, a thing of shiny tan satin spattered with sequins and edged with stringy fur trimmings, her too-thin legs were covered with black silk stockings that had heavy green seams on the back and spear-headed Frenchy clocks running halfway up the sides. She almost flopped on her French heels, she was so excited. "See!" She pirouetted. "Put on best dress for you, Roberto! People will say, oh, ho, big government bigshot, going with wifey to see sights! Hey, we go, Robertitito! Make plenty party!"

"Thanks for everything, Millie," I said, rising and shaking hands with my hostess. "Don't worry, I'll have her back safe and sound before tomorrow night."

"Send her any way you want," Millie said good-naturedly. "The doc'll look her over Saturday anyhow, with the rest. I run a clean house here."

"I can see there's nothing disorderly about this house," I said.

Natividad took hold of my hand and led me into the passageway, then down some back stairs. "Policía sometime in the front," she said. "They ass us we make traffic in back, for the looks." As we came out in the alley I heard the jukebox starting up again, a rhythm quartet doing close harmony on an old pop song. I got a gal in Kalamazoo, something and something and something, Kalamazoo. What movie was that from?

FIFTEEN   A block away I had to stop and catch my breath. I took hold of the black iron orchids topping a grill-work fence and leaned there. "It's nothing," I said. "I have weak arches, it affects my breathing." She seemed to take these words as coming from the fence. She fingered the carved orchids from petal to petal and answered straight to them. "Flowers hard," she said with interest. "Hit somebody on the head with hard flowers and finish with the breathing." The observation was accurate but not easily answered. Luckily the conversation was in no danger of running down. "Roberto?" she said, still to the iron petals. "Roberto who? Roberto the Big Stupid?"

"If you want to know my name, don't tell me, ask me."

"Roberto king of the stupids. Take ten year before he see ring," she told the fence. "What I suppose to do for ten year, scratch myself? How flower get hard?" Her tone and intensity were the same as before.

"Why did Millie play the trick?" I said. "Is she still a friend of Brod's, did she think—"

"Millie full of love and kissing for Señorita Peso-Eyes Millie." She turned her eyes directly to me, finally. I wished she hadn't. Her mouth was speaking the words, but they seemed to be coming from somebody behind her. She thought they were, too. There was haze in her wonderful big black eyes as she listened with interest to the words that came from over her shoulder and made her lips go. "Oh, she is smart, that one, smart. I say to her, my friend from Méjico is here, Roberto is here, and she think, maybe Roberto is friend of Miguel. Why friend of Miguel come to Milagro? Maybe to make troubles. If Roberto not friend of Miguel, still bad, maybe. Maybe he is policía or something. She want to know, these Roberto, he make fuggy with Natividad in Méjico, now he like to make more fuggy in Cuba, these is all, and no policía and politics? She is rat in the garbage, looking, looking." The voice behind her stopped talking and her lips stopped their ventriloquism movements. She took me by the arm and pulled. "We go, Roberto. Away from the Casa of the Garbage." We started up the street. "Go nice bar and drink the Scoatch-and-soda."

"What about Benjamino? Is he good friends with Miguel?"

"Benjamino solidarity with all exploited worker elements." She said it, word for word, as though still talking about how flowers get hard. "He my good friend, Benjamino, bring me the pretty ribbon and nail poalish of shoacking pink." Troubles like cloud formations went across her face, she seemed to be in a spotlight that kept blinking off.

"I like Benjie too. He is of much solidarity."

At the little park close by the Ministry of Health and Welfare she stopped to study the bums on the benches. She nodded, pointed to an empty bench set back from the street under a palmetto tree. "We sit," she said, apparently having lost interest in the Scoatch-and-soda. As soon as we took our places she came into focus, her edges stopped their melting and for a moment she fell into a kind of dehydrated, impersonal, cablese Spanish. "Miguel?" she said. "Does not come, sends you. Trouble, no?"

"He didn't send me, Natividad. I come for business with him but I cannot find him. That is why Benjamino called you."

But the concentration was going out of her eyes again and she turned her head to look at the hyacinths lining the path. She said in a puzzling voice, "All big ears, flowers. What do they hear, everything?" It wasn't a joke because her face stayed serious. "They listen to the air." She jerked her head back toward me and said, "So, mister. He give you words to bring? He want me to come?"

"When did you last see Miguel, Natividad?"

"How to see him when for all the years he is not there?" There was a quaver of hurt in her voice but it went as fast as it came. A silence: she lifted her foot and with a murderous kick ground a hyacinth into the dirt with her heel. Then, with a bored voice, as though reciting the multiplication table: "One year, then another year. I look for him one place, he is another place. There under the ground." She was taken with sadness, shook it off. "You take me to the place where he is? Now?"

"Natividad," I said, "don't you know where he is? Try to think."

"Colón Cemetery," she said placidly. She didn't see me jump. "Three weeks ago we go for the walk in Colón Cemetery. He says he must go away, come back soon. We sit behind the big stone of a dead Spanish general and he gives me pretty filigree earrings and feels on my leg. You want to make me feel sick and cry, you, Roberto? Give me the words and take me to my dear one." She turned away again and became interested in a bum on a nearby bench, a scrawny man with one leg missing and his exposed stump in filthy burlap wrappings. She reverted to English. "I do not know where a man go to lose a leg and hide it, Colón Cemetery? Friday I fall on the fuggy stairs and scratch my knee."

"I must find Miguel right away, Natividad. Can't you help me?"

"All of them talk and no words," she said calmly. "At Milagro they say to me, those others, find Brod, girl, find Brod. Do I know how to find him one year or next year? Brod find me, some years." Her attention was sidetracked again, she was looking up at the palmetto branches this time. "In winter leaves wither away. The state withers away, after the hegemony. It makes me feel bad when trees are bare and my knee hurts at night." She actually said it, in Spanish, in her little-girl recitation voice.

"You have no idea where he is? None?"

The lights came on in her face again: who was working the switch? "Long now that I do not see Miguelito. If you will not take me, and Coolio will not take me, then, all right. I will find him other ways. You will see."

"Why do you think he's in trouble, Natividad?"

"I hear them and their fuggy talk. They do not want for me to hear, those in the Casa, but I listen, for Miguelito. They say Miguelito is in bad trouble and try to hide but soon he go on long trip on boat, discipline, hard core, then more trouble when he gets off the boat." She was mixing words from both languages, at random. "Before, they are his big friends. Now they say he is in trouble and must go on the boat, and they laugh. Only Coolio does not laugh, and I do not laugh. I will kill them." She looked straight up at me and there were tears in her eyes. "You know I will die if he goes away one more time, Roberto? For all the years again? For the discipline and the hard cores, enough of that. Roberto, you promise, do not let him go without Natividad, or Natividad is sick and dies."

Hegemony: withering away: hard core: not a tongue picked up from American sailors with weekend passes in the whorehouses of Mexico City. From them and similar culture-bearers she had learned only the easy esperanto of fuggy and Scoatch-and-soda. "If we can find out where he is," I said, "I will take you there. Would Coolio know?"

"Make snakes to sing lullabies," she said. "Before you get the helping words from these one you see your left ear without the mirror. He is full of the needles."

"Then it is hopeless. You do not know where he is and I do not know where he is."

A sly, secret-hoarding smile came over her face. "There

are those besides Coolio. I know them. Some Coolio does not know."

I took her hand. "Can we find them now?"

"I go to them before, to do little businesses for Miguel. They will talk open with Natividad." She jumped up and tugged at my hand. "We go, Roberto! We go look!" On the way out of the park, passing the beggar with the bandaged stump, she looked troubled and said, "Leg withers away. In the winter? With proletariat dictatorship and the leaves?" After that, as we went by more flower beds, I thought she was saying flowers belong to the underground, flowers that listen to everything are fifth columns with their always listening.

Going toward the center of town Natividad was keyed up and chattering, pulling me by the hand. She was looking for Uncle Miguel, flower from underground, hyacinth that kills. I looked for an idea big enough to hold her against her flickering. All right, she was sparse between the ears, she was from Méjico and she had a Mexican jumping bean of a brain. She'd manage in a whorehouse. Customers do not come to whorehouses for high repartee, they would hardly notice how the Mazdas went on and off in a girl's face. Besides, in the Milagro, maybe, Natividad didn't dart so much. In the Casa, likely, when a man looked at her, the fact of his direct-statement eyes on her provided the center and she shaped herself as the immediate surround to that center. Maybe it was more like some blob of a marine animal who crawls into an empty anemone shell for cover and from then on is anemone-shaped. That was all. Except it was so far from all, it was nothing and less. This going-everywhere talk of hers was institution talk. The one thing to do with her was put her gently to bed and call the ambulance, but I let her lead me through the streets because her hand could lead me to Brod.

At our first stop, a rundown loft building two blocks west of the Prado, I had to make a decision. There was a risk to going inside with the girl. On the other hand, she wasn't to be trusted to handle it herself. And if I hesitated to go with her she might get suspicious.

I went along. The place was a dingy pharmaceutical supply house on the third floor, open shelves filled with boxes of patent medicines. We found a thin man in a turtleneck sweater, one shoulder higher than the other so he looked like he was partially shrugging at everything, who recognized Natividad and showed it by making his lips disappear and slotting his eyes. Did he know where the good friend Miguelito was to be found? An enormous urgency, did he know? He did not know, and he was delighted not to know, and if he were given the opportunity to acquire the knowledge he would respond by placing his knuckles in the kind one's eye. We left with many apologies for the intrusion, an odor of cooking hydrogen sulphide sharp in my nostrils.

Next, a tiny store with windows painted over black. On the door, in inconspicuous rough letters, were the words, COMMITTEE FOR SPANISH REFUGEE ASSISTANCE. Only four or five men were sitting inside, playing cards and talking Basque, and one of them, a flabby-cheeked man wearing a beret too large and too tilted, seemed to know Natividad. He was impersonal and businesslike when he came to one side to talk with us, he listened to the questions like a court reporter. No, he did not have these data, the whereabouts of Miguelito Brod were a matter of complete mystification to him, it pained him more than there were words for. He asked if I wished to play a game of casino for moderate stakes, and I said no.

Somewhere not far from Raimundo Cabrera Street we turned into a ratty structure, climbed four narrow flights to the top and entered a studio covered by a dusty skylight, the walls plastered with old passport and identity-card photos. Our host here, a big billiard-bald man with sagging moustachios that enclosed his liver-slack lips like parentheses, was a notary public and photographer for legal papers, also a scribe, translator and guide. Did he know where Brod was? He knew the location of nothing, animal, vegetable or mineral, with the name or the implication of Brod. Brod was the world's most repulsive word in his ears. He was going to make a life work of forgetting the name of Brod, and he would hold classes for those who wished to do the same. A very good day to all and sundry. Bye now, and go with God if you can but in any case, go. When he shut the door in our faces he shot the inside bolt.

"Pigs," Natividad said, reciting again. "Worms, spiders, dung flies. Yesterday they would jump like kangaroos and drip the oil from the mouth when Miguel said one nice word to them. Mud beetles, with mud eyes."

Somebody, it seemed, was spreading the word around town that Mike Brod was on the two-hemisphere shit list, and the town listened. Armies of more or less good folk were reluctant to mention his name. But we weren't giving up. "My knee hurts from where I hit it on the stairs," Natividad said, and led me down the street and then through some corkscrew turns that landed us in the Old Quarter, not far from the Ambos Mundos. "Once I met a beggar with the whole leg cut off," she said pensively. "He said the knee which is not there hurts very much when it rains. Rain falls in the ocean, the boat is big. Many cadres go on the boat." We went down some worn stone steps to a basement that was a musty, wine-smelling liquor warehouse, there were oval vats on wooden horses in the rear and shelves lined with empty bottles, some with rum labels and some with crème de menthe labels. Here a man appeared from the small office in the back, a man designed entirely with T-square and compass, square in the shoulders and body with a moon-round face, he came toward Natividad smiling and spilling warm greetings. Oh, unhappy day, he had not the first scintilla of the information. It hurt him to the quick because he, too, was fond of Miguelito, he, too, was withered in the soul by the lack of Miguel's sunny company. It worried me when he brought up the subject of withering but it produced no offshoot thoughts in Natividad.

"There is a place he goes," Natividad said. "Varadero. You would know this."

The eyes in the moon-face widened into subsidiary moons. "Is this possible, girl? In what connection do you mention Varadero?"

"Near Varadero you have your main business, true?" Natividad said. "The place to distill, where is distilled the rum and other things. This I remember, in the place of distilling, there near Varadero, sometimes Miguel stays."

The man looked brokenhearted. "It is not to be considered that Miguelito would be there and I not know of this. Besides, he is no longer friends with the director. Little one, if Miguel is in Varadero, I have string beans for hair."

There was one more place Natividad wanted to try, over on the other side of the Prado. We took a cab. The place was the small, unpushing, second-floor office of the "Greater Caribbean Air Cargo Services, Ltd.," and the only person on the premises was a fin-nosed thin woman who reacted to the sight of Natividad with outbreaks of passionate joy and a big motherly hug. Natividad stated her business.

"I look and look and do not find him," she said shakily. "I get sick and probably die from not finding him. They hit me all the time, the stairs. Maybe he is in Varadero, this I think is a strong possibility, but if they hit me and hit me—"

The chisel-faced woman perked up at this. She clucked. "Ah, but such a misfortune. This about Varadero would have been so easy to determine. One hour ago I could have put you on the plane."

"One of your planes went to Varadero?" I said.

"Yes, mister. A special trip by the charter of the Professor Brooke, an American. But there was space. Who knows, I might have arranged—"

"Professor Owen Brooke?"

"Yes, mister. He, exactly."

"He did not say why he was going there?"

"This is not for me to ask, mister. I know only he is friend of Miguel, and in the past he has chartered the planes from us also."

"Thanks without number," I said.

When we got out on the street I noticed Natividad had something in her hand, a rose. She'd been toying with the roses in a vase on the air-cargo woman's desk. "Be happy, Natividad," I said. "I think we are going to find Miguel. First I must use the telephone."

But she didn't hear. She said idly, "If they hit me," speaking to some point past my left ear, then she said, "A man could hide a leg in a boat, I have a bandage on a knee," still without expression. My eye was caught by some forceful movement of her hands. She did not seem to know it, her eyes were still directed to that point in the vicinity of my ear, but her hands were wringing the rose, wringing it with energetic twists as though it were the neck of a chicken, the knuckles of both hands white with the strain, and the lacerated bits of the rose petals fell over her open-toed patent-leather French pumps with the high, wobbling French heels.

SIXTEEN   I telephoned the Ambos Mundos from a drugstore. Owen Brooke had left a forwarding address, Internacional Hotel, Varadero Beach. The desk at the Sevilla-Biltmore also had a message for me: "Under no circumstances make any trips to Varadero without calling to me first. This is absolutely important." Signed, Benjamino Francisco.

Surprisingly, I still remembered Benjie's number. He answered the phone himself. As soon as he heard my name he took on the swallowed basso tone of a professional mourner.

"You keep up on current events," I said. "Who told you I was going to Varadero?"

"My good sense, plus your bad, your absolutely bad sense. Your no sense whatsomever."

"Why should I go to Varadero especially?"

"You are the big tourist. Today you make the tour of all lovely Havana."

He seemed to be experimenting to see how many different sounds he could produce with his nose and throat. Then: "I tell it to you once, then no more. Go to Varadero all you want, on the hour every hour, when there are no conventions in Varadero. When there are conventions, go quick in opposite directions, Roberto. You, especially."

"Benjie, I'm with a girl who's dying away for love. She's got to be taken to her dear one in Varadero or she'll die." I listened to his gargling exercises. "The *Easy Rider's* there, too, I think. I can't stay away from boats." More gagging. "Besides, they make good absinthe in Varadero, in crème de menthe bottles. I'm very partial to good absinthe."

"You will discover," he said, "it is hard to drink the absinthe with holes all over the throat. All the good absinthe will leak out. The worms will have a party with your absinthe."

"Yesterday I got a letter from a friend of yours. He asks me, as a special favor, not to come anywhere where he is. Today *you* ask me to be nice and not bother this fellow. Who're you free-lancing for today, Benjie?"

There was no sputtering at the other end this time, just a dead silence. When he spoke it was softly, almost with sadness. "I cannot keep nice letters of recommendations from each and all of my employers, I have not the facilities for the filing. From the time to time, I am my own boss. Some days, even, I free-lance for my big handsome dead cousin Oliviero, and other similar Olivieros."

"Yes. Would you know anything about our mutual friend getting ready for a boat ride? I hear he may take a trip."

"You have big ears."

"Where's he going?"

"I did not say he is going. He has the strong invitation to go, he must make up the mind in twenty-four hours. This is why you must make yourself absent, Roberto! He is under much pressure to make his mind up. You go there to make trouble, it is more pressure on him, he will not be happy with you."

"Where's he supposed to go?"

"His big bosses want to have convention with him in their home office, I think. They already ask him to come many time, but before he is not in the mood. That is why the convention in Varadero now, Roberto. It is a thing to do with should he or should not he go to the other bigger convention in the other place. This is my feeling of the matter."

"Who're you working for this week, Benjie? You going to the convention?"

"You shut up, mon! Hear! Ba-da-da, ba-da-da, stop with these always talka, talka!" I had to hold the ear piece away, he was yelling so loud. "Do I go to certain businesses, it is because, for the business, for that, for the work! That, and no else! Not for playing cops-and-robbing games and the tourism! You understand! I do my work!"

I began to say, "Yes, I hear you're a man of much solidarity with your work," but he'd hung up.

Natividad was sitting quietly at the soda fountain, her gaseosa untouched before her. "Good news," I said. "Miguel is in Varadero. We can take the plane."

She seemed not to have heard. She was playing with her fingers, counting the fingers of one hand with those of the other in some important stock-taking. "I like to buy some shoes of the alligator with the openings in the toes," she said seriously. "I like it very much to have the toes come out. Naturally, with these I have also to buy fingernail poalish of various color, not for the fingers but for the nails of the toes. Where is the good to have toes come out if there is no color on? It can be very expensive, these thing."

"I'll buy you the shoes and the polish in Varadero. Come on, little one. You can count the fingers on the plane."

We got a cab. It was only midafternoon but the neons in the center of town were sending off cheery bulletins about this perfume and those chic gowns direct from Paris, Hatuey beer and O'Sullivan heels, and couples were strolling down the street with arms laced together. That day, even in Havana, there would be quite a few people small as life, eating guacamole salad and watching television. All of them, these cafe and guacamole people, were on the other side of a foot-thick glass plate, and on this side I was in a cab next to the baby-face whore with whistling manifestos in her head, riding to conventions.

In a half hour we were at the Rancho Boyeros airport. We were in luck, the plane for Varadero was due to leave in twenty minutes. When we got aboard and settled in seats up front, the other passengers making funny low-pitched remarks about us, sure the moneyed Americano was off to Varadero for a toot with his sequined Havana tart, Natividad was still taking inventory of her fingers and I had to reach over and fasten the safety belt for her.

The plane went up but my stomach told me I was going down. The stomach, it was clear, was not a reliable altimeter: often, when diving, getting down to the deeper fathoms, I had the strong impression from the state of my middle that I was soaring. Now, going up, my stomach told me I was falling. Sending up reports that it was falling fast, forty fathoms, then forty fathoms again, down to where the last blue rays of light thinned out and finger-counting whores went on about cadres and proletarian hegemonies whose knees are skinned. Natividad was still turned, looking the plane over. Her eyes were open wide, her hand went up to point. "With the open toes?" she said wonderingly. "The red poalish cost too much? Pretty drums?" Then with delight she jumped up, pushed past me, and was off down the aisle.

I turned, not sure whether I would see cadres of leaping alligator shoes or flowers in whispering conspiracy.

There was a convention shaping up for Varadero, all right.

Natividad was bending over somebody in a rear seat,

chattering. It was Coolio in a stiff white suit, bongo drums in his lap. He was talking to Natividad, nodding to her excited words, but he was looking at me and he was grinning. He took a paper from his pocket and handed it to her, saying something meant for her but still grinning at me. After a moment Natividad nodded, pleased, and came back to her seat. She climbed past me and fell back, bubbling, talking in a jumble. "We go to Varadero!" she informed me. "Miguelito is in Varadero! I go see Miguelito." It had slipped her mind that we were on this plane precisely and solely for the purpose of going to Varadero, and to Miguelito the dear one in Varadero. The paper Coolio had given her was in her unaware fingers. It was an envelope, there was a name typed on its front: "Sr. Robert Heixas Garmes." Just the name, nothing else. I slid the envelope from her hand while she went on giving me her news: "These plane go now to Varadero! Miguelito there in Varadero!" I opened the sealed envelope.

It was a typewritten letter, from Brod.

SEVENTEEN

Dear Garmes,

As I thought: the lethargist moves fast when he finally moves. Today you've found Natividad. (How, precisely?) She knows the few contacts I still have. I must assume that before this day is over you will have heard rumors about Varadero.

I will confess something. From the moment it became clear that Barto had to be removed, you were my chief worry. The reason is not hard to see. A man in my position can cover himself reasonably well only so long as he can predict the behavior of those about him; and you, like most sidelines people disenchanted with the sidelines, were extremely unpredictable.

Not as to whether you would jump into the picture. Only how: with what methods, what intentions.

Do you know what, exactly, you are after? Don't waste your time and mine with easy moralistic formulas about avenging a killing. Suppose we meet: is it your intention to kill me (if you can)? Answer that question honestly and you will be shocked. What you want is to meet me. To meet me, to get involved in a situation, and then to improvise. Those remote from situations reach greedily for them when they begin to move; having lived too long in a vacuum, your first need is to feel surrounded. I would even suggest this: that to kill me would work against your own deeper interests here. If I am removed you will not easily replace me.

I simply cannot be bothered by a man who pushes his way toward me without the slightest notion of what he wants. Extempore is the sign of the actor, not the active. A professional worker avoids improvisation like the plague: too time-consuming. With us, minutes count. You have lifetimes: the amateur's incalculable advantage.

I know exactly why Vincent Caprio is after me. He wants something I have. I know, down to the last innermost detail, the nature and intensity of that want and what he will do to satisfy it. He is a professional, and I can deal with him. I know, too, that he is aware of my professionalism. It is extraordinarily difficult for either one of us to get something that the other has: we anticipate each other too well.

Vincent is quite well aware of the stalemate. That is why he needs an amateur in the picture; first Barto, now you. His hope all along has been that an amateur will—not out-maneuver me, certainly; he's too clever to expect that—rather, befog me. You are an utterly insignificant—and expendable—tool in Vincent's larger strategy. Key word: expendable.

Have no illusions about being a free agent. The professional has a goal and a plan; the amateur bumbles along with mixed aims and ambivalent improvisations; inevitably, the planless one becomes the instrument of the planner. Vincent has a plan and the means to carry it out: an efficient organization. What is your plan? To keep busy? Where is your organization? In your fists?

I remind you again that Vincent could have immobilized you in a minute if he had really wanted to. (*Just as he could have immobilized Barto and saved his life in the process.*) So much for your romantic notions.

Vincent, as he knows only too well, has me at a tremendous disadvantage. Until recently I had a large apparatus at my disposal, one which, with all due respect, put Vincent's to shame. (*Understandably; we on our side have had a rich experience in building apparatuses.*) Today Vincent still has his *apparatus,* a growing one; but I have lost mine. Exasperating, to a trained organizational mind. It is on that exasperation that Vincent is trading.

At the final point, Vincent underestimates me. (*That hurts, rather. But it means he can be fooled.*) No, Garmes, under this pressure I will not explode. But I will eliminate the source of the inadmissible pressure. I will get rid of you —the project does not need elaborate apparatuses.

All your life, I gather, you have made an indignant fuss about being used—by other people's compulsions, by your mother's drive or your father's dead weight, by mindless bureaucracy. You act (*even in the refusal to act*) as though you had a positive horror of being manipulated. You give the impression, often, that you were placed in the universe with an assignment: to take an arm-waving stand against everything that is not yourself. Sometimes you even seem to pick your women in order to oppose them. Some can be tilted at.

It comes to this: you choose to fight on fronts where you can't possibly win. Which raises the question of whether you fight to win, or only to fight. (*If not to lose.*) All of that is quite alien to me, as you can imagine. I see no point in going into battle unless victory is a foregone conclusion. But then, our purposes are radically different.

But I don't mean to criticize. The acromegalic Me has no place in our century, but you interest me all the same. I am intensely interested in leftovers; when I am in a new city I find time to visit the local cathedrals and look at the glass-enclosed relics—this old thigh bone, that abstracted tuft of monkish hair. If I had time for hobbies, one of them would certainly be archeology. I love to dig in the dust for shards like you.

I am trying to show you that you have no role in true happenings. Here I can get more concrete. Why, during the war, did you twice come close to a court-martial? I know your stock answers: you were rising up against all that Me-killing pressure, and so on.

No. It's not good enough, Garmes. The private commotions were more important than the public stand for human stuff against the machine.

Am I juggling the facts? Were you simply trying to protect yourself? Possibly. But how, then, would you explain your provocative attitude toward your superiors in both situations? That was a certain asking for trouble. Admit, in any case, that under your fierce insistence on freedom there is sometimes a deeper compulsion.

From time to time you have made quite a show of irritation with the bothersome "clutter" in the world. You were living a remarkably uncluttered life in Key West until two days ago: you had space on all sides. Why did you suddenly dive into things down here, unless you had a need to feel yourself surrounded?

All this means that you are not equipped to take part in the doings of professional activists. The mark of the professional is that he is scrupulously not moved by the compulsions of anarchistic inner need: he simply acts when thus and so can be accomplished, and refrains from acting when it cannot. It is all quite impersonal. He never says ME: only, WHAT CAN BE DONE?

Against the trained people, Garmes, you're bound to lose

every time. You can't get any satisfaction here. You can only be used and abused, to the point of extinction.

This is as far as I can go with words. Don't come to Varadero, Garmes. I make you this promise: Varadero will be the last stop.

By the way, I hope you will not jump—you're always jumping! I suppose it's your way of overcoming inertia—to conclusions about the effect I have had on Natividad's life. She is in a bad way, admittedly, poor girl. But the fact is that I have been a good deal nicer to her than may be immediately apparent.

Sincerely,
Brod

... and ...

Maui was where I had the first trouble. We got through the offshore phase of the mock assault all right, mining the crossbound steel rails and hardwood post clusters and other obstacles. The machine-gun tracers two feet over our heads were no more than an annoyance. But when we crawled up the sands toward the concrete emplacements and dragon's teeth, Barto just ahead of me, the whole damned beach began to wiggle under us with ferocious belching sounds —land mines going, to make it more realistic.

The use of live fire in training problems made me want to hit somebody, anyway. Those who stayed away from bullets in training would be the ones who tried to stay away in battle, was my thought. Those who were careless didn't learn anything, they were carried off in a stretcher. Simulation of reality? What enemy, for the love of sweet Jesus's brown eyes, would be obliging enough to keep his fire a nice two feet above all heads? Now, to round out the machine guns, here were land mines to make us chew on sand. Planted in patterns away from our path, no doubt, but I didn't trust their patterns and I didn't trust the demon realist sitting in a beach cabaña somewhere pushing the detonator plungers and eating a melted cheese sandwich.

Two-thirds of the way along I stopped and froze. A thing hard and flat and rough-edged was catching on the skin of my stomach. My fingers told me, then my eyes, that it was a TNT block. Such fine patterns they had. Arms prickly with bugs of sweat, I dug for the detonating cord and sliced it. I inched away, following the line, and when I reached the thicker main line I hacked that, too. Happily.

With that, the beach went dead. All explosions stopped. I had cut the master line in which several trunk feeds were bound together.

Three hours later I was standing at attention in the C.O.'s tent and he was asking why I had left my assigned position and by one uncalled-for move destroyed half the effectiveness of our most important training operation, on the eve of battle, when adequate training meant lives and more lives saved. He wanted sincerely to understand. There had been a mine under my stomach, I said. He said it was impossible, there had been patterns. I said all right, the Navy believed in its patterns and I believed in my stomach. He said my undisciplined attitudes could only undermine morale. I said they could not under any circumstances undermine my morale as much as that TNT mine under my stomach would have. I went on to suggest that the enemy would not in any case lay his mines in a safe pattern, he would try to place them under my stomach, where our own engineers had placed one last night, and that therefore, by accident, I seemed to be the only member of our teams who had had training under real battle conditions. I also stated that, in my opinion, war was an imperfect art, mock war as well as real war, and hence not one to be practiced by perfectionists. The C.O.'s face was red. He said that he would have me up for court-martial, except that our team was going into action and I couldn't be replaced fast enough. Did I have anything else to say? Yes, sir. There had been a TNT block on my stomach. He told me to get the hell out of there.

Barto and I argued about it all the way to Iwo Jima. We kept at it before and after Pearl Harbor, Eniwetok, Leyte, Hononhon Island in Lingayen Gulf, Kerama Retta and Okinawa and Ie Shima in the garden-spot Ryukyus. Barto agreed I'd done the only possible thing on the Maui beach. What he held against me was the way I'd spoken to the C.O. I said there was nothing in the Articles of War that stipulated a member of the armed forces was supposed to hand over his thought processes to his C.O. Listen, Barto said, you didn't take on with navies. You cut the detonating cord if you had to, then you stood at attention and saluted and said yessir, nosir, without philosophies. In private, locked safely away in the washroom, you beat your head and fists against the walls, where nobody could see, if you had to let off steam. Me, I had to take on all objects that occasioned my displeasure, in public, in full view, especially when they were bigger than I was. The navies were irrelevancies, was Barto's view. You happened to be there. No need attracting their attention during your stay. I looked at the bullet holes on his shoulder and thought to myself, at least once in your life, buddy, you attracted somebody's attention, at least once and maybe twice, but I didn't put it into words. This was after Brunei Bay and Daot Island, after the armada assembly at Morotai, on the night we were riding under convoy into the Manggar and Klandasan beaches of Balikpapan.

The night before a certain reconnaissance a young lieutenant (j.g.) came over to our destroyer from the command ship. He was from Intelligence; he was making a life work of sifting and collating and blending all available intelligence reports on the beaches and shore waters of lovely Borneo, and he was being assigned to our teams for this operation to give us the benefit of his intelligence.

True, he had no actual proof about the oil pipes. He couldn't show us any aerial photographs of the things. But they were there all right, we needn't think they weren't. It was simply that they were buried cunningly. Better too careful than too dead. (Smile. Pause. Look around. No answering smiles. Quick resumption.) We had better spend a lot of time and care during our reconnaissance tomorrow looking for those pipes or we might find ourselves in hot water. He would like to repeat that, hot water, he meant very hot.

"May I ask if you've worked with demolition teams?" I said when the briefing was over.

"No, I'm a Hydrographic man primarily. I've been thoroughly briefed, though. I think I'll be able to keep up with you."

"If it's in order, I'd like to go over some statistics."

"Fire away. Chances are I know them—but I'm always ready to be filled in."

"On a typical job we may cover almost a thousand yards of beach with close to fifteen hundred obstacle posts planted along it. We locate them, then we have to go back to blow them. In one reconnaissance we have to chart all fifteen hundred posts, as well as get an accurate and detailed picture of the reef, the undertow, the surf, the depths, and so on. We may be in the water two or three hours just to get that part of the job done. That's a long time, under close and heavy fire."

His face was turning less friendly. "I'm aware of those facts."

"More than once, sir, we've been given the additional job of looking for underwater pipes. We've suffered extra casualties doing it. We've never found a pipe, but we've lost men."

His face was not friendly at all. "Is it your idea that we ought to forget about the pipes?"

"Intelligence has never seen them, sir, and neither have we. The more we look for them the more our casualty lists go up, and that's the only effect it has."

"Chief Garmes, are you aware of what your casualty list might be like if those pipes are there and you don't locate them?"

"If the bay is flooded with oil and if the oil is ignited by shell fire, casualties might be one hundred per cent. On the assumption that the pipes are there to do the flooding. Most of us feel, though, that we can never locate them all and remove them all. Assuming the pipes are there."

It was what everybody had been grousing about for months. Heads were nodding all over the place.

"Chief Garmes," the lieutenant said, "do you know what happens when a man catches on fire and burns?" His eyes kept going from me to the others, to check on their reactions. "The human body, Chief Garmes, is larded with a considerable amount of fatty substances. They are extremely combustible. It takes a long time for them to burn. It might take many minutes for the topmost inch of meat and fat on the body to even char, and during that time you can remain fully conscious. The part of you slowest to burn is your skull and inside it you can be fully aware of what is happening, minute by minute, as the rest of you melts away and the smell of your own smoke comes to your nose. It is an unsavory smell. The head is the last part of all to go. It is very fire resistant. I am informed that there is nothing in your record, Chief Garmes, to show that you have taken any special courses in the slow and fully apprehended burning of the human body."

"Sir," I said, "may I ask where you took your special courses in flesh combustion? Do they have any correspondence courses at that school? Maybe I could enroll and catch up."

His (j.g.) face went dead white. The C.O. was on his feet and advancing to the table. Next to me Barto was pulling

on the waist of my dungarees, trying to get me back in my
chair and muttering, "Did it again! Hombre! This time you
did it good!" There was complete silence in the stuffy room.

"Your operation has been planned by the command staff,"
the lieutenant said in a dead white monotone. "My orders are
to see to it that you look for oil pipes. You will look very,
very carefully for oil pipes."

The C.O. said, looking directly at me, "Men, you were
called here to get your orders. You have them. Anybody who
does not carry them out to the letter—I repeat, anybody—
will answer to me. That is all."

Early in the morning, as the davit crews started to lower
our LCP(R)s from the destroyer deck, the fleet opened up
with a deafening barrage of all guns—three-inch and five-inch
shells from the innermost arc of destroyers, sixes and eights and
sixteens from the cruisers and battlewagons deployed farther
out, all the ships in the floating beehive zagging this way and
that in their grid patterns and blasting away at the shore
installations. Overhead the B-24's and Beaufighters and B-25
Mitchells cruised the beach, first for high-level bombing, then
for low-level work and strafing. From all the salvos and showers
and fragmentations, punctuated by the lower-keyed mortar fire
and lesser chatter of small arms, came an overall roar, a constant
maximum blabble that was like the sound of all matter
speaking out its Armageddon grievances. We were in an atmosphere of total sound. On the boat carrying our platoon,
along with the regular officers, was the lieutenant (j.g.) from
Intelligence. I didn't know whether he was coming along as
part of his assignment or whether he'd been shamed into it,
and I didn't much care. He was there. That was unmitigatedly
good. I couldn't help leaning over to him and saying, "I
hope you can make yourself comfortable here. This is going
to take a while." I wished immediately that I hadn't said it:
after all, whatever the reason, he was going to be there. But
I was a little feverish, and feeling generally yellow and nasty.
The jaundice was already doing its work, as I was to learn

a few days later. The lieutenant, to give him his credit, took
my pleasantry with neither rank nor haughtiness. He just said
simply, "Let's get this out of the way, then we'll make it as
personal as you want. I'd enjoy it." He did have guts, in a way.

The boat made its run and we dropped off in spaced pairs.
The enemy had us practically in point-blank range with mortars,
machine guns, sniper fire, tracked artillery pieces. The water all
around was choppy and spitting with their fire. If we'd had
just the regular job of surveying the post clusters it would
still have been bad, but possible. Our technique for that job
was to swim underwater from one cluster to the next and
come up only when we had some posts between us and the
enemy. The posts were no protection against the concussions
of mortar shells that landed nearby but they were a reasonably
good shield against small-arms fire. But if we had to crawl
over every square inch of bottom between the post clusters
to look for pipes we would have to come up for breath between the clusters, in the open and only yards from shore.

We did the job. Somehow or other, ducking from one
obstacle to the next, our group managed to get through the
entire line of beach assigned to it, charting on our Plexiglas
slates better than 1,000 poles. By this time I was chattering
with the cold, the cramps in my legs were so bad that I
couldn't move them, I was doubled up and swimming with
just my hands. Barto looked to be almost as badly off and
the other swimmers seemed in grim shape too. It took almost
two hours to cover our strip, then we started back, hugging
the bottom in long dives and looking everywhere for the pipes.
The shore fire was heavier now. Their aim seemed to be
improving. Suddenly about twenty minutes after we'd started
these bottom-hugging operations, there was an unannounced
commotion in the water, the silt heaving up in my face and
rocks from everywhere hurtling. Something hard hit me in the
head. My mouth was full of sand and seaweed. I was pin-
wheeling around in the rush of waters, head over heels. Maybe
I lost consciousness for a moment, I don't know. But seconds

later I was fighting my way to the surface, gasping and choking and spitting dislodged bottom from my mouth. My head hurt sharply, my whole body was one dull ache. I looked around. Barto was several yards landward from me, shaking his head and blinking. He pointed agitatedly to our left. Two of the other members of our team were bobbing in the water there but the third was nowhere to be seen. The two we could see seemed to be in trouble. I looked seaward. Our LCP(R)s were holding to their close-up positions there and running along in the same line were our small cover-fire boats, the LCI(G)s sent to protect us with quads and machine-gun fire. I raised my arm and began to wave it frantically in the distress signal. One of the pick-up boats left the line and headed in our direction. I was the first one picked up. One of the men helping me aboard, I half saw, was the lieutenant (j.g.), his face in knots. In a few minutes we had Barto hauled in, then the other two. We cruised back and forth in the area for a long time under heavy fire, but we never did find the fifth man. The faces around me kept coming and going, bits of their features oozing and dripping unaccountably.

I looked at the lieutenant (j.g.). Head on, for the first time. His left ear seemed to melt, part of his mouth was dropping away like soft ice cream. It seemed to me that his hair was rippling as though under water. "I'm sorry about this," his running mouth seemed to say, but I saw the words spelled out more than heard them, and the letters in them were inexplicably wandering and dripping too. I had the peculiar feeling that I was still underwater and current-stirred muddy fluids were between me and all objects. "Take your pipes," I said, thought I was saying, and it was at that point that I swung and hit him in the melting, rippling mouth. I vaguely heard the crunching noise and felt the crack of something breaking under my knuckles. Then there were a dozen hands all over me, holding me, throwing me down and pinning me on deck as I struggled and screamed, "Where were the pipes! Weren't any pipes!" After that I lost consciousness.

It was nothing serious, just the concussion effects and general strain. And, as I say, the detoured bile was beginning to seep through my body and make me hot and jumpy. They discharged me from the hospital ship after an hour. By early afternoon my vision was unclouded again and the cold ache had mostly gone from my body. I was able to make it under my own power when the C.O. sent for me. Everything was in focus and unwavering when I arrived and found the lieutenant (j.g.) sitting there with him. I saw without cloudiness how the lieutenant's upper lip was swollen and discolored and that an incisor was missing from his upper left jaw.

The C.O. got to it without preliminaries.

"You know what the penalty is for striking an officer?"

"Yes, sir."

"You struck the lieutenant?"

"Yes, sir."

"Do you have any explanation for your behavior?"

"We found no pipes. We lost two men." (A man from another platoon had been shot between the eyes by a sniper's bullet.)

"That's not the lieutenant's fault. He was doing what he was ordered."

"I had to hit something. The lieutenant was there."

"Yes. It's your custom to make everything personal. You'd like to make a whole war a personal matter."

"The war got personal with one man on our team today, sir. His person is back in the water."

The C.O. stood up. "I am not in this war impersonally. Neither is the lieutenant. We don't make a point of it." He came around the table toward me. "Garmes, after you struck the lieutenant you lost consciousness. Are you entirely sure you recognized him? The effects of concussion. . . ."

The lieutenant got up. "If that's the way it was," he said, "I want to hear you say it."

They were trying to be fair, I suppose. That made it all the worse. If I allowed myself to ease out the doors they were opening for me I would have to leave all my motivations behind. They would be robbing me of my motivations, my only property. It seemed urgent to keep that from happening. Maybe the jaundice had something to do with this reasoning but I won't claim that.

"I knew what I was doing, sir. We lost a man in the water, then I saw you. I hit you because we lost a man. I believed in my logic then, sir, and I believe in it now. Also, sir, you described how a body burns, and I hit you for the poetry of your phrases."

The C.O. seemed not to believe what he'd heard.

"What's this?" he said. "The poetry?"

"For not being burned," I said, "and for making poetry about it."

The C.O. stared at me. "All right. You've been asking for this for a long time. I think we can accommodate you. I'm going to leave the decision to the lieutenant, since he's the one who suffered at your hands. I think I know what he'll want to do, and I'm going to back him up all the way."

He turned to the lieutenant. The younger man returned his look for a moment, then turned and studied me. He seemed to be weighing a lot of things.

"I've been learning some things about you," he said finally. "I've been trying to get a picture of you and it's beginning to come. I'm getting a sense of how you think."

"I don't make a secret of how I think, sir."

"No. No, you don't. You don't like to be surrounded by anything—a crowd or a navy. Or a duty not completely de- • cided and defined by you. You've let that be known to quite a few people. That poses a question. If you dislike crowds so much—how would you feel about being thrown out of one?"

"Sir, I did not hit you in the hope of getting out of the Navy." It was hard for me to concentrate, I was feeling dizzy.

"No. You hit me under the impression that I was the Navy." He looked at me for a while in silence. "It's fairly clear what a court-martial would lead to. There are circumstances which might be taken as extenuating. You would get a dishonorable discharge, certainly. Maybe no more than that." I was still rigidly at attention. He came and stood directly in front of me. The C.O. was looking on intently, the beginning of a puzzled expression on his face. "How does a man like you feel about a certificate of dishonor, Chief Garmes? Do you recognize any labels applied to you by crowds?"

He didn't seem to expect an answer to that and I offered none. He went to the porthole and stared out for a moment. Outside from all directions came the bleats and blasts of war, at this moment somehow beside the point. "There are two elements in a dishonorable discharge, Garmes. The dishonor and the discharge. The thing that's clearest is that the dishonor would make no impression on you. As for the discharge. . . . No." He turned to the astonished C.O. "With your permission, sir, I would like to drop the matter. I don't care to oblige him with a court-martial."

The C.O. was open-mouthed. He studied the lieutenant, stroking his cheek. "Well," he said after close to a minute, "I hadn't thought of it like that. You may have a point." He shifted his eyes to me. "Garmes, the lieutenant is a more subtle psychologist than I am. Go and get yourself ready for the afternoon run."

"Afternoon, sir?" We usually made one run a day, in the morning. Ordinarily we would have no work after a reconnaissance but to prepare our explosives for the next morning's demolition.

"You didn't finish your job this morning. You're going back to make sure there are no pipes."

In an hour we were heading back for the breaker line in our LCP(R). Our platoon was on board, with reserve divers substituted for the missing, and the lieutenant was on board too. There had been one change. The pharmacist's mate who'd done a last-minute check of the concussion victims hadn't liked the way I was looking, he'd found a touch of fever and a general peaked appearance. I was not up to another long exposure in the water, he said, so another reserve had been put in my place and I was assigned to stay on the boat as a pick-up man.

We dropped the teams off and began our runs up and down, the small LCI(G)s running in and out of our line and peppering the shore installations. Occasionally mortar shells landed close by in the water, making us heave and rock for a while, but they kept on being near misses. It was about forty minutes after the operation began, at a moment when a string of our carrier planes were making a run along the beach some 300 or 400 yards in from shore, that there was a flash and a surging sucking roar and instantaneously the deck was gone from under my feet, the boat was gone, I was tumbling through blue smoky loud space and hit the water with a smack.

I was all right. I felt no pains and I was able to move in the water. Wreckage from the boat was heaving around me and men were swimming and treading here and there, some of them screaming. Close by me, yards away, there was a man screaming, making high nasal animal sounds. I swam over to him. It was the lieutenant (j.g.). His right ear was gone, just a hole there, and that side of his face was peeled off, it was a wall of meat with some bone and gristle showing through. I couldn't tell whether the eye on that side was left, everything was covered with blood. He was conscious, and though his throat was stretched to maximum with his screams he seemed to be aware of me approaching. I got a grip on him under the armpit and I said, "Easy, now. Pick-up boat be here in a minute. You'll be all right." The one eye looked at me while the screams kept coming from the blood-burbling mouth. The screams stopped. Maybe he recognized me, I don't know. The one eye went on looking at me, not blinking, and now he was making no more high sounds. After a minute or so he spoke. "You son of a bitch," he said. "What you trying to prove? You're still a son of a bitch." With that he pulled away from me and raising both hands in the water began to hit me furiously about the head. I grabbed his arms and tried to pin them down. He took hold of me with insane power and pulled me under, with a bear hug.

It was a sensation I couldn't stand, my father's dead malicious weight on me and pulling me down, holding me down. I had an awful need to break free and hit him. But I couldn't hit him, not with one side of his face gone. I struggled and broke out of his hold. He came clawing back at me, then in an instant the riot went from him and he was limp. I got him across the chest again and up to the surface and, treading water, I waved my free hand wildly to signal the boats. We were in the water for almost five minutes more, blood running from his face in a steady curtain and staining the water around. One of the LCI(G)s came alongside and we were pulled in.

That night was relatively quiet. The big guns of the battleships fired occasional salvos but there were stretches when the blasting subsided to a hum and less, which was still worse. We had gotten used to living with ultimate noise, any dips in the noise level made our nerves go tight. My fever seemed to have gone up but I didn't think it was bad enough to say anything about it. We sat in the magazine, preparing more Schantz packs for the next morning. There was a lot of bitter talk about the pipes. We exchanged notes. Nobody on our boat had seen a pipe. There'd been a report, though, that one of the men from another platoon working farther up the beach, one single man, had spotted what looked to him like the mouth of a pipe hidden in a rock pile, one mouth of one pipe. We didn't know if it was a fake, and we were never to know.

Sometime after midnight a PT boat pulled up alongside our destroyer and I was ordered aboard it. The lieutenant from Intelligence had regained consciousness and was asking, pleading to see me. Tomorrow, invasion day, the hospital ship would be piled high with lacerated Australians and slimy with blood underfoot, and thus no place for visitors, but tonight things were quiet there and the whims of a lieutenant with half his face shot away could be allowed. In the corridor outside the ward I was turned over to a doctor who asked if I was the Chief Garmes whose name the lieutenant had been mumbling, trying to tell me something about crowds, about there being gatherings and convocations that were more weighty than crowds, and I said I thought so. The doctor warned me that the lieutenant was not to be made anxious or stimulated in any way, and led me in. The ward was almost empty, a gray mouth waiting with no hurry. In a corner bunk the lieutenant was lying, a pancake of bandage over the right side of his face. Carved carefully around his nose and lips, the dressing made him look like one of those Picasso faces seen full on and in profile at the same time. Only his left eye was visible, it was open and following my movement across the room. His lips were parted, moving in the preliminaries to speech. On the left side, on the upper jaw, I could see the gap where the incisor had been. Over in back of the bunk, standing some feet away out of the lieutenant's sight, I noticed something extraordinary. It was a Navy flier, a boy of about twenty. He was standing absolutely still, staring down at the lieutenant from behind. The expression on his face was that of a man who has cunningly combed out the one fully significant thing from all his life's gropings to say, has found the words for it and must desperately speak them but at this precise moment discovers that he has been stricken dumb.

"Question of controls," the lieutenant seemed to be saying. "Controlling the variables. Not enough hands to hold all pieces. The job is to make the reach."

Each time his mouth opened I saw the gap left by the incisor.

"I'm sorry I hit you this morning, Lieutenant," I said.

"The joke, you see? The head is the last to burn. Head can split down the middle when it is not a question of burning. You cannot hold everything. Should try to hold both sides of face tight with both hands in the event something gets away. Half is variable and gone and that's it."

The young flier was still looking down at the lieutenant, his eyes wider. The doctor was looking at me, frowning.

"They'll fix you up when they get you home," I said. "They've gotten very good at it."

"You will not believe in the pipes. You are not a believer. Did you see the piles? Up to the ceiling. Piles and piles of files. Paper work is despised by some and crowds. Yes, it is for the bespectacled and office workers. Garmes, the control is to begin on the typewriter and the dictaphone. Poetry is something else. Lives saved in the interdepartmental memo. All but the halves of faces. We had reason to believe in the pipes." It was morphine talk, of course.

"One man saw a pipe," I said. "It was reported."

"Chief Garmes. Get them together and do your best. Only hold on both sides, tight. The pipes could have been there. Does it matter if they burn in pattern? The pipes can go everywhere and it is the worst thing to say no."

"Lieutenant," I said, "I wasn't in control of myself when I hit you this morning. I'd like you to believe that I'm sorry for what I did. You were doing your job and you did it well. One man reported seeing a pipe."

The one eye looked steadily at me.

"Chief Garmes, I despise you and everything you are." He struggled to get up on his elbows, his voice rose from deep in his throat. "You will not recognize that there are others in it. You son of a bitch with a whole face. All not glorious you are enemy. You do not know where the enemy stops. Do you think I want men lost and the half taken away? Swine son of a bitch." He was shaking now, almost up on his elbows but not quite making it. The doctor was holding him by the shoulders, easing him gently back. Behind him the flier stood in unmoving fascination, filled with big thoughts that were unmoving rocks in his mouth. The doctor shook his head warningly at me. "You think my face is not personal with me? Spit on you and all aloofness. Stand in the lone magnificence forever. Spit on you and I will defend the paper with half a face." I could not take my eyes from the gap in his teeth, there upper left. The doctor shook his head at me again, urgently.

I leaned closer. "One man saw a pipe," I said. "I'm sorry I hit you, truly. You'll be all right."

I backed away a few steps, the lieutenant's one eye following me over the doctor's shoulder. The flier behind him hadn't budged or once raised his eyes to me. I turned and went for the door. If it could have been done I would have arranged for this man with half a face to see that one mouth of one pipe in one pile of rocks. Fake or not. He had a right to see that pipe.

In the corridor a pharmacist's mate was catching a smoke.

"Aren't you one of the concussion cases? From this morning?"

"Yes."

He put fingers on both sides of my right eye and opened it wide.

"You don't look so good—bad color. You want to watch it. Concussions are tricky."

"I'm all right. Can they do anything for the lieutenant?"

"He'll be lucky if he lasts the night. Unlucky, I mean. With half a face."

"Who's the flier in there?"

"From the bombers. The ones this afternoon."

"What bombers?"

"Didn't you see those planes working over the beach when you were in there? They were supposed to drop their bombs three hundred to five hundred yards back from the shoreline and almost every run they stayed in the pattern. This one guy missed. You can't pinpoint them every time going over two hundred miles an hour. His eggs landed in the water. One of them was what blew up the forward boat the lieutenant was on. One of those things."

"Is that why the flier's in there?"

"He's the guy let those bombs go. When he heard what happened he went kind of crazy and kept saying he had to

see the lieutenant. He didn't know the guy but now he had
to come over and see him. They let him go. Funny thing is
he's been standing there for two hours almost, not saying a
word. Just looking. He's torturing himself for no reason, we
told him. They'll throw him out soon, I guess. Hell, if you
take everything personally."

The lieutenant (j.g.) died a half hour later. Scholar of
buried pipes, hard worker and believer in patterns, he had
failed to note the wayward bomb from the plane overhead
with MADE IN DETROIT on its warhead and it had sheared half
his face off, because at better than 200 miles an hour the
bombardier can't stick every time exactly to pattern. Before
that I had knocked his tooth out. All he had wanted was a
flawless correspondence between office and ocean. All I had
wanted was a flawless vacuum. I wished to Jesus I had never
hit him.

O, perfectionists!

BOOK THREE: *Varadero*

EIGHTEEN   Looking at me, with soapy eyes. Gold-toothed cadre: grinning still, fingers going lightly and testingly on the bongo skins. I was down the aisle and into the seat next to him before it occurred to me that talk was pointless: make snakes sing lullabies.

"You travel a lot."

"Gringo like the monopoly? Be big world imperialista of the travels, gringo?"

"You have monopolies on running down dark streets in Key West."

He nodded unqualified agreement, chin making dream-slow dips that his eyes seemed not aware of. "Artist of the people. Got to go where are the peoples."

His fingers seemed to be flicking at the drum heads without consulting him. His knee gave a jump from time to time, for no reason related to purpose or gesture. Apparatus man: and his own outposts up in arms against the imperialism of the central nervous system: what did that say about the mentality of willing cogs?

"You know the word expendable?" I searched through my Spanish for the sharpest insult I knew. "Pubic hairs like you are expendable."

"Thus O.K." He stuck to English: no accommodating

me in anything. His smile widened, but without involving his
diluted eyes. "You wig me, man. Some funny gringo, kill with
the mouth. You the most cat, gringo, gas me, sure." He
laughed, a series of phlegmed groans that left his eyes un-
changed and unmoored. "No, listen, funny man, tonight I
play in El Kastillito, nice club. My friends not be there. Dig?
Just me, you can kill me good. Thus O.K."

"You know about killing good. Do you people ever kill
anybody who's got his face toward you?"

"Man," he said, "you bug me, no hype. Break me up in
pieces. You should go on the stage, gringo, you know that?
Make big hit with these funny jokes. I get you booking in
Sain Loose and Weesheetar, you kill the people."

"Killing the people is your specialty. When their backs are
turned."

He looked elaborately hurt. "Thus a way to talk to people's
artist? Because he travel round to the peoples?"

"El Rey," I said. "El Rey of the alleys and the knives in
the back. Tell your friend I have an answer to his letter but
I'll deliver it in person."

When I got back to my seat I was trembling. Not because
of my words. The thoughts behind the words. My thoughts
were forming in marching columns, goosestepping from colon
to colon. I'd fallen into this short-go way of thinking, one
mental foot after the other. Colons, the onwardness and drill
spirit of colons, were to me altogether a way of marching, not
of thinking, and I had caught myself thinking to march music.
Brod's letter had been full of colons, the words eyes-front.
The colons in it were what had enraged me the most. Colons
brought to mind my mother, hands on hips, full of energy
and impatient, thinking ahead. To more and more energy
expenditures. My mother was the doer, all right. It was my
father who had rejected all lines of march, preferring to lean
back in his canvas beach chair and take in everything this side
of the horizon with no thought in mind but to see, just see.
All of this was behind my disgust for colons, which equalled

my disgust for beach chairs. Now I got a letter from Brod
and I was thinking in colons too. Only his went in a straight
line and mine went around in circles, which was often the way
I marched when I was forced to march. Once in Florida, in
boot camp, an impulse came over me when we were being put
through drill formations, and when the order came for
squads-right I didn't wheel smartly but instead headed off in
an easy semicircle away from the column. I did ten days of
K.P. for that hobo touch.

"He doesn't know exactly where Miguelito is," I said to
Natividad when I got back to her. "We'll have to look for
him."

"Mi esposo," she said in a whisper, and at first I thought
she'd decided I was her husband because she took my hand
and pressed it tenderly. "Mi esposo," she said again. "Miguelito
caro." Miguelito dear. Miguelito dearie. She thought of Brod
as her husband, or at least her intended, and was going to
this meeting as to a wedding. All she was doing with my hand
was rehearsing. Her life was one long string of colons too, and
all of them, all of the marching boots in her head, led to
Miguelito dearie. Adoration has its martial forms.

A few minutes later we unloaded at the Varadero air
strip. Coolio was out and gone before I could see whether he
was being met. We found a cab. It was just past sundown and
the moon was momentarily cut off by blooming land clouds;
the dark was as I remembered it from earlier trips, a custard,
with weight.

I looked about as we approached town, heading for the
unfrilled square where couples sat on the concrete rises. It
was all the same, one row of gingerbread wooden hotels along
the waterfront on Avenida Primera and another a block away
on Avenida Segunda, echoes of Victorian spas, and between
these seedy Saratoga transplants and around them, running out
to the slicker suburbs, newer homes, Bauhaus sweeps of stucco
and cinder block and glass, ribbed with sun decks and clean
curving overhangs, in colors from shy pinks and greens to

assaulting blood reds. A thick-sweet tropical baking odor over
everything, the ink night ambushing the few street lamps, along
the streets the long-bladed cocoanut palms with fraying bases,
and dotting these streets all the Casas, Casa This and Casa
That and Casa You Name It, the Casa Happiness run by
Happy Pete and the Casa Hello with an Approved by Duncan
Hines sign in front. Brod had programmed something for me:
his letters were aimed at pushing me toward his next stage:
what?

When the cab stopped at Casa Mañana, one of the lace-
work hotels on Avenida Segunda just off the square, I looked
down the cross street and saw the black waters of the ocean sending off cut-glass unorganized glints. Heard it, too. Slow, heavy-
limbed commas. Going nowhere all the time. I stood on the
street sucking the thick smells in, the anesthetic air, thinking
this was a place for breathing exercises, not programs. And:
what was behind those damned letters?

In the hotel I told the clerk there was no luggage and
didn't hit him for his smiling census of Natividad's sequins.
I registered for two rooms in spite of the sequins. After I took
a shower I met Natividad in the dining room and we ordered a
meal of chilled morro crabs and preserved guava shells.

Natividad was lucid. I asked her about Mexico and Brod.
Her parents had died in Tampico when she was a baby, she
said. For as long as she could remember she'd lived with their
friends in Mexico City, friends of Brod's, a bricklayer and his
wife, politicos. Brod came and went, sometimes a year passed
between his visits, but they were what she lived for. When
she was going on sixteen, the bricklayer and his wife moved to
Vera Cruz and wanted her to come along but she wanted to
stay and wait for Brod. He'd thrown one into her on his last
visit over a year before and she couldn't forget it, it was everything and then everything. From week to week, she hoped for
Brod. But he didn't come, her one true dearie, and nobody
would give her a job. Some man, a friend of the bricklayer,
also a politico but in addition a pimp, took pity on her and

offered to put her in a house. It was all right, many politicos
came there, they knew her as Brod's friend and at this time
they were Brod's big friends so they were nice to her and
threw many into her, but not like Brod. It was in this house
that Brod found her, seven, eight months ago, and from this
house that he took her to Havana.

My mind was three-quarters on Vincent Caprio: pushing
me away, he'd counted on my coming closer. And: Brod was a
man trained to think like Caprio. So: if Brod now warned me
to stay away, wasn't this warning to be taken in the same
light as Caprio's? Weren't his warnings, too, left-handed invita-
tions? Didn't all planners plan in and for everything?

I went with Natividad to her room and told her to lock
the door and not open for anybody. I suggested she take a
nap. I would finish my business, then come for her. She gave
me a big thank-you hug and went to sleep content. The world
was at the moment her sweet-talking esposo.

In the cab riding out to the Internacional I considered
Brod's letters. All phrases had to be given reverse translations.
Stay away: come quick. You don't want to kill me: try, please.
I could only hope the circles I was going around in were not
circles Brod had drawn in advance.

NINETEEN   The Internacional was a few minutes
out of town, facing the sea. From the driveway you could see
through the glassed-in lobby to the beach and the collapsing
breakers coming up. A pulse in the air made the concrete pavement seem flimsy and ready to go—the slow fall of the surf.

Only a few people in the lobby. I noticed some Americans
on the beach-side patio talking under the strings of colored
bulbs. It looked like a carefree group from a travel folder but
one of them, an erect, held-in man in long wool socks and
Bermuda shorts and rainbowed Hawaiian sports shirt, had a

go-getter hunch to his shoulders that troubled me. He turned his head and I was more troubled. Vincent Caprio, in work clothes.

I hurried past some people watching a troupe of Chinese jugglers on a television set, went by some rest rooms and came to the white rococo doors of a city-block-big nightclub. I went in. Up on the alto-cumulus of the stage an all-white girl angel in white gossamer wings and white mink G-string hipswitched through St. Peter's nacre gates and went into a mambo step, while the white-tuxedo'd band behind her beat the white celestial drums with their white satin wings. At the far end of the crowded bar, against the wall, I found a stool. Some of the shadow people at the tables were wearing costumes and masks.

The bartender said he had a house phone handy. He slid one over and plugged it in. The operator gave me Owen Brooke's room number, 451, and rang it. No answer. I told the operator to keep trying it, I'd stick at the bar. There were now twelve naked angels on the stage, bumping from cloud to cloud and beating their wings. From a group down the bar I heard somebody say, "Tell you why I wrote eleven hundred pages, I had eleven hundred things to say. I generally figure about a page per thing to say."

I'd heard this voice in the Late Watch three weeks before, saying these words.

"Next book I write," Nelson Boyar said, "I'm only going to say one thing. People like books say one, simple thing. Like, ouch. Or, wow. Or, hit me again, Jennifer. One simple, human thing." I'd heard that too, four weeks before.

"Nelson," somebody else said, "you wrote some excellent things in the thirties. I got a lot out of them." I knew that voice too. "That's funny," Boyar said. "I didn't put anything in them." I stood up to see. "You put a great deal in them," the other said. There it was, the back of the pinched Groton skull topped with the tired Groton hair, rising with kangaroo compactness over the barflies. "People weren't afraid of social content in those days," Professor Brooke said earnestly. "Your books came to grips with basic issues."

"Came to gripes," Boyar said. "Grapes. Sour gripes, doesn't sell. Only time Americans think of themselves as proletarians is when they're not working. Nobody was working, so everybody thought of himself as a worker. Novelists thought they were workers, they wrote worker novels."

"You can't deny that your books had a fundamental honesty," Owen Brooke said. "They said something."

"They said I thought I was a proletarian because I wasn't eating," Boyar said. "What they didn't say was that the reason I wasn't eating was, I was writing proletarian novels."

"I read all your strike novels," Owen Brooke said. "I made them required reading for my sociology classes."

"When they turn you in to the subversive board," Boyar said, "don't ask me to testify for you. Anybody who assigned my books to his classes *was* subversive. Subversive to the arts, the tarts, the muses, the fuses, and the sweet intimate Scotch tape of elementary grammar."

"With the reactionary hysteria that exists today," Owen Brooke said, "I don't consider that remark funny. If you would like the truth, Nelson, I think your war novel is a sell-out to the reactionaries. It's a shame, when a man of your talents yields to the hysteria and becomes a turncoat."

"Owen, laddie," Boyar said, "would you like me to let you in on a little secret? When I was a prolo novelist I didn't have a coat to turn, that's the truth. Listen. Best thing ever happened to me was the war. Gave me the formula. Thing is, in wartime all the streets have two sides. Learn how to work them both and it's the bestseller lists for you, boy. Know how much *The Determined Tigers* is going to make? Over two million fish, once all the movie money's in. Proletariat's crazy about this one. First time I was ever read by the prolos."

"That book is intellectually dishonest, Nelson," Owen Brooke said. "You spend 1,075 pages showing that the officers' caste of the army is reactionary, vicious, warmongering, and fascist-minded. It's a devastating exposé. Then, in the last 25 pages, you take it all back and say these fascist psychopaths won the war for the democracies. That's not intellectually honest, Nelson, I don't care what you say."

"Who said I was trying to be honest?" Boyar said. "I just wanted to write a new kind of strike novel where *everybody's* on strike. Bosses and bootblacks, coupon clippers and ticket takers—all picketing against the exploitation by clock and calendar, for shorter hours of insomnia and higher wages of sin. Get it, Owen? It's the larger view. Soon's you get the larger view, you write prolo-bourge novels. Worker-burgher novels."

"Nelson," Owen Brooke said emotionally, "you don't have an eraser big enough to wipe out the class lines."

"Don't want to wipe out anything," Boyar said. "Just want to be a mirror. Mirror of my times, Owen, mirror my God to thee and thine. I'm Jehovah's first witness, by appointment, from two to five. All I do is mirror the lies that are part of God's larger truth. Got the formula now, boy. The large picture. Something for everybody. It is not Christian charity to give to one and withhold from the other—all God's chilled ones got needs."

"You're being inconsistent," Owen Brooke said. "How can a professional soldier be a fascist and a progressive at the same time?"

"You, Owen, are a coupon-clipping professor who thinks he's a sharecropper—know how many volumes that'd take to tell? Haven't you ever learned to think dialectically, boy? Ever hear of the leaping, hopping, skipping transformation of a thing into its opposite—professor into sharecropper? You dance all the time in the daisy chain of irreconcilable opposites and you don't know it. History doesn't have points of view, like professors and sharecroppers. History *is* professors and sharecroppers, the sharecroppers trying to steal the coupons from the professors, the professors trying to steal the overalls and guitars from the sharecroppers—opposites in a bear hug. History's an avalanche of professors and sharecroppers hand in hand, each one's hand in the other's pocket. History's a mucking much of a muchness—"

"That's very well put, Nelson," somebody said. "It could very well be put in a box and buried in the ground."

Nelson Boyar was talking about the next book he was going to write, was just about to write, was on the precipice edge of writing, was indeed so close to doing that it might for all practical purposes be considered done and he was going to forget about it. He had turned around and was staring in my direction. "Say," he said, trying to see, "isn't that—" He looked harder and broke into a smile. "It is! The friend of the sharecropper and the anopheles mosquito!" He pulled away from his friends and came toward me.

He was the kind of figure you might get if you ordered all the parts from a mail-order house and found they didn't quite match. A man who had once held on for dear life to the idea that the universe was an engine, its cylinders pumping to the set iron rhythms of the dialectic, he was himself a shambles —but maybe it's just the disordered ones who have to grab for hard laws and hard cores, to steady themselves. His hair stuck up in back and hung down in strings over his chunky bohunk face, and for all his two million plus he still looked like the man who spent years on Gastonia picket lines, pushing through the slush and singing fisted lines about his soul belonging to the company store. He looked as though he would like his soul to belong genuinely to the company store, anything that definable and opposable, anything with an address, instead of to the absentee furies who had it now. But he was a man who had an enthusiasm bigger and closer to the roots than politics, or had had, and I liked him.

"Hello, Nelson," I said.

"Bobby Garmes! Bobby the Garmes! I was thinking about you just this afternoon. Owen said he saw you in Havana."

"He was with me. What he saw was another sharecropper lover."

"I know, I know. Amazing, how the sharecropper lovers love to share their crops of sharecroppers. What're you doing in these parts, Rob?"

"Thinking about a problem of punctuation. Nelson, when you were writing political action books, did you use many colons?"

Years of experience with sidewinding bar talk kept him from being disconcerted. He gave the question his undivided attention. "All the time. You know what the colon signifies, Rob? Expectation. Collection of things ahead. Politicians are bill collectors, my boy—colons are their way of dunning the future. You expect—I don't know what, better worlds, trips to Bermuda, equities, ice cream sodas—you lean forward with your hand out. Politicians make a career of panhandling the future. Colons are their tin cups."

They're using you, Brod said. He meant: come closer so *I* can use you.

"I'm making a discovery," I said. "I don't think the colon and I are in rapport."

Boyar was warming up to the subject. "Of course not, Rob! You don't want to carve your initials on the world. You just want to worry at things—nip at their heels to keep them hopping. When others make a dent in the world's face, you dash up and carp about its measurements. You know what's so dangerous about people who think in colons—who lean into the future? They think they're absolutely logical—when they say A, B and only B has to follow. And this, they think, is important—they attach great value to B, it's B they're leaning toward. So they feel justified in imposing B on the world, in case the world isn't quite ready to produce B of and by its own efforts. The first law of political life is—Colon-ize, then colonize. That's why we're all in the soup today. What form of punctuation you partial to?"

"I've always liked commas."

"The comma is fine! A series of commas—very soothing to the nerves, like a massage."

"With commas, you're just bobbing. Treading water and looking around. The semicolon isn't bad, either."

"Very accurate, Robbie. Denotes a rest, a pause for deep breath, not a quick tensing for the next plunge. That's Owen's whole trouble—needs his colons to sustain a tension—can't slow down because the life without leaning and shouldering isn't progressive—it's the old Puritanism about idle hands, etcetera. . . . What's this all about, Rob? Punctuation isn't your line."

"I've gotten involved in a little leaning myself, Nelson. I'm not sure it's for me."

He gave me a look keener than I liked. "Maybe not. You don't do much easy treading of water either, though. From what I hear, you go at this diving hard—as though you were going for something."

"Maybe just *away* from something. Puritanism about idle hands, etcetera." It was a subject I preferred to pull back from.

He swished the drink around in his glass. "Connie told me something about you—says your grandfather was once a pirate around the Caribbean. Is that right?"

"He said he was."

"My new book's about the Caribbean. I thought I'd tell a little story about your pirate grandfather in the book. Want to hear it?"

"Sure, Nelson."

"Well, I thought I'd make him a pirate that keeps his ship in this very private, secret bight, see. He wants this cove in tiptop shape, that's the point, so he dredges it, builds a dock, and everything. Only thing is, he works so hard on the cove, he's got no time to work on the boat. The deck of his barque begins to buckle, the masts fall off, the hull springs leaks. The pirate goes out to look at the boat one day and he shakes his head and says, 'Well, I may be a dog or I may not be a dog, but my barque's sure worse than my bight.'" I didn't laugh, and his face fell. "It's—just a small story. No social content."

"You don't have to make me like you, Nelson," I said.

"Quit working at it, will you?" He looked still gloomier. "When'd Connie give you my life story?"

"This afternoon."

I sat up at that. "This afternoon? Connie's here?"

"Sure. She flew down yesterday with some guy named Caprio."

"You know Caprio too?"

"Yeah—he's the guy told me about the fishing down here. Nice chap, friendly, I think he's in some import-export line."

"How did Connie happen to come down with him?"

"I don't know—he was coming down and offered her a ride." He looked away. "She came on down to join me."

"Did she say anything about Barto?"

"Not a word. Why?"

"I was just wondering. Where's she now?"

He looked vague. "Around somewhere. The mambo instructor's giving a hotdog roast, I think she said something about going." He looked away again. "You might look for her on the beach."

"I'll try it."

"Listen." He was sagging, his face forlorn. "Is that true? Was your grandfather really a pirate?"

"He worked on fishing boats for fifty years. Maybe he once was, I don't know. My hunch is, he worked so goddamned hard all his life, he needed a myth about some golden stretch in his life when he didn't work, just took."

"I know how that is," Boyar said. "I work so goddamned not at all these days, I need a myth about a time when I did work. I'd like to find one somewhere."

"Cut it out, Nelson," I said. "I told you, I already like you."

"Listen," he said, "let me tell you about this punctuation. Your grandfather was the true sharecropper—backbreaking colons every day of his life. He had to phantasize about some moment when the iron laws melted. And here comes Owen Brooke, born to a life without colons, everything greased—

and he can't stand it. And now I've got everything greased too, and I can't stand it either. It's a swindle, Rob! We've got what your grandfather saw shimmering in the clouds, the whole pie in the sky without a slice out of it—and we can't slow down and eat it lingeringly! For Christ sake—if you don't have to lean and reach—don't! What's worse and infinitely dirtier than idle hands is reaching hands." He looked at me with undisguised hopelessness in his eyes and said, "You're a guy who doesn't have to reach. Things fall into your hands—and you resent the lack of effort. You weren't built for the tropics." He turned away again. "I think you'll find her on the beach."

"I'll see you, Nelson," I said.

Pushing past Boyar's friends at the bar I saw Brooke's small elite head periscoping up over the others. He was looking at me. "Hello there, Robert," he said with his papier-mâché smile. "Good to see you." He got free of the group and held out his hand. When I didn't take it the smile fell off his face in pieces, like bits of egg. "What? What's wrong? You were friendly enough two days ago?"

"That was two days ago."

He was not worth any more bother. Connie and her being here with Caprio were what was important now. I didn't care to make my face smile at Brooke any more and listen to his apple-filled enthusiastic mouth.

"You gave no indication—"

"Brooke, you know what they were singing to you in that fake ñañigo? I'll translate—it would be nice to take the money from his pocket, and throw him in the shit behind the house. Hoo-wa, hoo-wa."

His mouth was wide open, the jaw flapping a little. Out in the corridors again I poked around until I found a side door that led to the swimming pool and the cabañas. There was a barbecue going on down the beach some distance from the pool, I saw a lively fire in a pit and dark figures moving around it. The patio was off to the right, nobody could see me

from there. I walked down toward the fire. Several people, some
in bathing suits, some in slacks and Marseilles sailor pullovers
but barefoot, were sitting in a group, harmonizing on "I Found
a Million Dollar Baby in a Five and Ten Cent Store." Connie
was sitting in an empty space near the fire, knees pulled up
and arms wrapped around them, a hotdog in her hand but
not eating at it, sauerkraut spilling. She was looking into the
fire and her face, with licks of light going across it, was composed and serious. Her thick golden hair fell away like another
spilling, exclusive fire.

She had a beautiful face, with special alcoves in the wide
green eyes and shadowings around the unskimped lips. It gave
the sense of sizable events inside, of their possibility, anyway,
a relief from the model's posed air of total lemony immunity.
Usually she covered herself with styled excitements, styled hip-
ness, styled drunkenness, for armor. Not conscious for once of
being looked at, she was absolutely serious, her true unease
on the surface, and without warning she had a more particular
kind of beauty that had nothing to do with good looks. You
would have something of value if you could freeze her in
amber just like that, hugging her knees and for once the day-
to-day bother puncturing the gloss. I bent down behind her
to put my hands along her arms and said, "You have a visitor,
miss."

She didn't say or do anything showy. Her torso arched and
she put her hands up over the backs of mine, her head tilted
against my shoulder.

"I was waiting," she said quietly. "I was worried."

TWENTY   "You're all right?" she said.
"Never better." I held my hands on her. "Let's take a
walk."

We started away from the hotel along the sand left tamped

by the breakers. After several minutes of going along, she slowed down and pointed to some large moving shape up a ways near the grass line. It was a loggerhead turtle close to twenty inches long, digging her tail end into the sand with slow, regular, backing-in movements. "It's a birth," I said, "but she doesn't know it. She thinks it's a funeral."

"Most animals look like they're holding funeral services when they're giving birth." She turned her face up to me. "Would you kiss me?" There weren't any pigtailed beseechments in her voice. I put my arms around her and she wasn't staging big moments. When we separated the kawama was still rump-tunneling and looking bereaved. "Their eggs bounce," Connie said. "You can play pingpong with them."

"I don't think kawamas know how to play pingpong."

Connie sank to her knees. "Let's sit here and watch. I like a ringside seat when basic things are happening."

The kawama was throwing out sand with all four flippers, swinging her body a little after each flurry so that a shallow moat was getting dug out around her. Her eyes were those of a rheumy grandmother watching her grandchildren being buried in droves. She was now several inches below the beach level.

"Connie, how'd you happen to come here with Caprio?"

"Well, Aristides said you'd gone to Cuba. I was worried. So, when I talked to Caprio—"

"How did that happen?"

"He came to the hotel and asked for me."

"There you are!" There was nothing else to hit, I brought my hand down on my thigh. "He wants conventions, too! Did he tell you what's happening here?"

"Some. He told me about Barto, and Brod, and Spain. . . . Poor Barto. I thought he was chasing girls." Her voice was getting a little tight.

"And me? What did he say about my being here?"

"How did he put it—he said you didn't have the perspec-

tive to see Barto's death as an event, you have to take it as
an insult. You take things personally, he said."

"They quote each other." I put my hand in my pocket and
pressed on the butt of my gun, to feel something hard and
cool. "Fight each other, quote each other!"

It was no optical illusion, the damnfool reptile was really
weeping. Tears had been welling up in her tragedian's eyes
even before but now they were going in a steady stream and
the sand being kicked up by her legs was flying all over, so the
eyes were getting caked with tear-drenched sand. Her expression said clearly that when she was having this much trouble
with her central work I ought to have the courtesy to tone
down my minor complaints. "Do you know why I'm here,
Connie? Because Caprio sent me. And Brod sent for me."

Connie sat back on her heels and looked at me in astonishment. "Sent you? If Caprio wanted you here. . . . He told
me you were in danger. He said maybe I could get you to
change your mind and go home. . . ."

"Think back, Connie. How did Nelson get the idea of
coming to Varadero?"

Connie rocked back again. She was thinking hard, and
more and more disliking her thoughts. "He came in one afternoon, he'd been drinking at the Late Watch and he said he
had this great idea. He'd been talking to a man who told him
about the fishing at Varadero. Somebody named Caprio, a nice
fellow, some kind of importer. I didn't give it any thought.
. . . But—oh. If Caprio *isn't* just a nice importer. . . ."

"Caprio wanted Nelson here. He needed him here."

"But why, Rob? Barto was still alive."

"I don't know. It was something to do with Barto. Barto
was bound to find his way here—Caprio knew that. . . . It's
tricky. Caprio wanted me to take Barto's place here. Maybe
I was the only one left who could—and would—play the part
Barto'd been supposed to play. And he still wanted Nelson
around. Now you. . . . There're *two* conventions going on

here. We're delegates to at least one—maybe both. . . ."

Connie had her arms wrapped around her, as though chilled. "Bad," she said, almost to herself. "Rob—let's get away from here. On Nelson's boat—tonight. Barto's dead. . . . The last man I knew who died, this was over in Cannes, he was driving his sports car at about a hundred miles an hour over the cliffs and the road took a turn and he didn't. He'd had so much Cordon Bleu he probably never knew what hit him, there was actually a silly smile on his face when they fished him out of the Mediterranean two days later. His friends held a mock funeral for the Mercedes-Benz. . . . The people I've seen die, they're playing some kind of game."

I searched for the right words. "Are you so sure Barto wasn't playing? He played with—not sports cars—oh, expectations."

"Then—what does that say about you?"

"Sometimes I go through the motions of expecting too. Since everybody's doing it."

"Rob." The trouble was deepening in her face. "Caprio told me something else. . . . He said the other afternoon, when I saw you so shaky, you'd gone down too far and almost drowned. I asked him why you took chances—"

I reached out and took hold of her arm. "Can you remember his exact words?"

"He said—your life was a sort of rehearsal. Some time before you die, you think, you may be called on to do something —oh, significant—anyhow, real. Until then, you rehearse. Just so your muscles will be ready. . . . He said there are some people who make themselves unemployed and then take their unemployment as a kind of prison. . . ."

I had seen the kawama's look of vassalage, the droop of the harness horse, before. Her hind legs kept flipping their loads, first the left, then the right, digging the cavity now.

"The ones who feel most moved to stage prison breaks are those who lock themselves up. . . . He would say that. A busy man has theories about unemployment."

"Why *do* you dive that way, Rob?"

The question had to be answered for one of the askers. "Have you heard of the drunkenness of the deep, Connie? It's what happens to divers when they go too far down. If this wonderful floating thing happens to you at thirty fathoms, you sense, what unimagined delights are waiting at a hundred, two hundred? It's a Marx Brothers world. Can you get too much of a thing this good? You keep going down. The jokes get bigger—a clump of seaweed looks like a corpse opened on a dissection table and that's a joke, a brain coral looks like an airplane motor, that's a joke too. You want to introduce the airplane motor to the corpse, so they can share the joke with you. A silk net becomes a rocking father."

I stood and looked with anger at the sky. It was a night almost without clouds, the crystalline light from the moon dripping down on the white oncoming ridges of the water to make them whiter still, everything in sight powdered in white. The flesh of my hands was no longer flesh but whitened out of life.

"And do you know what causes it all? What's behind this last and biggest exhilaration? Nobody knows for sure but it's most likely the extra nitrogen in the blood. A few lousy atoms of nitrogen—the deeper you go the more the pressure—the more the pressure the more nitrogen forced into the blood. A handful of nitrogen atoms and you're glowing, laughing, purring—down you go! You could work out a formula—so-and-so many atoms of nitrogen in such-and-such quantity of hemoglobin equals so-and-so many units of happy days! But nitrogen has less delightful effects too. You know what nitrous oxide is? Laughing gas, makes you laugh. But take enough and you die —laughing, of course. This same nitrogen is what gives divers and sand hogs the bends—one of the fiercest pains and no joke. . . ."

Connie was tracing waves in the sand. Without raising her head she said: "Caprio thinks Barto wanted to kill like a lover. . . . That you dive like a lover. . . ."

That made me angrier. "He and Brod assess projects in

terms of work—the worthwhile or the worthless job. It's not the whole story! There are explorations too—things you investigate without plans or thoughts of usefulness! Why did I go down too deep? You're right, it wasn't to collect plankton microorganisms, not primarily that. There was an experience to be had. Useful or not, I wanted it. To have it under my belt. But—understand—I wanted it on *my* terms. I wanted it, and I wanted to be able to control it, not be swept away by it— rather, to be swept away and still have control—I wanted to have it and then come back. And be altered and complicated accordingly."

"But you didn't make a move to come back that day. Barto had to bring you up."

"I made one mistake. I overlooked the fact that the nitrogen atom makes terms too. . . . It's hard to dictate your own terms and make them stick in anything but an absolute vacuum. . . . Everywhere you go you carry out orders. I saw an Ophiurian that afternoon, a brittle fish, he dropped his head and tentacles when I came close. I was *his* orders. Plankton is a slave to the light. . . . If you take offense easily. . . ."

That was as far as I could take it. But Connie saw how the sentence had to be finished: "You do take offense. Caprio says it's your career. If you didn't want to be insulted, as you say—why go where it's bound to happen? Fifty fathoms down the nitrogen is in charge, not you. You can't win—but nobody forces you to go and lose. . . ." There was a new kind of intensity in her face. "It's not just the diving," she said slowly. "It's everything. You say you want certain things from a woman. But you go back and back to a woman who you're sure doesn't have them to give. . . . You pick beds where you don't make your own terms either. Then you make a big point of your terms. . . . What nitrogen is in charge of you at no fathoms?"

Something was developing with the kawama. She'd dug the nest cavity as deep as her hind flippers could go, that phase of the work was done. Now she was smacking the flippers hard against her tail and cloaca to get rid of the sand sticking there.

"Let's get around in back of her," I said. "She's about to get basic."

We went up near the grass line. From the rear, watching from a slight angle, we could see that her tail had been lowered into the hole and the cloaca, serving now also as ovipositor, pushed down past the tail, inches below the plastral shell. The kawama was ready to send her encapsulated young into the world but she took little joy in this perpetuation of her being. With her teary eyes two patches of sand, she had her head raised high and to one side, giving the impression that her neck was broken or at least cruelly twisted, and her gash of a mouth was open, and she was making windy deathbed noises.

"She has a grievance," I said. "She's not the boss either, and she doesn't like it."

"Being the boss isn't everything," Connie said.

Behind us, in the stringy grass, there was a rustling sound. We heard whispers. In a moment two barefooted boys came out on the beach some fifteen or twenty yards from us, one of them carrying a woven grass basket. They were talking softly and gesturing in the direction of the kawama. They approached the kawama and squatted just behind her, watching her agonies with no curiosity and waiting.

"I hope you're not going to be a sentimentalist about this," I said to Connie. "They're after the eggs."

"I don't want to interfere in legitimate business. What do they use the eggs for?"

"In making cakes. Supposed to be very good."

"Turtles have to lay eggs, people have to eat cake. Round and round she goes."

The eggs began to come. By standing up and going close I could see them as they dropped into the cavity, two or three small whitish eggs at a time, a group easing down every ten seconds or so. The process was more than just an indignity to the kawama, Nature indifferently using her body as a corridor, it seemed now a positive torment. Each time the cloaca con-

tracted to push out another batch of eggs the kawama dropped
her high-held twisted neck and her head flopped on the ground,
chin slapping across the sand. Each time some eggs were
squeezed out she lay with her head throbbing listlessly on the
sand, neck muscles heaving and flippers quaking and all
through it the loud, panting sighs coming from the half-open
victim mouth. Her whole face was drenched with tears now.

As fast as the eggs dropped into the nest the two businesslike boys reached for them and deposited them in their basket.
For the sake of the order Chelonia, for the good name of the
family Chelonidæ, for the general welfare and all-around en-
hancement of the genus Caretta caretta, the good shell-backed
lady was going through ordeals by fire, and she had nothing
to show for it, and she didn't care. Her job was to suffer, and
drop, and suffer again, not to look around to see whether it
added up to anything. What was she weeping for? Nothing in
particular. It was her role and custom to weep.

"Labor and division of labor," Connie said.

It went on for some minutes and finally, with her last
shuddering breath, the kawama seemed to be emptied of her
commitment to the future. The boys seemed to know the
bonanza was over. They stood up and went off along the
beach, one of them carrying the basket filled with the kawama's
best efforts for the bakers and confectioners of the world.

But the kawama was against shoddy work. Now she began
to fill in the hole, her hind flippers shoveling sand from the
ramp around her body. She kept testing the sand with her
cloaca, picking the best sand and rejecting the rest—nothing
too good for her future citizens who were now on their way to
delightful batters. Once the backing and filling was done the
kawama began to tamp the sand with powerful blows of her
plastron, the whole weight of her body hammering. The more
the sand got packed, the louder the thuds of her jamming,
hammering body. Finally she crawled back and forth over the
entire area, erasing all signs and markings, then, mission ac-

complished, absolutely nothing accomplished but the motions, she turned her head toward the sea and began her slow, under-slung, lumbering trip back home. At the water's edge she stopped and looked back for a moment, with ancient unde-monstrative dignity, and what I thought I saw on the still wet and sand-plastered face was not satisfaction with the job done but a question as to what could be the next travail—since the sequence of events in this life is necessarily one travail on the heels of another, colon after colon. Another moment and she was slipping into the breakers and gone to her next scheduled duties. As though the last one had amounted to anything.

"What she needs in her blood is a little nitrous oxide," Connie said.

"Both of them!" I said. "Caprio and Brod—what are they dedicated to? Putting one foot after the other! Down when the sun comes out—up when the sun goes in—there's no dig-nity to an imposed rising and falling. . . . Flippers going. The digging must go on in any case. . . . I wish I'd seen it more clearly. I would have tried to say it to Barto. . . ."

Connie fumbled in the bottom fold of her poncho-style chino pullover. She brought out an envelope and handed it to me. "Caprio said if I couldn't convince you to leave I was to give you this."

It was a sealed envelope with the name of the La Concha Hotel printed in the corner, addressed to me at our office in Key West. Above the name of the hotel was Barto's name, in his writing. But there was no stamp on it and it hadn't been mailed.

"From Barto? How—"

"The night he was killed he wrote this letter. Caprio found it in his desk at home."

I began to tear at the flap. Connie pointed up to a small villa back of the beach, where a lamp was turned on at the en-trance to the pathway.

"Why don't you go up under the light and read it?"

TWENTY-ONE   There were some newspaper clippings in the envelope. They were yellowed and pressed sharply
at the folds, humped as though carried for a long time in a
wallet. One was from an anarcho-syndicalist paper published in
Barcelona, dated April 28, 1937:

Cuban Militant Speaks from the Heart!
*A Moving Appeal to All True Fighters
in Our Just Anti-Fascist Struggles*
BY *Professor Arturo
de Arellano Caro*

Comrades:

*I address myself to all anarchist militants, but I am not
myself an anarchist.*

*In 1929, in my native Cuba, I joined the underground
revolutionary workers' party to fight the Machado dictatorship. I became a responsible member of the leading cadres.
Important figures in our international movement slipped into
Cuba to consult with me. One of these was a man named
Michael Brod. He came often to my home. My son, Bartolome,
called him Uncle.*

*When the tragic civil war broke out in Spain, Michael
Brod came again to Cuba. His secret mission was to organize
volunteers for the International Brigade in Spain. Bartolome,
under my political influence, was one of the first to volunteer.
I offered to go too, to help edit the Brigade newspaper.*

*When we arrived in Spain, Bartolome went with the Cu-
ban unit to reinforce the Madrid front. He reported to me that
the political commandant of his unit was his "Uncle," Michael
Brod. But after some months, the communications from Barto
stopped. I heard that a contingent of Brigade fighters had
quietly been detached from the Madrid front and sent to a
mountain sector in the Aragon, below Huesca. This contingent
was under Michael Brod's command and its mission was a
secret one.*

The Huesca sector was not held against the Falangists by militants of my party. As you know, my party has not been able to make many inroads into Catalonia because of the strength of your independent workers' parties here. This sector was held by those whom my party calls "deviationists," the militiamen of your independent parties. These "unreliables" were now to be retired from the field. Michael Brod's mission was to accomplish this shift of forces on one sector of the front. His authority came from papers stamped at Barcelona military headquarters, which had been infiltrated by my party.

Brod's men were deployed with their machine guns on the side of a hill near the front. Brod went to the advance post and handed the unit commander orders with the official seal of the Cataluña Generalitat, assigning this unit to indefinite leave.

The "unreliables" surrendered their arms and marched away over the hill. At Brod's instructions the International Brigade men who were dug in there opened fire with their machine guns. No unreliable was left alive to tell the tale.

(On other sectors of this front, I am informed, the unreliables received the same type of leave. This, too, was arranged by Michael Brod.)

But my son Barto, like some others, did not fire his machine gun. He lay there with his hands over his eyes, and wept. This weeping was not unnoticed by his commander, Michael Brod.

After Brod occupied the post he organized discussions for the benefit of the "ideologically confused." Over and over he explained that civil wars cannot be won with split commands, that those who deviated from our centralism were fifth-columnists and wreckers and spies, and only our centralist party could lead the workers to victory against the Falangists. Barto could not take these explanations in silence. He was still sick with horror. He spoke up in these discussions with the eloquence I had taught him, denouncing Brod for doing the butcher's work of Franco for him. He no longer called Michael

Brod Uncle. He called him butcher. His eloquence affected several of his comrades, despite Brod's forceful clarifications.

Some days later the Falangists attacked this sector, with a heavy air barrage. Our troops were cut to ribbons. (There were few forces left to resist.) In the course of the retreat, in an olive grove on the side of a hill, Michael Brod was observed raising his rifle from behind a tree and taking careful aim. He was observed to fire twice. Bartolome fell some fifty yards away, with two bullets in his back.

This has been reported to me by Cuban militants who were eyewitnesses to the murder. The reports leave no room for doubt: either Bartolome was killed on the spot, or he was left behind to be killed by the Fascists. In either case it was murder.

This news reached me four days ago, in Madrid. In one moment I stopped being a political entity and became a father. I ran away from Madrid and made my way here, to Barcelona. Here there are still "irresponsibles" with papers and organizations of their own.

I am publishing this appeal as a father, nothing more. I will remain in hiding and go on publishing my appeal to all independent workers and militants until the butchers who called themselves my comrades and friends find me and destroy me. Hear this appeal of a mourning father from the agony of his heart:

Comrades, unite with me in tracking down and destroying the butcher Michael Brod, the murderer of my martyred son Bartolome Caro!

Help me to avenge my son!

Comrades, help me so that I can die with the blood of the butchers on my hands, not my son's!

Help a brokenhearted man!

Below this article was a box containing a description of Michael Brod. Another clipping was from the same anarchist newspaper, dated April 29, 1937:

Honored Cuban Intellectual Disappears
Rumored Kidnapped, Spirited from Country

. . . . *The comrade syndicalists who gave refuge to Professor Caro in our city report that last night a band of seven thugs, speaking to each other in an unidentified Slavic tongue, broke into the Professor's hiding place and removed him by force. There are strong indications, according to our private sources, that Comrade Caro was drugged, packed in a trunk, and secreted aboard a freighter in the Barcelona harbor. The freighter has sailed for an undisclosed Eastern port, but the precise port is of no importance. We know where such luggage is delivered. . . .*

One of the kidnappers, clearly the leader, was described as a thin, intense, blond man. He was addressed as "Mihail." According to Comrade Caro's description, published in these columns three days ago, Michael Brod is thin and blond, and speaks several languages. . . .

We have lost another courageous militant in another steamer trunk. For the sake of our vanished comrade, we hope that in the dungeon he is destined for he will manage to contrive for himself a speedy death. . . .

There was also a badly printed throwaway, published by some anarchist group, on which Barto had written the date, May 4, 1937:

Barcelona Under Siege! Civil War Erupts!
Comrades, Resist the Totalitarian Butchers
Who Dare to Call Themselves Loyalists!
Resist With The Last Drop of Your Blood!

The tragic hour has come.

Today they are marching against our city. Their agents are swarming in our streets, some in the uniforms of the Civil Guard.

They could not win Barcelona with "ideology." Now they

have brought in their bigger arguments—tanks and machine guns.

The arms which are so desperately needed at the front to shoot Falangists—they throw against us! In the name of anti-Fascism!

Now the bitter truth is clear. Now we know why they took their troops from the Madrid front, where they were needed, and "relieved" our militiamen at the Aragon fronts— sometimes with bullets in the back. Before they marched on our city, the last city in Loyalist Spain not under their iron heel, they had to dissolve or wipe out our independent armed forces. Even at the cost of leaving the field clear to Franco and his savage hordes.

Yesterday our printing plant was blown up. No doubt they will find our emergency press and destroy that too. But we must resist. Our comrades are at the barricades now, defending our city against these "Loyalists" from Madrid.

Citizens of Barcelona! People of Spain! To arms against those who come to us from distant places, calling themselves proletarian soldiers and offering us only manacles! They are digging the grave of the Spanish revolution! They are the worst of the Fifth Columns!

Resist! Street by street, building by building!
Resist!

Still another clipping, dated May 1940, was from a Mexico City daily. It told of a mass attack on the house of a well-known revolutionary exile who had found asylum in Mexico, an attack by twenty men with machine guns and incendiary bombs. Among the attackers was a man, apparently their leader, who spoke French and was addressed respectfully as Michel. He was rumored to be blond, and thin. He had eluded the secret police. . . . From an Ottawa paper, dated September 1946, was an item reporting that an atom-spy network had been uncovered, thanks to the defection of one of

its members. Several of the plotters had been rounded up but
it was feared that the most important supervisory and liaison
people had slipped out of the country and were hiding in the
States or Latin America. One of them was a man referred to
as Mike, a thin, quick-motioned blond man in his late thirties
who was said to speak English impeccably, with an Oxford accent, but was also fluent in several European languages. . . .

In addition to the clippings there was another envelope,
sealed, with the words "Open in the Event of My Death"
written across its face. Inside this was a letter from Barto on
La Concha stationery:

Dear Rob,

*In our talk tonight I made jokes about the danger I may
be getting into. To tell you the truth, I am sitting now in
the Concha lobby, waiting for Caprio, and I don't feel very
jocular. There is some chance I will not get back from Havana.
That's why I have decided to write you a note. I hope you
never read it but if you do, read carefully.*

*I will tell you only the few things you need to know.
It is a dirty business and it is a dirt that a man should not
share with his friend.*

*Only one man could kill me. His name is Michael Brod
and he knows the thing I live for is to kill him. The enclosed
clippings will tell you most of the story.*

*This man Brod did filth in Spain. He tried to make others
do it too, including me. In Spain I saw people giving up
everything, their families and their lives, to fight the bar-
barians and make things a little more bearable for themselves,
and the Brods came in and took this struggle over and killed
those who would not take their new barbarian orders. I was
sick to my stomach, and spoke up against Brod out of this
sickness. For this he shot me and left me on the battlefield
for dead.*

I was lucky. Some anarchist farmers came down out of

the mountains and found me and took me to their hiding place. They dug one of Brod's bullets out but the other one was too deep and they were afraid to go in for it. They nursed me for three months, until I got back on my feet. Then I sneaked down into Barcelona and found that my father, because he thought I was dead, had spoken out against Brod too. For this Brod had kidnapped him and smuggled him out of the country. Many disappeared that way during the war.

My anarchist friends helped me to get across the Pyrenees. I was in Paris for months, looking for signs of Brod, but no luck. I wrote home to my mother several times without getting an answer. Then I went home to Cuba and found that with his bullets Brod had killed my whole family. There was no more family. When my mother heard that both her son and her husband were dead in Spain she fell sick, and three months before my return she died. I had a little sister, Luz, only four years old when I left for Spain, but she was gone. Nobody knew what had happened to her.

My first year in Havana I went around like a demented man. Yes, I think I was out of my head. I thought only of Brod, the friend of my father, the man I'd called Uncle. Nights I lay in dirty hotel rooms thinking of how it would feel with my fingers on my Uncle's throat, and my fingers singing. I made up my mind there was one thing I had to do in life, to find Brod and kill him. Not for politics. Oh, no. Because it was necessary for the health of my fingers. Only for that.

I looked for him and for Luz. It was all a waste. When the war came I decided to go up to the States and enlist in the American forces because that was a way for a foreigner to get American citizenship. I will not pretend that I wanted the pleasure of being your compatriot, or anybody's. I wanted the pleasure of an American passport. I expected to do a lot of traveling, and an American passport is the best.

After the war, when you set up the business and offered me a partnership, I was glad to accept. It would be a lie if

I said I did it out of friendship. You were my friend, but there was no room in my life for friendship and such trivialities. I took the partnership because in Key West I would be in a good position to get to Cuba and other places in Latin America where Brod might go. Also, the business would give me money to travel.

Over the years I found traces of Brod, but only traces. (Look at the clippings from Mexico City and Canada.) But seven months ago there was a development. I have comrades in Cuba who were in Spain with me and whose stomachs were turned by the Brods. From them I received reports that Brod had been seen in Cuba. Also, that he was in some kind of trouble with his own people and therefore not so heavily guarded as before. Now, just today, I have confirmed that it is so. From Caprio, but from others too.

So I am close to him, after thirteen years. I intend to find him and kill him. But he is smart, he may get the best of me. If that happens I have two things to ask of you, who have been so kind already.

One, if there is something you can do, try to find my sister Luz. I would feel satisfied if I knew somebody in the world, one person, was still looking for her. A whole family should not be erased from the face of the earth with two bullets. And this was the most innocent of our family, a little helpless pretty girl, she should not be the final one to suffer when for the others the suffering is over. If she is alive her life should be made a little easy. It is a lot to ask, Rob, but with you I can do it.

Second, do not get mixed up in my troubles. Leave Brod to Caprio. These things are Caprio's business and he is good at it.

I say this because I know you, Rob. I know from our times in the Pacific and I know from our diving here that you have a strong brotherhood with trouble. It is with you in everyday matters as it is in diving, you have a tendency to¹ get in over your head. It is hard to understand, when behind *you there are no pitchforks. With you they are inside, of your own make, and this frightens me.*

I am going to confess something. For thirteen years I have felt the pitchforks, pushing me in one direction. I feel them now, that is why I am going to Havana tomorrow. But I no longer know why I am going, except for the pitchforks. They are not enough reason to do anything, there must be some meaningful prize at the end of an effort. I realize now, this minute, that I have devoted my life so long and with so much love to one thing that I have outgrown the possibility of prizes.

Do you understand what I am saying? There is one thing I fear in Cuba. Not dying, I am not afraid of that. It is the possibility that I will find Brod and manage to kill him. If I kill him now, after my whole life went into it, what will I have then? The base of all my existence has been the thought to kill him. If he dies, what will I base myself on?

I have been sitting by myself, thinking about the last things I said to you in the Late Watch, and I see they were lies. I said I was a hungry and a thirsty man and needed food and drink, but that is a lie. I am going to try and kill Brod only because my fingers need it, but my fingers are insane and I cannot stop them. If I kill Brod, I kill myself too. He, the idea of his death as the main event, has become my spine. How will I live without a spine? With no more main events to look for?

It is not easy for me to say this. But I feel obliged to tell you how it is with those who make wrong brotherhoods. If I could turn the calendar back thirteen years I would not chase again after Brod, I would forget him and—well, go fishing, take up oceanography. I envy people who can be interested in plankton. Anything not imposed. I would do this even with the two holes in my back and the bullet against my lung. Because to do what I have done means that not only my father and mother and little sister are Brod's victims, I am his victim too. When I filled my head with the thought of him and no other thoughts I did what his bullets could not do, I did the job for him, I killed myself.

With all the strength I have I say this to you. If you wish to do one thing for me when I am dead, look for Luz. This will be enough. Do not get on this bloody trolley, all the passengers are corpses. Some still with the eyes open.

I hope there will be no reason for you to read this letter. If you do: then goodbye, take care of yourself, thanks for everything, and salud.

Barto

P.S. Luz has two identifying marks. One, a heavy diagonal scar on the rear of her left thigh, under the buttock, where she was cut by a splinter on a seesaw. Two, a mole behind the lobe of her right ear, at the junction.

P.P.S. Another thing you said this afternoon on the boat, before you came to: "She keeps dropping her Red Sox cap with all the snakes." You're wrong. There are no snakes on the Boston Red Sox cap.

P.P.P.S. About the diving. You say you go down only to get plankton animals in your net. Did you ever ask yourself what the animals have in mind when they're obliging enough to swim into your net? Read an article about this the other day, in the Scientific American. *Marked a paragraph for you. Take a look sometime, you'll find it slipped under that calendar pad I keep on the desk.*

Included with Barto's letter were two cracked, browning photographs. I had kept them out, now I looked at them.

One, stamped "1936" on the back, was a group snapshot of the Caro family, the members stiff and looking straight ahead as though all necks were starched, Mamma and Papa sitting in the middle in their creased and crisp Sunday best and the two children standing alongside with hands on the parents' shoulders. Old man Caro was a peppery-looking man with long Spanish nose and fierce challenge eyes, runaway black moustache going from jowl to jowl like a brush mark, and Mamma Caro was all-over ample, with big dimples. The little girl leaning against the father was a cute four-year-old, all frills and mischief, and eyes flashing black. Barto, standing in sentinel angularity by his mother, must have been twenty, and was lean and concentrated, a younger edition of the Barto I'd known in all respects except the far-awayness and electric tautness weren't there yet, just unfocused young energy. The other photo was a close-up of the little girl Luz, showing her with bunches of flowers in her arms and a lace-edged white dress, maybe just come from confirmation services, dark-ish kewpie-doll face a little puffy, all her baby fat gathered and ready to bust out with the giggles.

There was another figure in the group shot. My eyes had gone around him the first time I looked but now I went back to study him. He was standing behind the parents, one arm on Barto's shoulder—the seersuckered figure was circled with a red pencil mark and over it was written the Spanish word for uncle, "Tío." This was a man in his thirties, somewhat shorter than Barto, five nine at the most, and lean like Barto, but with very fair skin that showed up chalky next to the sun-down Caro faces, and with quite blond hair.

It was the expression on his thin-featured condensed face, with scooped cheeks and trowel-angled jaw that traveled out as though there was no room for a structure that massive in the face behind, that held my eyes. He looked like a man who wore slightly smiling calm for a mask, for thermos wrapping, who had big excitement and cat watchfulness under the calm.

I wouldn't have taken this man for an East European or any European. Except for the under-surface tension, the hidden core of sleeplessness, the suggestion of quick triggers inside, he looked like a dozen lazy blond fellows in scuffed white buck rubber-soled shoes and cashmere sweaters who'd sat with me in Harvard classrooms, yawning at the lecture on the Albigensian Crusades.

TWENTY-TWO   Rather go fishing, he'd said. Barto, fishing.

A sneak dream of "fishing." Grandfather Heixas had had one of "buccaneering."

Both in quotes. Same dream. The quotes were a memo of its unlikeliness. Wake up, they meant, and back to work.

Long as muscles did not stir in their own good time, tensed to iron schedules—pitchforks at your back. The hoarded vision of a day torn away from schedules, that was something dreamed in and by the herded muscles. To register their complaint and counter their humiliation.

Muscles need their vacations too. Which can take the form of spasm, imp movement.

Even—especially—in those who dive without having to.

Many excellent divers, who dive not for a living but to spy on plankton, drown.

I stood under the beach lamp and slid the thick envelope into my pocket, and I think I said aloud to the insect-crawling lamp, with a feeling of enclosing nausea, and hopelessly, "He'd rather have gone fishing. He said he would rather go fishing." I added: "Rest in peace, Barto." Many excellent divers, some of the best, do not come up. No plankton is worth it.

I felt widening space about me, things roundabout expanding while inside I contracted, as though the physical world was backing off several feet to give me elbowroom in my precipitating thoughts. I took this not for abandonment but as true politeness, a wish not to interfere in my deliberations.

Connie was sitting on the sand looking up at me as though I was central in more than one scheme. I felt like saying something unguarded and nice to her, but what I actually said was, "Twice in a week."

"Twice what?"

"You'd think his work was done." I wasn't trying to be oblique. I was summing up for myself so I could explain it to

her. "He reached and grabbed for me at the last second again."
Over the spot where the kawama had dug, I saw, Connie
had drawn a big heart and across it printed in capital letters,
"VACANCIES." Her face was very serious. "He meant to do it.
It was one of his last thoughts, to pull me up with his words
if his hands weren't around."

"Does that change your mind?" She wasn't trying to force
any new course on me.

"Connie." The next thought was harder to shape. It had
to be approached by degrees. "You know how it works out in
a chase story in the movies. One man is injured, or his client
or friend, and he sets out to chase another man responsible
for the injury. They both run at top speed, without any slacken-
ing, and the virtuous man catches the unvirtuous one because
he can, with his virtue, run faster."

"They have to run fast. They've only got ninety minutes." It wasn't facetious. She was trying to say just enough
to encourage me to keep going.

"Sifting—that's the premise. But if you don't have good
and bad sifted in two separate packages how can you do any
effective chasing?" I squatted next to her. "You get your man
backed in a corner. All right. Suppose he looks like you—"
Connie folded her hands in her poncho flap as though cold.
She kept her eyes on me. "I've been down here for days," I
said more quietly, "chasing—what? The idea of chasing? Mirror images?"

Connie reached for my wrist. "I know something about
running. When there wasn't even anything to run after. No
excuse at all." She came closer to me. "What do you want
to do?"

The rest had to be said. "You see how it was? Barto had
been injured as much as a man can be, he had a legitimate
case against this bastard. But—tracking him for thirteen years,
dedicating his life to it, he made the issues recede. More and
more it wasn't the virtuous case that moved him but inertia.

Two people running around the same circle—who's chasing who?"

The next was harder to say: "The original issues get buried. . . . All you can do is stand to one side and hope your friend fires the first shot—not because he stands for the right but because he's your friend. If he gets killed all you can do is mourn him, because he was your friend." I looked up. How neutrally the stars stayed in their slots, remote as righteousness, unconcerned as clocks. "Barto knew that. He tried to say it in his letter."

With that the decision was made, almost by itself. No important or broad chemistry was interrupted to wait on my words. Far from listening, the elements were asleep or doing their work. "Do you still want to get out of here?" I said.

"Not without you."

"I don't have any involvements here that'll stand up." Everything in her face unfolded. But it still had to be planned. The exits could be trickier to plot than the entrances. "Where's the boat anchored?"

"In the lagoon just north of the airport."

"Who's on it, the captain?"

"No, Nelson gave him a vacation. He hired somebody else for this trip, a man who knows the waters around here."

"Who is he?"

"I don't really know." She looked troubled. "Caprio found him."

"That's not so good. If he's Caprio's man, if Caprio wants me here. . . . I'll figure out something. Wait in your room until I call. This is important—don't tell anybody about our leaving. Not even Nelson."

"Where are you going?"

"A friend of Brod's brought me here—she may be in trouble for helping me. I've got to go into town and get her."

She put her hands on my arms. "I don't understand it when people are hunting each other in earnest. There was a flier I knew in Tangiers, a Pole, he was what you'd call a soldier of fortune I guess, he'd hire himself out to any side in any war and he killed a lot of people but I don't think he did it for the killing. People said he just liked to fly and was too poor to get his own plane. He did it with a smile, the way people play tennis. It wasn't any the less vile but, well, I'd have been more scared still if he hadn't smiled. If he'd had just a work look." She put her arms around me. "Hurry, Rob."

Her way was to distrust what was soft in her. Only her hard parts could be put forward. Even in bed. Even in kissing the lips were offered warily, as reconnaissance from behind the armor. Yet the armor was down now. She turned her head to one side and pressed her cheek against my chest, holding on without caution. In this unexpected sag she seemed inches shorter. It was, exactly, the cupping, the openness, the offering, the needful receptivity, that I had time after time wanted from her. And with it the styles dropped away and for once she had true shape. Lesson in inturning and exposure. She was offering herself.

"Hurry," she said. "And be careful."

Immediately, at the sound of words centered on me with no thought to her own advantage, I felt a need for her. I started to pull her to me.

My arms froze and like a mouldy curtain a wave of revulsion went down my body.

Her hold was a dead weight. The pull on me. Body stripped of all attributes save mass, hanging on, wanting company in the drop.

Who wants to be dragged down?

For the moment, running from Brod, we forgot to run from each other, huddled together thankfully as refugees will. Once we faced each other again without the cement of spectacular trouble, no company but our irritations—

There was, further, the possibility that I'd run to Havana and Varadero partly because they were free of Connie. How

intent would I have been on vengeance and justice and other
banner words if our bodies had been meeting fittingly?

The thought made me wince. Large and public involvements could be an easy valve from private impasses. Another
angle from which to see political works—the Brods and the
Bartos. And me, though far from politics. Connie rubbed
against me and I had to strain to keep from wrenching away.

No going down again.

"Try to be careful," she said.

I took her fingers from my neck as gently as I could.

"It's an extraordinary thing. Brod—in a way he looks like
me," I said. "Go ahead. I'll call as soon as I can."

I watched her go down the beach with grace and lightness.

The stars were as far away as voluntary fishing and sweet
piracy. Separate as bodies.

TWENTY-THREE   I turned in at the swimming
pool, thinking that I might get through to the parking space,
to the taxi stand there, without seeing anybody I knew.

As I was passing the semicircle of cabañas a bellboy came
from the main building. He was calling out something in an
unenthusiastic singsong—it sounded like "Me, star, row, boat,
God, mays," over and over. I took a few steps, puzzling over
the sounds, stopped and went over to him. My guess was
right, he was paging Mr. Robert Garmes. Wanted on the
phone.

I found a phone in the hallway.

"Mr. Brew, Kay still does not answer, Mr. Go, Mays," the
operator said.

"I'm not calling Mr. Brooke now," I said. "I was paged—"

The door to the nightclub opened and a group of drunks

came out. All Americans and masked, the men got up as pirates and gypsies and lion tamers, the women as Madame Pompadours and harem beauties. One stout woman was wearing nothing but a leopard-skin bikini, high heels, and strands of seaweed trailing from neck and belly button, on her head an Empress Eugénie hat. Representing what? Spirit of the Nineteenth Amendment. One man was carrying a bottle of champagne under his arm and they were all laughing. From the nightclub came sounds of drums and trumpets. Saturday, carnival night.

"Mr. Brew, Kay does not answer," the operator said.

"You don't understand. I was just called—"

"I'm afraid that was my doing, Garmes," a voice said behind me.

It was one of the drunk Americans, the pirate with the champagne bottle. He was alone. He was looking straight at me, not drunk now, it was Vincent Caprio.

"There wasn't any call. I had you paged, to locate you," he said.

I put the phone down. "More work clothes. You must wear out a lot of them."

"No more than you do. Mine may be a little more varied."

"Thanks for sending me Barto's letter. I suppose you've read it?"

"Very carefully. I've been thinking about it."

"I can imagine. The question is, how does a Garmes react to a letter like that—right?"

"And? What have you decided?"

"Don't you know? You're the expert on anticipating me."

"I've got an idea. You're not really sore at me any more. You're acting superior, as though you've got a secret."

"And you know what it is?"

"What could it be? You were no doubt thinking how I was using you, and feeling sore about it. If you had a plan for ending *that*. . . . There's also Barto's letter. Very effective letter."

He was an amazing man. "Then why did you send it?"

"If you can ask such a damn fool question it shows how little you understand. About me, about anything." He pulled his mask off. "Garmes, let's go outside."

We went through the lobby and out the front entrance, began to pace slowly over the cushioning grass of the golf course.

"Of course you would resent me," Caprio said. "You thought I'd made elaborate plans for you, when you started to think." He bent to pick up a golf tee, studied it. "Sure I made plans. How do you think I could operate if outsiders insisted on sticking their noses in and I wasn't prepared?"

"Why didn't you simply stop me?"

"How! I threatened you with the Coast Guard and the police but it was just talk. You weren't breaking any laws, neither you nor Barto. Your passports were in order. How could I have stopped you?"

"You should be well prepared for Connie being here, and Nelson Boyar. And the new captain on Boyar's boat."

"Garmes, if ever some schoolkids form a secret cell to take over the third grade, don't join up. You're even too dense for third-grade conspiracies!"

I busted out laughing. It surprised me that I was already far enough out of it to laugh. "We seem to take turns. First I get sore, then you."

He calmed down, but not to the point of easing his face. "You've got one talent. For annoying busy people. It's a fine art with you." He pulled the pirate moustachios from his lip, shredded them and threw them away. "Yes, I got Nelson down here. I arranged that days ago, when I expected Barto. I kept him here because of you, brought Connie down because of you. Because without a lifeline you were dead."

"Lifeline?"

"Look—if you got in a bad spot here you wouldn't come running to me. Even if you could. Not you. You *might* go to your friends. I put the friends here, with a fast boat. I put my man on the boat. That way you've got at least one thin line of communication to the outside. To *me*. . . . Not that I expect any thanks. Anarchists don't thank the powers."

"Why do you keep calling me an anarchist? I don't belong to any wild-eyed organizations."

"You're the worst kind. You're so much of an anarchist you can't stand being in the same room with other anarchists. . . . Let me tell you—you'd have been dead in Havana days ago, after the Sociedad or even earlier, without a few powers like mine."

"In that case, thanks. All the same: why send that letter? If your plans called for me to stay here—"

"But they didn't. Not for a minute."

All I could say, stupidly, was, "What?"

"Look, my job is to anticipate *everything*. The possibility that you'd come here—and the possibility that you'd leave. With or without any letter from Barto."

No question about it, whether you had anything personal against him or not he was an exasperating man. "What gave you the idea I was so unreliable?"

"You're not likely to follow your Brods to the end, Garmes. You know how *you'll* get your name in the obituary columns? Heading for the ocean bottom to stake your one-man claims. . . . I had to count on your dropping out sooner or later."

We were down almost to the road, we turned and started back toward the hotel. I was examining what he'd said, trying to decide how much cause it gave me for anger.

"All right," I said finally. "Rightly or wrongly you expected me to quit. I repeat: why send me Barto's letter?"

"I was looking for some way to control the time and place of your quitting. The letter was bound to have an effect."

"Incredible." It was my turn to stop and stare. "You're—asking me to work with you."

"You can leave, I promise you. I just want to control the way you do it." He began to walk back and forth on the grass, holding on to his chin. "Look. Brod feels he can cope with me. He and I know each other pretty well—at times we've had drinks together. But *you're* an unknown quantity to him. Not that you've done one blessed thing to him so far. You've been slogging around here like a—like a blind man on the mud flats. But there's no telling with you. You worry him. At a time when he's got all the worries he can handle."

"You do know each other pretty well. Brod wrote me a couple of letters saying the same things you've been saying."

"We've both learned to analyze situations from a certain point of view. . . . Tell me about those letters."

"He talked about my background, my family, other personal things. My service record too."

There was undisguised admiration on Caprio's face. "Mike's a meticulous worker. . . . He couldn't kill you in Havana—we were watching you too closely. He had to tempt you off somewhere—and make sure you'd shake my people. . . . One thing's on our side. He couldn't know about Barto's letter. Garmes, our strategy here boils down to this—to make the situation intolerable for Brod."

"Why the squeeze?"

"We want him to move in a certain direction. If he does. . . ." He made a grabbing motion with his hands. "He's in a bind right now. There've been some shake-ups in his organization. Brod belongs to the Old Guard that's being purged— some of his closest friends have gotten the axe. He's been ordered home—he knows that almost certainly means the axe for him too. His people have gone out of their way to *help* us close in on Brod. A lot of useful information about him— his contacts, his hangouts, his bankbooks, the false passports he uses—has been mailed to us anonymously in Washington. Even his fingerprints, and some photographs. His superiors send this stuff, of course. It's an old trick of theirs to force their boys in line. . . ."

My head was swimming but I was beginning to understand. "His friends *are* turning on him, I've seen that. The people in Millie's and in other places Natividad took me to. . . ."

"Sure. They could have killed him long before this if they'd wanted to. He hasn't got much of an organization left —that's why you've got big nuisance value now."

"What's the move you're trying to push him into?"

"Can't you see? We move closer—so do his former friends, on orders—in addition, *you* keep at him with your unpredictable ways. He may choose what in this intolerable situation seems the lesser of two evils—and go home."

I was staring again. "How would that help you?"

"If he decides to make a break for it he'll bring out this thing we want. He can't go home without it. Unless he brings them the goods he won't even get a rigged hearing."

"If he tries to run—you'll be waiting?"

"That's the idea."

"What do you want of me?"

"Let him think you're still after him, and getting closer."

There was thus a second choice to be made, as a direct consequence of my first. "Decisions seem to come in pairs. . . . When I want to come in you say stay out. When I decide to leave. . . ."

"Whims—you can turn off whims. On a job you get into things more slowly and you stay longer—till the job's done. . . . What do you say?"

"Caprio—how do I know whether this thing you want from Brod is good or bad? Whether you should have it, or anybody? . . . You know how I react to the powers that say, Trust me and don't ask questions. . . . It's not a principle, I'm not offering programs. I'm not saying I'm right. It's not even an attitude—it's what I have to do to keep from feeling sick, and handled. . . . You say patriotism to me—"

When he spoke his voice was surprisingly mild. "I *didn't* say patriotism to you."

"That's what your argument comes down to."

"Patriotism doesn't have a thing to do with it." He looked

up at the unperturbed sky. I wondered if he saw belittling suggestions in the stars too. Maybe he didn't see objects that unfunctional. "It's a word for parades and public speeches. I'll be as honest as I know how, Garmes. My family lives in a certain place—I'd like to know bombs aren't going to be dropped around there—beyond that I don't have the time or the inclination to think about the big issues. Actually, in the sewers where I work the issues that agitate the public don't take hold. They're as high above you, as unimmediate, as—as those stars." He made an abrupt upward gesture with his thumb. "Know what interests me? Doing my job. Just that. I take pride in my job the way a carpenter does in his—there's no patriotism in carpentry either. I want your help because I'd like to get my work done. I can give you an equally non-patriotic reason for helping me."

"I'm still listening."

"You need a strictly personal reason for doing things, right? Listen. You help me force Brod into making his move and I'll promise you something. We'll take what we want from him—then I'll see that he's turned over to the Florida police to be tried for murder. . . . I'll testify against him if it's necessary. . . . Is that personal enough?"

He seemed completely serious. I took a breath. "You know more about me than I thought. . . . All right."

"Good!" His hunched shoulders seemed to drop by inches and that was all the visible reaction he had. "Where's that champagne bottle? I left it around here some—there it is." The bottle was standing near the first hole, where he'd placed it. He went over and got it. "Let's have a drink to the success of our squeeze, Garmes. This stuff's warm but it's still champagne."

He held out the bottle and I took it. "I despise everything you are and stand for," I said, "but I see no reason why I shouldn't drink with you." I took a swallow and he did the same.

"The next twenty-four hours should tell the story," he

said. "Brod's deadline may be getting close—with your help.
. . . I've got to set some things up. Meet you around the bar."

I started off. Then I stopped in complete confusion, feeling dizzy. I shook my head, trying to get my boiling thoughts
back in order. I turned and went back to Caprio. "I'm a fool.
. . . It just struck me. . . . At what point, exactly, did you
read Barto's letter?"

Instead of being thrown he looked at me with amuse-
ment. "I was wondering when you'd get around to that."

"You didn't find it on his desk."

"No. Absolutely not."

I shook my head again. "He says he was writing in the
lobby of the Concha, waiting for you. But he left the Late
Watch to keep an important appointment with you. It must
have taken him an hour to write all that. You wouldn't have
kept him waiting a whole hour. . . ."

"Better and better! Yes, I was with him. He wrote the
whole thing in my room. He put in the sentence about waiting
in the lobby at my suggestion. We didn't want you thinking
I had anything to do with the letter, you can understand that."

"But the letter says—he admitted he was going to Havana.
He didn't admit that to you. . . ."

"Not at first. I convinced him I knew what his real plans
were. I told him I needed this letter to handle you, in case
he didn't come back. He wrote it because he was worried
about you."

"You—dictated the letter?"

He stopped laughing. "Not a chance. You couldn't put
words in Barto's mouth, you know that. I only suggested he
write, and suggested some things to say."

"You suggested the letter," I said like an idiot. "You
planned this far."

"Part of the job, Garmes. I needed something to precipitate your doubts when you began to have them. If I could
precipitate them, maybe I could control them. . . ."

"I made the decisions. You planned them."

"Garmes—this kind of operation, essentially, is always a struggle to control the most anarchistic variables. Brod was trying to juggle your moods, to make you jump his way— that's why he wrote *his* letters. I needed to be one up on him. . . . Go and have a drink. Then we'll pick Natividad up and get started."

When I got inside I still didn't know whether he'd wanted me to stay away from Cuba or whether he'd backhandedly talked me into going. But I couldn't be angry, or superior. He'd very likely saved my life.

TWENTY-FOUR   When Caprio came back he was dressed in an olive-colored dacron suit and a lemony sports shirt grown over with fruits and jungle trees. He immediately took my arm and hurried me off toward the parking area. "We'll go and get Our Lady of the Miracles first," he said. "Better have her in a safe place."

We got into an avocado-green Pontiac and headed toward town. He began to talk: "I was guessing before but now I know. Brod's deadline is six o'clock tomorrow afternoon. That's official. Direct from headquarters."

"To be official it would have to be from *his* headquarters."

"It's official," he said happily. We were approaching the Casa Mañana on Avenida Segunda but he went past the hotel without slowing down. "Natividad'll keep. . . . Brod's dead- line has a name—the S.S. *Wolna*, a freighter loading sugar and henequén in Havana Bay. She's due to sail for the Mediter- ranean at six tomorrow afternoon."

"With Brod?"

"He's been advised that if he doesn't sail on the *Wolna* their whole organization will be turned loose on him."

"What about this thing he's got?"

"If they don't get it soon it's not worth much. This ul- timatum means they've decided to get it or him, now."

"Still, why should he go back? At home he's sure to be eliminated—here he might have a chance."

"If he could disappear. The world's got to be pretty indifferent to a man before it lets him disappear."

"But *you're* not after him!"

"If *they* write this article off, *we* write it off. In that case do you think we'd just let Brod walk away? We don't often get a chance to pin a foolproof murder charge on one of their people. . . . As of tonight we're out to get him for murder. Let me rephrase that. We're going through all the *motions* of a grade-A manhunt. They'd convince anybody."

"Either you're doing it," I said hopelessly, "or you're going through the motions."

"Garmes, Garmes—drop the either-or's. Brod's people are trying to make him produce this thing by pretending they don't care about it any more. Just what we're trying to do. . . . If he thinks there's a serious manhunt on he won't try to hide out. He doesn't have the resources any more. He'll run —toward the S.S. *Wolna*, if we can make him." Caprio removed his hands from the wheel and rubbed them together. "We've got him in a situation we control almost completely. We hold the major drawstrings. I've been waiting for this for a long time."

Just this side of the airport we'd taken a right off the main road and now we were moving along the eastern edge of the lagoon, out past the Club Kawama. Here and there in the blue-serge rippled waters were the dipping blurs of boats, small motor skiffs belonging to local fishermen, occasionally a more substantial form that was probably the cruiser of some well-off resident or visitor. Some of these craft were pulled up partway on shore, some were tied to moorings, others, the larger ones, were anchored at various distances out.

"Your job is to make other people reach your conclusions," I said.

Caprio's voice was mellow with pleasure over himself. "It's a time of decision. If people are behind the times we'll help them catch up." We had come to the mouth of the lagoon, the more demonstrative waters of the open sea in front of us. There was heavy surf, the breakers came in with a crack and boiled back with long diehard hisses. Caprio pulled up, keeping the motor running, and pointed to a cruiser moored to a matchstick-pinioned pier on the far side of the lagoon. "You were looking for Nelson's boat before—there she is. The *Easy Rider*'s back a ways, near the place they use for a basin." There were lights on the *Tiger*, we saw shapes moving about in the cabin. Caprio nodded in a satisfied way. "They're all aboard."

"Who?"

"My man, Nelson, and Connie." He backed into the driveway of a whitewalled Moorish-style villa, turned around and started off. "We've got a plan." He pointed across the lagoon to the bulbs strung in rows along the airport's single runway. "Airport, bus stop, cabs, shoreline—all covered. Most of them, anyhow. Brod's been given to believe they *all* are, and he can't check. Patrols on both roads out of the peninsula, the highway back to Matanzas and the one east to Cárdenas. Some men on them at check points anyhow—Brod thinks we've got more."

"How do you get all this information to Brod?"

"If a man can talk to the east he can talk to the west. All he has to do is turn his head." He demonstrated. "What kind of rendezvous Brod's got with the *Wolna* I don't know. We've found out he's got a seaplane, the one Brooke chartered to get to Varadero, hidden in a cove the other side of Matanzas, around a place called Bacunayagua. He may try to reach the plane and fly out to the *Wolna* after she sails."

"How does he get from here to the plane?"

"That's the whole thing. We've tried to set it up so he can only move out of here by water. Brooke's over on the *Easy Rider* now—getting it ready."

"If he knows you're watching everything else, why wouldn't he suspect you're watching the *Easy Rider* too?"

"First of all, he's got to move *some* way. Besides, there's a question of logic. We know all about how he's been using the *Easy Rider*—ordinarily that's the last place we'd look for him now. He's been told that that's the way we're figuring it."

"You're *not* watching the *Easy Rider?*"

"Don't have the men, and don't need to. That'll be *your* job."

"I thought my job was to get out of here."

"Sure—on Nelson's boat. Half a step behind Brod, so it looks like you're chasing him."

"Looks?"

He seemed downright hurt. "The *Tiger*'s at the mouth of the lagoon. The *Easy Rider* will have to pass it to get to open water. All I want you to do is be on the *Tiger* and ride herd on Brod up to Bacunayagua, so he won't take any detours."

"Suppose Brod turns around and rides herd on me?"

Multiple grievances came out on Caprio's face. "He knows *I* wouldn't open fire on him if I could help it. But you— who can tell what crazy notions *you* might get? No, he'll try to run faster. Straight to the plane and the *Wolna* if all other avenues are closed—and they will be. You are going to be the final unmanageable pressure to convince him the Western Hemisphere is no place for him."

"How will he know it's me on the boat?"

"Why should the *Tiger* be chasing him? Because Nelson has a friend named Connie who has a friend named Garmes. He'll think it's you coming after him with blood in your loner eye, period. He won't want to tangle with you." He was full of congratulations for himself again.

I watched the palmettos go by. "It's his dislike of improvisations. That's what you're counting on."

"Sure, he can't predict you. It's his biggest weakness—the way he likes things in order."

Instead of getting angry I felt a seizure come over me. "When I was looking for Brod I couldn't get anywhere near

him. Now that I'm retiring from his life and projects. . . ."
The hysteria was hard to control. "It's a wonderful, wonderful
way of leaving. I admire the dialectical thought that went
into it. No either-or's for you."

"You'll have your friends for company," Caprio said seriously. "My man will handle communications and all technical
problems. You just take a nice boat ride."

But, knowing that he essentially had me, he'd lost most
of his interest in me. Talking directly to the windshield, he
said quietly: "We know the when. We know the how. We've
got the big variables in *our* hands, for once. I don't think he
can get out of this one. I don't think so." The same almost-
concealed inward sweat I'd seen in Barto.

Near the central square I sensed a bustle unusual for this
late at night. The music from the Kastillito and the Pullman
sounded livelier than you would expect, excited cries and
whoops came from the clubs and from the streets too. Of
course—carnival weekend, there were groups of people in the
street or sitting in the open cafes in costumes, some with
masks, about them the overdone cheeriness of the liquored-up.
Cars full of party-going or party-coming people began to pass
us both ways, their riders in gay costumes too.

"Carne vale," Caprio said. "Means the leaving of the
flesh, doesn't it? Maybe soon big caballero Mike Brod will be
taking leave of his flesh."

"Isn't this a pretty roundabout procedure?" I said. "When
and if he goes for the *Easy Rider* you could just grab him."

"His pockets would be empty, Garmes. He's not the one
to take chances. Maybe he's arranged for somebody to bring
this stuff to him at the last minute, I don't know. The only
sure thing is—he's got to have it when he leaves for the
Wolna."

"But if I'm chasing him—maybe he won't stop?"

"Make sure he's taking the last step toward the *Wolna*—
then you can beat it. Leave it to your captain. You just sit
on that nice boat and smoke your cigar."

He took a right at the square and another on Segunda, went along the block and stopped across the way from the Casa Mañana. He raised his finger in an offhand gesture that seemed directed at any and all, and immediately a man in a loose guayaberra shirt stood up from a rocking chair on the hotel veranda, drifted down the front steps and off around the corner.

"The back entrance is covered," Caprio said. "Better if you go up by yourself—Natividad's touchy with strangers."

There were groups of costumed people on the veranda, drinking and making a lot of noise. Inside, at tables in the dining room, were more revelers in various unhinged states, singing and jabbering, one couple doing a teeter-hip and spastic-headed comedy tango to the tune of somebody's guitar.

Upstairs I knocked at Natividad's door, calling her name. No sound. I tried the door and found it, surprisingly, open. I swung it back and went in.

The room was dark but I could make out the vague form on the bed. "Natividad. Wake up. It's Robert." I found the light switch and snapped it up.

It was not Natividad on the bed. Rather, a man, dressed in billowing clown's costume of dazzling white with large black polka dots. Flopping oversize hat of the same material on his head. What was past understanding was that the face too was a ground of dead chalk white with black perfect circles scattered over it, one over each eye and eyelid, others camouflaging nose and mouth, more still on the cheeks and running over to ears and neck, the effect being to erase all contours. It took me a moment to figure out that the face had been carefully painted to continue the outfit's pattern. The hands too, outrageously. The man was up on one elbow and looking at me. The revolver in his polka-dotted right hand was pointed at my stomach.

"No funny stuff," the big dot under the dotted nose said. "You could get the monopolies on no breathing."

The glaze was off his eyes and the coma cleared from his voice, but it was Coolio. Nobody else could have exposed that much shining gold in one black polka-dot mouth.

TWENTY-FIVE   He got to his feet and approached, making a circling movement with his finger. "Turn? Slow and nice, ah? Hands to the wall, mister."

I did as he said. He pressed the gun to my back and felt in my jacket pockets, took my automatic.

"The hands down now."

"Where is Natividad?"

"Someplace." He laughed, a series of high-pitched pump noises from his sinuses that made his gun jump. "I tell to her, Miguelito, he throw big carnival party and he ask for his sweetie pussy-baby Natividad to come. I bring her the costume to put on so she look like condesa and not five-cent whoor and the condesa go, and the smart ones to make the watch by the door, they sleep. Smart, ah? Ah! Ah! Ah!"

One variable in all this Caprio had not fully harnessed. The sometime craving of a bubble-brain girl for her Miguelito, when she was not too dim to remember his name.

Coolio backed to a chair in the corner, picked up a manila-wrapped package and threw it across the room. It landed on the bed.

"You are invite to party too. Look in there." I stood where I was. "You don't hear good? Snap it up!"

The change in him was impressive. He moved with coordination, even with a certain cool economy and springiness, his eyes were clear. He made a sideways rocking gesture with the gun. I went over and reached for the package.

"Nice, nice," he said. "Beautiful and pretty."

I got the string off and the wrapping paper came open.

Inside was a complete Chinese mandarin outfit, a long robe of green-and-gold brocade, temple headgear to match, a full-face mask shaped into unperturbed Buddha plumpness.

"Where is this party?"

"Too hard for you to find. I take you." He gestured toward the costume. "First you get dress, dig?"

I unfolded the robe and slipped it on. It was so long and full that it covered my jacket sleeves and shoes amply, that was one thing. Also, there were heavy layers of padding, pillows, to give the comic impression of a fat man. It was so stuffed and hung in such deep folds that nothing of the wearer's stance and gait could come through.

"The hat and the mask," Coolio said.

I slipped them on. I was totally gone from view, dropped into a hole.

"Now I explain you somethings," Coolio said. "Better listen. I keep like this—" he slipped the gun inside his ballooning shirt "—we walk in the street by your friend. First you, then me. You do one things, one teentsie little things not to my likings, I shoot. You like to give me these chance, I be gas."

"What about Natividad?"

"You make her to do things against her true friends. How you think her friends gone to like these?"

"What has Brod done to her?"

"So far, nothings! Absolutely! He gone to talk whole things over with you, ah? Maybe you save nice little whoor-baby. You see these now? You maybe save her. Ah? You make me kill you, girl is finish, all accounts of you." He opened the door and beckoned to me to go first. "I tell you true," he said as he followed me out, "one funny business, and over. You hear the birdies that ain't there."

We went down the stairs. The lobby, I could see as we came into it, was overrun with more merrymakers, some in costumes, and the restaurant-bar just beyond was livelier than before. I felt Coolio's finger at my back. "In there," he said in my ear. "The bar. For the kicks."

He put his hand on my shoulder and steered me across
the lobby, his other hand in his sacklike blouse. In the bar
wigged and masked figures ranging from monks and Robin
Hoods to snake charmers and can-can girls were milling
around in hit-or-miss hopped merengues, colliding and veering.
Three weed-mired musicians were slumped in the corner, playing guitars and whining in close harmony an idiot song:

> *Todo el mundo con la lengua fuera*
> *Todo el mundo con la lengua fuera*
> *Un poquito pa' 'lante y un poquito pa' fuera*
> *Un poquito pa' 'lante y un poquito pa' fuera*

Everybody's got his tongue hanging out, everybody's got his
tongue hanging out, somewhat to the front and somewhat out,
somewhat to the front and somewhat out. Nothing more
pertinent than that.

Several people, men and women, were in the corner with
hands joined, snaking around in a circle to some jogging tempo
not the singing trio's. From the full-lunged blasting way in
which they brought out the words "Agua! Agua!" time after
time, as unrelated to the musical accompaniment as their
everywhichway feet, it was clear that the faces behind the
witch and Frankenstein masks were American. Whirling with
their shouts of "Agua!" and heel-heavy unpatterned steps, they
swept toward us and the nearest ones tried to pull us in.

Coolio's hand tightened on my shoulder. I stood rigid.
Coolio managed to pull free but his manner was altogether
merry as he took his hand from me and caught the ringleader
of the group, a heavy man in the uniform of a Scots High-
lander, complete with bagpipes. The man stopped trying to
wheeze bongo rhythms from his pipes and said to Coolio in
English, "Well if it isn't Emmett Kelly. Wuhyuh want Em
boy?"

"Listen, my friend," Coolio said pleasantly, "you want to
go to a hot party? My friend, American fellow, has house
here, he give big party. He say to me, bring nice people from

all over. Free drinks, toprates band, have a living ball. You go? O.K.?"

The group had stopped dancing while their leader talked with Coolio. The man turned to the others and said, "Wanna go a party? How's bout it folks? Plenny a hootch!" The others began to pop their enthusiasm: "Ess blow iss dump!" "Lead a way Georgie boy Georgie!" "Off to the races!" "Agua! Agua!" One of the women did a lead-footed pirouette and shouted, "I'm Carmen Meander and I'm wi-yild about parties!" A man slapped her across the rear. "Carbine Marimba don't come from Cooba beautiful," he said. "From Payru Boliviar there-bouts and she's got bananas in her hair. Whatter we waiting for let's go!"

"Less go!" Coolio said. "Hot party! All nice good Americans! Please to come with me, folks!"

We headed for the door. Coolio kept his hidden gun against me while with his other hand he kept tugging at the drunks until we were in the middle of the group. As we came down the steps and along the walk to the street I saw Caprio in his car look over at our party carefully but with no special interest.

We got to the sidewalk and turned east, following Coolio's instructions. We started past the green Pontiac.

In movies, in such spots, the lead actor can at the right split second execute a faster-than-the-eye turn, slamming the wind out of his captor and simultaneously slicing the gun from his hand. What constantly amazes in these pictures is that the gun so seldom goes off. But the statistical fact is that, fast as the fastest hero's arms and legs can move, a finger poised on a gun trigger has less distance to travel and must therefore complete its move faster. As we passed the Pontiac sweat was crawling over my back. "No funny moves," Coolio said low in my ear. "Be nice good Chinamans." "Boliviar is where they have the tin mines," somebody said. "Venezoola." "Venezoola what?" a woman said. "Venezoola is where at Carbarn Veranda comes from." "Rio dee Janeerio," the woman said. "Now you listen to me it's Venezoola," the man said. We went on past the Pontiac, my teeth aching at the roots with tension.

We went two blocks east on Segunda, turned right and continued on for a block. Everybody was joking and making funny catcalls and yodeling snatches of song, something about you will see her standing across a crowded room, a few bars from "La Cucaracha." We came to a Chevrolet sedan parked in the grassy road and Coolio stopped.

"Listen, friends," he said with all his amiableness, "I juss remember, I got to pick up other people from by the Club Kawama. Beside, hell, car too damn small. Why you don't to take taxi from over there by El Kastillito and we meet you at the party, O.K.?"

They were confused by the turn of events. They stopped singing about enchanted evenings. Where was this place, they wanted to know. Would the man let them in. Who should they say sent them, for Gosh sakes. If it was going to look like they were a lot of free-loading Americans crashing a party, well, heck, etc., etc.

"Thus O.K.," Coolio said. "You tell to the taxi man, take you up Avenida Segunda, Second Avenue, to where is gate for Du Pont estate. You say to gatekeeper, where is house of, ah, Mr. Vincent Caprio, hah, hah, nice American man. Vincent is my excellent friend. You say him I send you, happy clown name Bartolome Caro send you, he give you the big kiss and open door wide. We see you over there, ah?" He turned to me and said, "O.K. you take the wheel, Nicolaso? My lousy damn eyes no good to drive at night."

I went around and climbed in on the driver's side. Coolio slipped in next to me, hand still in his shirt.

"Have good time, friends!" he called to the puzzled group standing in the gutter grass. "Agua! Agua! O.K., friends! Less go, Nicolaso."

I started the car and drove off. At his instructions I con-

tinued along on a parallel to Segunda, going over the pitted
narrow passages of the fishermen's section. He was laughing to
himself, making those high sounds in his sinuses.

"It pleasure me to do the business with gringo peoples,"
he said. "Very good neighbors, good. Do all to help the backward nations and colonials and the ones without the shoes.
Yes, yes."

He was so pleased with things in general that he began to
beat with his big gold signet ring on the dashboard, a fast,
syncopated rhythm. To this accompaniment he sang a couple
lines from the song about everybody with his tongue hanging
out, then in midpassage shifted the tempo and began on new
words:

> *Tome chocolate, paga lo que debe*
> *Tome chocolate, paga lo que debe*

Drink some chocolate and pay what you owe, drink some
chocolate and pay what you owe.

How make a whole arm traveling several feet go faster
than one finger going a fraction of an inch? Sing about that.
How do you beat the muscle-speed statistics? No songs about
that.

TWENTY-SIX   "Straight," he said when we got
past the lagoon and were approaching the junction below the
airport. Left was for Cárdenas, ahead was the highway running
along the coast to Matanzas.

Matanzas—sounded like a yawn that went with plump
fruits and green growths, but it was Spanish for killings. Bill-
ings, Montana. Killings, Cuba.

"I can't see with this mask on," I said.

"Take it off," he said in a bored voice. "Nicolaso my
friend."

Caprio's men were around but he let me drop the mask.
Datum.

From the black circle overlaying the mouth his tongue
came out and moved over the lips. Going vague, and mouth
dry—a datum. Head dropped to an extent.

He had a gun—his advantage. But he had some kind of
habit, one I didn't have. That could be my advantage.

"I'm thirsty," I said.

He gave no sign of hearing.

"Is it far? I'm very thirsty."

The hand on the gun shifted a little.

"You know about thirst," I said. "You hate the Yankee
dollar but want dollars. Want to blow up the States and look
for bookings in the States. If you didn't get your language
and needs from the Americanos you wouldn't have any language or needs. Plenty of imported thirsts. Zoot thirsts, cool
thirsts, hip thirsts, go thirsts. Tome Coca-Cola, paga lo que
debe. Sing that, if your mouth's not too dry. Todo el Coolio
con la lengua fuera. Sing it, why don't you? Your mouth too
dry to sing?"

His free hand came down from the dashboard and closed
over the other one. To hold the other back or what?

"Make the jokes," he said. "Smart Nicolaso."

"You're too thirsty to shoot anybody. Agua, agua. Wouldn't
you like to have your mouth all wet and not with such an
itch? Agua, agua. Anything, to stop the itch. Tome alguna
cosa, paga lo que debe."

"Keep on to ask for it," he said tonelessly. Tongue curled
over his upper lip, going back and forth. He raised the gun
until it was level with my chest. "Talk some more."

With eyes on me he bent and took hold of something
at his feet. He lifted it to his lap and rested his free hand on
it. The bongo drums. His fingers moved with slow cat
crawling over the skin.

"What kind of stuff are you on?" I said. "Something you
pull up the nose? They say it's terrible when you're overdue

and keep on not taking it. Your mouth gets like blotting paper. Tongue hangs out, all the way to the front, all the way outside."

"I tell you true," he said softly, "I shoot you in the head. Drive or not drive, what I care."

"Tongue like burning hot dust. Water won't help. Nothing helps only—"

"Fookface talk! Talk and talk!"

His free hand took the drums and turned them upside down in his lap. His fingers moved over the wooden plugs covering the undersides of both drums.

"No liquids help," I said. "The stuff causes the thirst. More stuff is the only thing. . . ."

His fingers were at the edge of one plug, where there was a small recess. They pried. The wooden disc came loose, he dropped it between his legs. His hand, trembling, reached inside and brought out a small bottle.

"If you take a stiff dose," I said, "the bad feeling goes away. Mouth gets wet, it's the first thing that happens. One real dose. . . ."

His fingers clamped hard on the bottle. They came away and went to the metal cap. They played with the cap, jerked away, went back.

They began feverishly, twistingly, crushingly, rushingly to unscrew the cap.

The cap was thrown aside. The long fingers gripped the bottle. His eyes did not leave my face. They did not blink.

"Talk, talk, talk! Dirt! Bastard!"

It was a hope-relinquishing groan. The bottle went to his mouth. His head tilted back and he drank, one long after-everything gulp. His eyes stayed on me.

There was a thanksgiving gargle from deep in his throat. He drank again, then a third time, making more salvation-time noises.

"In bastard fook eye," he mumbled. "One bullet each

eye." But the fullness of purpose was out of his voice and he was losing some of his hard-core look.

A heavy, pungent, bitter-prune smell in the air. His hand was cupped loosely under the bottle, by the dim light from the speedometer I could make out the label on it: JUGO DE CIRUELA. Prune juice. I had heard that the young hip set back on the Key had a new kick—ashes scraped from opium pipes and mixed into ordinary cooking wine from which the alcohol had been boiled away. Yen Shee Suey. Smelled and tasted like prune juice.

Opium could slow up the reflexes by significant seconds. Datum. Opium ashes mixed in cooking wine—

We had just passed the cement road marker reading KILO-METER 14. Almost halfway to Matanzas.

"Left eye first," Coolio said without moving his lips. He was looking at me but his head was down and a little loose.

We passed the KILOMETER 13 sign. He sat up with an effort and he seemed again to be held together only by skin and containing clothes.

"Left," he said.

There was a dirt turnoff immediately ahead. I slowed down and took the turn. All the way, I noted, we had seen very few cars and nothing that looked like a patrol.

We drove for what I judged to be almost ten minutes, jogging over the bumps. Then Coolio pointed again and said, "Right." It was a narrow lane just wide enough for one car. I turned into it. Ahead, some distance off, was a large barn-humped structure. "Park there." He was pointing at another car standing near the building. When our headlights swung over to it I saw that it was an old Cadillac. It looked familiar—the car we'd driven to the Salsipuedes ñañigo in.

I pulled up. Odor of rank ferment everywhere, sharp and biting in the nose. I switched the motor off. There were piles of open-sided crates near the building, filled with empty bottles.

Liquor bottles. The fruit-working smell was a distillery smell.

Coolio was out of the car and around to my side, moving water-slowed, beckoning to me. I went along with him toward the building. He walked as though his parts were not in tune, arms making brusque at-something movements and hips floating in a less linear time.

There was no ground-floor entrance at this side of the building. A flight of rough wooden steps led up to swinging barn-style doors about twelve feet up. There was a sort of loading platform there with block pulleys hung overhead, and one of the doors was open. Coolio pointed to the stairs.

I stopped when I reached the platform, near the door that was closed.

"Inside." He prodded me with his gun.

"Where's Natividad?"

He backed up against the closed door and called toward the opening, "Hey, whoor-baby! Natividad!"

Natividad's voice from somewhere inside, childish and tentative, not so much in answer as to register uncatalogued grievances: "Here. I wait."

"No more wait!" Coolio called. "I bring the boyfriend! Come, I send him in!"

He came toward me and pressed the gun against the padding over my back, pushing me to the open door. Natividad's voice floated out again, coming closer, excitement growing in it: "Miguel! Miguelito!"

My mouth was dry, Venezoola, Killings, lengua fuera, Nicolaso, tome chocolate, Yen Shee Suey dry as I swung my elbow into his stomach and twisted my body. Wild sound of pain from him and the gun went off.

With the same movement, smelling something scorched and thinking without fully believing it that the bullet had gone through the back padding without touching me, I brought the edge of my palm down on his wrist. He made another abdominal sound, higher, and the gun dropped. Both my hands were clawed in the material at his shoulders and heaving him through the open door before his groan stopped.

Yen Shee Suey could make fingers go slower than arms.

I was on all fours, reaching for the gun as Coolio from inside began to scream, "No shoot! No! Is me, Jesú, no— Ah!"

Three guns had gone off, maybe it was four. One bullet spanged into the closed door above my head, then another. Coolio was wailing.

Three or four people shooting at Coolio from inside. Thinking it was not Coolio.

Natividad's stretched voice, still closer: "Miguelito? Why do you shout? Miguelito? Why do they shoot?"

She seemed to be near the door. Coolio was screaming and blubbering. The shooting stopped, started again.

Natividad once more: "Aaaaiiiiiii." High and sirening, the far end of grievance.

Feeling silly but not knowing what else to do, I dropped to my stomach and crawled through the door.

TWENTY-SEVEN   To my left a shape rocking and making thin sounds, ai, ai. I turned that way. Footsteps, yelling. Someone, Coolio, was running down a flight of steps, screaming, "Shoot! Shoot! I told you no! Sons of cockroach mothers!" Sounds of running below. A voice from down there and far back: "How could we know? We thought—" It was an easy, complacent voice, familiar to me. "Thought! As good as shoot my arm off!" Another voice, false-friendly: "You were to stay outside!" Footsteps again. "Now you are happy with your games?" This third voice was gruff, full of quick business. I knew it too. I knew them all.

My eyes were adjusting to the dark. I saw that what I lay on was not a full floor but a staging. From this strip extended two more walks, thinner ones, that cut the big room in three. Bulge-sided wooden vats rose up from the ground floor, up above the level of these stagings, separated by the catwalks. Rank smell of fruit and vegetable ferment, more than the nose could take.

Downstairs they were shouting and cursing and accounting. Natividad, when I reached her, was sitting on her heels, holding to her shoulder and rocking.

"Natividad," I whispered, "it's me, Roberto. Do you understand? It's Roberto. Are you hurt bad?"

"To love me and to shoot me," she said, rocking. "Is this the way? To love and to shoot."

"Listen to me, I'm Roberto, not Miguel. Coolio tried to kill us. If you make noise he will come and try again."

Coolio: "Droppings of a goat! You wish to take the arm off totally?" The fawning voice: "Necessary to cut the sleeve. To approach the place." The no-nonsense one: "Always your way is the way. They are far in the fields now. All you know is games."

"Soon I will fix your shoulder," I whispered. "We must hide or Coolio will shoot at us again. Be very quiet. Come with me, quietly."

There was no way to get outside. The moon would silhouette us in the open door. If we got through the door, the outside platform was creaky and so were the stairs. If we made it down I could not move fast with the girl. If four of them came looking, they would find us.

"This way," I whispered. "Very quietly, if you wish to live and see Miguelito."

Slowly, testing each plank, I crawled toward the nearest catwalk, helping Natividad along. At the first vat I stopped her with my hands, rose and pointed to the wide mouth, almost at the height of my shoulders. The vat was open, inside, three feet from the top, was some darkish pulpy mass from which came an odor of spent fireworks, turning wines, curdle, swamp drainage.

From a railing overhead a great iron pulley hook hung down into the vat, and suspended from the hook was a bucket partway dipped into the muck. Iron rungs ran up the vat from the catwalk.

"Come after me. Remember, say one word and they will find us and shoot us."

I started up the rungs, pulling Natividad by the hand.

There were not four of them. Five. Far to the rear a new voice spoke.

Voice with no one narrow quality but used with full deliberation, like an instrument. Meaning its words, expecting all who heard to take this meaning and follow it. I had never heard it but I had been waiting for it and in some way recognized it, its fine inner jewel balances. I felt almost a proprietary interest in this voice:

"I told you there must be no guns."

Footsteps crossing the suddenly still room.

Natividad froze on the iron steps. I reached down and put my arm about her, stroked her cheek, ready to stop her mouth.

Absolute silence. Unseen crawling, squirming.

The new voice: "My orders were: get them and at the proper time bring them to the boat. I made this clear."

Coolio: "You agreed there was necessity to remove them! They could interfere!"

The quiet one: "Now they are removed? Now they will not interfere?"

Natividad began to tremble. "Mig—" she began to say.

I clamped my hand over her lips. "Natividad," I whispered, "you will have to wait to see Miguel. Only a little while. If you talk Coolio will kill you and you will never see Miguel again." I took her under the arm and urged her up the rungs. "Now we must hide. Come with me, quietly."

I slipped my robe off, looped it over the mouth of the vat. More voices from below. "We must leave," the quiet voice said. "There are fincas near here, I saw them when I was hiding in the fields. Somebody will have heard the guns." Coolio: "It is necessary to find those two." The gruff one: "You lost them. You find them. Go and whistle and they will come to lick your hand. Play them drum solos on your empty head."

Holding to the pulley chain, I swung over. One arm looped on the hook, I held out my free hand to Natividad. She held on, lowering herself until she was cradled in my arm. Our chins were just free of the mealy liquid. In the slimed pungency that rose from this slop was a wormy, wood-rotting, sickly sweet edge that I thought I recognized. Some abomination that, subdued and infiltrated, prettied partway out of noxiousness, was yet present in absinthe.

The fawning one: "Would it not be good to look for them?"

The gruff one: "Perhaps there is a sign upstairs. I will go."

The lazy, complacent one, after his long silence: "Do not trouble. I will do it."

The quiet one: "Look if you must. But quickly."

Footsteps. Creaking on stairs. The walker reached the upstairs staging near the door, evidently went to the door, came back, hesitated, set out on the catwalk leading to our vat. I was holding Coolio's gun in the hand that supported Natividad. I raised it and got a firmer grip on the butt. "No words now," I whispered. "One is coming to kill us. Be very quiet."

The footsteps came closer. They stopped only yards from us. A moment of silence, then with a snap an overhead light went on. The man had found a hanging bulb and pulled its chain, the light rays slanted into the mouth of the vat across our faces. I raised my gun higher.

More footsteps. They stopped directly outside our vat. I watched the rim, waiting for a face to appear. I tried to keep the gun pointed at the spot where it would come.

Two hands appeared, the fingers curled over the rim. A face rose up between them. Dark, sweat-run face, lean and sober under a stiff straw hat. Benjamino Francisco looked down into the vat, lips drawn back against the smell, peered down like an observer at a cockfight pen and saw us. One of his hands had a gun in it.

He looked at us. His gun remained as it was, drooping. He looked at Natividad, then at me, with curiosity, then with disapproval, then with full and unalterable disgust. I watched the gun in his hand, keeping mine aimed at his face. His gun still drooped.

The quiet voice from below: "Benjamino—put that light out."

The face stayed another moment. It scowled, the head went from side to side. It disappeared. The light went out. Footsteps again. They went along the staging, down the stairs, across the loose-planked floor below.

"Find anything?" the gruff voice said.

"They left not even their halitosis," the lazy mellifluous voice of Benjamino Francisco said.

"Of course," the quiet voice said. "When our friend loses a thing he loses it well. This is his true work."

"Is the boat not too dangerous?" the gruff one said. "Now, with Garmays dung knows where?"

"We have no choice," the quiet one said. "My staff of geniuses in short pants does not give me choices."

"We follow the same plan?" Benjie said.

"The same," the quiet one said. "Repeat your orders."

"To go to Bacunayagua," Benjie said. "To leave the car at the appointed place. To take the bus to Havana. There, all afternoon, to have the other car in readiness, on the Malecón, for when the professor comes."

"Past Matanzas you will be safe," the quiet one said. "I do not think you will find trouble before Matanzas. Perhaps Caprio does not have the men to watch the road. In any case it is not known that you are with me. You can start now."

Sound of one man leaving the building. In another moment the Cadillac started up and drove off.

"Now we go," the quiet one said. "If something apart

from the plan happens, we will have to invent. It is not good, but my staff of chickens has made it this way."

Feet scraping across the floor. They went outside, crunched fragments of bottles on the hard ground, stopped. Car doors slammed. The Chevrolet motor started up, raced, the car took off.

They were gone, that improbable crew, the gruff beret-wearing doorman from Millie's, the taffy-toned clerk from the Havana cellar office of the false-label absinthe industry, Coolio, who was partial to the flavor of prune and lost things, Benjamino Francisco the swivel-headed, who talked to the east and talked to the west, and Miguel, Michel, Mihail, Michael, Mike, alias mi esposo, the soft-spoken, the granite, who hid in henequén fields and loathed to improvise, but would. Off to new improvisations.

Natividad spoke up for the first time: "Oh, Miguel, it hurts."

TWENTY-EIGHT   We kept to the back road. I carried the Chinese robe in my hand. It was hard to see, the moon was gone again, but we passed through what seemed to be orange groves, then fields of tall and thick sugar cane. After fifteen minutes the rows of spiked henequén started and from then on it was all henequén, most likely the International Harvester plantation.

We trailed behind us a raw absinthe reek. The slime was in my hair, on my eyelids, over my skin. Natividad seemed to have forgotten about her wound, as she stumbled along her head was down and only occasionally she opened her mouth to say something unfastened like "They leave, one by one. All, in time," or "He brings the pretty bracelet from the Canada." Once she stopped in the road and said to me significantly, "I fell down today and hurt my knee." Shoulder cut open but it was the knee that held the hurt. Under one arm, I noticed, she was carrying a bottle of absinthe with a crème de menthe label, she'd picked it up as we were leaving the distillery.

On foot, over the winding back roads, it would take hours to get to Varadero. Still, I was afraid to go to the highway and try flagging a car. There was no guarantee that Brod's people had gone straight to the lagoon.

Without warning, Natividad fell to the ground, holding her knee and moaning. She told me, face full of child's hurt, that the knee was in pain something terrible and she couldn't take another step. Her shoulder was bleeding again—she was weak from loss of blood.

I carried her into the field and set her down between two chest-high henequén plants. She was crying, not loud, a low rhythmic humming to herself. With the pipe reamer on my watch chain I pried the cork out of the absinthe bottle and gave her some to drink. I tore some strips from the lining of the mandarin robe and made them up in pads, washed her wound with the absinthe, put dressings on it. When I removed her gummy court dress and underthings she seemed not to notice. She took more gulps from the bottle, murmuring something about "Mamacita makes very good wine from bananas." Her body was delicate and undernourished, the flesh thin and full of hollows, the unused and previous body of a child. I wiped off her skin as best I could, pulled her to a sitting position and slipped the robe on her.

"Now," I said, "lie back and rest. Your knee will be better soon."

She dropped back, lost in the folds of brocade, and lifted the absinthe bottle to her lips. Lips pouted, body in a crib huddle, she said in a singsong infant lisp, "I like the wine from bananas. Mamacita makes it the best." Her lips made sucking reaches at the bottle, rhythmically. "Mm, mm, mm," she said in greedy nursery rhythm. She giggled. "Funny! Huh-hay! Hah-hai!"

The sky was mottled, with black-centered and wisp-edged laminations of clouds. On her back, bottle in mouth, "Mama makes the wine," she said to the clouds. "Papa takes the boat. Mama gives him the bottle of the wine. Because they have not the bananas and the banana wine there in Spain. In Spain they have the olives, little one. How can they make the wine of the olives. From the olives comes the oil. One does not put the bananas in the oil of the olive, no, little dear. Olives are one thing and bananas are a thing again. Stop asking all the questions, little love." She was almost singing the words, a disheveled litany. "Come back to us, papa. Always wear your muffler." She sat up suddenly, spilling some of the yellow liquid down her chin. She was quite drunk now. "Putsch, what is putsch? Not an olive. Against the Messerschmitts the firm and bold cadres and down with dung caudillos. Do not forget the muffler, my prize. Come back, little papa." She began to cry again.

I took her in my arms. She was frail, shoulders too small and thin for opposition, and all her body abandoned to an ancient sorrow.

"Do you remember your parents, Natividad? Why did your father leave Mexico? To fight in Spain?"

"You have the delicate lungs, my husband," she sobbed. "You are for the books not the guns. When there is a cold five miles away, you catch it the first. The winds blow there in the olive trees. Do not go from us, Arturo. It is not your country. This little baby girl, this is your country. A family is also a country, Arturo. Dear one. My only."

Some leavetaking had been witnessed and heard at the beginning of years by a child and the child was back, speaking all parts, sobbing another's sobs and believing them her own, appropriating to herself old losses seen and overheard but not then comprehended.

"Your mother didn't want your father to fight in Spain? Was that it, Natividad? She wanted him to stay in Mexico with the family?"

She was beyond reach. "Beat down the Messerschmitts from the sky. With the one proletarian fist. The fist as big as the world. To smash down the generalissimo and the Moors and this will make my family safe. My family has many members, most dear to me. Those in the olive groves are also my family. Can the muffler keep out everything?" Her voice was surprisingly deep now, filled with ringing male energies. But in the middle of the eerie salvaged speech she collapsed and her tone became stretched and lamenting again. "There they shoot at him among the olives. Where are the bombs and the Moors? There they steal him away in the Cataluña city, in the trunk. Are these the Messerschmitts? Where is his muffler now." Sobs began to shake her whole body. "One by one, they go. All go, and we wait. We wait, and they shoot. They will not come back with the bracelets. Dear one, dear one. Oh, my husband."

I felt my scalp tightening. "In the trunk, Natividad? In the olive grove?"

There is no banana wine. A cordial is made from bananas —in Cuba. Arturo is a Cuban name as well as Mexican.

I felt along the edge of her ear, to the junction with the neck. Behind the edge, at the joining place, was a small hard dot, a mole.

"Lie back," I said. I pushed her down gently. "On your side, yes, so the shoulder will not hurt. There. Close your eyes and rest. Soon the knee will be all better."

Her eyes were closed. Her head dropped in drunken looseness. As carefully as I could I lifted the robe back to expose her skimpy thighs. I leaned over to see but there was not enough light. I put my fingers under her left thigh, below the buttock, and moved them around. "Go to sleep," I whispered, though there was no reason to whisper. "Everything is all right. Go to sleep now." Close to the buttock, over on the inside, I found it, a thick diagonal welt more than an inch long.

Her eyes opened and she watched me, a knowing and trained voluptuous smile widening the mouth.

"Hey, sport," she said in English, voice beery and from the gut. "Little jiggoo cost you ten bucks, hey, O.K.? I give it to you like nobody's business, sailor boy. Ten bucks, what you say?"

I turned the coat down.

"It is all right, little girl," I said. "Go to sleep."

She woke up fully. She sat up and threw herself on me, her hands reaching for my hands to bring them back.

"Miguel! You are the only one! I die of the waiting! Now! I have been waiting only for this!"

I got her hands to her sides.

"Miguel is gone. You will see him later. Here." I gave her the bottle. "It will do you good if you sleep."

Once again she began to cry.

"Always go," she said bitterly. "They go, always, one by one."

I stroked her forehead.

"Go to sleep, Luz," I said. "Sleep, Luz."

The grievances went out of her face. She looked only puzzled, vastly puzzled, as her eyes searched my face.

"Luz?"

She did not turn away when I put the bottle between her lips. She took one long swallow, another. When she dropped back and closed her eyes her face was remarkably peaceful, beautiful again in its purest little-girl way. The sobs came only now and then, irrelevantly.

"Luz. Luz." She was murmuring to herself, lips curved in a secret child's smile of contentment. "Oh, Luz go up and Luz go down, and Luz go all and all and all around," she half sang, half whispered, in some forgotten playground rhyme, a song of seesaws. "Scratch my head." I put my fingers to her head and rubbed her scalp. "Nice, Barto. Good, Barto. All and all and all around. Uh, ay, ah, ai."

I stroked her head. The humming stopped. She was fast asleep, a smile curling her pigtail, pink bow, confirmation flower lips.

Nice, Barto. Good, Barto.

The shoulder bandage was already soggy with blood. I had
to get a doctor—go into Varadero or at least find a phone
nearby. Had to locate Caprio. I made sure she was covered,
and started out.

After some minutes of walking I came to a crossroad that
seemed to go in the direction of the highway. I turned into it.
In ten minutes I was at the highway, the ocean pounding just
the other side. I began to walk east, keeping close to the henequén rows. Twice cars came along and I was tempted to signal
them, but each time I got too worried about the risk and
ducked back into the fields.

Good, Barto. Nice, Barto.

I passed the concrete marker for KILOMETER 11, then the
one for KILOMETER 10. I must have been going for upwards of
twenty minutes when I heard something approaching—the
sound of horse's hooves.

Round and round.

I hid again. In two or three minutes a shape rose out of
the darkness ahead. It was a typical country horse, small and
pony compact, with an expression of what-can-you-do-about-it.
Astride him was a campesino, a slight Cuban dressed in coarse
white-cotton pants and blouse, kerchief around neck, raveling
soft straw hat pulled down over eyes, heavy knee-length laced
boots of the usual country style on his legs. The man seemed
almost asleep as his horse jogged along, body bent and loose,
head rolling. He had a burlap pack slung to his saddle. Likely
he owned a small finca hereabouts or worked on the planta-
tions. It was Saturday. Saturdays these guajiros went to town
to buy supplies, returning to their field huts dog tired. You
saw them by the highways at night, going along half asleep.

When he was some yards away I stepped out.

"Hello! Good evening, friend! Have you got a minute?"

It was hard to talk because I was crying.

His head jerked up and he pulled the horse to a stop. He
shook his head, trying to come awake. I could hardly see his

face, what with the kerchief over the chin and the hat down, but he seemed to have a friendly though alert look.

"Good evening," he said, with the soft tones of country speech. "Is there something wrong, friend? You have trouble?"

"Someone is hurt. I must get to Varadero and find a doctor."

"I am sorry to hear of this." His hand came up from the saddle, a heavy military revolver in it. "Mr. Garmes," he said in brisk English, "drop your gun. Two men are watching you. They will shoot if necessary."

The English was as perfect as the country Spanish of a moment before. A quiet voice, extraordinarily quiet, but with the suggestion of power in it, the tone of a man used to giving orders and having them obeyed. All and all around. I let the gun drop.

TWENTY-NINE   "Avelino," he said. "Ipólito." Two figures came toward him from the trees: the bouncer from Millie's, the absinthe-warehouse clerk. They stood on the roadside close to the horse, covering me with their guns. "Come over here, please, Mr. Garmes," Brod said. He dismounted as I crossed over.

The face remained partially hidden. I had only the impression of efficient cool eyes, a nose without curve or larding and the nostrils meager, lips in a ruled alert line, indications of a narrow but square and outslanting jaw behind the kerchief. A face cut to functional minimums, bones compressed and asserting themselves, all parts built close to a long up-and-down median line. He was my height and remarkably lean, even in the loose peon cottons his structure seemed one of springy wires: mechanism needing only fingertip triggerings for total and fast reactions. His air was Barto's, essentially—a superficial laziness which was rather muscle economy: a constant mobilization for basic calls and only those.

"We had not hoped for this," he said. "We were watching for patrols. You are, we might say, a bonus." There was no rise of humor in his regulated voice. "Where is the girl?"

"I don't know."

"She must have been with you."

"You might consult Caprio. She'll be with him soon."

"Not too soon, I think. It's a long walk to Varadero, and she does not have a notable sense of direction."

"Would I turn her over to you?" I said in a rage. "For more target practice?"

He seemed to be nodding. "Certainly not. Coolio's sense of play would not amuse you any more than it does me." He was intolerably on my side. "I'm told she was hurt. Is it bad?"

"Not bad enough to keep her from getting to Caprio."

"I'm glad to hear that," he said, with a simple sincerity that made me shake. "Natividad's been hurt quite enough. Merely staying alive is a terrible matter with her." He turned to his men. "Wherever she is, she can do us no harm. We will move fast." He went from English to Spanish without a pause.

"Natividad?" I said. "Call her by her right name."

"Ah?" For the first time his tone rose above the military-command evenness. "Barto never knew—you understand? I kept it from him."

"To save him pain?" My fists clenched.

"Precisely for that reason."

"Not, just possibly, to keep him from coming after you twice as fast?"

"Mr. Garmes, for thirteen years he was coming after me as fast as his legs would carry him. How can you make a man going at top speed go faster?" He addressed the other two: "Take him to the car. Keep back from the road. I will ride down and meet you." The two men moved over to me, one on either side. Brod spoke to them once more: "You are not to harm him. For a thing even small you will answer to me."

He swung up on his horse and rode off to the east. I started for the tree line with the others, then along with them eastward.

"Phew," the bouncer, Avelino, said in his hoarse, barking voice. "He stinks."

"I have not yet met an Americano who did not stink to the Milky Way," Ipólito the clerk said.

"Not to touch him. I could put six bullets through his ribs and not touch him once."

"I could make a steak from his face with a whip and not one touch."

"As a friend he comes to our house. A nice boy from Mexico City. I tell him, feel that this is your home. Have some on the house."

"In our warehouse he is one of us, I discuss the matters of the distillery with him. I give him the location. I regret that I cannot give him all the desired news of Miguel. If Miguel is in the distillery, I say, I have string beans for hair. It is all between friends and comrades."

"Why does Miguel wish such a stink alive? Alive, he stands up and we must look at him and smell him."

"He would be of immense value dead, this stink. Dead, he could be thrown to the barracudas and the sharks. His nice gray suit would fit me as to order, if the stink of Yanquis could but be removed."

We were in the sweet perfumed open, above us the stretch of cloud-stacked sky, off not far to our left the pocked coral beach and beyond the riding wide sea, openness to all sides, but with these two soft-talking pigs at my sides and my hands useless in my pockets, and with Brod waiting ahead in the woods, I felt barrelled, smothered, in a vat and obscene liquids lifting their scummed top higher and higher. It was difficult to breathe—there was pressure on my chest.

We entered a lime grove. There, safe from eyes in a small clearing, was Coolio's Chevrolet sedan. Coolio and another

man were leaning against a fender and standing with them was
Brod, his horse off to one side tethered to a joshua tree. Coolio
had removed his make-up and was dressed in a zooty purplish
suit with a deep-blue stripe running through it. His left arm
was in a sling, the jacket sleeve hanging empty. His eyes stayed
with me as the three of us approached. "Big cowboy," he said.
The thin and drawn-in man next to him, with his reticule
moustache, I recognized too: the technician from the Sociedad
store who concocted superior drums.

Brod raised his hand: there was an immediate coming to
order in everybody.

"There will be no more games. The next one who departs
from his orders, I will kill." He looked around at the serious
faces. "We have now a better way to go than the *Easy Rider*.
Nobody, nobody imagines I will go near the boat of Boyar,
the *Tiger*. Mr. Garmes will help us to use the *Tiger*. Pupi."

The drum technician stepped forward.

"Pupi, you will swim across the lagoon from this side and
board the *Easy Rider*."

"Miguel." The man looked worried. "Is it entirely sure
they will not be watching?"

"They have not enough men to watch everywhere. They
wish us to think they have more than they have. If they are
watching at the lagoon—"

"They will stop me, no?"

"You must not make yourself to be seen."

"But if they see me?"

"Perhaps they will take you. Perhaps. I am not sure." Pupi
looked more puzzled. "If they see you from a distance they
may think it is me. Will they want to take me?" Brod seemed
to be occupied with his thoughts for a moment. "It is a question of what they want. They act now as though they wish
only to take me for murder. Benjamino has reported this. It
is to be considered whether this is their true wish. . . . Tell
Brooke not to go too fast. I wish to meet with him one half

hour after we start. This is important." Brod turned to Coolio, pointed to the bongos under Coolio's good arm. "No un- needed luggage," he said. "Get rid of those."

Coolio clutched the drums and smiled at me with a mean- ingfulness I could not understand.

"They are my best instruments, Miguel. I need these."

Brod took the drums and weighed them appraisingly in his hands. He shook them vigorously. There was the rattle of a loose object inside.

"Yes, you need them," Brod said. "They are filled with your needs." He handed the drums back. "If I see you open- ing them once, the drums and the bottle go in the sea. This is a promise." He gave me a quick look which I also could not understand. He went to the car and opened the front door. "Pupi, you will drive. Ipólito, in back with us."

Brod held the back door open for me. He and Ipólito took seats on either side of me while the others squeezed in the front. Pupi backed the car out to the road and turned toward Varadero.

"You think the road is safe?" Avelino said without turn- ing his head.

"We have seen no patrols," Brod said. "Caprio cannot cover everything. The lack of men is his weakness. If he watches the highway it is only at the Matanzas end and the Varadero end. We will leave the car in back of the airport, be- fore the place where there may be watchers."

He was reciting dry syllogisms and checking them against each other for consistency. He nodded: the propositions had passed the test. But even in logical exercises his voice had un- derplayed strength and command ring, hooks on it for all neighboring minds. I was breathing rapidly and the sweating was worse.

"I owe you an apology," Brod said to me. "What hap- pened in the distillery was unforgivable—wanton."

"So long as you're sorry."

"I'd like you to understand my position. We knew you

might interfere with our leaving. You had to be stopped, of
course. Coolio insisted and I had to agree. But my plan did
not include that wretched incident, you must believe that."
He tapped his knee with his fingers, with precise, metronomic
movements. "I don't have much mobility at the moment,
that's the problem. I have to let others handle these matters—
their tastes are not mine."

"No. They shoot people. You use knives."

"Not as a matter of taste, I assure you. Do you think Barto
would have had an *easier* time of it if I'd turned the job over
to—somebody else? I could have done that, you know. One
of the reasons I did it myself was to spare Barto more brutal
treatment. You won't take this in good faith, but it's so—I felt
a certain obligation to him. We had a relationship. If it had
to be done it called for my hand."

"The personal touch." All the venom I was capable of
went into the words.

"It was, among other things, a personal matter. Much as
I dislike having the personal intrude, it was there. It would
have been an evasion to leave everything to outsiders." He
rubbed his nose reflectively with his finger. His hand was surprisingly small and delicate, with the well-tended look of a pi-
anist's. "Our wayward friend there—he's excitable. Under tension he gets more so. He's under considerable tension now—
he and the others have a good deal at stake. A great deal, in
their terms. That doesn't condone what they did under his
overenthusiastic and insufferably sadistic direction, but it may
help to explain it."

"You disapprove of their excesses but you're still with
them. I see no big rifts."

His words, too, were smothering me.

"That's foggy thinking, Garmes. I'm not engaged in es-
thetic pursuits here any more than you are—any more than
Barto was. Where it's a matter of personal taste I'd prefer by
far to associate with Oxford dons. Where unpleasant jobs are
to be done, I work with the unpleasant people who won't

shrink from the job. Do you know what my real love is? Astronomical mathematics. I'm quite good at it, too. But I don't know any astronomical mathematicians who could or would efficiently get me aboard Nelson Boyar's boat." His patient, objective, fact-marshaling, slightly professorial tone did not change as he added: "Lately, as you know, I've had some personnel problems. Rather acute ones. I have to work with the few lumpen leftovers who have a stake in my future. Who can be made to think they have."

Calmly, with no sign of passion or self-tenderness, he was detailing his reasons for working with dregs, and for tricking them into a minute-to-minute loyalty, and the dregs sat there, looking out at the scenery. The most intolerable part was that it was me he chose to confide these monstrosities in. The clear implication was that, by the golden bonds of the elite, I was his natural ally, I would sense and share his nice premises.

"You have my sympathy," I said. "It must be hard—a blow to your sensibilities—to have to associate with people who would shoot at such as me."

But the conversation between spiritual brethren was over. We were coming close to the turn that the highway makes over in back of the airport, the lagoon was just ahead.

"Here," Brod said, leaning forward to tap Pupi.

Pupi drove off the road and parked in the shadow of some palms. We all got out of the car.

"You can start," Brod said to Pupi. "Brooke is to move in exactly—twenty minutes. Swim so as to be not seen."

Pupi went off. In a moment Brod said, "Mr. Garmes, come with me, please," and started east, signaling to the three men to follow. We kept to the trees where there were any, then left the road where it turned south toward the airport. We continued on across the fields, Brod and I in the lead. Suddenly I was aware of someone walking along with us: Avelino. He had come up noiselessly from the rear.

"Miguel," he said in a low, rasping voice. "There is one thing."

Brod said: "He of the drums."

"He will see the true plan and try to spoil it."

"It will need guns to leave him. This is not the time for shooting and noise. Also there is this—we could yet have need for him. We have not many now."

"Already he suspects there are things. This is why I allowed the thing of the distillery, though it was insanity. To show to him it is done his way."

"He suspects nothing of Bacunayagua. He imagines the car of Benjamino in Havana is for Brooke and the plane and car here are to take me to his places."

"He has the eyes. He will see the indications are otherwise. This could make him wild."

"I have the ways to control this. It is of the utmost foolishness to leave him. This could make the others think and worry."

"It would satisfy me to put him aside. I have given the word that all will work as planned."

"I have given the word equally. It will be done my way. Go back now to the others."

Avelino dropped back.

"He of the drums is not going to be happy," I said.

"Happiness," Brod said, "is not on the program here."

We reached the west side of the lagoon, where the bank was weedy and swamp-soft. We were at a point not too far from the entrance to the lagoon, before us was a cluster of small fishing boats and some distance past them was the *Tiger*, its cabin lights on. Brod stopped and called the others.

"Listen to every word," he said. "Ipólito and Avelino, all depends on you. You are good swimmers. Go until you are past the *Tiger*. Those on the boat must absolutely not see you. Swim to the boat underwater and come up only for air. Hide there on the other side of the boat and be ready."

"Where will you be, Miguel?" Ipólito said.

"We three will take this dory. We will row toward the *Tiger* from this side. Mr. Garmes will be seen by his friends.

When we are close Mr. Garmes will call to his friends. They will come to our side. When you hear the call, you will board the boat quickly. There must be no guns. They must be surprised."

The two men nodded.

"Go now," Brod said. "You have five minutes. Wait for the call. Then to move with absolute fastness." The two men left. "Mr. Garmes—into the dory, please. You will sit up front, facing forward."

I climbed in and took the forward seat. Brod and Coolio shoved the boat out until it was floating clear. They stood in the water for some time, holding the small boat against the current. Brod kept looking at his watch. "Now," he said finally to Coolio. They eased themselves into the boat behind me and each one took an oar. The dory headed out from the bank, turned left and began to move toward the sea.

"You don't like to improvise," I said, staring ahead at the leavening shape of the *Tiger*. "Who's going to improvise my call?"

"I make you call," Coolio said.

"Make me. I invite you."

"Be quiet," Brod said to Coolio. "Garmes, you don't have to do anything but be seen. If you try to make a sound I shall be obliged to use my gun on you. I would not like to do that."

"Use a knife," I said. "My back's to you."

The waters lapped with tired slow slaps against the prow. I strained to see the cruiser ahead. I could see its outlines distinctly now, I thought I saw movements on the port side, the side toward us. One shape—two—they seemed to separate and fuse again.

The oars made dripping sounds as they rode out of the water. We pulled closer. I could make out two people leaning against the rail. One moved—a gleam—Connie's golden hair. I heard a low mumbling voice—slurred, drunken—Nelson Boyar's. I could not see a third figure anywhere.

"Coolio," I said, "you are going to be unhappy at Bacunayagua. You think your friend is going to one place but he is going to another place. He and Avelino are planning nice surprises for you—"

"You're wasting your breath, Mr. Garmes," Brod said softly. "Coolio and I are planning the surprises. For Avelino. Coolio has worked out the details himself."

Closer. A stillness behind me. They weren't rowing any more. I looked around. They were both crouched behind me, hiding their faces. Brod pressed his gun into my back.

"Connie!" he called. "Nelson! It's me! I want to come aboard!"

It was uncanny: my voice coming from his mouth. Almost mine, anyway, just bluff enough, nasal enough, with the right amount of Massachusetts salt in it and pitched nicely to my grumbler range. There was a third shape in motion on the boat, hurrying down the steps from the wheelhouse and to the rail to join the other two.

"Robbie?" Connie, prayerfully. "Rob? Is it you?"

"Connie!" Brod called in my voice. "Nelson!"

I simply couldn't breathe. I jumped up.

"Don't listen!" I yelled with all my might. "Connie! They've got me! Look behind—"

As I was rising, spitting the words, my body was turned and heaving at Brod, and in that split second I could see Coolio rising more slowly at the side, oar put away, gun raised by the muzzle in his good hand, mouth open with rage, poised to hit at me. Brod was coming at me as I threw myself his way. With all my strength I closed my arms on him and wrenched to one side, outward from Coolio.

"Robbie!" Connie's taut voice. "Rob! Oh—"

Into the water, locked tight. Down, down into the muddied water, shout stuck in my throat as I was being pulled by the powerful arms and clawing at him but he held on, down and down, and wouldn't let me go. Then—

... down ...

"Son! Son!"

He lay on the deck where I had dumped him, face in the fish entrails we cut up for bait. He stared ahead at a rotting mackerel head which wholeheartedly stared back.

Near his nose, on some decomposing halibut livers, lay the copy of The Golden Ass he'd been reading when I pulled the canvas chair from under him.

I kicked him in the ribs, not hard.

"Son, son," he said in Biblical solemn cadence. "Do you think I'm happy either?"

He'd been sitting too many years in that canvas-backed chair, sketchpad and book on his knees, idle while we others hauled and mended and packed, his embarrassed lips apologiz-

ing for his uselessness even as he held to it as his one anchor
and, with a malice I think he never sensed, kept shoving it
under our noses. Long Fifth Avenue legs crossed, given over
completely to the idea of leisure, to the slump born. Sunday
painter to whom every day was Sunday. With sketchpad to
establish for our proletarian eyes that he, too, had his projects
and his seriousness. He never knew, I suppose, that his lips
were almost always knotted with giveaway apologies. Shame can
get localized.

I kicked him again. Not hard. It was important to know
if there was some slap in the world that would make his eyes
widen.

"Oh, I'm not happy either," he told the mackerel head.

You couldn't even rebel against him, he refused program-
matically to be there.

The book was lying open to an illustration showing a
little jackass, head down, face hopeless, studying his forehooves.
Behind him towered the lovely goddess, dressed in black many-
folded and tasseled mantle embroidered with stars and moons,
bronze rattle in one hand and boat-shaped golden dish in the
other, asp curled round the vessel and its head dancing out,
her breasts jutting free and coiled with snakes, a bright disc
like a mirror circling the goddess's forehead, vipers rising from
both sides of her head to hold this disc and interspersed with
them some ears of corn. Jackass rooted there in his misery,
in a neck-sagging listlessness, goddess lit up with laughter and
outthrusting.

Why didn't he get up and fight? I was seventeen then,
and I had been waiting patiently for ten years for my fists
to get big enough to hit him.

"I know I offend you," he said. "I deserve it and more."

He was talking in his Groton sinusoid way of happiness
and its remoteness, and lying in patched-elbow tweed jacket
and white raveling oxford button-down shirt he began to cry.
His old Harvard Yard-Montparnasse clothes were becoming
older and rattier, from the spread of the patches could be

charted year by year his passage from country-squire Bohemia to plain Skid Row.

"All the perfumes of Arabia in my nostrils," he said to the stinking fish bits. He knew his Apuleius by heart, of course. After twenty years he could recite the attributes and accoutrements of All-Goddess Isis backwards, his one excuse for sitting. "She alone can disentangle the knots of fate, end spells of bad weather, restrain the stars from harmful conjunctions. At her nod winds blow, seeds quicken, buds swell. Pessinuntica, Mother of gods, to the Phrygians, Cecropian Artemis to the Athenians. On Cyprus, Paphian Aphrodite, and for the archers of Crete, Dictynna. Stygian Proserpine to the trilingual Sicilians and ancient Mother of Corn among the Eleusinians. Juno, Bellona of the Battles, Io, Demeter, Hecate, Rhamnubia, but to both races of the Æthiopians the truly named godhead, Mother of the wholesome sea-breezes and the lamentable silences of the world below, Queen Isis, true mistress of song birds and asps."

The mackerel head went on observing him neutrally, nowise enchanted by this recital.

He often pulled this kind of face-saving random scholarship on me. His mind had a tendency to retreat from harsh real sounds into safe quotations anyhow.

"Who told you her name was Isis?" I said. "She doesn't have any fancy name like Aphrodite or Proserpine."

"They all have the one name," he wept. "They nod to the song birds and asps."

"She doesn't send the perfumes of Arabia into anybody's nostrils," I said. "What she smells of is the stink of three-cent fish. Her name is Annie Florence Heixas and she wears a Boston Red Sox cap, no asps. If you thought she was Isis when you married her you ought to get your money back."

"I don't blame her for anything," he got out between his gasps. "Nothing, nothing. They nod as it's their business to nod and we're transformed. That is our business. Son, try to understand, I'm not happy either."

"She didn't turn you into a jackass. She didn't, and your nodding Isis didn't. You took on the shape you felt most at home in."

I could retreat into quotations, too. I was quoting my mother, who liked to give him the facts in her own unclassical language.

"Lucius wanted only to be changed into an eagle and to fly," he whimpered. "Fotis and Pamphilë gave him the wrong magic ointment and instead he became a wretched ass and never flew but was kicked. Did the women give him the wrong potion deliberately? I wish I knew, I would like to know."

It was weird. Through the babble he was keeping up a touch of the game he often played with me at home—the funny catechism he liked to give me to see how well I'd absorbed all the useless information he fed me from all the useless books he bent over.

"Meroë in that inn didn't turn her lover into an ass. She made him a beaver. When the beaver gets scared by hunters he bites off his own testicles and leaves them on the river bank to fool the hounds."

I watched him closely to see if he would react to that, at least. It was one thing from Apuleius he might not remind himself about on his own. Though my mother, without knowing Apuleius, had given him similar reminders many times.

All he said was: "To the hunters it looks as though the beaver has mutilated himself. How are they to know that the beaver would be a man, and never think of mutilations, if not for the magic spells of Meroë?"

And that was all I could take. It was an effort, but I broke out of the magic spell of this game.

"Her name isn't Meroë either!" I said emphatically. "She's Annie Florence Heixas and nobody else, and she never did a thing to you but marry you! If you lost your balls it was your own doing! And not even to put the dogs off the track or anything! Just to lose them, just for the mutilation, that's all!"

The family doctor back in New Bedford had told us over

and over it was not willfulness that made him, an outwardly robust man, into this unsalvageable lump, but a deep sickness in his mind, some strangling rope around his will and application powers. But all that was words. He sat and we worked, this was the daily fact to be gagged on. Who could you blame, unseen rope?

The Apuleius was still there, with the dirty lie of a drawing. I took a swinging kick at it. It sailed up over the railing and dropped away into the water.

"You're not even a beaver or a jackass!" I shouted. "Beavers and jackasses work, they do the jobs they're given to do!" It was one of my mother's strong points.

I looked around in a fury. There, against the base of the winch, was my father's sketching pad. It was open, on the top sheet was a charcoal drawing my father had been working at earlier in the afternoon. While my mother and I had been grunting over the nets he'd been raising his eyes to us and sketching us.

I grabbed the pad and looked at the drawing. There was cunning in it. I was a fair amount bigger than my mother but he'd made me a shrunken and insignificant figure beside her, runty, down-pulled, bent over the heavy nets with the dropped-head and spine-sagged resignation of a donkey or mule. But my mother stood there flared and breast-jutting, the baseball cap she wore was somehow luminous and its long visor shone over her forehead like a crescented halo, looped with squirming snakes, in her hand the fish knife looked to be some magical vessel of gold and the torn strands of net she was cutting away had the thick-bodied writhing quality of eels or snakes, and the polka-dotted red bandana she wore around her neck to catch the sweat had long thick loose ends that somehow had been given the air of live winding things too, asps or whatever, with the dots at their ends largened to beady snake eyes. I had a drained and do-me-in look, of course, and my mother was triumphantly smiling, of course.

I was wild. I tore the thick pad in half and hurled the pieces overboard.

"I wish Ma had some goddamned magic ointment to rub over your goddamned face!" I yelled. "Maybe there's some new stuff that could make you get the hell off your ass and go to work for a change!" One of my mother's oldest prayers, reworked.

"Rob, Rob," he said. "Try to understand, son. Manuel has his story of doubloons and that sustains him. I've lost all my dreams of doubloons."

All morning we'd been hauling catches that would bring three cents a pound in the depression markets, heaving and heaving again because Ma would have taken any interruption of the work as an affront to the sacredness of effort. All morning, partly bent and hip-clamped in his brittleness, mopping his pinkish bald head, old Manuel had kept up his running fable about how in the year 1887, when he was joost a small kid, there east from the Bahomas, in this little coove on a small key, he'd seen the ocean bottom sprinkled with lost gold doubloons, whole damn bottom, and maybe this sommer he and I'd buy us one hell of a boat and go down there and scoople up all these doubloons. All this my father heard from his seat over behind the winch. He listened to all our conversations to prove to himself that nothing that went on among standing people was worth the ultimate sacrifice of standing up. Manuel's stories about the doubloons always made him shake his head. Even fantasy was too much work for him.

"I never saw the doubloons," my father said to the piled entrails with a sob. "You cross your legs and listen to the clock roar and that's all."

It was a slap-wind May afternoon, with too many tenting thrusts in the sea, and I was dogtired, strings of ache running over my shoulders into my arms. I couldn't forget about the lousy three cents they would offer us in the New Bedford markets and I wanted no more talk about who sees what doubloons under which lovely circumstances.

I prodded him once more with my toe.

"Get up," I said tiredly. "Try to pretend you're alive."

His arm moved, pushing the entranced mackerel head aside. He raised up on his elbow. The tears were still coursing down his face as he got to his knees and then hesitantly stood. "Don't think I get any happiness from being what I am," he said. "I don't know what the word means, Rob. My contempt for myself is a thousand times stronger than anything you could ever feel for me. That is my load. It's not a light one, son."

Then he did something completely surprising. With energy and an almost captivating litheness, with one ballet spring, he jumped up on the rail, feet coming down exactly on the top beam, and at the same moment caught the winch line there to steady himself. Against my will I felt a small lick of admiration for him. He was an extraordinary athlete, my father was, and one of the less primary reasons why he ought to move once in a while was that he could move so very beautifully.

"I'm a burden to you!" he intoned. His voice was climbing to a shout. "My gift to all is knots and bad weather and the lamentable silences! No wholesome breezes from me and my buds no more will swell!" Damn him and his memorized poetry. Some days quotes should be a capital offense. He got louder: "Your mother's the only one who's worth your thoughts, Rob! The only present I can make to you is to remove myself from your eyes!"

If he wanted to jump, it was his inalienable right under all the constitutions that count. These were not the words in which I put it to myself, at seventeen, but this was the main sense. And wasn't my mother always saying he was self-formed, even in his nothingness, and that was that?

So I said: "What are you doing up there? Are you going to make speeches, or jump?"

My total approval of all his reluctant plans must have come as a shock.

"I'll do it!" he said. He was shouting now. "I've made my mind up! Nothing you can say will stop me!"

Nothing in what I'd said was calculated to stop him. But the volume of his pronouncements wasn't quite in keeping with their meaning. Because the louder he yelled, the surer it was that my mother and Manuel would hear him and come up. They did. There were hurried steps on the stairway out of the hold, and the two of them were there, looking over at my balancing father with complete unbelief. They weren't used to seeing him upright anywhere.

"You out for a walk, Charlie?" Manuel said.

"Come down from there," my mother said.

"Don't come near me!" my father yelled. "I'm going to do it, Annie! What do I have to live for? Nothing! Nothing!"

"What do you have to die for, Charlie?" Manuel said in a puzzled way.

"Charles," my mother said angrily, "you stop this nonsense and get down off there."

My father began to weep again, with his whole body.

"I know what you all think of me!" he sobbed. "You're absolutely right! Let me go and forget about me! I'm only in the way!"

He said these things with complete and unalterable conviction, but still studied my mother's expressions to see how far she agreed with him. It was as though there was no smallest doubt in his own mind as to his own nullity but he fully expected, even demanded, that there should be plenty in hers and that she should talk him around to her view.

"It's too easy," my mother said with a grim look. "You will always take the easy way." She took a step toward the railing. My father moved a step away. "Get down, I say! You don't deserve to have it all over! Get down here!"

"Come on, Charlie," Manuel said. "Don't give us no trooble, Charlie. We got a lot of work to do yet today."

"Robbie," my mother said to me, "get him." I did not move. "Robbie! Get him down from there!"

"I'm not going to touch him, Ma," I said. "I can't tell him where his doubloons are."

"Robbie," my mother said. "I'm not going to tell you again. You wouldn't let even a starving dog die."

"He's not a dog," I said, "he's a beaver." I kept looking at my father as I said these things. "What are you waiting for?" I said to him. "You want a push from me? Can't you do one job by yourself?"

"That's no way to talk, sonny," Manuel said.

"Maybe you'll find your lost doubloons down there," I said to my father.

"Robbie!" my mother said with terrible iron.

"He's not going to jump," I said. "The only doubloons he's looking for are in our eyes. The more damned aches and hates he sees in our eyes, the more doubloons he's got."

It was a knotty and lamentable way for a seventeen-year-old to talk, but he had taught me. He and my mother both, in their Thirty Year's War of accusing looks.

Bless us all if he didn't give me one last waking-up look, one sudden look of so-that's-the-way-it-is, and then a quick help-me-but-you-won't glare at my mother, and then jump without another word.

Manuel and my mother stood still. Then they came to life and rushed over to the rail.

One thing about my father, he was not even in extremes indifferent to form. When he moved, he moved gorgeously. Almost absent-mindedly, I'm sure, just because the instinct to right form was trained into his athlete's muscles, he had, halfway down, started the jackknife move of fingertips to extended toes—just routine for the champ. He'd remembered the more important work at hand and pulled himself back, of course, but all the same I had seen the automatic beginning of the perfect exhibition dive and it had stunned me.

Also, I really hadn't thought he would jump. I was stunned by that, too. Things were going on in me that were not all of a piece.

"Don't be a fool!" my mother yelled. "Come back here! What do you think you're proving!"

"Charlie!" Manuel called, still not believing it. "You better come back here, boy! That water is cold!"

But my father was swimming like fury away from the boat. He was some swimmer. Even with sneaks on, and wrapped in tweed jacket and Brooks Brothers oxford shirt, he was going a blue streak.

My mother came to me and fiercely grabbed me by the shoulders.

"You go and get him before he drowns!"

"I won't!" I pulled away from her hands. "For years you've been after him to take some job! Now he's going to work! Today he's finding the one profession and career for him! Leave him alone!"

Little bent Manuel was dancing in front of me, slicing the air with his agitated fish knife.

"That water's cold, Robbie, cold! He'll get the cramps like anything! You hear, boy? He's all the hell away and going more, look!" Then he was tearing at his blood-streaked denim shirt and peeling it off, exposing his yellowed coarse-knit underwear with the long wrinkled sleeves. "All right! Stay here and make jokes! I go and get him! I go, Annie, all right!"

He was bending for his sneaks and clawing them off.

"That's right," Ma said. "Stay here and make your speeches and let Manuel go. He'll drown too. He won't come back."

Manuel ran to the rail and painfully hoisted one leg over. I rushed to him.

"Come on, Manuel," I said. He struggled but I pulled him back. "Never mind. I'll go, for you."

I guess I really wanted to go but needed some excuse that

was not my father. Maybe the old man had understood that —he understood a lot.

"I get the boat going," he said.

He dashed stiff-hipped up the stairs to the wheelroom and a minute later, when I was stripped down to the waist, I heard the motor start up and we were under way. It took us minutes to catch up with my father. He was still going with his long, efficient shoulder pulls, fresh as a daisy. I climbed to the rail and jumped.

The water was sickeningly cold. I was only yards from my father. I went straight at him, with the long even strokes he had taught me to perfection, and in a couple minutes I was up to him and grabbing at the sodden coat stuff around his shoulders.

"This is what you've been wanting, son," he panted at me.

He made a strong pull with his shoulders but I held on.

"We fed your body and kept it warm! It's ours!" I said. "You've got no right to throw away our property!"

It was an observation not shaped to win his co-operation.

"I'm through being a boarder and charity case in my own house! Let go, I say! Rob!"

He yanked again. This time the coat slipped away from my numbed fingers. That infuriated me. He was even going to make me work to keep him alive. He was swimming desperately away from me again. I set out after him with every ounce of strength I had left. Luckily he'd made me as good a swimmer as he was, and I was the younger and not soft from years of sitting. I caught up with him again. This time I got a bear hold around his neck with both my arms.

"Ma wants you back, Christ knows why, and I'm bringing you back!" I was clamping on his throat, choking him.

He thrashed about with his arms, making snorting and grunting noises.

"I won't sit and be sneered at! I am dirt but all the same! That's over with!"

With maniacal strength he reached behind to me and got a grip on the back of my neck. The mighty yank he gave brought me right over his shoulder in a somersault and then I was gliding head down into the water and I saw his stylish unstained tennis shoes wobbling past me in still another flight. I lunged and caught him by one ankle. He knifed his body around and twined his arms around my chest while his feet hooked behind mine and held them tight. All the commotion was forcing us farther down and I felt with despair that the air was squeezed from my lungs and I had to fill them again, immediately, but his death grip on me was taking me to the bottom. I squirmed, I tried to kick, I clawed at his ribs and his back, but he held on, arms around me like barrel hoops, and I couldn't breathe. I had to get air into me. I simply had to. Immediately. I was already opening my mouth for the intake, already against my will gasping in small experimental drops of green icy water, tempting myself with it, pulling it inch by inch toward my lungs. Still he held on and still the salvation top with its thin openness was far away.

With one enormous eruption, wild against his loathsome crippling weight on me, I broke his hold. I turned on him viciously. As I swung around I saw his retreating face, the look of saintly single-minded pure dedication for once on it, intent as the severed mackerel head, and with all the force I had brought my elbow up and against his jaw. The head jerked back, the face looked startled, slightly displaced to the left like a slipped mask, and above it the hair danced slow weed-winding tangos. In a split second life came back into the face and his body, loosened for the moment, snapped into stiffness again. He darted away from me—down, down, toward the boat's hull.

I catapulted myself to the surface. I treaded there for a few seconds, gasping, my lungs crying for substance and not getting enough. I dove and started under the boat. There he was, immaculate white shoes in beautiful even rhythm pumping sternward, into an agitated white froth there. Froth—

stern—it was the propeller he was going for. Down and down, straight for the propeller. He'd already been under a minute or more, but he kept going down. Down, straight down and back, into the propeller froth.

I swam as fast as I could after him.

Once, only once, he looked back over his shoulder. Right at me. He must have seen me. His face was as clear to me as a white basketball close up. What was that on his face? Direction—the sudden triumphant sense of aim regained and installed up front. A focusing on one sharp and fixed point, and the point almost, oh, infinitesimally almost, just not quite, there, at hand, waiting. I think he was laughing, behind his closed lips. The face of the young fierce water polo demon was back. Maybe it was the joy of being in motion again. The athlete long immobilized would know about that.

I swam with all I had, but it was too late. The churning white mix was just ahead, and he was there and rushing into it.

There was a kind of click, a muffled brisk impact, that communicated itself through the waters to my skin more than my ears.

My father revolved fast out of the spume, going almost sideways, in perfect slow spiral, shoulder over shoulder. Abandoned to the sweet movement, curled in a ball, the something like a smile on his face.

It was late afternoon and the rays from the strong May sun slanted deep under the hull, lighting up the whole scene in rich alfalfa greens and livening the bubbly froth around the propeller with perfect dazzle.

My father lay motionless for a moment. Then he started back.

It could not be the propeller suction pulling him back. He was thrown clear of it. He had even to fight against the wash to get back, but he put his all into it.

He was working for something, finally. Like a pack horse, like a beaver, all beasts of burden into one.

Back he went, right arm dangling useless, oddly twisted.

Another faint impact. Out he came, tumbling through the lovely barm. Face lit up.

Was it snake-bristling Annie Florence Heixas he imagined he saw there in the propeller? Arms going like a windmill, tossing him out each time he came near?

Was it to Annie Florence he kept going back each time, to get another bone cracked at her spinning hands?.

A new color was added to the incredible soft greens and overwhelming unsmirched whites. Something dark, rising in strings and small blotches.

Blood was rising from him, staining these ingratiating woodsy shades with driblets of black. But still he smiled. As though bathed in some last-minute beneficence, and blood embroideries spilling from his cheek.

And back into the miraculous foam he went, with his thirst.

To Annie Florence, to beg for more transformations? My father was at work. Like a beaver.

He came out flying again, while the crack was still vibrating against my skin.

He lay there, inert. The blood was stringing all about him.

His work was done. He stayed motionless, floating, rising slowly. Something like a smile still on his mangled face.

I got to him as soon as he drifted far enough up from the propeller. He stayed limp as I pushed to the surface. There was no opposition in his body now. It felt like a bundle of crumpled slats inside the patched-elbow tweed jacket and oxford button-down shirt.

I draped him inside the lifesaver they threw me and Manuel pulled him up with the winch. He dripped blood all the way. But as he rose out of the water, bent in two, I could see his face and on it there was yet some kind of triumph unknown to me.

Three days later they let me in his hospital room for

a few minutes. He was in a cast from his neck to his ankles, and one side of his face was humped with an enormous wad of bandages. His face, half seen from the front, looked like a multiple-vision Picasso head. He was conscious and his eyes were alert to me when I came in.

"My bones have been largely reduced to meal," he said. His tone seemed that of mere statement, if anything serene.

"You got banged up all right," I said.

"The doctor says I'll be able to walk inside of a year. The left leg may not be too good, but I'll walk. That's all right."

"You'll be O.K.," I said. "Listen, I'm sorry I dumped you out of that chair." I moved awkwardly to the window, came back. "Pop," I said, "can I ask you something? What did you think you were going after when you went into the propeller?"

His mild gray eyes looked keenly at me.

"I don't know, Rob. You look for the ointments in the damnedest places."

"Yes."

My hands were tightened into fists. I wanted to raise them to my ears, press them there.

How old had I been? Five, six. Lying stiff, fists against ears, but I heard them through the thin wall. "Dear, do you have to wear that cap in the house? It's not very feminine." "Slaving over dirty fish nets isn't very feminine. Should I wear my Easter bonnet gutting the fish?" "But you're not gutting fish now." "I look like what I am." Sounds of moving around. "No. Not that way." "You feel good on your back. Stay that way." "Please, dear. It's not good for me." More sounds of movement. Sounds of low crying from him. "Ah. All right. I'm soft. Yes. You marry a man who's soft and demand of him to be hard." "When could you be hard? At what? Even now." More crying. "No good for me. Can't help it. Grinding, grinding—humiliating." "Where else do you work? Don't ask to do the work. I wouldn't want you to strain yourself." "Please. Please. I can't stand it." My fists did not keep the crying out.

"Rob?"

That old comical, quizzing look in his eyes.

"Yes, Pop?"

"After a long and arduous search Isis discovered the mangled and chopped remains of her dead husband Osiris, the once mighty king."

The joking expectations in his eye.

"And took them back to Egypt and with the assistance of her son Horus recovered the sovereign power that had been usurped."

"Good boy, Robbie."

"See you, Pop. I—sorry about the chair. . . ."

"Sovereign powers get pulled. . . ."

BOOK FOUR:

Bacunayagua–

Havana

THIRTY   The white basketballs congealed into faces and grew features. The one directly before my eyes became Connie. "It's all right, Rob," she said. "It'll be all right." She was dabbing a spot on my head with a washcloth. My head hurt intensely at that point. The other faces cleared. Behind Nelson Boyar, Brod and Coolio were standing. Near them was a heavy man in a sports shirt. I had seen this man and this shirt before. On the Key. He had followed me from Barto's that morning, in the same shirt. The room jelled. We were in the cabin of the *Tiger*. I was sitting on a canvas chair and my hands were down at the sides, tied to the uprights of the chair. My clothes were soaking wet.

"Very derring-do," Brod said, "and very foolish." He was wringing out his wet peasant cottons. "If we'd surfaced a little closer to the dory Coolio could have hit you much harder."

But his eyes were on the man in the sports shirt. "I've seen you before."

"I doubt it," the man said. His expression was very serious. "This is an act of piracy. What do you mean by—"

"I have very definitely seen you before," Brod said.

"I'm a fishing captain from Key West. A lot of people have seen me."

"Not Key West," Brod said. "Ottawa. September 1946. The railroad terminal." The man looked puzzled, then startled. "The old lady—crippled foot—dropped her box of peppermints—you were good enough to pick them up. I thanked you. Yes. The name is—yes, Feltus. Dean Feltus. You were watching the terminal."

"The old lady with the built-up boot?" the man said, stunned. "There were reports. . . . They didn't add up. . . ."

Soft important sound of a diesel engine off the portside bow. I looked out through the glass window. It was the *Easy Rider* slipping up dimly in the lagoon waters.

Brod went to the door and called down back, "Avelino, Ipólito, cast off." To Coolio he said: "If nobody follows, we move in five minutes. First, carry him out on deck." He pointed to me.

Coolio came around in back of me and lifted my chair by the arm rests. I heard Brod say, "Be good enough to step out on deck—all of you." Coolio set me down directly in front of the cabin, then went back inside. The others came out, followed by Brod. Connie came to me and put her warm hand against my neck. Nelson Boyar leaned heavily against the cabin wall.

"*You* change the picture, Mr. Feltus," Brod said finally. He kept surveying the lagoon. "*You* would not be on a fishing cruise. . . . I see. Vincent *expected* me to use the *Easy Rider*. *You* were to follow me. . . . Yes. Very good, indeed. . . . But—clearly—if *you* were here on the *Tiger*, waiting for me to move with the *Easy Rider*—Vincent was *not* planning to arrest me. Not at this point. . . . Yes, yes. I see. If the report does not quite fit the reality. . . . Benjamino. Ah. Benjie. Vincent worked that very astutely. Oh, indeed, yes. I never suspected. . . ."

He turned from the shaken Feltus and approached me. The *Easy Rider* had cut by and was heading into the open waters.

"I begin to understand, Mr. Garmes," he said. "It puzzled me that you were able to get into Millie's with such ease. . . . Benjie. He handled himself brilliantly. I didn't see it. . . ." He saw that still more followed: "Vincent, then, has his heart set on the *Tiger* following the *Easy Rider*. That will suit our plans." He looked through the glass partition into the cabin. "He'll be wanting your progress reports."

By twisting my neck I could see what he was peering at. Down on the starboard wall inside was a very high frequency transmitter-receiver. Brod nodded. He went and stood directly in front of Feltus, his face only inches from the man.

"You filth," he said. His voice, up till now emotionless, was tight and boiling with rage. "You set your feeble-minded traps. Why don't you learn your business? Did you really think you would so much as delay me for one minute with your schoolboy ideas? I deal with your kind with my little finger. . . ." He spat with deliberation into Feltus's face.

Feltus's jaw quivered. His hands rose, wavered, fell in frustration. His shoulders shook with held longings. Finally he exploded:

"Stupid and inept! Sure! We had you buffaloed all down the line! Spit that away, bright boy! You didn't know a thing about Benjie, you never even suspected about the *Tiger!*"

Brod stood absolutely still, staring straight into his eyes. When Feltus ran out of words Brod simply nodded, precisely and with something like satisfaction.

"Thank you," he said coolly. "The speech characteristics come through clearly when a man raises his voice. . . ." He motioned, and Coolio came out from the cabin. "Watch them carefully," Brod said to him.

Coolio leaned against the railing, weighing his gun in his hand and looking from one of us to the next. Time after time his eyes came back to me and each time he puffed his lips. Brod was inside now, unscrewing the top panel of the short-wave set. When he had the set uncovered he searched around in some drawers and came up with a length of insulated wire. He found a knife and carefully scraped the insulation from one end of the wire. Then he leaned over and lowered the wire inside the set.

"What the hell's he doing?" Boyar said grumpily.

"Winding the ends of the wire around the grid leads of some amplifier tubes," I said. "To set up a feedback. There'll be static at the other end."

Low voices from the stern: Avelino and Ipólito in earnest discussion. Brod now was reaching for a box of Kleenex on a table and removing one sheet from it.

"You of all people," I said to Boyar. "You, working with Caprio."

"You lose your ardors you lose your plots," he grumbled. "Put it that way—I'm unemployed author in search of a plot. You sure provided me with a couple new story twists, you crazy bastard. *You've* got your ardors."

Brod was painstakingly wrapping the Kleenex over the mouthpiece of the short-wave telephone.

"He didn't need a sample of my voice," Feltus said. "With that wire inside and the paper over the mike nobody's voice going through that set is going to sound human. He's a thorough bastard."

Brod snapped the toggle switch of the short-wave. He held the paper-covered telephone piece close to his mouth and said, "Feltus calling. This is Feltus. Emergency. Come in, please." The voice might not have been a dead ringer for Feltus's in all phonic respects but it was close enough: American all the way, terse and flattened, yet with just the trace of Carolina slur the original had.

A voice crackled from the phone: "Feltus? Is that you?

No sign of Garmes yet. Maybe Benjie was mistaken about his getting away. Anything at your end?" It was Caprio.

"Garmes is here! He's here, Vince!"

"What was that? I'm getting a lot of bleeps. Anything wrong with your set?"

"I think there's a short or a tube going. No time to check. . . . Garmes is here, I said! On board! He got away!"

"He's there? On the *Tiger?*"

"Benjie knew what he was talking about! Garmes is right here! He's O.K. He's all right. The *Easy Rider* went out five minutes ago. Garmes says he knows for sure Brod's aboard her. We're going after her!"

Feltus took a step toward the cabin. Coolio lazily moved out in front of him, gun raised. Feltus went back to the railing and slouched against it, looking hopeless.

Caprio again: "You sure he's all right?"

"Positive. Want to talk to him? I say, do you want to talk to him? I'll put him on. Hold it, I'll put him on."

Brod lowered the telephone. He swallowed, he was making experimental movements with his lips and twisting his head. He spoke into the mouthpiece again, this time with his expert duplication of my voice: "Hello? Caprio? I'm O.K. They gave me a bad time but I'm in one piece. Don't worry. This time the son of a bitch is going to have to improvise plenty. . . ."

"Impro what? Improve, did you say?"

"Improvise. I said, improvise, we'll make him improvise plenty. We'll get back to you."

"Thank God you're all right. You had us worried. Get Feltus to fix that goddamned set if he can. The racket is fierce, I can hardly hear you. . . ."

"I'll tell him. I'll tell him. . . . Oh, Caprio. One more thing. I had to leave Natividad in the fields—around the International Harvester plantation, I think. She's hurt. Try to find her, will you? . . . Call you later. . . ."

Brod switched the set off and replaced the telephone. He

nodded, wiped his face with his sleeve. He came out and joined
us on deck again.

"Due west," he said to Coolio. Coolio began climbing to
the wheelhouse set over and just back of the cabin. "Avelino?"
Brod called out. "Come forward, both of you." In a moment
Avelino and Ipólito appeared from the passageway alongside
the cabin. "Those," Brod said, indicating Connie, Nelson and
Feltus, "in the bunks. Each in a separate bunk." The two men
stood ready. "I regret having to do this," Brod said to Connie
and the others. "We can't watch all of you. The rooms appear
to be comfortable."

Boyar walked unsteadily toward the cabin. He stopped in
front of Brod and looked searchingly into his face.

"To think that I used to set them up for you," he said.
"For such as you."

"You exaggerate, Mr. Boyar," Brod said. "I assure you I've
never picked for an associate anyone who suffered from your
especially silly brand of literary proletarianism."

Boyar started as though he'd been hit. Apparently, with
Brod, his renegacy was not the issue. His original endorsements
and acceptances were.

"You—you disapproved of my early books? They were
very popular in the movement."

"Movements are inane literary critics," Brod said. "They'll
acclaim any written word that acclaims them."

Boyar shook his head as though not hearing right.

"In that case—you mean you thought more of my *last*
book? The one your movement opened all its guns at?"

"Come, Mr. Boyar. Let's face it. When you wrote a litera-
ture of slogans, you helped only to manufacture a smokescreen.
You see, the true prime movers, the ones hidden under the
slogans, ultimately come to operate in very much the same way.
It's unavoidable, the conditions of professional invisible life are
everywhere the same. And so long as no eyes are upon us, we
aren't obliged to hide this extremely interesting fact from each
other. . . . Expose us *both*, Mr. Boyar—Vincent and myself,

and all our counterparts. Expose the laws and workings of the invisible life. That could be useful—more and more is getting submerged today. . . . I'm sorry, Mr. Boyar. I have no time for this, really. You must go. You tempt me to hold forth. . . ."

He signaled to Avelino, leaned back tiredly against the railing. Boyar, too shocked to say a word, turned and went off toward the cabin. Connie gave me a troubled look and followed him. They all went single file through the cabin and disappeared behind the curtain hiding the narrow passage to the bunks. In a moment Avelino and Ipólito passed back through the cabin and went out to take up their positions astern. I tried to move my wrists. The cords would not give.

THIRTY-ONE   We were in the open sea now, heading west. Brod sank onto a chair.

"I hope you're not in too much pain," he said.

"No."

"Tell me if your wrists are bound too tightly. I hate the idea of tying anybody down, but you're too impulsive. . . . Have you been impressed tonight, Garmes? I deduced a lot of things from Feltus—even Benjie. I carried on a very delicate conversation with Vincent. You learned that I was once a convincing old lady with a surgical boot and a box of peppermints, in Ottawa. . . . Aren't you impressed with my accomplishments?"

"You've learned your trade well, I suppose."

"That's precisely it." His voice was almost inaudible. "It's only application. Make-up and impersonation are easy to learn. So are speech characteristics. Most people don't make themselves experts at miming and such minor arts simply because the idea of putting on other identities—professionally—is so outrageous to them. I wonder if that isn't the real lure of the theater. People don't go to watch the insipid dramas—they want to see and marvel at grown men and women who make a business of pretending to be someone else. . . . It's very tiring, though. I don't enjoy acting."

"You're doing some very complicated acting with Coolio and Avelino. Maybe with the others too, I don't know. Are they convinced? I wonder."

"You've seen all that, have you?" There was approval in his voice. "Yes, it's a delicate balance."

"You can't please all your friends at Bacunayagua."

"You don't understand the nature of obsession, Garmes. You know about the *Wolna*, I suppose? One faction among my friends is obsessed with the idea of getting me aboard that ship. The other faction is equally obsessed with the idea of keeping me off. As long as I stay on a higher level of self-control than they. . . ."

"By tomorrow night you've got to go along with one side, and offend the other."

"Of course. But the direction I go will be *my* direction—the one I choose."

"You've decided which way you're going from Bacunayagua?"

"Oh, yes. I decided two days ago. . . . Coolio, of course, thinks I'm going to run away and hide. He has quite a stake in my hiding, you see. He has been encouraged to believe that the thing I have in my possession—you've heard about that from Vincent, surely—will bring quite a price from my superiors if I hide out successfully. One-tenth of a million dollars can become a strong obsession. . . . Avelino, on the other hand, is very sure that I am going to fool Coolio and make for the *Wolna*. He was sent to me to make certain that I would obey instructions."

"Miguel."

It was Coolio, calling down from the wheelhouse.

"What is it?"

"There."

Almost directly ahead, though still some distance away, was

a small light. Brod was immediately on his feet, approaching the side of the cabin:

"Avelino. Get those grappling hooks. There, by the fishing seat. Be ready, you and Ipólito."

It was again quite clear, except for an occasional thin puff of cloud over the shoreline, and the air was only faintly stirred by currents of breeze from the north. I could make out the running black line of the shore to our left. Here and there a small flick of light punctuated the line. Ahead, and far off, there was a pinkish glow from the more concentrated lights of Matanzas Bay.

In some ten minutes we were alongside the *Easy Rider*. Pupi and Owen Brooke appeared on its deck. On our side, near where I was sitting, Avelino and Ipólito stationed themselves with long-handled gaffing irons and, when the boats drew close, reached out and got holds on the rail of the *Easy Rider*. The two hulls rasped against each other, their structures creaking.

"Michael!" Brooke said. "Thank God! I don't like any of—" He saw me and leaned over his rail to peer at me. "What —Garmes! It's Garmes!"

"Who did you expect?" I said loudly. "Barto?"

"Barto?" Brooke said, bewildered. "Is he down here?"

"Never mind about that," Brod said. "You're going to—"

"You ought to mind about Barto!" I shouted. "You ought to mind plenty! Brod killed him, and you helped!"

I could barely make out Brooke's face. It was seething. He swung his eyes from me to Brod.

"Dead?" he whispered. "Oh, no. Oh, no. You only wanted to talk to him. Talk, that's all."

"No, Owen," Brod said coldly. "You thought I wanted a pleasant conversation with him. Because you are stupid, and your horizons are limited to conversation."

There was a note in his voice I hadn't heard before. It was contempt iced and final, a dismissal of this man's existence, a wiping the slate clean of even his name. Brooke heard it too. His face was twitching.

"Not Barto," he said softly. "He was our friend. He fought for us."

"You know what you are, Owen? One of the dumb agreeable nonentities who incline their heads to everything. . . . You created me. And one of the jobs you gave me was to eliminate Barto—because he *wouldn't* incline his head. Stop whining. It's disgusting. . . ."

Brooke turned away, hands over his face.

"You used me. That much. . . . Everybody. . . ."

"How could you survive without being used, Owen? It's your trade. . . . I've got another job for you now."

"No. . . . No!" Brooke raised his head. "No more jobs! I'm getting out of here!"

"You've no place to go, my friend," Brod said flatly. "I was your one link with vitality. Now that this vitality's given a name and a face—a rather bloody face—do you imagine you can just back away? No, no. It's the price you pay for living all your life in someone else's footsteps. You stay until *I* tell you to go. *Your* hands are bloody too. . . ."

"I'm through listening to you. Murderer!"

"Owen. . . . You're going on to Bacunayagua. You're going to drop anchor there. To give me a chance to get away. . . . You can't afford to have me caught. If they get me, they'll find out every detail of the help you've given me for the past fifteen years."

Brooke stared at me with demented fixity. He jerked around to Brod again.

"Ipólito," Brod said. "Avelino."

Ipólito drew a gun from under his guayaberra and leveled it at Brooke. With his other hand he kept a hold on the gaff. Avelino followed Brod to the other side of our deck. The two stood there and talked in low voices, indifferent to my presence.

"You and Ipólito will board the *Easy Rider*," Brod said.

"Go to the place where the plane is hidden and anchor off-shore there. Caprio's men must be nearby. There or by the car. They must see the *Easy Rider* and think I am on it."

"Pupi is there," Avelino said. "Let Ipólito go also. There will be two against Brooke—it is enough."

"You forget—Pupi and Ipólito are with Coolio and wish for the plan of Coolio. There must be on board one of intelligence who wishes for *our* plan and who can control the others."

"I am ordered to stay with you through the last part. This was emphasized."

"The orders do not apply now. The situation is changed."

"You ask that I leave you with this pig of the drums and no other. Then there is none with you who wishes for our plan."

"*I* wish for our plan."

"It is possible. Not until these last days have you been for this. You could change your mind again. Coolio could have some influence. A third must stay to guard against this."

"You do not think but only say words. I control Coolio only by this, that he thinks I am with him against you. To prove this, you must go now. We cannot kill him. I have need of him yet. For the letting out of the small boat and the pulling back after. You know this is the biggest thing. He will pull back the small boat and know nothing."

Avelino was silent. His face was tense.

"Miguel. For many months you made promises and did not keep them. Is this one more promise not to keep?"

"Before I had the time to maneuver. You know that I have now no more time. It is over. I will do as planned."

"It is my neck if you betray now. If they are displeased and wish my neck, I will try very hard to get yours first. . . . You believe Caprio has men at Bacunayagua?"

"Benjamino was not of our side. He talked to Caprio of our plans. . . . He has left the car in the decided place, of this I am sure. But the place will be watched. . . . There is this you must do at the place of the plane. . . ."

Then Brod put his arm around Avelino's shoulder and drew him into the furthermost corner of the deck. His voice dropped so low that the words were lost to me. I twisted around to see if Coolio was still up in the wheelhouse. I could see his face behind the pane of glass. He was looking down at Brod and Avelino with dead set intensity.

In a few moments Avelino went back to Ipólito and whispered a few words to him. Ipólito nodded. Avelino hopped over the railing to the deck of the *Easy Rider*. His released gaff dropped with a clatter on our deck. Ipólito threw down his iron in turn and vaulted over to the other boat. During the jump he did not take his eyes from Brooke, nor did his pointed gun waver.

Brooke stood where he was. He looked from Avelino to Ipólito, then his head dropped. He sank into a deck chair. His hands were over his face again.

Pupi ran inside to the *Easy Rider*'s wheel. The cruiser's engines started up, she began to move off. Avelino stood on her deck, looking over at Brod with serious eyes.

Brod waved two fingers at him in a neat, abrupt gesture. Then he looked up at Coolio. He nodded his head quickly, just an inch or two. With no change in his expression, he winked, once. I turned to see Coolio's expression. The worry went out of his face. He broke out with a broad smile. He nodded in turn.

A moment later we were under way again, following quite close behind the *Easy Rider*.

Nelson Boyar's voice boomed out unexpectedly:

"Bye, Owen. Farewell, lonely trivialer traveler. Dear Owen, forever owing. . . . Robert H. Garmes! Do you hear my thunder?"

His voice was a growl, his words run together.

"I hear you, Nelson," I called. "Take it easy."

There was the sound of glass breaking. Brod straightened, hurried out of sight around the cabin.

Connie's voice: "Nelson. Please. . . ."

Brod came back, holding the jagged top half of a bottle in his hand. He was smiling.

"Bourbon," he said. "He must have found it in his room. He's lying on the floor."

He threw the bottle overboard and sat again.

"Bye, bye, Varadero," Nelson sang huskily. "Bye, pretty pen'n-pencillar. Pen-*in*-sewer. Need no eyes here just flowering flutteral nerve-ends, skin to plug in'n feel's it turns fluorescent. Flower isn't. Floor essence. Yeah. Place where y'disconnect thought'n turn on synapses'n live by Braille. Sun shares y'bed'n board here, boy. Y'wedded t'sun. Sun insinuates self in skull and y'host t'heat'n days pass inna lemon-n-lime'n blur. . . . Bye, Brod. . . . Work, work. . . ."

His voice sank to a low humming in which there were no words, petered out entirely.

"You see why some of them suck up ready-made programs," Brod said. "They have no plots of their own."

"You're running out of plots yourself."

He looked at me queerly.

"That's your theory, is it? You think that at Bacunayagua—"

"You shake Coolio and go with Avelino. You're going home because your story's over."

"You're very sure."

"Why did you kill Barto? He was a danger only if you stayed around here. If you were planning to go home—"

"The *Wolna* came in the next day, Garmes. The tragedy was in the timing. If she'd come twenty-four hours sooner. . . ."

"No!" I was straining at the cords around my wrists in my fury. They held tight. "That's what you'd like Avelino and your superiors to think! You'd like to believe it yourself, wouldn't you? The *Wolna* came with strong new orders for you—an ultimatum—their arguments finally convinced you—oh, neat! But it's a lie!"

He leaned forward in his chair, listening with full concentration.

"You accuse me of deciding to go home—and *then* killing Barto? You think I'm that maniacal? To kill without reason—the thought sickens me."

"The thought of welcoming a bullet sickened you more!"

"You're talking in riddles. . . . Listen: I do what the situation requires but I'm not a wanton killer. I had no reason to harm Barto if at the time I hadn't been determined to stay. . . ."

"You wanted to *feel* you were determined. . . . To *deny* the growing need you felt to go home. . . . You killed Barto for one reason. To show *he* was the one who wanted to die, not you. And *you* talk of avoiding obsessions!"

Brod sat perfectly rigid. I watched him closely.

"Garmes—when do you think I decided to go home?"

"Months ago, I suppose. The moment you first got the orders."

He stood and walked over to the rail, his back to me. Finally he turned.

"An ingenious theory," he said quietly. "Your very best effort—it has all the deviousness an idle and active mind allows itself. You make only one mistake. You imagine how *you* might act in my position—then attribute *your* motives to me. . . . I tried to tell you something in my letters, Garmes. We're two very different people. . . ."

"That's the mistake *you* make." At this moment I became aware of how strangely calm I was, surer of myself than I had been about anything in a long time. "We're alike."

"You're the one who toys with his own extinction, Garmes. Your diving—all of that. . . . I've wanted one thing—to get things done. You've wanted—excitements. . . ."

"I dive one way—at odd moments, and come up. You submerged yourself in the sewers fifteen years ago, and you've stayed there. You're telling me there were no excitements in that, no creeping sensations down your spine? You denied them and your pleasure in them. You could cover them up with the thin excuses of—practical affairs, professional projects, changing the world. . . ."

Something powerful and exhilarating was gathering in me. The sweet sense of triumph.

"What about those letters?" I said.

"The letters?"

"Why'd you write those letters to me? The thought has been eating at me."

"That's a blind alley, Garmes. Believe me. . . . I can see what you're thinking—"

"You see what I'm thinking! I see what you're thinking! We keep anticipating each other—isn't that strange? For two people absolutely unlike!"

"Logic remains logic. . . . You understood that my letters were phrased to whet your appetite for me—to make you come after me. But I'd already decided to go home, and you were accordingly no threat. If I didn't have to kill you—why did I try to taunt you into coming closer—that's your question, isn't it?"

"I know your answer: you wanted to convince Coolio and the others that you were staying."

"That's it. That's all of it."

"Oh, no. . . . Why didn't you let Coolio take care of me any way he wanted? Was I so precious to you?"

"I told you—I can't stand wanton killing."

"These last few days a wild thought has been growing in my head. Every time I heard something more about you, every time I read a description of you or your activities—it got stronger. I realized what it was, finally. I was *looking forward*, somehow, to seeing you. When Benjie asked if I was going to kill you—when you needled me with the same question—I couldn't answer. Because what I was after, more than anything, was just to *see* you. To get you in sight. . . . It began to terrify me. . . . Then, last night, I saw an old picture of you, one Barto had. On the spot I decided to quit all this and go home. That's what I was up to when Coolio caught me—I was picking up Natividad so I could go home. I think now—yes—I'm almost sure—it was that picture that made me want to run. . . .

Brod was absorbed in every word I was saying, head slightly cocked to hear better.

"You really were going? How extraordinary. . . ."

I was feeling wildly elated. There was a tremendous bubble in me. I wanted to break free from the cords and get to my feet and jump, dance.

"You know what scared me off, Brod? The thought that when I got to you I'd find I was looking at myself in a kind of distorting mirror."

I wanted to shout for joy. I almost did shout:

"You were drawn to me for the same reason I was drawn to you! You had to treat your eyes to this rare picture of another variety of yourself! That's why you wrote the letters. Not to fool Coolio. To see yourself in another skin—without your usual costumes on! . . . You said I just wanted to meet and talk with you. Right! But you were accusing me of what you felt yourself! The minute you decided to go home to that bullet—you had to see me, you couldn't wait! . . . We're the same man, Brod! With slightly different covers! You can see through mine—but I can see through yours! That's how I know you're going home with trembling anticipation to that bullet —how you've been leaning that way for months! You're exactly like me. You've got to dive a little deeper each time!"

Brod made no answer to this. He turned his back to me and stood looking out over the waters at the lights on the *Easy Rider*. The pink-tinted glow of Matanzas was closer now but had shifted over to our left. We were headed northwest out to sea, apparently to skirt Matanzas.

"You're right about one thing," Brod said in a queer in-turned voice. His back was still to me. "I did want to talk to you. . . . Let me tell you a few things about Natividad—Luz. It will help pass the time. . . ."

THIRTY-TWO   Do you know Huesca? I shot Barto near there. April 21, 1937. I'll come back to that.

I was sure I'd killed him. Four months later I learned he was alive—seen in Paris.

Barto's father heard what had happened. He left his post at International Brigade headquarters and went to Barcelona. There he began a press campaign against me. Barcelona was not yet controlled by my people. Opposition papers were being published there, and their editors were glad to give him space.

I had to stop Arturo. We were about to bring things to a head in Barcelona and crush the opposition parties—Arturo's articles called attention to our plans. At the end of April I went down to Barcelona. We found Arturo, took him from the anarchists, and shipped him to our country. He was put in a labor camp—many dissident elements from Spain were sent there.

By the way, Arturo died in that camp. 1945. Four years ago, when I was home, I checked the camp records and found his death certificate. The cause of death was listed as tuberculosis. Of course, life in the camps was not easy.

I'd done what I had to, no more. But the Caros were more than political comrades. They'd been kind to me during my visits to Havana. I had spent pleasant hours in their home. Their children were fond of me and called me uncle.

I asked friends of mine in Havana to check on Magda—Señora Caro—and her daughter Luz. Through these friends I arranged to send them money.

Magda was destroyed by the news. She died three months

later—one week before a letter arrived from Barto in Paris. I am not a sentimentalist. But I remembered the little girl, Luz. I'd seen her dozens of times with her family, crawling about and being petted. I'd held her on my lap and played with her. Those who loved her, all three, were gone. She was being cared for by friends of the family but her life was hardly the same.

Some of my concern *was* sentimental, I suppose. I had no family of my own—nobody. I'd been moving about too fast to acquire possessions. . . . Curious. Politics eventually gives you a fearful craving for one absolutely *non*political tie.

The war was going on in Spain—I couldn't leave. By letter and courier, I located a childless couple among my comrades in Mexico City. I made very sure these people were reliable and would treat a child well. The man was a building laborer who worked steadily but made little money. I provided funds for Luz—quite substantial funds. Friends of mine got the girl away from her guardians and brought her to her new Mexican home. Nobody knew.

Why did I bother with Luz? You may say—I'd learned that Barto was alive and my conscience was troubled. I didn't want Barto raising the girl and, when she was old enough, telling her what her Tío Miguel had done. I wanted one Caro left who would think well of me. . . . Conscience money.

Too easy. . . . Certainly it would have pleased me, pleased me inordinately, if Luz María de Arellano Caro could have become a young woman devoted to me, respecting me for my work—calling me uncle out of ideological as well as personal sympathies. It might have made me think less about the other Caros. . . . Remember, I had no children of my own. Nobody.

Nonsense. All that's quite academic. Luz could never be a woman. . . .

She shocked you, of course. You were shocked further to learn she was Luz. Your first thought, surely, was that this was my last Caro victim—I'd pulverized the family.

Victimization—magnetic idea. Confronted with a particularly awful case of distress or distortion—we shudder—shift from foot to foot—we're painfully reminded of our own distresses and distortions. We try to explain it away in terms of some awful blow from the outside. For our own peace of mind: otherwise we'd all have to take responsibility for our own deficiencies. You found this girl so horribly twisted and you thought: Brod did this. Crushed by terrible blows in her delicate years—the sudden loss of those near and dear to her—under these blows she fragmented. Brod delivered the blows. Luz is Brod's victim.

No. Luz was twisted from within. From the beginning.

Oh, her family thought she was a gifted child—spontaneous, given to delicious fancies, full of sparkle—naturally. They doted on her and, consequently, saw nothing. The most glaring symptoms they took as merely the marks of a precious being. . . . I could be more objective. I liked the child but I found myself watching and listening to her with mounting horror.

I would take her on my lap and raise three fingers. I asked her how many fingers were up. Two, she would say, or five, or none. I would change the number of fingers and ask her again. Again she said any number that came into her head, and laughed. Her parents laughed with her. So did Barto. Her face was always so pert and lively when she gave the laughing answers, she was so cute—her family took all this as a kind of enchanting mischievousness. It never occurred to them that Luz gave the wrong answers, not to play amusing games but because at times she could not grasp the meanings of the most elementary words.

That was it, I think. Two and five and nothing were not numerical terms to her—she often had not the slightest sense of number. They were sounds she had learned. She produced those sounds which pleased her or which she thought would please the adults. If you gave no indication of which sounds you wanted to hear—only held three fingers up and waited for her to associate her own sound with that cue—she was at a loss and had to experiment randomly with sounds, watching your face to see when she was right. . . . Magda and Arturo were amused by the "game." But it was played so often that it began to bother me.

Once when I was alone with her I tried a test. Instead of asking her for oral responses I held three fingers up and told her to raise the same number of fingers, to do exactly what I was doing. She raised one finger. When she saw I was not satisfied she looked puzzled and raised all five fingers. Again, patiently, I explained what I wanted her to do. This time she began to laugh and held up *both* hands with all ten fingers raised.

She was trying to please me. Her fantastically primitive sense of an act was quantitative rather than qualitative—if the elders aren't pleased by a *little* of something, give them a whole lot of the same, bowl them over with a muchness—the infantile idea of largesse, of the cornucopia of nice things. But my three fingers were directly before her eyes. It was a horrible thing to watch. . . .

I live by words. Do you know what that means? More than most people I have to assume that words mean what they say, exactly that and no more—do their intended work, name the things they're designed to name, convey firm meanings and logical sequences. Short of that, politics is a demented exercise in sound—a babble. If that were so, what would then have to be said of us who work under and behind the words, with no aim but to infuse them with life and give them the body of a breathing community? Communities are based on the common acceptance of words and their meanings: they're cemented by language. If language is mere sound—societies are founded on pure noise and those who work to bring them into being only contribute to the racket—no more.

A sweet-faced four-year-old looked at me with mischievous black eyes and told me words were random sounds. Marbles. Hoops. Modeling clay. That one was as good or as bad as another. She was not going to change her mind.

I'm not making my point. Can you grasp this, I wonder? The words of politics are up there. The professional workers of politics, the true movers, are down here. The words don't do the work. They only make it possible for us to do ours. We're their silent partners—we make actual what they only make desirable. But you know—to be obliged to work always in a dead silence, out of sight, gives you moments of eerie doubt as to whether the cover words mean *anything*. Anything at all. I was possibly more sensitive to Luz's reduction of words to their common denominator—noise—than some might have been. . . .

Some time after that Luz showed me a pair of roller skates she'd gotten for her birthday. She asked me how I liked her hegemonies. She was beginning to pick up the "sounds" of politics she heard in her own house. I felt a frightening chill and I suppose it showed on my face. She did not understand, of course. She thought I was displeased, just that. Trying to please me, she held the skates up and said the words, thesis and antithesis, questioningly. Then a rush of words tumbled from her mouth: leaping transformations, seesaws, hard core, carousel, the nice ponies, the withering aways. Faster and faster they came—she was getting into a panic. She was terrified by her inability to manipulate my face with her words, you see. She wanted so much to produce the sounds that would take the grim look from my face and make me happy. But she could not locate the sounds.

Of course, she wasn't always like that. These disconnections appeared only at moments. There were times when she hopped about in a reasonably organized and related way. Unless you were alerted you might not have noticed the occasional "lapses.". . .

There are no blows to explain Luz, Garmes. Be very clear as to that. She was hopelessly fragmented *before* her cruel losses. In the *midst* of her happy and doting family. It's nice and terribly comforting to trace personal troubles to the loss or lack of love—they're infinitely more bearable when they're

somebody else's fault. I repeat: Luz came apart in an atmosphere of the fullest love.

Why did I keep the girl hidden? Well—I'd discovered
that Barto was alive, and in a sense I was relieved by the
news. He was no danger to me then. He was removed from my
world and as long as he stayed away I wished him well. It was
only in the last few months that he got close enough to be a
serious nuisance. . . . Suppose he had found Luz when he
went back to Havana? He was bound, as time passed, to see
her for what she was—not an ingratiating little thing but a
monstrous cripple. She was all that was left of his family. He
deserved to be spared this nightmare.

Oh, there was more to it. Yes. I had my own involvement
in the girl's fate. Remember: I'd given myself body and soul
to a movement whose premise is the perfectibility of the human
animal. We believe, we've *got* to believe, that the failures in
people are due to faulty surroundings and harsh treatment.
How can you devote your life to overhauling the world unless
you're perfectly sure that as a result of your labors *people* will
automatically be overhauled? Nothing must shake our conviction that what's bad within flows from what's bad without, and
in a one-one ratio—that the evils in man are an *invasion*.
Wherever my people come to power they mercilessly liquidate
biologists who don't believe, as an article of faith, in the in-
heritance of acquired characteristics. The Darwins and the
Mendels—certainly the Malthuses—get what they deserve: a
firing squad. We need a kind of biological hope to sustain ourselves. . . . You should understand this kind of perfectionist
hope, Garmes. It's very American. Some of its roots can be
traced to your own founding fathers.

Victimization—it's the premise of the professional rebel.
Scratch any really working world-changer and you'll find a victim: I mean to say, a maimed creature *mythologized* by himself
into victim, given the air of the plagued and set upon. You're
not driven to a career of assaulting the world unless you're the
sort who blames his troubles on everything and every source

but himself. But the corollary of that fancy is this: perfect the world and you yourself will be perfect. Your premise is your own potentiality for perfection—your squelched, interrupted, hampered perfectness.

Luz by her very existence made a shambles of programmatic optimism. Of mine, especially. Imagine: her people were *my* people, the very best examples of them, intelligent, sensitive, supremely civilized. Their ideas were entirely my ideas. In this entirely benign and favoring climate, a foretaste of the world I was laboring to bring into being—she was turning out a monster. Do you wonder I was shaken? For my own peace of mind I had to assume that the Caros had failed in some way I couldn't detect—as human beings, as the conduits of ideas, as carriers of culture. There must have been some poison, some foulness in that household which had escaped me. This taint of Luz's had to have a source that I could locate and cope with.

Think of the temptation: she would be in an environment I could control. My work took me to Mexico constantly, I could watch over her. Somewhere in my mind was the idea that I could give her the needed climate, free from taints, and so erase the taint in her.

I would not have dared to put it in so many words then. But I see now what I was doing. If such emotional rot could be self-generated and self-perpetuating—no, I couldn't allow for the mocking possibility. The mere thought aroused in me the fiercest sort of—yes, ideological fury. I wanted to bring Luz to sanity as a vindication of everything that guided my life.

The years passed. Luz did not get well. Each time I returned to Mexico I found her in a more disintegrated state, the "lapses" more and more frequent, more and more total. The bricklayer and his wife were intelligent people, they did everything they could for the girl. . . . She steadily declined.

A few years ago I was given a complicated assignment. In Canada, as you may have guessed. It was over a year before I could leave Ottawa. I came very close to not getting away at

all. I owe a lot to surgical boots and the world's awe of crip-
ples. . . .

When I got back to Mexico Luz had just turned fifteen. I
was in a rather tense and upset mood. The greater part of our
Canadian organization had been smashed. Almost everything
I'd sweated to build up was gone: our secrets were exploding
all over the world in sensational headlines: there were repercus-
sions at home: already some of my immediate superiors were
being blamed for the mess and falling into disfavor. The more
responsible people out in the field expected that they would be
recalled, to face charges. It was only a matter of time before my
turn came.

Luz was in a particularly bad state the day I arrived—making a hash of her words, using political phrases to address her
cat. My political world was at the moment enough of a jumble
without that.

I'm afraid I was rather short-tempered with her. Here, at
least, I wanted a touch of order. Words and objects holding
fast in their assigned positions. I couldn't bear any more confusion. And here was Luz—Natividad now—actually crooning
to the wretched cat, with her eyes vacant and her voice that of
a whining baby, the words: "When the transitional dictatorship
dissolves its brass buttons and instruments I am going to pull
your big bushy tail out, pussy, and it will wither away, wither
away. I promise you."

I knew where the words came from. Natividad had been
sent for a short time to a party school where the classic writings
of our movement were used as texts. In one book by an early
theoretician there occurs this sentence, which our people know
by heart: *The transitional dictatorship of the proletariat will as
its final act dissolve its own policing instrumentalities and the
state will automatically wither away.* We had had to withdraw
Natividad from school because her senseless shuffling of words
disconcerted and frightened the other children. But she had a
fantastic memory, she retained everything she'd read or heard.

I keep a tight grip on myself under all circumstances. But

that afternoon my feelings ran away with me. It became insanely important to me, in my troubled state, to hear Natividad speak that sentence, that keystone sentence in my political credo, as it was written. Without the brass buttons and cat's tails. In a strong, mature, convincing tone of voice, rather than with this infantile singsong.

I took her by the shoulders and shook her. "Natividad!" I said. "Say it correctly! Word for word, the way you learned it! Let me hear it now—*The transitional dictatorship of the proletariat will as its final act. . . . Say it!*"

She was frightened. She held the cat tighter to her and whispered, "Your eyes are transitional and I will pull them out. Your tail has no police, and when I pull it out it will wither away."

I shook her harder. "You must say it!" I shouted. "That's enough about transitional eyes and tails withering! Come on —*The transitional dictatorship. . . .* I want to hear every word. . . ." I was beside myself. I can't begin to tell you what a fury there was in me.

She began to whimper. "The transitional dictatorship of the proletariat will as its final dissolve," she began, "will as its wither final, police act, instrument away. . . ."

There was a wild screeching from the cat in her arms. The animal was suddenly squirming and clawing and making the most frightful howl. Natividad, with her eyes on me and reciting this nonsense solemnly, had sunk her fingers in the cat's neck and was viciously choking it. The cat tore away and streaked out of the room. Natividad's fingers had been slashed and were dripping blood, but she did not seem to notice. The tears were running down her face.

"I want you to understand," I said. "I don't care what happens. I'm not going to let you go until you say those words correctly. . . ."

Her answer was to sink to her knees with a terrible moan and reach for my privates with both hands.

I think even then I sensed what she was doing. She was

fifteen, she'd been to a progressive party-school, she knew as
well as she could know anything what sex was. I was the father
in her life, in spite of the new parents she'd acquired. She
looked forward to my visits eagerly. Her one aim was to do
and say the things that would please me and make me laugh.
Something had gone wrong that afternoon—she'd tried and
tried and couldn't produce the words that would make my face
light up. She sank to her knees and reached for me because
that was the only other thing she could think of doing to get
close to me again and please me.

You won't understand this—I didn't push her away. Desire had taken hold of me with an intensity I'd never felt before. No. I didn't tear her hands away. I lifted her and carried
her to the sofa. Nobody was in the house—her father was at
his job, her mother was at party headquarters doing clerical
work. I placed her on the sofa and I lay down beside her.

Desire is not the word for what I felt. So many utterly
different things take the form of sex. . . . Suspend your moral
revulsion for a moment. Try to understand. I had done everything in my power to make this girl wake up and come together
in one piece. It would have been the most important thing in
my life, I think, if it had worked. Nothing had worked. Do you
know what can happen in a man's mind when he sweats and
strains to make some impact on a woman or a girl and finds
her impervious, out of reach inside her hard shell? Can you
imagine what a defeat that can be, not to make one contact
with such a girl in ten years—what wild ideas can suddenly
come to you in your defeat?

This genital fever is so little sexual that its object need not
even be a woman. When I was young I used to take part in
fierce political debates. More than once, when in spite of all
my intensity I found I was having no effect on my audience,
I found to my astonishment that I was getting an erection. . . .
The last time that happened to me was at Huesca. I was explaining to my men the necessity for executing political wreckers and saboteurs and Barto began to attack me violently. I

shouted back at him—and this same extraordinary thing happened. The more I shouted, the more intense it became. Barto was swaying some of the more naive men, you see, I could tell from their faces. I assure you, I had not the slightest sexual interest in Barto. I have never had any homosexual inclinations, the thought itself disgusts me. . . . It was at that moment, I think, that I realized I would have to kill Barto. . . .

When it's a *woman* you can't reach you think—no, not think: you *feel*—there is one power in you you haven't used yet. Don't deny it—every man harbors the secret conviction that his own phallus has magical powers that can uproot mountains and turn night into day. Why else do *you* pick the maimed creatures you do? . . . And Natividad was in such crying need of a jolt, a crack of the whip, to bring her alive—and everything else had failed. . . .

It's a terrible thought, a terrible feeling, to come to a man who lives his life under the sign of rationality—believing that among civilized people the reaching and influencing is done with words and thoughts, with sweet reason. . . . Perhaps in my submerged world I had secretly come to have some doubts about the civilized modes of appeal. . . . Yes. I had nothing but contempt for myself. But somewhere inside the most confirmed rationalist is a club-swinging savage with the sure knowledge that in his stiff phallus are the seeds of all miracles. . . .

I was out of my mind with excitement. Somehow I thought: this girl must before I leave her say the words, simply, intelligibly, in sequence—I needed that. Somehow I thought, hoped, phantasized, that what I was about to do would shake her into compactness and sanity and make her say the words. . . .

I took her. She was clawing at me with her demands, which had little to do with sex, but I was not obliged to take her. I did it voluntarily, out of my own demands. Which had no more to do with sex than hers did. . . .

She did not come to orgasm. Something else happened

to her—there are no words for it. She had some sort of violent
convulsion. I'm quite sure it didn't involve her genital areas at
all—there were no signs of that, on the contrary I had the
impression that genitally she was almost completely anesthetized.
This was a spasm of the whole body, of the giant muscles of
the legs and torso, and of the face. The most terrible thing was
the transformation of her face. The flesh seemed to be writhing
—the teeth were grinding together in the most fearsome way
and foam was bubbling from her tightly pressed lips—and her
eyes were wide open and glazed, they were looking straight
ahead but I was sure she did not see me. I thought then and
I still think that it was some kind of epileptoid seizure. The
fingers twitched, the body grew stiff and arched away from the
sofa.

It went on for two or three minutes. Toward the end the
lips relaxed just a little and she made some noises in her
throat. She was trying to say some words. I caught a few of
them: Will as its wither final, she said once, and a moment
later, Instrument away, instrument dissolve. . . .

I have never touched her since that day. Never. I would
give a good deal if I could undo the ten minutes I spent on
that sofa with her. . . . I know this about her, though. She's
had hundreds of men in the last two years. Never once has
she had another such fit—she feels nothing, she's a typical
whore that way. But she remembers that epileptic fugue and
she has come to equate all delight with it. Since I was the
magician who gave it to her, she has been begging me for
two years to sleep with her again. I've assumed godlike pro-
portions in her mind. I can give her the fit she identifies with
orgasm and all good things.

That's what came of my ventures into the practice of
black magic. I am the god who bears golden gifts of epilepsy.
I suppose it's what a renegade rationalist deserves.

Don't shed too many tears over what she's come to. That
would be a mistake. She didn't have to go into a house in
Mexico City. When her foster parents moved away she could

have gone with them. If she preferred to stay and wait for my return, no one forced her to sell her body—she was provided for. She went into that whorehouse for one reason. There was no other place in the world where she could feel at ease. Nobody would give her a job, obviously. Wherever she went she knew that people shied away, looked at her queerly, made sneering remarks. She had no way to relate to people except through her body. Whorehouses are tremendously democratic institutions, Garmes—especially for the queer and unconnected. It reduces all of them to bodies, and they all have bodies.

I suppose, too, that Natividad couldn't stand my being away. She'd had one taste of glory and she wanted more. Unfortunately, she hasn't been able to recapture those epileptoid delights.

Are you beginning to see? She begged me to take her with me when I came back to Havana a few months ago. It wasn't heartlessness that led me to leave her at Millie's. That was the only place I knew that could approximate home to her. . . .

Well—I'll not be seeing her again. . . .

THIRTY-THREE   Matanzas Bay was half an hour behind us. We were following the coastline westward again. Just ahead were the aft navigation lights of the *Easy Rider*.

Brod stopped talking to watch the other cruiser. She changed course, heading in sharply toward shore. Brod signaled Coolio to follow.

The *Easy Rider* stopped. Brod motioned to Coolio to do the same. A powerful searchlight from the *Easy Rider*'s deck began to sweep back and forth across the heavily wooded shore. The beam picked out a tiny inlet whose mouth was almost completely hidden by foliage and came to rest there. Behind

the curtain of leaves, in gaps here and there, I could see the
outlines of a small blue-and-yellow plane, riding on the water.

Flashing the light was smart. It meant Brod was on the
Easy Rider and felt safe. He was being followed by sea, by the
amateur, yes, but he hoped one way or another to cope with
that. He was positive nobody else was around—the searchlight
was intended to and would say that to Caprio.

Figures appeared on the deck of the *Easy Rider:* Pupi
and Ipólito. They dropped anchor, I heard the splash. A few
moments later their searchlight switched off.

Twice during the trip Brod had interrupted his story to
go inside and call Caprio. Both times, speaking as Feltus, he
had made a routine report: the *Easy Rider* was proceeding
west, we were following, no replacement parts to fix the damned
transmitter. Now Brod went back into the cabin. He fooled
with the inside of the set, making the feedback still worse, I
suspected, then called Caprio. He reported now that we were
at Bacunayagua—the *Easy Rider* had anchored off the cove
where the plane was hidden. Caprio complained about the
reception and Brod had to repeat his words several times.
Caprio said he knew the *Easy Rider* had arrived—he'd just had
a report from his people on shore.

"Do we go ahead as planned?" Brod said in Feltus's
voice.

This was the ticklish moment for him. He had no way of
knowing what Caprio had planned from here on.

"No sense in your hanging around," Caprio said. "We've
got Brod covered from shore. Our plane's standing by, too.
Let's give him some room."

So the *Tiger* was supposed to go away. But there was no
indication where she was to go.

"Garmes is pestering me with questions," Brod said. "He
wants to know why Brod won't get suspicious if we just leave.
What do you want me to tell him?"

That was taking a chance. But it was pretty good.

"Tell him he's a jackass," Caprio said. "Are you listening,

Garmes? Do you hear me? You can beat it. Brod'll think the plane scares you—you can't stop a plane. You're going for help. He doesn't know *we've* got a plane in the neighborhood. . . . Take Connie dancing at the Tropicana tonight—it's on me. . . . And thanks. . . ."

"He heard you, Vince," Brod said. "He says his opinion of cops just went up two millimeters. . . . Correction. He says he doesn't like to exaggerate. *One* millimeter. . . ."

He came back out on deck, signaled to Coolio to get under way. The uprightness of his body did not seem a natural alertness now but something forced. The engines began to pump and we were off westward again. Brod sat down on the bench near me. He kept running his fingers through his limp blond hair with slow, deliberate, pressing movements. It was several minutes before he spoke again:

"There—see that cluster of royal palms?" He had raised his hand tiredly and was pointing toward shore. "Benjie was supposed to leave the Cadillac there. I suppose he did. I suppose Caprio's got somebody watching *it*." He looked at me speculatively. "I gave myself the choice of two ways to travel. Vincent's blocked them both. . . . Well. I'll improvise another. Don't think I'm *bad* at improvising. I just don't *like* to do it. . . ."

"You're not staying on the *Tiger?*"

"Come, now. Vincent's going to have a reception committee waiting in Havana with Benjie."

He stood and walked around the deck, making a boxer's hunching movements to stretch his shoulder muscles. He stopped and looked at me: "Incredible sky. How many stars do you suppose there are up there? Do you have any idea?"

"How many were there at Huesca?"

"I'm not wandering. . . . Did I tell you? I did advanced work in astronomy at Oxford. Of course, I studied languages too—I had a knack for them. But that was routine. Astronomy was my passion. . . ." He was bone tired but he managed a smile. "You should understand that, I think. Astronomy's an upward sort of oceanography, really. Ten years before you went to Harvard to learn about marine plankton, I was at Oxford investigating the celestial planktons—nebulæ, supernovæ, dust and gas drifts, globe clusters, all the migratory intergalactic stuffs. . . . That leads in a straight line to Huesca and Barto."

He pointed up at the sky.

"Does that fantastic sight do anything to you? It does to me—makes me furious. Always has. . . . I'll spare you the mathematical calculations. But we've arrived at some reasonably accurate figures, you know. There's a supernova explosion in each galaxy every four hundred years or so—from which it follows, never mind how, that there must be better than one million planetary systems in each galaxy. It's entirely reasonable to suppose that in our galaxy alone—that Milky Way up there —there must be a minimum of one hundred thousand planetary systems in which there is at least one planet similar enough to Earth to be capable of generating and supporting life. . . . And there are at least one hundred million galaxies in the Universe. Each with the same number of planetary systems in which there must be some forms of life. . . . Doesn't that make you boil, Garmes? Doesn't that make you want to shake your fist—smash something?"

I cringed. At La Jolla Barto had asked why I worked up so much emotion about the plankton migrations.

"Imagine, Garmes—*we* look up and wonder how many millions of planets carry living things, and what they're like. But on millions and millions of planets *they're* looking down here at us—and many of them may not have to wonder about us—they may *know.* . . . We're very young, as planets go— from the radioactivity of the earth's crust we know quite precisely that Earth was formed only four billion years ago. But the Milky Way is *five* billion years old. Other galaxies are fantastically older—so, accordingly, are many of the planetary systems within them. . . . We can't have evolved very far, in other words. We're still taking our baby steps, we're hardly out of the evolutionary cradle. What are the living things like up there that have billions of years of seniority on us? . . . We're the promise. They're the fulfillment. Most likely they *know* we're down here—and they're just not interested. Methuselah can't be bothered looking at Tar Babies and Chicken Littles. . . . At the observatory I used to sit at the telescope and literally quake with anger. The affront of it! To know that all you lack for that perfection is a few billion years—and nobody is going to give them to you, nobody! There's your potentiality up there, fully flowered—there's where you could arrive, given the time—what glorious shapes and expansions must exist out there!—and they're all incipient in you, you're seeded with them—but you, you yourself, will never know what it can feel like to be all you, totally realized you. . . . *That's* where our biological hope is—thousands of light-years away. . . . Our senses are so coarse. Their range is so puny. Up there—do you suppose there are some who see the ultraviolet and infrared worlds—who smell and hear cosmic rays and beta-rays and all the other emanations and great shimmers lost to human receptors? Is there a music of the spheres? There may be ears attuned to it, but not ours. . . . Up there you will find stellar bodies so dense that a matchbox filled with substances taken from their centers would weigh *one billion tons*. They're spinning so fast, some of them, that their surfaces go at the rate of *one hundred million miles an hour*. Are there some of our older brothers up there who have explored these bodies—felt these ultimate densities with their fingers, experienced these ultimate speeds with special kinesthetic receptors? . . . We've felt so little, that's the dirty part of the business. One trillionth trillionth of the marvelous sensations waiting for us. We *could* feel and know everything, if they'd give us time to grow up. But they won't. We'll never get what's owing to us, you and I. . . . I tell you—I think of them looking down at us from their perches up there, *seeing* us, and I want to throw bombs. . . . But we don't even have bombs for such work. . . ."

"You got impatient," I said slowly. "Wanted to speed things up. . . ."

Barto had said: For the sensation of everything at once.
To telescope now and later—you're tired of waiting for one
measly thing to follow on another.

He clapped his hands together forcefully.

"Something like that! Yes—that's it, Garmes! You can
rattle on all you want about social justice and the oppression of
man by man—that's not the reason you become a *professional* revolutionary. There's a deeper malaise—it doesn't have
to do with classes of men pitted against each other, but with
Man against himself—his possibilities as against the wretched
nonentity he is. . . . You can get impatient with history,
certainly. But the wildest impatience—exasperation—is with
the lumbering, indifferent, eon-by-eon evolutionary amble. . . .
It leaves you, the particularized small blob, so out in the
cold. . . . I have come to see this. You don't turn to revolution, finally—on the obsessive *career* level, that is—out of a
desire to improve the human lot. Far below the surface
humanitarianism is a disgust with the human condition—a
raging protest against the impossibility of being anything more
than human. You get fed up with being so irremediably
paltry. . . . It's not really wages and hours and the social relations of production you're attacking, hateful though they may
be. But what the devil else can you attack? You're stuck and
you've got to hit something—your reach is so damnably
short. . . ."

"All right," I said. "And Huesca? The two bullets in
Barto's back?"

"You don't see that yet? Look here—I was impatient, you
put your finger on it. I couldn't stand things being so paltry
and static. . . . All the more so because of my father, I suppose.
He was a mousy sort of man—a civil servant—worked all his
life as a clerk in the tax department. All day long, every day of
his life, he sat on a high stool, entering figures in a ledger. All
evening, every evening of his life, almost, he sat in the same
sagging easy chair, in the same pair of carpet slippers, reading
Dickens. . . . So compact in his inconsequence. So immova-

ble. . . . Fathers riveted to chairs, with books—you know that story. . . . Well, I became a rebel at the university. There were others who flared up the same way—I knew a lot of them. They were young poets, mostly—we had quite a core of incendiary poets at Oxford in the early thirties—some of them have gone on to make considerable names for themselves. . . . They disgusted me after a time. There came a general strike—they wrote poems to it. Hitler swept in—more sonnets and odes. Reichstag fire trial—odes; gas chambers— quatrains. They stood in one grassy place—sat—writing their poetic invocations to bustle and change. As though words, even the most artfully fashioned words, could do the trick. One thing they never realized—people write words sitting down, and people read them sitting down. The problem is to get them all on their feet and running. . . . I dropped my literary friends. I joined the party while still at school, worked hard for it. I came to the attention of our leaders—I knew languages, I was a good speaker, I had a sharp organizational sense. Before long I was recruited for underground work and dropped out of public party life. . . . I was a courier for a time. Later I was given more important assignments. The fighting broke out in Spain. The soft oratorical ones wept into their poems about it—I went there as a political commandant. . . ."

I nodded.

"You went to Spain," I said dully. "I went to the Bering Strait. When you're in a hurry. . . ."

"You were in a hurry to everywhere. I had my direction picked. . . . Until that afternoon at Huesca I had never been called on to kill a man. But Barto refused orders. He attacked me during our discussions. I had finally allied myself with a force, a lever, that was hurrying history along—you need the centralist organization for that, Garmes, by yourself you're powerless to do anything but write charming couplets. Barto stood up against that force—he had to be removed. . . . I *had* to shoot him—it was my baptism as a professional—it was to mark my final emergence from the subjectivity and sentimental qualms that immobilize people. . . . But I wasn't as professional as I'd hoped to be. Some remnant of sentiment, possibly, spoiled my aim. A last tear for Tiny Tim. I only wounded the boy. . . . What was I doing at Huesca? Oh— pumping bullets at the poets and sitters. The ones who don't realize we have to hurry—and that hurrying takes technique, planning, discipline. . . . I saw the collected works of Dickens on Barto's back, there in that olive grove. . . . Amateurism, with all its squeamishness! We won't get any stretching of horizons from the squeamish—just poetry. . . ."

His voice had been changing during the past hour as much as his physical bearing. The cool controls were going—an unsteadiness had crept in, a shakiness, the words faltered and then came in quick rushes. But now he broke off to study the shore carefully. There seemed to be a narrow strip of beach there, fringed with trees and bushes.

"The end of the line," he said in a low voice. He turned to wave at Coolio. "We drop anchor here," he called out.

Coolio cut the engines. In a moment he was down on deck, cranking the anchor down by its line.

"This is a good place," Brod said. "There is danger for me on the boat. From here I go by land."

Coolio's eyes opened wide.

"If you go, better that I go with you."

"You are a fool. If Caprio finds the *Tiger?* His friends will tell him where we landed and he will follow and catch us. You must stay and see that no one comes on the boat. You must take these to Havana. Bring them to the car that is waiting. Benjamino will help. Do no harm to them—this is my first order. Only to keep them in the Sociedad where they cannot talk. Until I am away and safe."

"And then, Miguel?"

"Then we meet in the agreed place. We make the offer to sell. It is not too much to hope that we will get one hundred thousand dollars. You will collect the money yourself and take your share and give to the others their shares."

Coolio looked uneasily to me, then back at Brod. He coughed, ran his tongue over his lips.

"You will meet with me in the agreed place, Miguel? Truly? You do not go to the other place with Avelino?"

"That is a stupidity. Why do I send Avelino away and keep you with me if it is my plan to go with Avelino and not you?"

Coolio thought this over.

"Then good, Miguel. You will go to the car or the plane?"

"They are watched. I will find a way to go."

"You wish to go to the shore in the small boat?"

"Yes. If it is found it will tell where I have landed. There is much rope in back, by the fishing seat. Tie it to the rope of the small boat and keep one end. When I flash the light you will pull the boat back."

"As you say, Miguel."

Coolio left.

THIRTY-FOUR   "Benjie is sure to have some of your friends waiting for you," Brod said distractedly. "Coolio doesn't know about that. Just take it easy with this idiot— once you get to Havana you'll all be quite safe, I'm sure. . . . Yes—that was the thing about Huesca. I stepped over the line and became a professional. . . ."

"And at Key West?"

He looked angry.

"At Key West—I finished the job."

"Did you? What job? You had no reason to kill Barto in Key West. The practical reasons of Huesca were done with."

"I'll tell you again: I was determined then *not* to give up and go home. . . . Don't look for hidden meanings when the bald facts are so unambiguous. Digging for the undersides of motives doesn't become you—you of all people."

"How do you suppose I spotted you for a parodist? That's what I am myself, essentially. Takes a thief."

"I *had* to get rid of Barto!" he burst out. "I was not going to be finished by a bullet from him—after these fifteen years."

"A bullet from your superiors, in some soundproofed basement—is that better?"

"There are contexts—even for bullets! If I'm to be shot when I get home, at least it will be my own people who do it! Going home—going as a matter of choice—that means I still dictate the conditions, in a sense. . . ."

"You're dodging and dodging," I said with no urgency. "Other agents defect and drop from sight—become truck farmers and stamp collectors—even some from your side. . . . When they do go back it's often because members of their families are being held as hostages. You don't even have that excuse. . . . You've got a genius for improvising. No one's better than you with masks and make-up. You'd have no trouble hiding, if you wanted to. . . . You *had* to kill Barto, sure. But not for the seemingly practical reasons you had in Spain. Just to make sure everybody would be gunning for you—so you'd *have* to go home to that comradely bullet. . . . Killing Barto was a parody of an act. . . ."

With one detached part of me I was listening to the sound of my voice and I was astonished by what I found there: the unmistakable dropped accents of boredom. The reversal was complete. He was getting wild, and I was just bored. Oh, it was all so elementary. Looking into a mirror—where's the controversy in mirrors?

Both his hands were tight on the railing.

"Death-hungers—good. Very modern. . . . It's not much of a theory, Garmes. It leaves out entirely the question of *why*."

"Your father just sat, you said. You haven't said one word about your mother. . . . She wasn't by any chance what you'd call—a windmill?"

"Oh, no, Garmes—that's too easy, really! The supervisory ghosts of Mamma and Papa—no, no. A man is driven to become a revolutionary out of the need to be *self*-determined. You wouldn't know about that. . . ."

"Driven. There you are. How self-determined can you be when you're *driven*. . . . And you forget. *Barto* wanted mightily to be self-determined."

"Childishly. Romantically. By setting himself up against the only agency that would give him his freedom."

"I see. Your freedom needs designated agencies—whether you want them or not. If a man feels free to buck your agencies—you give him the freedom to be shot. . . . Where do you people learn your corkscrew logic? You rage at existing authority—in order to bring into existence harsher, much harsher, new leaders and authorities. You're not rebels—all those fists are a lie. You're the most submissive people around. Looking for an excuse to lie down and be squashed. . . . You still haven't told me about your mother."

"If you must know—she was in the civil service too. She was one of the few women employed as investigators by Scotland Yard. . . . Be as glib about that as you want."

The legs of my chair banged against the deck as I rocked back and forth, howling. Brod stood looking at me furiously until I got over it.

"Mamma was a policeman!" I said, choking. "Sure—it had to be something like that! The joke wasn't complete. Mamma wore the brass buttons. You hid in the cellars to make trouble for the brass buttons. To make the brass buttons wither away! And in the process became the worst kind of cop yourself! And you talk about being self-determined! You were only driven! Oh—nice. Nice. . . ."

He looked at me and shook his head.

"You're becoming a bore. If all you can see in a grown man's behavior is the long shadow of the nursery. . . ."

"I don't know any formulas. Look at the facts, they're hilarious. Flexing the muscles is supposed to be the manly pose.

Most people get the habit from their fathers. You had a flabby father, with muscles of wax. It was your mother who had the fists. That's enough to confuse you—your old man sags around and your old lady is the policeman—the windmill. You get the mistaken impression that any form of muscularity is womanish. Still, you've got muscles that have to get used. . . . Naturally you'd be interested in me. You thought I represented the same parody. With less elaborate subterfuges. My mother the doer—me *over*doing to the point where any and all movement's a joke—to ironize her and her image out of the picture. The indifference to political and other subterfuges fascinated you. Everybody's attracted by the image of himself with his clothes off."

"Fantastic," Brod said quietly. "How little you see. If you think we have anything in common. . . . You think in terms of parodies, don't you? It's not simply that your mother was the go-getter and your father the sit-and-taker, contrary to the accepted scheme of things—"

"Your family and mine may have been just exaggerations of the common thing. With the decent coverings pulled off."

"In your case," he went on, "your mother was a *parody* of action and your father a *parody* of relaxation. Because you never truly stepped away from them, out into the open where they couldn't reach you, you could neither sit back nor flail around with conviction and single-mindedness. . . . You're not fit to discuss the idea of free movement."

"I wonder—how would you come to make such close guesses about me? . . . Lethargist who's always jumping— that's me, absolutely. It's also you, the professional midwife of new worlds. . . . Our jumps take slightly different forms. We dive in different media. That's all—"

Coolio called out: "All is ready, Miguel."

"All is ready, Miguel," I said. "This time you'll get what you've been diving for for fifteen years."

His face was knotted again.

"Pull the boat to this side," he called back. "Around to the steps." He went inside the cabin. I saw him take a flashlight from the table next to the short-wave set. He came out again and stood juggling the flashlight. "There's also a matter of discipline," he said to me in a hoarse voice. "There are rigidities a man must bow to if he wants to be a man. . . ."

"Hail the rigidities," I said. I yawned. "You're a disciplined little soldier. You'll soon be a dead little soldier. In your permanent easy chair. Bon voyage."

Coolio appeared, pulling the skiff around by its line.

"I'll tell you something, though," I said. "We both had parodies for families. Each one of them was the essence of family—therefore the caricature of all families. But you're right—you don't have to be yanked by them and their echoes all your life. It's possible to pull away and take a good look back and have one hell of a laugh over the sight. It's the funniest damned thing if only you can see it from a distance. You can chuckle over a joke that big all your life—Pop squatting like a hen and Mom marching in police uniform—if you're far enough away from it. Some people do, I guess. Not you and not me. It never occurred to us that we might just walk away and start laughing. We only pretended to walk. You more dramatically than I. . . . But stay close and you're driven—right to the nitrogen and bullets, sometimes. . . ."

Coolio was holding the skiff close by the steps. Brod walked out on the platform that led to the steps.

"I thought we might have had something to say to each other," he said huskily. "I'm genuinely sorry."

"What can twins say to each other?"

"There are light-years between us, Garmes. Words can't travel that far."

"You know what you see up there on your heavenly plankton, Brod? Somebody with no imposed tunes to dance to. No pitchforks at his back but those of the future. All the light-years are between you and your dream."

"Coolio," Brod said softly, "you are not to harm this man

and his friends. This I emphasize. Only take them to Havana
and meet Benjie and hold them there."

"Thanks, brother," I said. "Save all the bullets for yourself."

"We meet the approaching Thursday?" Coolio said.
There was a touch of prayer in his tone.

"Thursday," Brod said. "At the decided place."

Coolio went down two steps and bent over to secure the
skiff. Brod looked up at me.

"There's a difference between us you won't see," he said.
I was not prepared for the total breakdown in his voice. "On
your own you're an insignificant speck, a piece of dirt. It takes
an organization, an apparatus, to translate your desires into the
urgent force that shakes up the world. Without that implementation—you're thrown back on yourself and your own puny
fists!"

"Would you feel the need for implementation so much,"
I said, "if you didn't feel your fists were so puny?"

His voice rose still more. No doubt he had sounded just
like this in those fierce Oxford debates, or in the olive grove
near Huesca when he screamed at Barto the need and glory
of firing squads:

"I won't have it! To be cut off like that—it makes me
like you—nothing! *That's* why I'm going! I will not be reduced
to shaking my fists in the nursery dark and denting nothing!
You—all those like you disappear without leaving a trace!"
His voice was fluttering wildly. "There will have been alterations because I was here!"

He started down the steps.

"At Maui, at Balikpapan—right or wrong, I at least
thought," I said listlessly, trying to fight off the immense drowsy
blankness in me. "You, you would have had to call a conference. To the last minute you were holding conferences—your
last parody of an apparatus in your last parody of a conference.
You're running because you've run out of conferences. You're
afraid to stay alive without a crowd. . . ."

Brod was standing in the full moonlight, with his hat off. I looked into the face of my neighbor from Harvard classrooms, a hundred years of strain written into the curiously young but diminished features, caving in the cheeks, shrinking the flesh down tight against the small purposive bones. And the cheeks were wet. His eyes were blurred with tears.

I realized what it was that had begun to haunt me about this face from the moment I saw it in the old snapshot. Its rigidities, the forces that knit the features together and held the head at iron angles and made a compressed undeviating shaft of the neck, the strains that pulled and flattened the lips and gave them their tense angularity, weren't those of toughness and determined male push. This was a face that had been mobilized all its life against its primary urge to break into tears. That was its deepest drive, toward lament. What really accounted for its enduring youthfulness was the child's readiness to break down and cry under all the man's overlaying controls. The face was fulfilling itself now, all the masking hardness of purpose and program and dedication dropped from it and the baby coming forth, the indomitable baby, with its wracking sobs. He seemed very young and very overwhelmed at that moment. An infant with many wrinkles.

"You are right," he said. "There may be a bullet waiting for me. Is that the worst thing? . . . Death to you is not a presence—it's a topic. Up to a certain point you're young, which means, between you and dying there's a barrier of old age. You haven't reached this barrier yet. In secret you're convinced you never will. Yes, yes, logic tells you you will die, but logic is only a concession to your mathematics teacher, and full of jeers. . . . The terrible thing is to cross the barrier and feel the different, cooler climate. Each year now, if I lived, I would be a little more dead. It's all downhill now, a daily fading. . . . Do you see? I cannot allow just anybody to kill me. I must arrange the circumstances myself. As a last act of will —it's important, because will is the sign of life. I want you to understand: my last act of life is to choose the circumstances

of my death. Choice for me is easier than for most. Many
people offer me death. I have only to pick that death which
will run against the wills of the greatest number of other men.
I'm lucky to have such a choice. Most people who are dying a
little every day don't have it. This is why I'm going home. Because, don't you see, it is what you and so many others don't
wish me to do. . . ."

He put the straw hat over his head, pulled the kerchief
tight and disappeared down the steps.

I heard him pulling back the stiff tarpaulin covering of
the rowboat. There was the sound of oars being inserted in
locks. In a minute he appeared off the portside, facing me in
the little skiff and rowing slowly, steadily.

"You wanted to feel the billion-ton matchboxes," I called
to him. "What did you feel? The cosmic thrill of sinking a
knife in an honest man's back."

His tense set face was turned up to me. He went on
rowing.

"You wanted to live ten billion years," I called more
loudly. "How many days have you left? Did you commune with
the marvelous beings of the galaxies? All your talk was with
your lumpen opium-eaters and pimps. You turned your face to
the future and you were strangled from behind by your own
diapers. . . . Listen! Brod! What made you do all that research
on me? Brod—you're a parody of me!"

Coolio stood on the platform above the steps, paying out
the line as Brod rowed, staring at me with slacklipped puzzle-
ment. Brod continued to look at me, his face growing smaller
and smaller in the darkness.

What a picture: the lean campesino in straw hat and modest
cottons, rowing to his soundproofed cellars, tears streaming
down his juvenile Harvard face. It woke me up.

"You were going to work wonders in the world!" I
shouted. "Change everything! You brought epilepsy to one
deranged girl! You dreamed of celestial powers and couldn't
get her to speak the sentence! That's your defeat! That's what

you're running from! Luz paid you for Barto and all the Caros! Row! Row, Brod! You'll never forget that defeat! The bullet will drown it out! You need the bullet! Row, Brod! Faster! Faster!"

I did not know whether he heard me. I could hardly make out the skiff now, it was a small white patch near the beach.

Then his voice came across the water, distant, thin:

"I had to kill Barto! Do you hear? I'd had too much of pressure! Too much!"

Coolio went on feeding the rope for some time. Then he stopped. Holding the line, he looked to shore.

A flashlight went on at the point where the skiff was. It snapped off. It came on again, then a third time.

Coolio began to haul the line in. He worked at it for several minutes, the empty skiff with its folded-back tarpaulin riding closer. Finally it banged against the side. Coolio pulled it around to the stern. Soon he was coming toward me again, this time with gun in his sling-held hand. He kept me covered while with his free hand he untied the cords around my wrists. He straightened up, watching me.

"Inside," he said. "No tricks."

I went into the cabin. For the first time I noticed that the horizon to the east was beginning to mist and glow. He pointed to the narrow passageway to the rear and I pushed through the curtain and went past the first set of compartments. In the one to my right I heard heavy snoring—Nelson Boyar, probably. Coolio pointed to the second door down on the left. I opened the door and went in. The door closed behind me. I heard the key turning in the lock. Coolio's footsteps retreated.

"Connie?" I said, as quietly as I could.

"Rob?" Her voice came from the bunk next door. "Is that you? Are you all right?"

"Don't be afraid, Con," I said. "We're going to Havana. Everything's going to be all right."

The engines had begun to run. We were moving. The glow to the east was brighter.

"Con," I said. I could hardly speak, there were weights on my lips. "He couldn't get her to say the sentence. He wanted slogans and got epilepsies. She foamed and wouldn't say the words, she beat him. . . ."

Then I was stretched out on the bunk in my still damp clothes and asleep.

THIRTY-FIVE   I awoke with a spasm of my muscles. I sat up. A ferment of noise—drums, trumpets, klaxons, whistles, hand claps, firecrackers, chants, yelps.

It was daylight. The boat was not moving. The insane racket seemed to be coming from all sides, infesting the air.

I stood and looked out the porthole. We were tied up at a pier—Caballería Pier in the channel of Havana Bay, the place where the Morro Castle ferries docked. The sun was slanting into the porthole from the west. It was pretty far into the afternoon.

Elaborately decorated cars and trucks were moving back and forth along the Cespedes extension of Malecón Drive, filled with costumed passengers. Other people, many in costumes, were walking and running around on the street.

Sunday afternoon: I remembered. The second day of Carnival. The vehicles and costumed people were going toward the parade assembly point on the Malecón.

Somebody was standing on the pier just to the left of the porthole. I looked up and saw Coolio with his eyes on me. He smiled and pointed to the hand in the sling. The hand was hidden inside one of the cavities of his bongo drums and the face of the drum was turned toward me. He raised his hand to his lips, still smiling. He patted the drum, wiggled his forefinger as though pressing a trigger.

He disappeared from view. I heard footsteps coming through the cabin and into the passageway. The key turned in the lock of my door.

"Please to come now," Coolio called. "You be nice and careful."

I opened the door and stepped into the passage. Coolio was standing at the entrance, the hand in the sling uncovered. In it was a gun.

"Open now all doors," he said. "Tell the people come out nice and quiet one and one."

I took the key from my door and unlocked the other doors.

"Connie?" I said. "Nelson? Feltus? Come on out. Be careful."

Connie was the first one out. She came to me and put both her hands on my shoulder. Nelson Boyar and Feltus came out. Nelson looked mussed and scratchy-eyed and walked as though his joints hurt. Feltus kept watching Coolio.

Nelson got his eyes all the way open and turned them in my direction. He squinted until I came in focus. He saw Connie pressing against me and jerked his head away.

"Hit by a Mack truck," he said. "Spent night in cement mixer. Oh, oh, my."

"You listen and good," Coolio said. "You go first down steps to pier and to right on the street. I follow. Any time one run or make little move or noise I shoot the whole nice bunch."

He took the drums from under his arm and slipped them over his gun-carrying hand again. He signaled to us to move into the cabin and backed into it himself, holding the curtain aside. He stood away as we came through, keeping the drum up.

"Outside now and by the steps," he said. "You better walk like you just walking."

We filed out and down the steps to the pier. Coolio was right behind us. We set out for the street, Feltus and I in front, Nelson and Connie a few steps back. Coolio kept close, drum over his hand.

When we reached the street we turned right. The noise was deafening. There were hundreds of people in motion and a steady crush of crazily painted and festooned cars inching along toward the Prado. The people were dashing in and out between the cars, whistling and making peppery long-voweled sounds. We kept to the sidewalk along the water, moving west with the traffic. We came to the mouth of the channel and followed along into the broader drive.

"Benjie's meeting us," I said softly to Feltus. "Brod told him to wait all day with a car."

"What the hell for?" Feltus sounded worried. "If Brod had a car and a plane at Bacunayagua—"

"For Brooke, I think. Last night when he sent Benjie here he thought he'd be traveling on the *Easy Rider*. Brooke was supposed to take her on to Havana."

"Maybe."

"Caprio *must* have some men here."

"When we get there you watch the north side, I'll watch the south."

"One of us'd better find them. They may be needing our help, in this crowd."

I judged from the position of the sun that it was around four o'clock. Still two hours before the *Wolna* sailed.

We were approaching Martires Park at the foot of the Prado. The crowds and traffic were denser now, making still more of a commotion. The whole damn city seemed to be howling and blabbing with one mouth. Huge gaudy floats were lined up along the Malecón on the far side of the Prado, slowly moving into the parade of comparsas that was in progress along that boulevard. Running around them on all sides were the smaller cars, many of them disguised with elaborate papier-mâché painted overlays to resemble elephants and gape-mouthed monsters and trolley cars and great sparkling beer bottles, all of them swarming with screaming riders piled on top of each other.

"Still more crowded," I said. "Think one of us might make a break for it?"

"Too dangerous," Feltus said. "This is a wild man. He might really start shooting at everybody."

And suddenly there was Benjamino Francisco just ahead, standing very still and looking at us, first at Feltus, then at me, with eyes wider open than any eyes should be able to go. In his candy-striped shirt without the collar, straw hat pushed informally back on his head, hand resting on the roof of a large touring car almost totally covered with twisted paper strips and fluted swabs of bunting—eyes bugging from his skull.

He recovered fast. His eyes narrowed and his face went flat again.

We had only a few steps left before we reached Benjie. I beseeched him with rolling eyes to give me some hint as to who was around and where.

No suggestion of reaction passed over his composed face. But his eyes moved—once, then a second time—just two quick flicks to his right. I looked in the indicated direction without turning my head. On the edge of the park were two men dressed in ruffled blouses and silken striped trousers, evidently the uniform of some comparsa.

"Across the street," I said quickly to Feltus. "Those two. Against the statue."

Then we were all at Benjie's car and Coolio was right behind us, saying, "All in the car. Got the nice passengers for you, Benjamino."

He was opening the rear door and moving his head to indicate that we were to get in, and his drum-covered sling-supported hand was pointed at us.

"In," he said. "Fast now, no little games."

The two men in ruffled blouses had moved away from the statue and were heading across the street toward us—no agitation showing in their walks, heads turned partway aside, hands limply in blouse fronts, but coming fast.

"In, I said," Coolio said in a low grinding voice.

There was an agitation in the disorganized crowd. A bunch of girls dressed in identical harem costumes, evidently all members of the same performing club, had begun a squealing stampede across the Malecón from our side, pursued by a gang of boys in pasha outfits. The whole group swept around the two men in the ruffled blouses and engulfed them.

Coolio was saying still more softly, "I tell you the last time. You get in or—"

Benjie's eyes had been going from Coolio to the scene across the street, face stayed unperturbed. Suddenly he moved. With one violent sweep of his hand he slammed the door shut.

"Aaaaaaaah," Coolio said from his throat. He dropped to his knees and made the sound again.

Blood was gushing from his free hand. Benjie had slammed the door on his fingers.

But his eyes were still on us and his other hand was still inside the drum, now at rest on the sidewalk.

"Run!" Benjie screamed. "Run from this madman!"

And he was shoving us into the crowd, driving at us, heaving us. On the sidewalk Coolio, moaning, mangled hand lying palm up on the pavement, was trying to raise the drum in our direction.

"Quick!" Benjie screamed. "Run! Run!"

We were in the crowd, being shoved this way and that. Connie was at my side. I grabbed her hand and pushed ahead, trying to make a path. We were forcing our way into the Prado, toward the heart of the parade, Benjie close behind and yelling, "Run! Yes! Fast and fast!" I couldn't see where Feltus and Nelson Boyar were. I kept pushing and dragging Connie behind me.

"Hold on!" I shouted to Connie.

"Go ahead!" Connie shouted back. "I'll keep up!"

Somehow, reeling and tripping, we got past the park and

up into the solidly packed boulevard, first one block, then two. We had veered out of the traffic stream in the street and were cramming our way along the arcades, in back of the benches lined with chattering people. We got up through the third block and partway into the fourth before we found ourselves stopped. The arcade ended in a blank wall. We couldn't move out into the street at that point because the bleachers were lined up there solidly.

"Could we rest minute," Connie panted. "Catch breath."

"In here," I said.

I pulled her up a couple of steps into the grillwork-gated entrance of an old office building. We were back several feet from the sidewalk, it looked safe.

Connie was leaning against the wall, head down and breathing fast.

"Boy," she said. "Got to cut out smoking."

Then her head was up and all the muscles in her face stretching as she stared out past my shoulder and began to say "Oh—oh—"

I turned. Down the arcade some thirty steps away, stooping under the bleachers, was Coolio. One hand hanging at his side with a blood-soaked handkerchief over it. The other in the sling and bringing the drum skin up slowly.

I jumped back. The grillwork door was at my shoulders. I reached for Connie.

"Down!" I said. "On your knees!"

But she threw herself at me, pressing with all her might against my body.

I reached for her shoulders to shove her down, yelling, "No! You can't—"

Over her shoulder I saw Coolio's drum come to a stop. Face turned to us.

I was pushing at Connie's shoulders with all my might, she was holding on tight. The drum jumped just perceptibly. There was a small black mark on its face that hadn't been there before.

"Mm," Connie said. She went limp against me and began to slide down.

I caught her. As I was lowering her I saw Coolio looking wildly toward his left. Benjie had appeared there alongside the bleachers, being swept along by the crowd. He had his gun raised over his head and was trying desperately to get it pointed at Coolio.

Coolio looked quickly in both directions. He darted into the crowd and was lost.

"Benjie!" I shouted. "Over here!"

He heard me. In a few seconds he was in the doorway.

"Bad?" he said, looking down at Connie.

"I don't know." There was blood seeping over the front of her dress, on the left. Her eyes were closed. "Take care of her. Get her to a hospital."

I took the gun from his hand and ran into the crowd in the direction Coolio had taken. I knocked a man over. Somebody else, I didn't know whether a man or a woman, I sent spinning against the wall. Voices barked at me. I got down to where the bleachers began and there in the middle of the crowd, fighting his way east from the Prado into Emilio Nuñez Street, was Coolio. He jerked his head around and saw me. He began to burrow into the mass of people again.

I went after him, slamming people away from me.

"Coolio!" I shouted. "What's your hurry?"

He went faster, bent low.

Halfway down the block the crowds thinned out, there were open stretches. Coolio got into the street and started to run, weaving his way around the strollers. I ran after.

"What're you afraid of, Coolio?" I yelled. "I've only got one gun! You've got a gun!"

He kept on running. He was fast on his feet, he crossed Morro Street and then he was sidestepping the traffic over the wide Monserrate boulevard, still going full speed. He turned here and dashed up to the park across from the Presidential Palace, then east through the park. Just before heading into Cuarteles Street he turned and saw I was gaining on him and fired twice at me. His drum was under his loose arm now, his gun was in view. I fired three times at him but he was sprinting again into Cuarteles, up the narrow curved road going to the old church on the hill there.

I took off after him. He reached the church, at the high point of the hill where several lanes come together like curling spokes, and bolted around the corner. In a second I was around the corner too. He heard me coming and he faltered.

"Coolio!" I yelled. "Don't run! Got something to tell you!"

He sped into a down-slanted alley alongside the church. I got to the alley with my gun raised, ready to fire. Then I stopped and began to laugh.

He was thirty feet away, standing still. The alley was a dead end. Directly behind him was a high weather-etched stone wall that abutted the church.

"I've got something to tell you!" I shouted. "It's not nice to run away! Where are you going to run now?"

He raised his gun and fired at me.

"Where you going to run now, Coolio? Run up the wall!"

He fired again.

I raised my gun and took slow, careful, delicious aim at his left thigh.

"Big news, Coolio! Very important for your future!"

I pulled the trigger.

He screamed and dropped to the ground. The gun clattered on the cement walk. He was rolling on the ground and screaming.

I walked over to him. I bent down to press the muzzle of my gun into his right thigh.

"All you do is bleed," I said. "You bleed a lot. From one arm and then from the other hand and now from the leg too. All your nice blood is running out for your good friend Miguel and Miguel is running and running from you. You know where Miguel is running now, Coolio? To the S.S.

Wolna with your money and your future and your blood. With your nice friend Avelino and the nice hundred thousand pesos you will never see."

He was rolling around and wailing but his eyes were open and fixed on me.

"One leg still is not bleeding," I said. "Would you like me to make this leg bleed too, Coolio? For the good friend Miguel who sends you into Caprio's traps? So you will bleed all over for your Miguel whom you will never see again? What do you say, Coolio? Would you like Nicolaso to break one more bone and make more bleeding for you?"

I was beginning, slowly, deliciously, to pull the trigger as footsteps raced down the alley and then two men in ruffled shirts were bending over the whimpering figure on the ground. I stood without raising my eyes, a hand reached for my gun and Vincent Caprio's voice said in my ear, "Steady, Garmes. It's over. You won't be needing this."

THIRTY-SIX   We sat on the steps of the old church. Somebody was playing the organ inside, a thin out-of-breath reed sound like the blubbering from Coolio.

The ambulance had gone off with Coolio. Benjie, Caprio said, had taken Connie to the hospital in a cab. A police car would rush me there as soon as she could be seen.

The organ piped out tremulous Coolio laments. Tone poems of robbed flesh. My thoughts were beginning to settle.

It was absolutely quiet in this side pocket of the Old City, with the weather-chewed chunky Angel Church at our backs. Practically no sun came in, very few sounds from the carnival crowds only blocks west got through. The organ was not so much raising hysterical fuss as stating said and done facts. What its clear reed threne was saying was that the blood was spilt and no more need for guns.

I looked at the deserted pinched streets slanting out of sight, the peaceful tall face-gouged buildings with shuttered balconies and awning-topped roof gardens, and began to relax. I told Caprio everything that had happened from the time I'd entered Luz's room in the Casa Mañana and found Coolio there.

With each step in the story his face got grimmer. When I was finished I said:

"What about Brod? He's still got an hour or more before the *Wolna* sails."

He looked grimmer still.

"The *Wolna* sailed over an hour ago. At three-thirty."

I sat up.

"You said she was leaving at six."

"She was. Just before noon her captain informed the port authorities that he wanted to clear for an earlier sailing. I flew in to see what was going on."

"Did Brod get aboard her?"

"The captain yelled bloody murder but the Cuban police searched every inch of the ship. All they found was henequén and sugar."

"Could Brod have changed his mind at the last minute?"

"He'd made his choice. We forced him to it. . . . Besides —where else would he go at the last minute? We closed all doors. No. . . . It's a puzzle. . . ."

He had been speaking mechanically, his mind on something else. Even now he had no interest in my questions: he was looking down at his feet and frowning.

"You didn't even look up when I told you who Natividad is. . . ."

"I've known about her for the last three years."

The organ was making plodding bass sounds of nothing-will-avail.

"Three years?"

"Three years ago I stopped off in Vera Cruz and located the bricklayer who'd adopted Luz. He was still a party member, but I got the local police to give him a scare and he talked. I got the whole story from him."

"You never told Barto. . . . You helped him look for the girl. . . ."

"You want the full facts? I had an understanding with Brod. He was never to let Barto know about Luz and I wasn't either. The guy was obsessed enough. Neither one of us wanted him wilder than he already was. We *both* had work to do that he could interfere with. . . . Sometimes our interests overlap. . . ."

This topic was not absorbing to him either. His thoughts were still away. He made a face, pulled a folded newspaper from his pocket and opened it. He made whistling sounds as he studied the front page. It was a copy of the *Havana Post*.

"Here's a story broke in Washington today," he said. "May interest you."

He handed the paper to me. The screamer headline read: TOP DIPLOMATS MISSING! Caprio tapped his finger against the text under these words.

Two officials in a friendly embassy in Washington had disappeared. The rumor was that both had been feeding top-secret documents, including many from American sources to which they had access, to agents of a foreign power. There was no trace of these men. They had dropped from sight two days ago. Preliminary investigation pointed strongly to the possibility that these diplomats had been playing their dual role for years. Both of them had been at Oxford during the thirties. It was said that they had come under the influence of certain extremist political elements while undergraduates.

Pictures of both men were printed alongside the story. They were both youthful in looks, delicate-faced, with the slight aura of campus thinker about them, and might have sat next to me in Harvard lecture halls.

"Those extremist political elements at Oxford had a name," Caprio said. "Mike Brod."

"These two disappear while you're after Brod. Is there—"

"Brod was their contact man. Somewhere in the last few months he collected a batch of stuff from them. Then he was ordered home—ostensibly to deliver the documents. He knew it was a setup to get him back. This stuff gave him some bargaining power, so he held out. . . ."

He put both hands between his legs and squeezed his knees together, as though cold. Calmly he said:

"That's why these diplomats were told to beat it. If we got Brod they were in trouble. . . ."

He stood up and rubbed the back of his neck with both hands.

"I've been sitting here trying to figure the thing out," he said. "It makes no sense at all. Brod leaves the *Tiger* and slips ashore at some point not far west of Bacunayagua. He can't go for the car or the plane hidden there—he knows they're both lost to him. He starts out on foot, dressed like a farm hand. Through a section where it's highly unlikely he knows a soul. How's he going to get from there to the *Wolna*, Garmes? Tell me that." He rubbed his eyes and cheeks with his hands. "Tell me again how he left the *Tiger*. Tell me every least thing."

I started through it again: Brod's last talk with Coolio, his last words to me, the extra line attached to the skiff, the flashlight. Caprio paced back and forth as I talked, staring at his feet. The church organ now was playing slow full-bodied chords that went up and up in chain-gang steps.

"And he was crying. You saw that clearly. He was crying as he rowed away. That meant—it's got to mean—he was really going to the *Wolna*. But there was no way for him to *get* there. . . ." He stopped moving. "Listen. He made a big point about Coolio pulling the skiff back. . . . Look: you can pull a stiff up on shore and hide it. You can shove it out from shore and let it drift away. . . . He told Coolio there was extra line on the aft deck? Think—is that what he said?"

"Yes. He said there was a lot of line near the fishing seat."

"Then he must have looked around the boat. He must

have looked for rope right after he got on board. Before you came to. If he looked for it that early—he must have had this idea about landing and pulling the skiff back from the first. From the time he got on the *Tiger*—even before. . . ."

"He said something to Avelino about a plan they had with the small boat."

"He was planning to do something like this when he used the *Easy Rider*. . . . He'd worked out this plan for the *Easy Rider* and shifted it over to the *Tiger*. . . . *Why was it so goddamned important for him to get that skiff pulled away from shore?*"

He was standing directly in front of me, looking at me, but he did not seem to be asking me the question. He wanted no answers from me.

"Unless," he said. To me, through me.

He put both hands over his eyes.

"Oh . . . my . . . God. . . ." he said behind his hands.

I stood up.

"What's your idea?"

He didn't even hear.

"Come on," he said. Before the words were out of his mouth he had turned and was running down to the corner of the church.

I started after him. He tore down the inclined street toward the broad Monserrate boulevard below. There was a car parked there, in front were sitting the two men in ruffled shirts. Caprio jumped in back and waved to me to get in beside him.

"Caballería Pier," he said. "Fast."

In a few seconds we were racing down the boulevard toward the waterfront. The traffic was less jammed now going east along the channel. In a few minutes we were parked at the pier and running across.

The *Tiger* was not there.

Caprio grabbed a man in uniform who seemed to be some kind of attendant.

"The cruiser that was here?" he said, pointing. "The *Tiger?*"

"She left, sir," the man said.

"When?"

"I think—perhaps an hour ago there came two men who boarded this boat and looked there. They were there for a time and then they went away. Soon the boat went away."

"Did you see who was on her?"

"No, sir. It is very busy on the pier today, sir. Many people. We have been very occupied with the launches and the ferries. I did not see."

Caprio let him go. He turned to me and spread both arms as though embracing a thick tree.

"See?" he said. "How nice and easy it is? Brod takes the *Tiger* to the *Wolna.*"

Both the men in ruffled shirts stared.

"How could that be, Vince?" one of them said.

"From Bacunayagua to this pier," Caprio said in a flat voice, "Brod was towed behind the *Tiger*. In the dingy, under the tarpaulin. When the *Tiger* docked he stayed there. He knew we'd be with Benjie. He was smart enough to stay where he was until we searched the boat. It would never occur to anybody to search a damned dingy with the tarpaulin half rolled back. When our men left he sneaked on board and got going. It was hectic on the pier today. Nobody noticed him. . . . Benjie's car *was* for Brooke. Brooke didn't know it but he was supposed to be bait, to draw us off while Brod headed out to sea in the *Easy Rider*. . . . The plan worked even better with the *Tiger*. . . ."

Caprio looked unpleasant.

"Get to the car," he said to his men. "Call Carlos—tell him to get some planes out. Fast—Brod's been gone a while and that boat really goes."

The men hurried away.

"A formality," Caprio said. "They'll never get him inside the three-mile limit."

"The *Wolna* must have been waiting just outside the limit."

"We *could* stop her and take Brod off by force. But that's violating the freedom of the high seas. It could lead to a major international incident. These days international incidents can develop into more than incidents. . . . If they find the *Tiger* abandoned out there, we pack up and go home. . . ."

We started down the pier toward the car.

"That's the trouble," Caprio said. "You work out the pattern in your head—it looks good. But getting all the elements *outside* your head to behave themselves—that's another matter. Too many variables you can't control. . . . And when one of them is named Garmes. . . ."

"I was going along with your patterns. You recruited me into them, remember?"

"No pattern is going to last very long when you're included in it. That's a fact."

"I've seen patterns break up when I wasn't anywhere near."

"Then some protégé of yours was there."

But he was composed, through with strong hand gestures and lip biting. We got to the car and started to climb in.

"What've you got there?" Caprio said to one of his men.

The one he was talking to, the one next to the driver's seat, was drumming his fingers against a set of bongos in his lap.

"Rodríguez was carrying them," the man said.

"Let's see," I said.

The man passed the drums back. I turned them upside down. One of the wooden plugs had been removed—this was the hollow in which Coolio held his gun. There was a bullet hole in the skin on this side. The other hollow was still covered.

"Know where the sweet music came from?" I said. "Prune juice." I weighed the drums in my hands. "Feel heavier than they should. Maybe. . . ."

I pried at the plug until I got it open. Inside this hollow

was a small bottle, held with strips of adhesive tape against the side. I pulled the bottle free and gave it to Caprio. He read the label.

"Jugo de ciruela," he said. "Uh—I see—prune juice. That opium stuff. What he was on."

"What's this?" I said. "Something—"

Moving my fingers around inside the hollow, where the bottle had been, I'd felt a bulge along one of the wooden strips. I'd clawed at the projection with my nails—it had moved slightly. I was working at it harder now. It came away from the side entirely. It was a separate slab about four inches long and two across, coming away from the inside of the strip but leaving the outside intact. Inside the gap were two envelopes of calling-card size, taped against the wood.

Caprio's fingers were inside the drum, pulling the packets loose. He opened one. Several very thin strips of film fell out in his lap. He held one up to the light, close to his eye.

"Is this the way the chase ends?" I said. "The thing falls into your lap with the prune juice?"

"Looks like printed matter," he said. "Don't jump to any conclusions."

"The Thing of Things! Dropped from the skies into the mouth of the pattern-maker! Neat! Counterbalances the other pattern-maker's dingies!"

"Garmes," Caprio said, "don't ever at any slack time in your life consider taking up police work. Don't fool with anything that requires the exercise of logical faculties. Would the stuff I've been running myself ragged after be in that hophead's drums?"

"Brod let Coolio hold the films to show he wasn't going back. At the last minute he couldn't ask for them. Coolio was worried about Brod going off by himself. If Brod asked for the films *too*. . . ."

Caprio sighed, very slowly.

"Sure—Mike would have left *something* with Coolio. Worthless stuff. He had to have the important stuff on him or sent ahead. If he went home with empty hands. . . . He wasn't a playboy."

"Suppose he didn't *want* to stay alive?"

Caprio looked deeply pained.

"Was he acting like a man who didn't want to live?"

"He acted on the surface like a man who wanted to protect himself. All the same. . . ."

"Brod also knew Coolio was walking into a trap here. He knew we'd be waiting with Benjie. If he didn't take these films from Coolio or warn him about the trap—"

"He *wanted* the films to fall into our hands? To throw us off?"

"Give me another theory that fits the facts."

"Where do you want to go, Vince?" the driver said.

"Sevilla-Biltmore," Caprio said. "Garmes and I are going to get drunk. Call me there the minute there's news."

From my room I called the hospital. They said Connie was still in surgery but was not on the danger list.

It was three-quarters of an hour later, when we were on our sixth drink, that Caprio's call came. The *Tiger* had been found adrift almost four miles northeast from Havana. Nobody was aboard.

THIRTY-SEVEN   Benjamino Francisco was back in Vedado with the retired madam and picture window and bougainvilleas. I phoned and he agreed to meet me. When he arrived in the Sevilla-Biltmore lobby he was the same, except for sleeve garters of a new color. He began apologizing for his lousy bad aim in the distillery. He felt very badly for only winging the diseased iguana of a Coolio. The light was not good and the richly scabbed and eyes of mucus weasel had been moving too fast. Most times he could put his bullet through any fly-attracting guano heart he aimed for.

He cleared up the main questions. Yes, he'd shown interest in me at our first meeting because he'd heard certain things. Caprio had said I was a man looking for this and that and Benjie was to help in my quests, all of them. But he had been much upset about the specifics. Had he had the specifics in advance he would have fast departed for Madagascar someplace. I asked as a favor that he not look with displeasure next time he saw me floating in any absinthe vat with a girl. Next time I was coming to town, he said, *he* would go and hide in the vat.

"Benjie," I said. "In that bar when I asked about the Milagro."

"My ulcers had children."

"You went to the telephone."

"I wished to go to Honolulu."

"Before you called Natividad—did you make any other calls?"

"Sure. I called to Colón Cemetery to make two reservations. One in your size and one in my size."

"I'd like to know. Did you make another call?"

"How do I know? I call on the phone for many this and thats. I do my businesses on the phone."

"Before you called Natividad—didn't you call Caprio? Didn't he *tell* you to help me with Natividad?"

"Robert, I have no clear thoughts of this day when you put the fleas in my ear. Ask did I call the girl Natividad and this I cannot tell you either, truly. It is entirely a big cloud in my head now, believe me."

"All right. Tell me. Ever thought of making an honest living?"

"It is the dream and happy hope of my life."

"Would you like to come up to Key West and help me run my sheds?"

"This could make me honest and dead."

"It's a tame business. You only work for one side."

He put his hand out, knuckles up, next to mine.

"These two hands together in one shed in the nervous State of Florida—trouble, my friend."

"We can handle small troubles. You've got executive talent, Benjie—you're good on the phone. You'd be a help in the business."

"If they make a big fire from your sheds you do not have any business."

"We've got fire extinguishers. Take the job for your big handsome cousin Oliviero. I've developed a liking for him."

"For his talent to get himself shot?"

"Because he went on being a mouth when they told him to be a gun. What do you say?"

"Mon, you are a crazy mon. You got to have for yourself some nice troubles each and all days. You eat up the troubles like some folk eat the cream cheese." He stood up. "I give it my best consideration, Robert. In two weeks I come up there and we talk around the subject somewhat. Maybe if I am not require to wear the tie I will take to the up and right path. I cannot sell out my immortal soul totally."

Later that morning I took a cab out along the Via Blanca throughway to the sanitarium. Caprio was waiting for me in the administration building. We went into Luz's room together. She was sitting in an easy chair by the window rocking slowly, she hardly noticed us entering. Tranquillized with such doses of reserpine she could not, the doctor said, be alert to much. I told her she was coming up to Washington where the doctors would make her well. I said I would come to see her and Caprio said he would too. All she responded to in this was the name Luz. She repeated it and began to sing seesaw verses to herself, head dipping with the tune.

Going back to town Caprio told me more about the Washington hospital. They promised no miracles. Luz might be too far gone to be reached by anything. But they were doing pioneer work there with schizophrenics and had had results with some cases. He was returning to Washington and he would as agreed upon make arrangements. I gave him a check for the first payment.

He had news: Owen Brooke was being extradited to Florida. Coolio, Avelino and the others were in the hands of the local policía. Brod? Brod was a closed file. Caprio was anxious to get to Washington and the next job. The subject of Brod bored him. I told him my idea that Brod had under everything decided to go home *before* he killed Barto, had killed Barto to hide the meaning of that decision. At this Caprio got almost as angry and derisive as Brod had. That showed you what a mind at loose ends could come to, he barked. I was simply incapable of understanding busy people. Brod was a practical man, he killed when there were obstacles in his way, killing for gestures was foreign to his nature and realistic purposes. He couldn't have decided to go home before the *Wolna*; the *Wolna* came and put the heat on, adding to the heat from him, Caprio. Brod killed Barto because at that time Barto was a real and active danger, and for once would I quit seeing people upside down?

I thought Brod hadn't needed that pressuring because he was driven to go home by his own collapsing? According to me, Brod hadn't wanted to harm me, just talk to me? Caprio got more snappish. He, he himself was an organization man. Organizations work on the premise that people make sense. People think ahead and defend themselves in rational ways. He couldn't see that the ass-backwards idea of a man endangering himself for a little conversation and wanting to go home to bullets because a weak-minded whore couldn't get her sentences straight was much of a contribution to the understanding of Brod or any man. You couldn't plan or predict much in this world if you allowed a Brod could get hungry for talk and haunted by schitzy whores. To the point of running to bullets. No: the trap had had to be set. It had been a damned good trap. But Brod had wiggled out. That was the story, and there was its end.

Caprio was ready to confess something, though:

"Mike and I were too evenly matched—that was the whole trouble. I know damn well that unless a piano or something falls on me Brod could never get anything I had. I knew from the beginning that it worked the other way, too."

"You acted as though you had hopes."

"It's my job to have them. You can't run organizations on the theory that things *won't* work. . . . It's this simple: I was almost certain Mike had taken care of those films *before* he started for the W*olna.* There are so many safer ways to handle stuff like that—send it ahead, give it to a pick-up man, use a drop. But I had to cover every possibility. . . ."

"Have you looked over the films yet?"

He made a face: "Backwards and forwards."

"And? Is the stuff important?"

"Some, some," he said. He made a sound through his teeth. "We were after something *big.* The big thing isn't in those films. But it most likely is in Brod's pocket. This minute."

"You're losing me," I said. "I don't know what bigness means to you people."

"I know. Big to you is big stands and big trouble and that's it. Other bigs you take as funny." He turned exasperated eyes to me. "Forget your own two-bit dramas for once. I'll tell you about something with real dimension. We've been learning their techniques, learning them well. We've got some, more than a few, men at work over on *their* side. Some of them pretty strategically located. I'm not telling you anything you can't guess. What we're afraid of is that these two bums in Washington slipped Brod a list of our men *over there. That's* the thing we've been knocking ourselves out to intercept, and there's no sign of it."

Well, it did have dimension. All I could say was, "Wow. That is something. I suppose these people get pretty vital information for you."

"That's a brilliant deduction, Garmes. Yes, from time to time they get us nice tidbits." He was drumming on his lower lip with his fingers. "This couldn't have happened at a worse moment. Some of our men there have worked their way pretty far in. They were about to get their hands on something that would have made the difference. . . . If they could just have had another few weeks. . . ."

"Difference in what?" I was duly impressed. "Something military? I'm not asking for details. . . ."

"Military? No, not military. Not *primarily*." He went on playing idiotically with the humped lip. "You know what we were about to get? There's no harm in telling you, I guess. We were after a complete list of all *their* agents operating in the Americas. Another month. . . ."

At first they were just words to me. Then the words began to come together, I got the drift of individual phrases, then of whole sentences.

Spasms began to shake my insides. I bent over, holding on to my ribs, howling.

"No, no," I gasped. "Oh. . . . Really. . . . No. . . ."

"Have you lost all your bolts?" he said unpleasantly.

"That's what it was about?" I groaned. "You were chasing *him*—because he was chasing *your* men—because *they* were chasing *his* men. . . . Oh. . . . Best daisy chain of all. . . ."

"See?" he ground out. "What did I tell you? Everything that's not you is one big laugh."

"It *is* me. I was in the ratrace too. . . . Shadows taking snapshots of shadows. . . . You do run beautiful circles in your sewers. . . ."

It took me minutes to calm down. I still had the impression that I was standing off to one side watching my head do loop-the-loops. The cab pulled up at the entrance to the Sevilla-Biltmore.

"You'll find this hard to understand," Caprio said. "You with your slapstick view of all efforts. Chasing people—in the movies it's always assumed that the chase is a perfectly normal form of behavior. It's not—it's monstrous, except when you do it for a living, and with a true purpose."

"Don't be too sure. Maybe all the chasers, the professional ones included, are just chasing themselves. Getting on a payroll doesn't make the thing any the less circular."

I got out of the cab. Caprio leaned toward me intently: "What about Connie?"

"What about her?"

"Nelson's gone. He said you'd see after her."

I was sober again. After my outburst I felt cold all through, and depressed.

"She'll be all right. I'm taking her back to the Key with me."

"You going to teach her diving? You'll both get your names in the obituary columns."

"I don't have any plans. I may try an experiment." This wasn't easy to put into words, I'd already tried it with Connie. "I've spent a lot of time fooling with women who are all surface. It's just possible she's more. I'd like to—I'm going to see how deep I can go with her."

"There you are!" He was jabbing his finger through the air at me. "Backed into an event again! Nelson says you're a guy who backs into events. . . . Well—a guy should at least once in his life get in something over his head. On dry land. There's less chance of drowning. . . . Nelson says if he could write another novel he'd write it about you and call it *The Undetermined Tiger*. He says that's the most ferocious kind. I said I had a better title for him. *Portrait of An Edgy Man.* . . ."

"Edgy's too narrow a word. Diffuse might be closer. . . . You don't get a man who's just looking around with no job to do, just looking. You wouldn't know how to look, without a Brod to focus on. That's narrow, too."

"You've put your finger on it—you're incapable of narrowness—some containment of the energies. You know? That's the quality of the pre-twenty-one. The ones in apprenticeship."

"It's not something to be lost entirely. . . . You're the

sort who always apprentices others. That may be the worst kind of limit—to be always in the grip of *purpose.* . . ."

"So long, Garmes. You interest me because you can afford the luxury of doubting the things you undertake. But I hope to hell I never see your face again. If there are many like you around I might as well close up shop. All shops might as well close because nothing's going to work."

"If you had less faith in things working, and made *that* part of your work plan—you might be a better cop. One millimeter better. Pianos do fall."

"All professions are founded on reasonableness and optimism, Garmes. You'd see that if you ever had to profess anything yourself. . . . Good luck."

"I'm sorry I can't wish you the same."

"Spoken with your usual grace. Spoken like the Garmes we know and can't lose."

"I'd be out of my mind to wish anybody luck—down on your levels. I hope no bombs fall on Chevy Chase or anywhere —and that you wipe each other out in the sewers."

"Thank you. I hope no sharks get you on *your* levels."

"If anything gets me on my levels it'll be myself. Sorry. I know you can't stand theories about people chasing themselves. But it's just possible that this tendency in people is the biggest variable you fellows can't control. How could you? You don't even recognize it."

"So long, Garmes. Go chase yourself."

"Make sure you're not doing a little of it yourself, Vincent. So long."

... and ...

(from "The Deep-Sea Layer of Life"
by oceanographer Lionel A. Walford:
paragraph underlined by Bartolome Caro)

"What happens in the depth when a plankton
net drops at the end of a wire and is drawn through the
water at a rate of two or three feet per second? What effect
does this lumbering, insentient object have on the cosmos
down there? Does it stir up a cloud of light in its path as it
pushes ahead myriads of the small luminous creatures that
inhabit the sea? And as these concentrate in the net, transform-
ing it into a terrifying cone of luminosity, do larger creatures

dart out of its way to escape? Then for what distances around the net is the order of things disturbed? We can only assume that as the net is hauled through the various swarms of animals, it takes from among them those so unwary, so inagile or simply so unfortunate as to get into it. When it is at last emptied into a pan on deck, how can anyone reconstruct from that chaotic jumble of organisms the pattern of life below? How can anyone know what species and what quantities escaped? . . ."

A NOTE ON THE AUTHOR Bernard Wolfe was born in New Haven, Connecticut, in 1915. A graduate of Yale University, he is the author of REALLY THE BLUES (the life story of Mezz Mezzrow) and of two novels besides IN DEEP. Sections of his study of Negro symbols in American culture, THE CONGO ON MAIN STREET, have appeared in Commentary, Les Temps Modernes, and other magazines. He has done occasional plays for television, and has recently finished his first full-length play.

A NOTE ON THE TYPE The text of this book is set in Electra, a Linotype face designed by W. A. Dwiggins. This type is not based on any historical model, nor does it echo any particular period or style. It avoids the extreme contrast between "thick" and "thin" elements that mark most "modern" faces, and attempts to give a feeling of fluidity, power, and speed. The book was composed, printed, and bound by Kingsport Press, Inc., Kingsport, Tennessee. Paper manufactured by P. H. Glatfelter Company, Spring Grove, Pennsylvania. Designed by Harry Ford.